GUARDIANS OF SIN

Published by J.P. Schimidt at Amazon.com

Copyright 2014 J.P. Schimidt

Translated by: Michael John de Souza

License Notes

INDEX

THE "NO MAN'S LAND"

"And what is the shadow?" the creation asks the creator.

"It is commonplace that sharpens fear of the unknown and where ignorance becomes stronger;"

"It is also where from mystery, curiosity is piqued and from the revelation, innocence is sacrificed;

However, fear and curiosity are interwoven and pull with the same hunger."

By Marin Bey, a saint of the Yellow Monastery

The limit of the perimeter between the various sovereignties was mostly peaceful. Whether for military or political reasons, the landowners avoided that their limits touched the borders of their neighbor. The area between borders was called "No man's land".

The village of Miller was a clear example of this kind of land. Its geography was nothing exceptional, it was another one of those places between the forest and the woods, with pockets of stagnant water that became a dry and brittle land. Except, of course, in a place westward, where, with clever use of drainage of the remaining water pockets, a farmer prospered and others with him. Thus, without the world noticing, "nowhere" became "somewhere". Allied with this, thanks to a caravan route, an inn was built, and soon the place became a village thanks to the opportunities created by this establishment. The area grew on its own, that is, without encouragement from the king or the nobles.

Along with the prosperity, however, diseases became constant, and although fatal, the biggest problem was the abductions. The militia formed hastily was unable to intervene, or either, determine the origin or causes of the disappearances.

Could it be wild animals? Monsters? The forest plains, where the village was situated, was not so dense and it was less somber and fearsome than the black forests at the base of the mountain, where the way to the throne of the Great Empire lay.

Could it be a local and isolated horror, or maybe it belonged to greater fear patterns and magnitude? Anyway… Whoever becomes responsible for the protection of these unfortunate people would have rights to the land? Could it be that the king, once aware of the facts, would create a new protectorate and order a military or a knight of his confidence or any unfortunate man with a title won by bravery, dedication and service time such as a marquis? On the other hand, whomever simply took the place or aided the people could declare war against the domains of another noble. A delicate matter… and, given the issue, treated carefully by nobles and those well born. How long could the village of Miller survive without aid? Would the nobles do something besides discuss rights and duties, defensive and hesitant policies?

Sartre, a peasant, born a farmer, with calloused hands from using a club to beat wheat, straitened his green shirt. His hairy body would never be a mild combination with it. He felt like a silly bear chewed by scabies in a green vest. Although the color was appropriate, over the years he learned the healing craft.

His hair looked like soot from the road dust and still, he stood in the living room of one of the four nobles to whine and cry out for attention and mercy like all simpletons.

"Diseases and the abductions progress, general, they grow like weeds in the rosary, how to avoid them is a mystery."

The man before him was no general, officially at least, but for sure it was an appropriate title for the one who commanded the maximum defensive against the reptilian invasion. A rich land owner that nowadays wished only avoid unfounded hysteria about abductions and epidemic diseases.

"People disappear on account of frustrated love, debts and…"

His speech paused as he recurred to his memory. Epidemics of incurable diseases like leprosy and influenza transformed cities in fatal locations. Especially as they spread among the poor and miserable. The proximity of their homes ignited the contamination and lack of care, understanding or money would turn scratches in gangrene and moderate injuries into lethal ones. But he would leave the theorems aside and would debate based on unmoved and impervious reasoning, however, the question insisted on galloping from his mouth.

"Let's talk only about the disease… Is that what really concern you?"

"Yes! Evidently!"

"I respectfully disagree." said the nobleman. "It is happening far away, and who knows, maybe it has already ran its course…"

"Forgive me again," Sartre pressed, "we know nothing about it and ignorance kills the same way."

This was true. The nobleman still struggled to banish old concepts. Dirt was considered a layer of body protection. A bath was harmful to one's health. Two…

Maybe three per year were enough. Thanks to this reasoning, skin diseases were common. Quite common.

"Humph! A spoonful of wisdom for each dose of idiocy." The nobleman declaimed an old saying in the land that today was part of the great empire.

"I drink of the ignorance that you provide so that you don't understand what I represent." Sartre replied, the man of healing, quoting a sentence of an ancient tale.

A fierce expression, not contained, of inflated, but wounded ego, was directed to the healer. If someone was watching them, the dispute of wise inflated egos would be increasingly clear inflated by conceit. Including the debaters.

Sartre lowered his eyes and controlled himself. He backtracked and spoke in a calm and mild tone.

"Please understand… To consider the illness a lack of virtue or divine punishment of dead gods should offend our intelligences even more."

"I Agree. But I still think the seclusion can avoid exposure and perhaps the epidemic."

"Yes! But how does the disease manifest? Under what circumstances? Is it transmitted by contact? By the water?"

"The northern rivers supply the entire region."

"And the towers of silence?"

"Huh? Are you insinuating that we drink the broth of the dead?"

"It may not go that far."

"If such a thing had happened, it would affect everything around that territory."

"Alert your armies, my good sir!" Sartre said.

"That would be an exaggeration, wasting the time of soldiers with assumptions."

"Sir! By any means, the army's duty is to defend the homeland in times of war and by designation, take care of the weak and sick in times of peace."

"Do you think I should take over the obligation of the others?"

"By omitting yourself, 'the others…' What would they do? Is that what haunts your Excellency?"

A dry break. As if the air dried to the point of interrupting breathing.

The healer expected a skewed answer. Instead, the nobleman grinned as he looked at his guest with a teacup on his lap. Sartre imagined his head falling by the saber that decorated the place where they were, but instead…

"Master Sartre, where are you from?"

The extension of the gesture to the left to leave the teacup as right in front of the saber, made the frightened peasant flutter his eyelids like the wings of a moths against the wind.

"I'm afraid I don't understand." Sartre said finally.

The lord laid quietly another leaf in his tea, only then Sartre relaxed and stopped watching his posture. The ritual of the questioning was just an inevitable fact, even expected. But Sartre refused the idea of getting out of there without help against the abductions, against the diseases. Not without guidance, without a name, without nothing.

"Where does the blood comes stronger?"

In his rich speech, he only wanted to know about the peasant's origins, his roots. Sometimes people are too complicated, Sartre thought. Especially the nobles, but he was his guest and had no shortage of good and simple manners. However, before answering he raised his own hypothesis as if it was an affirmation of the obvious.

"From the valleys, the plateau of extensive lawn and home of the horses."

"From the center, sir."

"Certainly the fable of the three wishes made to a genie is known there, isn't it?"

Sartre did not know the relationship of the fable with the theme they were discussing, and, most likely, would never have the understanding of the knight, but the host gave him a tip.

"That one that brings on the war?"

Plézoun Raymovick, knight of Kleitos and the Oromb and Therao hills, stretched his body to accommodate the rest his refined drink on the ugly and elongated piece of furniture by the peasant's understanding. Only one of the stones mounted in the silver ornaments would be able to pay for a month of patrol and food of their mounts. The nobleman, combed his eyebrow with the tip of his index finger in an extended gesture as one who chooses the words in his vast vocabulary.

"His first wish was to be the richest man in the kingdom. The second was to be the healthiest and the third was…"

Unnecessary. And absurd. Sartre was born ignorant and remained ignorant for lack of money and sponsorship as most of the people in the kingdom. Therefore, even a duck understood the outcome arranged by the snob lord of so many lands and lives, so he decided to interrupt him and spare the sad comparison.

"The first wish bankrupted the kingdom making all the treasury disappear, making him and his skinny cow and the few coins in his pouch the richest man in the land." The peasant said. "The second wish made everyone around ill with all kinds of diseases, a simple wound caused bleeding and death. Of Course, without money, without basic resources to import remedies and herbs. Should I get to the third wish?!"

"Master healer, I am uncertain of your understanding."

"Good understanding, I would say. I remember the tale in detail, including its outcome."

"I'm shocked. I'm in shock, you misunderstood my…"

"Intention? Words? The moral of the fable?"

"I just wanted to allude the mission of the other characters." the nobleman suggested. "To locate the holder of the wealth and health of the entire kingdom and convince him to return, or even influence the fool, so that he did not wish any more insanity."

"If you will excuse me…". the peasant said raising from the table.

"Sartre? I urge you to come back."

Urged or ordered? The peasant ignored him. He knew this was a risk, but anyway he risked other things just for being there. If the other land owners knew the order in which he decided to visit them. Jealousy, violence, indifference, whatever it is, he was prepared for each action or reaction.

Contact with them, as far as he knew, had never been easy, it was costly actually, for both sides.

How many like himself visited him to cry and appeal? How much whining would be legitimate? Which should have greater importance? All these questions; Sartre asked himself each one of them. He could relate to the nobleman's routine exactly for being in a similar position. At the village he was seen as a leader, so any action that needed a judge or an advisor required his attention. However, Sir Plézoun Raymovick, knight of Kleitos and the Oromb and Therao hills demonstrated hastiness.

The lack of preparation, the careful choice of words and the difficulty in expressing himself concealed in poses, postures and parables unmasked him. Regrettable. It was a shame wasting time visiting the nobleman who lived closest to the village. However, village issues of this mount had to be discussed with the nobles. In his opinion, it was pointless to discuss issues as diseases and disappearances with merchants for they would quickly change their routes to avoid possible losses, and without them, the village would die.

One of the peasants who abandoned his home to serve the nobleman looked lengthly at him as he was passing. Submission and convenience; the plague of the world. As Sartre grew closer, the peasant lowered his eyes and went on sweeping the floor, burying his head into the ground to avoid being judged by him. As soon he passed, the sweeping silenced.

The walk through the inner courtyard took a quarter of an hour, a quarter more if he had to go through the winding path delineated by fine carpets weaved with golden threads. The chosen path had violets and petunias planted in placeholders, laced by small charming walls of low and trimmed shrubs. At the end of each rug there was either a metal clasp to weigh it down or a pair of tall vases decorated with strips of fabric at every turn.

Peacocks pecked freely and certainly were there more for the beauty of their feathers than by the value of their flesh.

Handmaidens and servants riddled by hunger and hopelessness, turned their faces as he passed, as if Sartre was the personification of bad days. They all sacrificed their freedom without a second thought.

After all, what else could these humble cowards think of? The tall walls protected them from the truth outside, from the monsters of the world, from hunger, hopelessness and misery. Could anyone criticize them? Never. They thought with their stomachs, ill treated by the bitter years and the unseen horizon. To raise their eyes would surely go beyond what they could stand.

Curiously, there were no children there. Not a trace, not a corn or rag doll in a corner nor a spin top, neither a silly scribble on the walls or on the floor. Certainly if they existed, sir Plézoun Raymovick, took care of them and sent to them to distant lands under the pretext of good education and learning a trade. Especially if such patronage was due to being the secret father of those children. Thus avoiding unwanted gazes due to of the remotest resemblance to their landlord. Either that or merely there were no children.

Angry and frustrated, the healer scratched the wrinkles between his eyes as if he could just rip out the petty feelings. He then realized that he was already in front of the stable and there was only the heavy double gates of lord Raymovick's village ahead of him. A real shame. A young and well positioned nobleman, but with a terrible choice of words. All that was left to Sartre was to mount his old and lame mule, that looked more like a cancer amidst so beautiful steeds, and return.

On his way back, while riding down a hill, he thought about what went wrong. Was the visit at an inopportune moment? The way he approached the matter? The arguments? Did he expect too much?

Time would answer such questions. Yet his mind was restless wondering if there would be some reflection, a hint of repentance in the nobleman and maybe he would send help. The mule stumbled on something and jolted Sartre out of his thoughts.

Meanwhile in the village of Miller a sad entourage. On an ugly banner, a shabby fabric with the framed figure of a young mother who died in childbirth. A young boy, her widower, with a dry and lifeless face, was followed closely by a couple of siblings, guitar players, who, as was the custom of that rite of death, laced the guitars to their chests and finger sound melody. After the guitar players, at a respectful distance, the people, with their children held by hand or carried, cried together to the skies, home of the gods, good and evil, their singing and moaning.

Close up it was a feline and acute cry backed by the hard and heavy sounds of the drums. The chaotic sum of voices and sounds in the distance enhanced the simple spectacle making it a beautiful celebration.

Life and death, destiny and fate. Duplicity of ideas and sensations.

Nothing of the rite could be criticized, the people paid attention to the slightest details, even the rhythm. And despite their precarious conditions, they were accommodating and receptive. Everyone was invited to take part in the divinity celebration. It's like they say… There are no better hosts, even among the nobles of the known realms. One should be good and simple like the revered mother Goddess.

Even when outsiders visited the village and rejected their beliefs and values, they acted like wise elders with kids, raising the visitor's immaturity with dignity, instead of arrogance.

Even to the north, well beyond the simple cemetery in the mountains, Sartre could hear the echo of the rites and high singing.

It was already too late to continue his journey so he decided to stay overnight at the Yellow monastery before nightfall. He would have to stray away for more than two hours from the path of smooth stones in the icy mist. But he preferred that than to risk sleeping outdoors. He didn't want to be another one to disappear. After all, no one knew what was happening. There wasn't a single person in the village, a hunter, or anyone else able to see, decipher or locate possible tracks clearly. If there were any. Sartre avoided thinking about the supernatural, but there had to be someone who could help them in good faith. Finding the monastery at night was easy. The stones on the path had a light shimmering pollen that lead to the rustic and walled monastery with two or more paths of pollen attached to its door. Even in the darkest night, as long as there was a faint moonlight, the fluorescent color of the stones would guide to the monastery or the road. The simple door of long, thin sticks united by wooden nails opened and the healer was surprised to see Marin Bey, the saint, in person, greeting him. Before she answered by Montilla. A thief with a dirty past, immersed in deceit and lust in her youth. After the disappearance of her lover, sir Morcant, the vicar, amidst the mists, she toiled through many trials until she found her faith. The same faith as her beloved.

Sartre, abiding by the protocol of good manners, knelt and begged for shelter. Marin Bey didn't speak… She reserved her voice for singing. They said that everything she did was focused on the obsessive idea of bringing back her lover and to help his return, she painted personal symbols on the stones of the path and on the gates with the extract of mushrooms from the region. Over time, wanderers and others who got lost in the dark found the Yellow monastery thanks to the active presence of the fungi. Those who are reborn in faith will be guided to salvation. Guided to the Yellow monastery.

Montilla, that is, Marin Bey's hands and parts of her body always shone. Some believed they were illuminated by her faith. But those with sense and a knowledge of the world of wood knew about the pollen, and healers like Sartre knew it in detail. Bards and devotees sing songs about the monastery, about the saint and her beloved man of little faith lost in the heart of the mist. To the healer, it was more likely that Morcant plummeted from the waterfalls close to the monastery. Stones and walls have an equally simple explanation, albeit far from the romantic ideal. She painted them to avoid the same mistake and to easily find the way back home.

Sartre already felt his old back and his mind was exhausting him with its ceaseless thinking. He crossed the simple internal courtyard and almost stepped on the vegetables stored for the lady and those who lived with her.

Marin Bey, in a friendly and silent gesture, smoothed the straw bed and fluffed a thick fabric. Sartre smiled tiredly, and the lady removed his boots, stood up and came back with water in a copper color bowl. She knelt gracefully in front of him and began to wash his feet, then she dried them carefully, using her long and simple gown.

Who could say if what the stupid and gullible people believed, wasn't right. Marin Bey maybe really a sanit. Once again his mind manifested itself, trying to establish facts, pondering about who could this woman be. It didn't matter, at least for now, he concluded. True or not, who cares? The freckled lady with orange hair knew how to welcome strangers, regardless of good faith, rules of worship and moral issues.

And that's all that Sartre did before passing out from exhaustion.

HOLY ENCOUNTER

"The world is a jumble of nonsense subject only to the degree of importance that we attach to them."

Was she talking? Montilla, or rather the saint Marin Bey was talking to him? He was impressed with her low, soft, almost whispering voice.

"I heard that in other bands a group of princes choose their emperor."

Spectacular! For years the beauty hid herself from dialog, strange and profound changes stick its teeth in her soul mirrored in some ways Sartre's own. The peasant, thinking of the story of many and his own, drops his mouth, but pulled back the reins of emotion, swallowing a bit of saliva before answering without measuring the importance of response.

"In other places."

"Yes, indeed."

Sartre had grown in pagan lands without religion, however, he admired, in his own way, the religion's power to make people think, and, with justice, of some devotees.

"And elsewhere advisers act on behalf of incompetent kings."

"Govern in his place."

She didn't even look at him. Focused on her chores, Sartre's presence didn't seemed to disturb her. The woman also didn't despise his company.

"My saint… What would you say if I told you that I will seek another nobleman to mediate the situation?"

"Only that you continue."

And that was Montilla: distant and present. Duality, uncertainty and still with agile hands enough to break your neck with a single movement. Watching her with her knees on the ground clearing the area around her simple, although beautiful, rosebush, there was no way of knowing how mortal the saint was.

"Should I find another nobleman to mediate the situation?"

"I like roses. They are simple and like water and need only a little sunlight to thrive."

The healer felt foolish, she didn't even hear him. Loneliness and retreat spiritualized and maddened. And in both cases, spirituality or madness, easily deepened. The healer felt foolish, she didn't even hear him.

Loneliness and retreat spiritualized and maddened. The beautiful lady was uninterested in everything, and he suddenly understood that he was the guest, someone who the lady of the Yellow monastery sheltered against the misfortunes of a night slept in the open… And now, he, the visitor, had to go.

"Lady of the monastery, I enjoyed your hospitality and I am grateful to you, now I must go and not abu…"

"You're a farmer, are you not?"

"Huh?"

"Some time ago, the roses ended up here. I didn't even notice them, at least not at the beginning, I think. After all, who would notice a dot in the middle of nowhere?"

"Seeds come with the wind, with the bees. Only a few buds later… I don't know. If I may, I would remove the fine mane around the rose garden. Open a two meters long rot in the ground so that rainwater runs easy to it."

"Humph!"

The eyebrows rose up together, the hand was retreated cautiously, a smirk appeared on the saint's face.

"Councilmen on behalf of incompetent kings…"

Sartre was outraged. At that moment he didn't know the difference between what he thought of her and what she really was.

"Saint! From those who have been through here, I learned your splendid voice was reserved for singing, I found it poetic, beautiful and endowed with love and righteousness. When you began this conversation, I said to myself, 'why not?' I wanted to hear your ideas, someone else to share the mind. My anxieties… Someone to solve my problems."

"Are they your problems? Are they yours? Or are they problems?"

"Don't even mention it. I learned long time ago that riddles are an easy way to dodge answers."

"Of the good and praiseworthy ones, which you don't want to hear."

After hearing these words, Sartre asked for a blessing from the saint and said goodbye. Outraged, he walked through the short space of the almost garden. Picked up the stick that served as a support in the woods and left without looking back.

"There must be someone to help my people."

VILLAGE OF MILLER

The coming and going of the healer took two whole days. Upon returning he found his house opened, as always. In the ceramic jars, some saffron, in another corner hyssop; strong purgative for washing guts; almost over…

To the innocent eyes, there were no known remedies, except a lot of leaves and herbs, which were useless without knowing what dosage to mix and what it was for. And therefore could be good or cause poisoning. On the window, facing the rising sun, a full stomach spider slowly wove a thick web. Her shadow on the pots was an omen. Scared, Sartre grabs a handful of smelly herbs from a bunch on the table, place it in his mouth and threw a bit of salt over his shoulder before leaving.

He would go south now.

To the lands of father Cyrus. He was described as centered, although active.

It was a four days trip and the ride would once again be welcome. Lucky for him, he had a few coins. Well… not luck. He received them as payment that he initially refused. A weak refusal, because he needed some money to buy a little of everything that was not produced in the village from the caravans and occasional traders, .

Undoubtedly, such caravans were like mobile villages that brought herbs, ointments, liquids and compounds necessary to his craft. In addition, he admired the craftsmanship of his payment. It was a machete covered with pierced coins sewn side by side on the curved edge. For the ill woman, the piece under the pile of rags that served as a pillow, had the purpose of paying the demons that tormented her. A request for mercy to those who never complied. The woman went through nights howling in pain and, as the smiling gentlemen of pain did not put down their invisible whips, the ill woman family called Sartre.

He intended to treat neuralgia using powerful compounds, but, in the absence of those, he would use bleeds to reduce the pain and the small demons' inflamed tempers. However, the patient's age would be an obstacle to the simple treatment. She would never withstand the extraction of the excess blood in her veins. Because of this initial problem, Sartre soon found that the only evil was the swelling caused by gases and the smell reported by her was never from the breath of demons nor sulfur.

Anyway, bringing his mind back to the present, he removed the discreet necklace he wore under his robes and together with the coins, he bought a mule. As much for the price, as for being a lower animal.

In the village, amid the dry and thirsty afternoon, villagers carried bags of dirt on their backs and stored them in points furthest from the large and oblong hole they dug. If they didn't find water this time, they would make the cavity into a cistern, hence the reason for the wide edges. The earth soon would be dry again.

The windless period was a short hell and to deny its strong influence, was to put death in their homes.

However, although the families were still quite fragile due to the disappearance of Mili, son of Beonder, the cross-eyed. The community had to rebuild. Survival lacked sensitivity and who ignored it would have a violent reality drying up their mouth and their skin sticking to their bones. Right or not, some believed the Little Ones were to blame, the so-called "Demons of the forest" and other beasts and reigning monsters of the neighboring forest. The brushfires provided a withdrawal of the forest who always wanted to cover and choke the village with its greens. And if green was to triumph, then may it be that of the vegetables in their gardens.

Despite the vastness of the area, houses were built increasingly closer for safety reasons. Each neighbor gained extra protection from the family next door, like birds that travel in a flock would be less prone to predators.

With the joint effort on the new artesian well, neighbors put aside their phobias, reservations and oddities to share the work towards the common good.

At that moment, a row of people with sticks in their hands, scratched the earth in front of the houses. As a poor cousin of the well, the ditch followed to the cistern as straight as possible. During the rainy season the water would trickle from the lower straw roof to the ground, running lean, slow and dull on the almost plain ground to the cistern.

Now the queue of workers he was digging in front of Beonder, the cross-eyed, house. A hapless house like all others there, but with his daughter missing, it had a stain of ill omen and sad amazement. In the dark interior with dirty floor, there were clear and washed leather drums sprawled in the corners, stretched by two-color braided ropes. Mostly the color of leather, the braids contrasted with the poor and untreated wood, giving an air of wear and rudeness, taking away the beauty of yore of the ceremonial drums.

Sartre, riding an old animal, without luggage, had the appearance of a pilgrim and thus would be unlikely to meet road robbers. Besides, it would be pointless to deviate from the road without knowing the spouts and forks of the road, or follow the rivers with an old animal that could certainly split a hoof and suffer until it died. He would only have to fear the predators and, in particular, the nocturnal ones, but his mission was too important for personal fears.

"Confidence, man. Your purpose is fair. Destiny must be complacent."

On the way he noticed the small graves dedicated to the dead and erected rods with a coconut on top for men and clothes for women, he counted a dozen at a quick glance. His breathing became shallow, who else was gone? And what family would be harmed by the disappearances? Did they still blame the anger of the gods?

Well, the decision between to find and store water or build any temple, altars and prepare rituals and offerings to the gods was outvoted. As he was also a farmer, Sartre knew that without water, despair would gradually open the door to violence and would claim up to the last life. And nothing would be left for the gods.

That is why he really had to rush. However, how would he address the matter? How should he proceed with a devout man? Sartre was a rational man and rationalizing the problem was, for him, the only way to understand it. He knew about the mistake of thinking for others, but according to another more illustrious person,

"To understand the rulers of a land, just look at its people."

The man of healing, was how he would be called in the southern lands. He could already see himself among the people of the prairies of the priest with them saying: "Everything happened by the anger of the gods;" "the gods were unhappy." They would say it with a pointing finger, it was the lack of prayers. "The people had moved away from their beliefs". And the speech wouldn't divert much from that. There was no reason for a thorough look over the whole. A good number of villagers from his beloved village came from the south.

"If it was such a blessed land why did they leave?"

His voice escaped, but he wouldn't say anything in front of them, because they would say that the newcomers brought the foreboding and wherever they go, misfortune would follow, hungry and desirous to get its dues.

Suddenly he stopped on the road with his head down and clamping his hands.

"That's not it."

He stooped and suddenly surrendered to despair with hands suffocating the sides of his head, hoping to forget the answers that his brain had just revealed. Minutes were lost while he suddenly looked up and a gentle breeze gained strength, and from some distant point in the sky, thunder heralded changes. The ugly and gray mount heehawed and pulling the reins, it trotted back home.

In the village, between the wide spans of the wall, light helped the child to hunt the lice on the wool blanket. Sick of being bitten, she decided to bite them while they slept, just to see if they liked it. After revenge was served, she picked up a milking stool and jumped up, trying to reach the pot with honeycombs on the shelf, but as she accidentally made noise when she hit the hung pots, mugs and utensils, she ran under the old board, that functioned as a table, mounted on a double easel. Not that the idea was to hide, but to grasp quickly the gourd of water. And so she left the house with a "it wasn't me" look on her face.

Mendeli, a freckled and naughty girl, always preferred to get water instead of the household chores. The brooms, besides their basic attribution of keeping the floor clean, were used lately to whip her skinny ass. She didn't even consider running away from home. After all, at such a young age, would there be a place to go? Her imagination was not that great. She was a child, a silly and wicked child at the height of her seven years of age. Along the way, she balanced on fallen twigs and even in the shadows of the trees. She pretended that the sun, the fat enemy, would not touch her thin and dirty feet and would not give her deadly blisters. All she had to do was find the shadows and she could always find them.

And so, the valiant Mendeli, carrying the big gourd, walked through the path and called Mirtes and Miguel to come along, but she won't call Donovan because he always wanted to show her what he had in his pants. Yet, he went with them to the creek. On the way back she intended to pee in the gourd to give Geitel, her stepmother, a stomachache. After all, who told her to steal her mom's place? And so what if daddy put earth on top of her when she was cold? She was still her mom and her Mendy still knew where she was.

The other day, she dug on her mother's grave and found her little fingers. They were smelly and full of white little milky worms that tickled Mendeli as she held them in her hands. Mommy was funny and very strong for not laughing while the worms tickled her.

"The stream is this way. Why are you going that way?"

"Get out of here, little baby."

"I won't and… I'm not a baby. I'm not breast fed anymore!"

"Get out of here; go get your water!"

Donovan and Mirtes were almost the same age. From what Mirtes said, she was almost two Mendelis old, but she thought nothing of it as her father was two Mendelis and two Mirtes old.

"Go on, go, girlfriend." Mirtes said lightly.

"No way!" Mendeli didn't care if Donovan wanted to show that to her again. Anyway she wouldn't go alone "Come on! I know where we can find guava." she couldn't resist that. He knew how much she loved guavas.

"I'm coming, okay?"

"No!"

"What a dumb girl. Get lost!" Donovan said, closing his fist in front of his mouth.

Donovan was a fool and she had already decided that he wouldn't be the boss of her.

"You go. Stinky melon head!"

"Ha-ha-ha."

Miguel always laughed at her jokes. Mendeli was good at it.

"Leave her… Who knows, maybe she will want too."

"What? She's only a baby!!"

"I'm not."

"See."

Mendeli didn't get it, she became suspicious, but soon her face clouded, like her friend had done. Fresh and larvae free guavas for today.

"Mendeli, we're going home now!"

"No!" Mendeli thought about the broom beating for not bringing the water.

"Apparently she's more inclined to…"

"Shut up, Miguel!"

"Tsc! Come here, come…"

"Don't be an idiot."

He perversely put his hand on her newly formed bosom and was slapped on his face. Her nail bruised his left eye and he cursed.

"Run Mendy!!!"

She ran and soon heard a thud coming from the trees and, looking back, in her shy and uncertain race, didn't see her girlfriend, but she saw him running after her, screaming and howling like an animal. Scared, she started running for real. Dorky Donovan was fast and when he caught her, he almost choked her when she fell. In tears, she picked up a rock and hit his soft head while he had his knee on her lady part. The fool fell sideways, cockeyed looking even more stupid than he already was. His tongue fell out of his mouth and she laughed.

Suddenly a noise hushed her.

Donovan was dragged backwards. In a moment of fear, she leaped forward trying to rescue the poor kid, but he was still out with his tongue hanging and Mendy could not catch him. She locked her eyes on his and tried again, but his body began to zigzag between the trees, and he disappeared.

A quick bang, like something hard being broken, made the girl stand up and hold her mouth with her index finger, in a self imposing silence. She spun around and ran and ran and ran. A thick hand grabbed her by the neck. And in a spasm, the girl turned to her enemy. What took Donovan was there…

"Mendeli, you useless child, stop playing."

It was Geitel, her hateful stepmother. Although she hated her, she was grateful. Holding her wrist with a shaking hand, Mendeli looked back. She could not believe what she had accomplished… Suddenly, like a dream, several voices, like those that echoed in her head, said the same thing: "The latest abductions took place when people went alone to the creek for water."

However, she still had to fetch water.

And if she stole it from her neighbor? Stole some water from Bernardo, the pig? He was a small pig and he wouldn't need so much water until tomorrow, not after tomorrow, not after the name given to the day after and after. She would never go into the water, only in the bath with the water stolen from the pig. No river water, and don't even think about swimming.

Not even if Mirtes asked, no and no. No way. Let Miguel and silly fat tongue Donovan go alone. Then suddenly she cried hugging her hated stepmother, because she remembered that something got him and he will never return…

FOREIGN HOPE

In the village of Miller, inside Darrell's tavern, Phillip Darrell, an emergency meeting with the entire council of villagers was underway.

As usual, they started with routine discussions and lesser problems while awaiting for the remaining council members, but there was turmoil upon the arrival of the elves from faraway and strange lands. It was as if they were the saviors from all evil. After all, they were such rare beings these days that it was inevitable to think it was a miracle, a divine providence. Therefore, they were direct and ignored the rites and protocols. They told them about the disease and the disappearances, about their failed ideas and the pretense theses about the reasons.

When questioned if they had reported such calamities to the rulers of their land, they shied away, waiting for someone to speak for them. Then an unknown voice spoke from the back of the crowd:

"We can't wait until the king resolves this matter, we have children, family!"

True. The answer was quite correct. They had greater interest in this and less ability to handle it.

A man with a sad look spoke to the woman who arrived with the venerated elves. He felt unworthy to speak directly to the beings of divine ascendance, but he said:

"Waiting is impracticable. We secretly carry a little, but honored amount in coins."

The sad man raised his eyes quickly from the ground to the woman's long hood that shrouded her body. On her abdomen and chest, interwoven metal plates with overlapping leather straps showed that she was evidently a missionary warrior. The face under the hood, almost totally thrown back, he noticed her eyebrows slightly arched design contract and, before he realized, she lifted a warning finger and spoke firmly:

"Save your money so you may build a good divine house."

The intense red stripes on her arms and face identified her as an emissary of the high clergy, but only Yuri, a talkative man with plump face and body, from distant Caleb, noticed its real meaning.

The warrior looked at everyone and continued.

"Faith and weapon training could prevent the need for outside help."

The haughty elf as nature made him, reclined on the table, with legs and arms crossed, looked contemplatively at the floor. He was sagacious and paid attention to every comma pronounced there and spoke quickly.

"To solve this mystery we need more information."

"And equipment." Osiris added. That was the given name of the warrior of faith.

"Don't you believe in what we said?" some argued.

"We only want to go to the places where they were last seen." the elf replied quickly, before his partners.

A lot of discussion arose from there on. After all, they would have to identify what they were dealing with and when they accepted the challenge, they received a discreet cork brooch in the form of notched leaf. The traders absent from the meeting would easily identify them and thus, attend them with discretion and preference. Discretion was everything, if the events became public, it would withdraw the caravans the village was so dependent on.

Leaving the tavern, they decided to start with the blacksmith's house, since Osiris needed to fix her weapon, especially because the last time she used it, Osiris had insisted in skinning some animals, "for practice". The rounded and bit long rod had a link at the end to hang it to the horse and on the other side, a thick ball of spikes, made from a single piece of cold iron. The name given by the nobles was "Cavalry Mace", but Osiris called it: "The Peacemaker".

Not that the priestess was bad or foul, she only had a strict opinion of good and evil, a vision shared by all priests warriors of her order. Months before, this same "vision" made Osiris the champion of the Great Valley, when she destroyed an altar of evil creatures. The occasion was dubious, given that, while she toppled the totem of these creatures' god, she met the other two elves, Tarson and Jupita, who bravely fought alongside her. For the warrior priestess there was no greater honor than to make allies while fighting. Their friendship has since tightened.

Arriving at the blacksmith's house, a young man recognized the brooch attached to the tattooed woman's cape and offered to fix her weapon and its balance as it lacked a piece of metal. Osiris issued a strange laugh compressed and suffocated between her thick lips remembering that something flew off together with part of the rock and the rival creature.

The blacksmith took advantage of the slow customer movement and relayed good information regarding the conditions the first and third disappearances took place. However, the insistent pounding of his hammer made many of the questions hard to hear. And he spoke proudly of a large order of meat hooks and knives made by the butcher. Curiously, the missionary became interested in the subject and listened intently. Tarson and Jupita realized what her real interest was and excused themselves, leaving immediately. Osiris said she would listen to that man's story and take a nap, as early next morning she had some offerings and obligations to fulfill.

Relieved, they followed down the street until they found a hovel with a hanging plaque with a chemist symbol. The elf chose to take care of the borrowed horses while she went in alone rolling her eyes with a slight air of disapproval.

It was a well assorted store of items from local vegetation and roots and ointments bought from traders. It was very common to minister any quantity and mix just about anything to make remedies, however the desired effect was only achieved by experienced healers and skilled apothecaries. Charlatans and frauds huddled in cities and commercial routes with their wagons claiming to have an elixir for the ails of the body and soul. The villagers, however, trusted Sartre. Him, and his excellent teas. Actually, such compliments and referrals were heard in other lands kilometers away. Initially, Sartre attended the stranger with a strange look.

"Take this one also. They are invigorating potions of splendid nature. They preserve the muscles and strengthen the body of…"

The doorbell rang twice and three men came in. The beautiful and attentive lady elf accepted the potions and left quietly. But conferring with the other elf, they decide to seek the council.

"It could have been a mistrustful look." said Yuri Caleb, who gradually made it clear he was the council leader.

"Or maybe, they didn't want to alarm the village with their ideas." said another person.

"I'm will go personally with you tomorrow, to hear him."

After Caleb's promise, they left to get some rest.

"Maybe she was afraid of strangers." said the elf with a sober and placid voice.

"Or is it guilt?" added the lady elf.

However, the next day the apothecary shop was abandoned, apparently, everything was in place, except the empty space behind the counter where Sartre was supposed to be.

The news could not be contained. Everyone found out about the disappearance of the apothecary and, at the council meeting, everyone wanted to speak. Many threatened to leave the village and go to the capital. Others maintained that if a nobleman acted as a burgomaster there, all local economies would be under his tutelage. He would, of course increase taxes to defend the arrival of troops. Therefore, some caravans would avoid them, thus resulting in the end of the village of Miller.

A tall man, with a closed and thick beard ran his hand through his ruffled brown hair before turning to the complacent face elf and introduced himself as the woodcutter of the village.

"The others say you are the only one with some weapon experience?" the elf was uncertain, he despised innocent types who tried to be heroes.

"Weapons? What kind of weapons? Tarson, we won't need a guide." the lady elf of sinuous walk says, aware of her sensuality.

"Jupita, we can't do it alone." Tarson said, without looking away from the woodsman.

"Wait!" Phillip Darrell, the tavern owner, said. "No one will say that I didn't help."

With an elusive look, Phillip took an old piece of leather from somewhere behind the counter, wrapped a cheese in it and gave it to Tarson.

Meanwhile, the woodcutter stared at the lady elf, running his eyes over her silky hair wrapped in light twirls, firm skin and youthful as desire. The curves of her hips and lap were just the way you wanted, all inside a smooth leather dress. The lady elf was a sin waiting to happen.

The leader of the council cleared his throat, drawing attention to himself.

"I'm sorry. But Dominescu…"

"No, Yuri! I'm negotiating." the woodsman said. His serious and decided gaze silenced the councilman, and turning the elf he continued without delay. "My brother and I…"

"Have private interests in this." Jupita completed offhand.

The firm, resolute look, different from the harshness of arrogance, of the woodcutter impregnated even the air with his seriousness and gravity. Such look fogged any other comments, then another member of the council decided to ask about the fellow.

"Elves, I can assure you that Dominescu would be of great value to your pursuits. A professional woodcutters has to know their workplace very well."

Taking advantage of the small hiatus, the woodsman went on to speak for himself:

"My brother and I spent the entire spring and summer either in the dense forest or in the woods ahead, seeking and cutting the right kind of wood for each application and use. But then, I got an excellent order for meat hooks.

I insisted that he hired a youngster to help him, but that wasn't his style."

"Wooden hooks?" the beautiful Jupita says, in a provocative tone.

"Iron. I learned the craft with the blacksmith a year ago."

Osiris raised an eyebrow inquisitively and in an outburst said:

"We met him." she then tried to hide the smile when she remembered the confused conversation she had with the boy hard to listen and with agile muscles.

"Then I discovered I was good at it. It would be a very good extra. So we split up. My brother would take care of the order for long boards and that was when he disappeared."

Tarson noticed the humbleness of the woodcutter's clothes. Certainly, as it occurred in other places, poverty forbade prolonged rests. Even during winter, in front of the forge, they most likely did all kinds of things especially horseshoes for the rich caravan owners, repaired old pots, cauldrons, etc. The woodcutter seemed to study him for a moment and said:

"The trails are not the problem, but where the kind of wood ordered from brother is found."

"Huh?"

"I know where he might have disappeared."

Meanwhile, far from the village, Shasta, Adoriel and little Gódi like any child of the Little Ones race, enjoyed themselves. Now they played jumping among the trees of the forest, far away from their village. As a hasty covered wagon passed by, they jumped from the leafy branches hoping to catch a ride to another tree farther.

Shasta laughed victoriously from the top of the wagon while the other two crashed into a bush. Curious as her mother and aunts, she peeked inside the wagon and was terrorized when she found Sartre tied and injured. She stretched her fat little fingers and managed to remove the gag, but she wasn't strong enough to remove the straps.

"Tell the village master…" Sartre said hastily "I need Sargauss."

She retracted her body and, suddenly, a calloused thick hand tried to grab her. Scared, Shasta dodged, kicking the bad man's face. She jumped into the bushes rolling over the ravine slope.

She heard cursing, and put her hands over her ears, like her dad had taught her. The wagon stopped on the road. The bad man wanted to take Shasta also.

The girl ran desperately into the tall and dense woods. Her tininess was an asset when it came to hiding, and this time the intention wasn't only to avoid a cold water bath or to play.

"Little tramp, come here! I will be very angry if I have to come find you" the man threatened with some sweetness. Sweeping the area, walking slowly with watchful eyes. "Jumping like that… You must be hurt. I have some medicine."

"Liar!" she screamed innocently.

"There!" he said to his partner and ran.

"Forget it! Let's get moving." the other man said with disdain.

The pursuer hesitated.

"She saw me!"

"So what? You never show yourself in the village anyway. Who's going to believe a child?"

The guy walked a little more, the endeavor in the imperious vegetation would be enormous. He never knew how to kill children and he wasn't going to start now. Frustrated, he struck the bushes, cursing a good number of profanities and gave up.

Shasta shrank even more. She knew that adults only spoke like that when they were angry and she covered her mouth to contain her fear. The little girl saw the tall boots of her stalker pass nearby. She didn't have the courage to raise her eyes. She felt that her attitude, somehow, would protect her.

After a strong holler, the wagon wheels began to click and the snap of the animal hoofs sinking in the hard ground marked the compass of that noise, which, in the distance, became silent. Shasta, still hidden, with her hands pressed over her mouth finally stopped crying.

BACK TO THE HEROES

The woodcutter's tip led them to a semi buried ruin. Every turn and door created doubt about where they came from, and when they reached the exterior it was morning. They were all hungry.

Osiris blew her nose strongly, making Jupita sick. The horses rented from the tavern owner were not there.

Suddenly, Tarson, the last to come out was ensnared by his arms and pulled back. While his body was dragged and suspended, a mysterious figure came down holding the other end of the rope.

When the others tried to react, a hail of arrows blocked their passage and warned them.

A loud laugh was heard through the trees.

"Bravo! Nice shot!" fat Yuri Caleb said in a wide gesture displaying his muscular arms as he came out of hiding.

"I came to pick up the horses. And of course, to collect the rent."

The man with the crooked broken nose and strong arms that was holding the rope tied it around his waist and now, hands free unarmed them, taking everything of value. When he removed the knives from Dominescu's boots, he immediately recognized him as Maqui Bone Breaker, one of the tavern's regulars.

"I will take your belongings and, when the villagers arrive, they will conclude for themselves that you died." the fat tattooed man joked. "Losing all hope. Or maybe if we just said something else? I don't know… I will decide later. For now, brave adventurers, dead or missing, please be kind enough to climb on your new ride."

He was referring to the wagon with iron railings covered in fur and thick fabric roughly covered by branches and a newly cut bush.

Jupita's sensitive ears noticed something in the distance, moving away. She whispered:

"I heard a wagon leaving, didn't you?"

Dominescu took advantage of their proximity and kicked Maqui on the side of his knee. Even before he fell, the bastard was dragged up by the rope, while Tarson dropped from above. When they passed each other, the elf kicked him in his mouth. Once on the ground, he picked a barbed hunting arrow from his quiver and took aim.

"Open your mouth and close your eyes."

Tarson's anger accelerated in such a way that the action became a thing of legend, the first arrow pinned Yuri Caleb's shirt to the wagon, the second aimed to destroy the crook's wrist missed, while the last metal tipped arrow stuck the tray that the fat tattooed man used to cover his face. The fat rascal ripped his shirt and jumped on the horse tied at the side of the wagon and ran away. Dominescu reacted too late, he jumped on one of the thieves' horses and chased the fat man through the forest. His conscience begged him to return, because his route through the valley was obvious, but there were personal reasons involved also.

Maqui Bone Breaker was once kicked by a cow and didn't pass out, thus, he would not faint because of an elf's light kick. He was more stunned from the fall than anything else. Shaking his head, he put his hands on the ground and quickly stood up. As he was still pretty close, he was considering what to do with the elf and it would be something really painful.

Jupita, still angry, wanted to expose Phillip Darrell, the barkeeper, so she insisted with Tarson.

"We should kill him for what he put us through."

"I've never heard you talk like that!" Tarson said before he missed the opportunity.

"I'm Sorry…"

"The cheese was wrapped in a map was quite subtle and… Undoubtedly ingenious."

Maqui saw the metal hook on the ground. He decided to gut the elf. Suddenly, abruptly and violently, Maqui fell into a small crack that opened under his feet. When it fell, the ceiling took the appearance of a blue pupil eye moving away. Still attached to the rope, his falling body hit the walls of rocks and earth. The rope still slipped and his hands were burning and then in a jolt, he stopped falling. Suddenly, something with icy and spongy fingers grabbed his leg. He kicked the thing and from the sound, it understood that something had broken. On the surface, someone tried to pull him up while below more icy fingers of dead hands pulled him down… to the earth… to the grave.

Osiris smiled when she realized that something else was weighing on the rope she held.

Absorbed in the situation, the elves continued to discuss.

"Don't forget to hear his version of the facts before you condemn him."

"I…"

"I know it's not like that."

"I hope it's the last time we enter ruins. I hated everything, dirt, mold, cobwebs and all those slimy and disgusting insects." as she spoke, her face squirmed with disgust.

Tarson laughed and Jupita poked him gently, smiling…

"You are so quiet, Osiris." Tarson said watching from a distance.

"Leave her. She must be praying and thanking." Jupita said.

"Right. Are you ok? Injured?"

Osiris thoughts were back to the to the chaotic underground battle. The warrior priestess was the first to be hit and as her anger grew in the heat of battle, she pelted the bold creature far away. Unsatisfied with the damage, she turned her thorny mace on the others until black blood splashed.

It must have been at that moment, she thought. Surrounded and with little room for her heavy and thorny weapon, "The Peacemaker", the almost lifeless creatures were gathering to catch her. The names and occupations of the gods from her lips were and will always be powerful weapons and by screaming their names with fervor, the rotten mass of the creatures' flesh exploded.

They had been separated and when finally Jupita, Tarson and the woodcutter managed to reach her, they saw only Osiris's sweaty face emerging from the dust with dried and torn bodies. Only then, they felt the pain in their backs.

"No." her eyes widened noticing not the scratches on her arms, but her bitten wrist. "Tarson, listen to me." she said with some urgency.

"Tell me later. Ok?"

"Errr… Sure."

In ecstasy, remembering all the strange and mystical points by which they passed in that antique and abandoned underground building, the devotee of the gods of war understood somehow that the temple, because this was the closest term, and the closest… that the temple had requested a new sentinel. So she ponders: should I pull the rope held under his feet or should I let the scoundrel fall? She decided to let fate deal with him and raised her foot. The rope hissed whipping quickly the edge of the crack as if it was the restless tongue of a lizard, before it disappeared.

"Someone has to go after Darrell." Tarson said, with a thoughtful look.

"I'm coming with you!" the lady elf said.

"Take a look around. Osiris was injured and, despite being a warrior priestess, she will need someone clean her wounds."

"But…"

"I will be fine. The barkeeper won't want to lose his reputation. Things went quietly, even for him. At least I got that impression. Well, it doesn't matter, I want to check the extent of it."

"Dom went after the fat guy."

"Dom, huh? You are already fond of him? He is strong and skillful."

"No doubt."

"What if he doesn't make it?" Osiris says startled, because the conversation was high enough be heard.

"We can't do nothing for now." Jupita replied quickly, walking toward the androgynous figure with short spiky hair that was Osiris and placed her hands on her shoulder and continued, "and we're tired and our friend is injured."

The smile was candid and smooth. There was no way or reason to disagree with his friend.

"The road they took doesn't lead to the village, so Dominescu will have to come back this way." Tarson said as he gathered his things.

He took a long look at a spot in the woods, he was exhausted and the pressure of so many dangers in that place messed with his eyes. He rubbed them hoping to clear his mind and not become hostage of his imagination. He turned around, checking if he didn't forget anything.

"I'm going to the tavern and try to surprise Phillip Darrell, case he is guilty."

"Why don't we go together?" Jupita suggested .

"And spoil the surprise?"

Jupita dropped her eyes, her concern was clear.

Tarson didn't know if he was ready for a new life. A life together. There were more urgent things at the moment. The chatter in taverns, brothels, weapon houses and markets always said a lot about direct and indirect activities of the communities. And Phillip Darrell was the man behind a counter. If he was guilty, he would crumble at the sudden appearance of the elf and give up the his accomplices. If he was innocent, he would help to find out if what they faced outside the ruins was an isolated case or connected with the disappearances.

Tarson glanced quickly at the two brave women, his body was covered in a blue glow and he began to levitate.

"Be careful!" Jupita uttered silently.

Flying, the elf instantly entered the low clouds of the morning fog, going farther and higher.

BACK TO SHASTA

"I must find dad, tell him about Sartre and the bad man", Shasta thought repeatedly. She ran through the trail made by animals in the woods. Running and running. She should have never left her mother's side that morning, Shasta thought. An almost dry stream was an easy obstacle to jump. Shasta was good at that. Her feet sank into the mud on the opposite bank, but she continued to run.

Suddenly, her tiny body spun around fast and her slim weight avoided the shock of her head and delicate arms against the ground as she was suspended by her feet. The surprise tore a small cry of surprise from her.

The woods moved, something was coming towards her. Surely a predator. The young lady was speechless with panic.

A huge cat with long yellow hair and black vertical stripes emerged. Noticing the hanging snack, it approached calmly, roaring low.

"Zork!" Warned a raspy voice coming from afar.

The owner of the voice was near the dry stream. His sensitive tact told him he had stepped on something. He squeezed his toes on the object and raised it twisting the leg without changing his posture. Lifting it, he ran his hands over it.

"A shoe?"

He squatted and ran his fingers in the small and evenly spaced tracks that were followed by the heavy paws of a quadruped. Intrigued, he sniffed Shasta's lost shoe deeply.

"Smell of fear." he whispered to himself while he squeezed the shoe between his hands, remembering his old promise to defend the Little Ones, and in raging voice, said:

"Zork!"

The man followed the footprints in great strides, his sight had been blurred for days. The brute tree sap and herbs infusion were useless. So much work for no result. Between the tall and thin trees he made out a figure, hanging and swinging. "I should have removed that foolish villager's trap", he thought…

"Zork?"

He hoped that the noise and the yelling would scare away whatever pursued Little One. The figure was short and very thin. Maybe it was already too late, because the large feline pounced very well. The blur that he could hardly see, could might just be someone's remains. Zorak got angrier. When he got to the small clearing opened by the fall of a great tree, he saw the tiger.

Removing the short bow from across his chest, he pulled one of the arrows from his small and practical quiver at his waist and shouted to the beast:

"Evil creature! Any scratch on her and I will split your thoughts with a single arrow and skin you just for the fun of it."

The tiger roared, indifferent to his approach.

"A young lady! What…"

CERTAIN FATE

Further ahead, in the same rustic and badly maintained road, in the big wagon that left ahead of Yuri Caleb, two people with pasts free of innocence and guilt, took turns as driver and executioner. Inside, sad and frightened faces prayed and accounted for the happiness and bitterness they committed. They called that certain fate. For irrational reasons, they were absolutely sure that the reason why they shared such suffering would only be revealed to those who made it alive to the end of this narrow road. The new wooden floor didn't even bend under the load, but the sight between the spans was clear, and their fates, uncertain. Two riders switched between flanking the mobile prison, sometimes riding ahead, sometimes behind.

Sitting on a bench latched to wagon's raw iron ceiling, two mercenaries chatted about daily events. But suddenly one of them became silent and when the other one touched the driver's shoulder, he fell aside, revealing a blow to his forehead and blood smudged eyes.

"Ambush!" he screamed at the top of his lungs.

He searched for the other hired warriors, but found nothing. Desperately, he took the reins and whipped the horses, but their thrust dragged him away, leaving the wagon behind. Scared and surprised, the second and last kidnapper let go of the reins, stopping a few meters ahead.

He went looking for a site less vulnerable to any kind of projectiles. He unsheathed his broad and curved blade, like the overseas ones, and took a defensive position with his scimitar.

Whistles are heard from all directions, demonstrating they were in great number. He ran to the back of the wagon and opened the grid, tugging on one of the prisoners.

"I only have these to negotiate!" he screamed.

A stone hit his hand making him drop his weapon. Scared, he surrendered.

There are howls of celebration and effusive compliments to someone called Morgause, while a hooded person, that looked more like a beggar, walked toward the prisoner transport.

"Miserable bums." he hissed to the bruised man, who was still dazed from the fall.

The bruised man pulled a knife from his inside pocket and ran to attack the ragged figure.

But, a second later, the ragged man grabbed his attacker's wrist and twisted it in a circular motion throwing him to the ground while with his right hand he grabbed strongly the attacker's throat.

"Mercy! Spare me, I have children."

"Children without a father."

"No!"

"What can you say about yourself that would make me spare you?"

"I was hired by Yuri Caleb."

"The bohemian bard?"

"No, the merchant. I am but an employee, someone without profession, besides, these people are meaningless."

"I believe that they themselves have their own opinion about you."

"My boss said they are drunks, beggars and peasants who did not pay their taxes."

"And where do you take them?"

"Gods! To the port merchants."

IN THE SKY

It was difficult to define to those who were not air natives. The breeze, the humidity of the first cry of a virgin cloud. From the ground, they are mere clouds, heaps of fluffy white tufts escaping from their gentle shape when they grew darker and took the gray color of rain and the sullen dark of storms. Tarson-Romanei always liked them, not their shape or color, but the feeling of emptiness among them. Air without ground. There he daydreamed about the first home of his ancestors, without the ground or sky, without the sea, nor sun, nor stars, nor nothing.

Plenitude.

There, in the subtle shelter, a wide range of feelings and sensations soaked his senses, and no other place would ever give him that. There was no hurry that day. Not after facing the underground and its darkness and the nightmares of meat and/or bones. He would go back to the village, as he said to his beautiful and brave friend. And if the man behind the counter of that human beverages trade was guilty or an accomplice, he would certainly be surprised by his presence.

Osiris and Jupita would certainly take twice as long to get there, given the sinuosity of the way back. He had time.

The sun, the tireless fireball, burned wilder in the summer. His back burned both because of the dry and arid climate as because of the extra and unexpected exercises in that stomach of earth men insisted in calling caves. Humans had this habit, they invented shorter names believing, with all their characteristic pomp, that it was the best thing to do. Believing with all their shortage of virtues, to have solved the unfathomable mysteries through this habit. And they still believe they invented the wheel.

However, it was even older, before their time… before the time of emptiness… prior to despair even before the gods died… Before we accepted that they wouldn't come back. Not everything happened that way, of course, but it was how memory worked. The brain composed his own journey… Remembering so much suffering from that lifeless time was useless, because what happened and took place is fact and it belongs to the common history of peoples and creatures of this world. A world built to replace another, a coarse copy that had already lost its meaning, but gained another.

Now, there was only life to live and responsibilities inherited by tradition from the ancient races. After all, in the absence of the gods, there should be order. And no one was so close to the old gods as the descendants of the ancient races. Aiollius, Nymphs, Earth-gem, Orcs, Flekk, Unicorns, Simurghs, Hair-Hands and others. And these others, as far as he knew; embraced the void and remained there. Today, there are those who descended from fire, children of the sun, coming from the lands beyond the sky. Nested under the land were the rock people to who Tarson held true apathy. Especially because those of the air had little or no interaction with those of the rock. After all, what could or should Tarson-Romanei, the person, say about them? And, according to a passionate account of his lady elf friend and partner, the sons of mother water are parasitic beings dependent of the warm bodies of mammals. They use them as living nests, that is, whenever they surfaced, they attacked the unsuspecting people of the coast and riverine areas around lakes and rivers. Jupita really had reasons for her hatred and Tarson for his bitterness. However, although today they were so few, almost non-existent, the offspring of the fire were the worst, well beyond the savages that once existed. The fire reptiles, described as having a corrupting nature, lived cloaked, hidden inside living bodies, warping moods, distorting character. And what could be more disgusting than that? Maybe only the ravenous ambition of humans. However, how can one blame such a young race for its ignorance? As for the rock and mud people, Tarson had no comments.

And during this reflection of the world he caught himself questioned. How would he describe his own race? The air natives? Some remained in weak joy, even when deep lines on their faces betrayed their old age. They kept this extreme childishness, hoping to deceive the rings of time. And besides, most of them avoid using the powers. But how can one deny what one is? Deny the extent of their own souls? They fear that, by using these powers, they made their bodies weaker and bring on a speedy death.

For the air natives the initial signs of age and death are the loss of weight and gravity. The body becomes increasingly subject and interested by air and the constancy and/or need to use the powers, a matter of time. Of course this was a private conception of life, defined by Tarson-Romanei, survivor of war and battles.

Death, however, was the same for everyone, death wasn't exclusivist, classist... It came for everyone. Well... If it had reached the gods, why should it be any different? It is said, however, that descendants of the ancient races can transcend, enlighten themselves or merely decay, die. Truth or myth? The elf didn't have a formed opinion.

Halfway between the village and the highlands, a rocky ridge was caressed by long blocks of clouds from the coast, a nice cluster involved the rock with fingers of fog producing a light circle, imperceptible from the sorry ground. He decided to go there, fast, of course, however, when he was closer, he decided, wisely, to reduce his momentum and approach from the bottom up, so he wouldn't risk hitting some hidden rocky peak. At this very moment, he knew that, there, among the humid and cold clouds, there were only sensations. A welcome freshness to the heat of the day. Tarson took the opportunity to sip the moisture of his long collar and shawl. Would it hurt if Tarson relaxed between his beloved, placid and calm clouds? Of course not. He deserved it, he craved it, and, therefore, did it. He sighed with pleasure as soon as his lungs took in the air and freshened him up. There, in that void, he abandoned his body and, carried by the light inertia of the coast wind, he allowed himself to roam absent-minded.

Suddenly his ears wiggled. Is there something with him? His body left the tranquility, and took a stance between being seated and crouched. Stillness helped his trained and sharp ears, as those of his race, he recognized sound patterns from a distance. Suddenly something shimmers in front of Tarson in a scarlet tone and high speed. Sensing danger, he tried to remain motionless, hoping the cloud won't dissipate and reveal him. Whatever it was, it was humongous and should be avoided. The wind tilts down, attracted by the mountain slope. Looking down, he sees the cloud becoming increasingly thin, opening a window, showing the village tens of meters below. The secular trees at the foot of the slope would provide a favorable hiding place for landing. However, caution was the miraculous liquid of life extension. He would wait until he was sure he was alone. But, enormous eyes with yellow elongated iris and black veins, saw his…

THE LITTLE ONES

Voices, sometimes nasal, sometimes sharp, called three names: Adoriel, Gódi and Shasta. Out of the woods, three small furry creatures emerged with infant faces and bodies. They wore pants, shorts, shirts and vests like humans, however, they were all barefoot. An old tale said that the Little Ones are the ones who never lost contact with mother earth. Truth or not, those known only as Little Ones were always kind and, among the forest creatures, they were by far the most intelligent and smart.

"Greetings, human and lady elf. Have you seen our children by any chance? Better yet, what were you doing in this forgotten building?"

"Little Ones! In the land I come from it's so hard to see them that the mere sight of one is a sign of good luck to my people."

"And where is that?" says smiling to the lady elf and the others.

"My homeland is not far, south of Almokaryr village…

Many of the faces became sad.

"A place that no longer exists. We left during the first invasion. Many of our families were killed." said one of them.

"Sorry to intrude on your sadness. But we're looking for someone too." An anxious and tense Osiris said.

"And who would that be, woman?"

"Sartre." they replied in unison.

"On this side of the forest?"

"Yes, we came here at his request."

"I see." they resumed walking. "We will tell him should we find him in our search."

"No. He was here when we came in." Jupita cried to the Little Ones who moved quickly.

So they stopped. Some took their hands to their mouths, others hit their cheeks and demonstrated amazement in a long sigh. One of them, propped on a stick, laced with knick-knacks, bones, birds feet and a bag that poured water, much bigger than his small stature, suddenly stopped.

"Excuse me?"

"He stayed here while we entered to dissolve a mystery."

"Mysteries in stacked stone?"

"We thought that it was an animal's den."

"Crazy ladies." several said.

The others continued talking, trampling each other.

"A beast would never hide from intruders in its lair."

"The beasts fight without truce or flight."

"They become furious when cornered!"

"Listen." Jupita said, trying to redirect the conversation. "We had to go in, the people of the village were complaining about missing people."

"And did you see them?"

"We saw many things, and I think we solved everything. Sartre was supposed to wait for us here, that's all."

"Seriously? Where is he?"

Growling with rage, Osiris drew her mace and the Little Ones took a defensive stance.

"Unless I'm blind, deaf or insane, I heard the lady elf say that he wasn't here." She cried, in revolt.

"What only complicates the story you told us" said the one holding the staff.

"True. And who's to say that you are not responsible for everyone's disappearance?" one of the Little Ones argued.

"Including Sartre" added another.

"Brothers, relatives, see?" the one closer to Osiris alerted. The woman's weapon was blood-stained.

"Listen to me, broccoli head…"

At that moment, a thick book made a deaf sound when it hit with the ground next to the Little Ones. Everyone's aim and attention danced to Dominescu, the bold newcomer.

"It wasn't only Sartre and the villagers that disappeared." breathless, he pointed with his head and put his hands on his legs.

"Who are you and what is this?" the quieter one among the Little Ones asked.

"I'm not important. And that's the wicked one's ledger."

"That may well be yours! Your handwriting."

"Letters? Gods! He's a mere peasant! He may not even know how to write." the warrior priestess replied.

Disregarding the comment, Dominescu continued, although gasping.

"I chased one of them and almost caught him… If my horse didn't fall in that ditch… I had to put him down. I saw this fall from his mount's saddlebag."

"How can I believe you?" said the one with the staff, stepping ahead.

Dominescu took a deep breath and drank, in a single swag, the water from the wooden canteen, lined with leather. He poured the rest on his bearded face and continued.

"I'm sorry, I wouldn't dare to teach reading obvious ground signs to people bred in the woods like yourselves. It would be disrespectful. You can see for yourself, almost a kilometer from here, on the road. Or look up and see the birds of prey circling the feast."

When one of the Little Ones picked up the book in his hands, the sounds of the woods prickled everyone's senses. Then a far roar echoed sharply.

"The beast was attracted by your screams and came to kill all of you." Osiris said in a low-toned, intense voice, common to the guttural singers of her faith.

Everyone was alert. A single beast threatening to attack so many? How could it be natural? It was most likely a monster. Shrubs are ruffled, denoting that something was moving through them. Maybe there were more beasts, taking advantage of numbers and suspense. Suspense yes, after all there was no way to predict what, when and how many would attack. Wolves acted the same way. The bushes stopped moving, hiding its real position. Whatever it is, it waits for the right moment, a lapse…

Immediately, weapons were removed from their resting places, arrows were prepared, stones were placed in leather and thin cloth slingshots. Maybe someone would have to throw stones at random. Would they hit or just make it angrier? What if the beast was as scared as some of them? A scene almost frozen by tension. Hearts beat loud, releasing adrenaline, ears trying to identify the faintest noise, eyes scanning the area like zigzagging snakes. Suddenly a thin laughter surprised them.

What could that be? Was the beast able to roar and mimic other sounds? Sounds of laughter instead of that dreadful roar?

"Stripes!" one of the Little Ones shouted.

"Prepare yourselves" another one commanded.

"Father? Father, is that you?"

"Shasta's voice?" someone else shouted, astonished.

A new roar in response and suddenly, a beast jumped in front of them.

"It's Shasta! Alive! her father rejoiced and most of them sighed with relief.

The great coated beast was the same height as the tallest of the Little Ones carrying a little girl on its back . It was amazing to see her riding a tiger that size.

"Daddy!"

She jumped with the peculiar agility of the Little Ones. An agility that maybe only a few squirrels, monkeys and cats could match. Running quickly, she jumped into his lap and embrace of her father.

"Father, a bad man almost caught Shasta. I was scared, father."

"How dare they…"

"No!" one of the Little Ones in the back, with squinted eyes, peering thought thick lenses interrupted. "They speak the truth. At least that. This is a book achieved with the cost of men; women" he took a quick glance at Shasta. "and other considerations…"

The noise of the wooden wheels of a wagon approaching created new panic.

"Friends or yours?" the Little One with his quivering daughter in his lap asked. "Maybe reinforcements?"

"They are no one's friends, Little Ones." said a hoarse and heavy voice from the woods.

"Zorak?!" whispered the Little One with his daughter still attached to his lap. He cradled her with an expression between serious and surprised on his face.

The splendid tiger that had disappeared quietly, returned bringing an old man, dressed in tatters and barefoot. If it wasn't such an odd situation, Jupita, Dominescu and Osiris would have thought him a beggar. Although beggars have only stray dogs, when not, a bottle as companion. It was clear that this man couldn't be an old beggar.

Suddenly, a series of whistles agitated the Little Ones.

"And it is true. The news they report are the same I bring." said Zorak, showing proficiency in the whistle language.

The hairy creatures, whose height barely reached the waist of a man, changed their face and body expressions to horror, fear and anticipation. But they didn't forget to watch the lady elf, the strong man and, above all, the woman with the wild gaze.

Osiris fainted.

"Give her some room." one of the Little Ones shouted, trying to get to the fainted lady.

Jupita, suspicious of their sudden change of attitude, intervenes. A stalemate arises. They stared at each other. No one moved a muscle.

"Fuck you all, and get out of my way." roared the old tattered man as he made his way between them. "I know a lot about diseases and how to identify them. Fever, apathy. What happened? Was she injured?"

"Old man, if you try to hurt…"

"Should I leave your ignorance or theirs to complete her illness?" Zorak asked with his eyes closed, and clearly upset.

Everyone stepped aside.

"A lot has happened in those three floors." Jupita replied.

He looked frightened like someone who remembered a secret. The old man started a prayer and drew a diagram on Osiris's chest. Her wounds are closed, and even unconscious, she screamed of pain, revealing sharp teeth that weren't there before.

"I need to know how she was injured."

Her wounds reopened issuing a terrible sound of cloth being ripped.

"Plague!" cried the old man.

Everyone moved away.

Zorak, who nowadays was called "The old bush man", examined each of the adventurers, rudely and quickly. Confused and fearful, no one reacted.

"I need long branches. A litter! Build a litter, now!"

"What happened, old man?"

"Heed me!" he said imperatively.

Dominescu and Jupita stared at each other.

"It may be her only chance." said Dominescu. He turned around inquisitively. "Are you sure you know what you are doing?"

The old man continued watching the stampede of the others as they tried to gather what he asked for.

"Tight knots. Fasten her legs and arms, tie her firmly to the litter with the rest of the rope!"

His orders were promptly carried out. Without hesitation.

"Be careful! Don't touch her."

The old bush man went to one of the Little Ones and spoke briefly with him. The Little One said,

"Ok. I need volunteers."

"If it is to go with the taste… Well, I will go with her. I liked her errrr, resolved voice."

So the lustful young man came out of the crowd.

"Hello, my skinny goddess. I Am Hans Ranni Ramiro Roder." The indecent and bash hairy Little One, like those of his race, rubbed his hands as his eyes scanned the lady. Like someone who examines a nice, juicy piece of meat.

Jupita knew it wasn't the moment to beat his crooked teeth soft, she spared him by issuing only a quick offense.

"This is the greatest rat I have ever seen."

There was a chuckle among them. Hans hid his buck teeth with his thick lips.

"Big rat, if you please, my dear." he replied with a sly look and the glory of youthfulness.

"Hans Ranni Ramiro Roder, do you know the woods between here and the humans village?" asked the Little Ones elder, whose age was only revealed in his voice.

"I have three women this way, dear grandfather." he said bowing his head as if confessing.

Almost lost in shame, the elder looked to the others until he found his king in humble garments, who subtly agreed. Turning back to Hans, he hugged him and whispered in his ear,

"Boy, if you are thinking of only lowering your pants with your indecencies and Sartre is lost in this kidnapping, I will make you sing thin forever!" he ended the message with a weird smile, making the young man quiver and walk bowed over to the adventurers.

"Sweetheart, your big rat will take you faster than…" he seemed to remember what he was told and quietly departed. The woodcutter and the lady elf followed him.

The forest was thick in many places and the advantage of his size became evident whenever shrubs and thorns meshed ahead. The others opened passage with either with a sword, or just by crawling under the vegetation.

Jupita hurried the others.

Hans Ranni Ramiro Roder jested, but she didn't even listen to him because Tarson was alone and something told her that he was in danger.

Dominescu followed her closely, and found out that the elf had gone ahead to anticipate the adversary's moves. A good general, although a bit rushed for solutions.

"Soon we will arrive at the tavern", the lady elf thought, "hold on Tarson, don't be hasty".

When they arrived at the village, the moment was perfect.

When they looked through a crippled window, they could see the slow movement in the tavern with rich pink marble floor that needed only a good wash, obviously it was a luxury in the village.

Dominescu recognized some of the drunken patrons from his last visit.

The buck teeth Little One left without them noticing, which was, without doubt, a relief. They went in calmly. Just by walking, Jupita attracted everyone's eyes, soon Darrel noticed Jupita standing next to him and Dominescu sitting at the counter.

"You have solved the disappearances!" Phillip said gratefully.

"Where is the Tarson-Romanei?"

"Who?"

"Tarson, the elf. Where is he?"

"Did you get lost from each other?"

Trying to control herself, Jupita canvassed the place, every corner and window. She drew her sword from its sheath and held it to the innkeeper's neck.

"Calm yourself!" Dominescu suggested. "After all, this pig is well liked in the community. His coming has contributed greatly to the growth of trade."

"I Agree." said a shadow that went past Dominescu quickly, close to his feet. "Jupita, my dear girl," the shadow was Hans, the Little One resurfaced from somewhere "if someone comes in here he will run out and return with others and soon there will be a lynching of little hairy here!"

"I see." having said that, Jupita twisted her sword and with a swift wrist movement, struck heavily the barkeeper's nose with the hilt of the sword.

"You're crazy! I already said I know nothing." he said stepping back and trying to stop the bleeding.

"Liar!" You knew about the port and said nothing. You expected us to die so your little secret would stay alive. If the news of our failure spread, the caravans would come through alternative routes and for being farther, they would end up here anyway. If we were successful, the routes freed used by your accomplices had to be used so carefully that certainly would reduce the profit and as these parasites would have no means of paying off any debt, they would continue to provide favors.

"Was this bitch a victim of some thorn or juice to be raving like this?"

"Look fat man… honestly…" Hans argued, "at least she didn't use the blade to hit you."

"I have a fixed address. What ensures my survival?" the innkeeper said promptly.

"Simple." said Dominescu, cutting a piece of cheese on the counter. "She is calm."

The dissonant look of the lady elf said something else. The woodcutter took a bottle hanging from a nail on the wall, and said:

"Oh, and of course. Being accused of the disappearance of the village healer wouldn't be good for business."

"Ok. I also wasn't sure that Caleb and Maqui were responsible for all these disappearances" Darrell agreed.

"You know those bastards? Hans crossed his arms "how well?"

"In the past, we were, shall we say, sea dealers. The kind of dealers the local bourgeoisie didn't appreciate."

"Tell me about the east port." Dominescu demanded.

Darrel was intrigued, however, hiding what he knew would be more dangerous than telling the truth.

"There is a secret port to the east. They ship slaves there to the overseas realms."

"Slaves?" the indignation of the beautiful lady elf flushed the former pirate.

"To the salt mines, where their labor is allowed and common."

"Your friends became greedy." Dominescu said with malice.

"There are other things in these parts" Darrell pointed outside to emphasize what he said "everyone knows of the beasts in the region." the innkeeper perspired "the growth of this place was substantial and they had to clear a large area for sowing. It is not unusual to find slaughtered animals at the residents' door seeking food or new prey."

The merchant realized the chance to confirm his story on the Little One's face.

"The whole area suffered the same problem, isn't it, Little One?"

"That's true!"

"Forest areas were burned down to make place for sites and farms. The hairy people intervened."

"And even after our guidance and help in the plantations area." the hairy bucktooth continued, "arsons occurred without explanation last year. We fought the blazes many times."

"Except, of course, that half man half beast, Zorak."

Hans, the big rat, listening to the description, knew he spoke about the old bushman.

"Two days ago, no one said anything about this Zorak." Jupita said, narrowing her eyes.

"What do you want from me, after all?"

Dominescu, took a large step and moved to the old former adventurer, who retracted.

"Timetables and port handling days, possible routes and the names used by that fat tattooed arms man."

After a few minutes they left with all the information regarding Yuri Caleb, and, mounted on fresh horses, they followed toward the east harbor.

As he didn't have the size nor riding ability, big rat rode on Jupita's saddle. He took advantage of the situation by embracing the lady elf and enjoyed the swing of the cavalcade, delirious with indecent thoughts and dreams. Jupita never noticed any of his intentions because her thoughts were focused on the absence of her beloved friend. Slavery was an unspeakable horror to the lady elf, a disciple of Darkay, who grew up free and learned long ago that every being is free. Thus, what she faced was serious. She gave the stable boy an old coin she found in the ruins and told him to show it to the elf called Tarson-Romanei, and to tell him that Jupita and his friends followed the trail eastward. If he did that, the elf would give him another coin. Therefore she could proceed in peace because he would soon find them.

The horses ran through the trail and as soon as they reached the woods, big rat whistled and listened to the repetitions. It soon became clear that it was an effective means of communication.

"They are still working on your friend."

"How is she?"

"I already asked. The answer is always the same. They are working on her."

Jupita silenced.

"This path is too sinuous. I know a couple of shorter trails. The horses can pass easily." Actually, Hans wasn't sure. The trails were useful to the forest dwellers and the horses were common to the open plains. He hoped that Ttississ, the Great Snake had already fed, because if only its smell scared him, imagine what it would do to the horses. Besides, Hans feared failing. The path used by the kidnappers ran along rocks and mounds, difficult obstacles for a wagon, thus delaying its haste. If they were lucky, they would catch up soon.

On the way they met Adoriel and Gódi. Big rat became serious and jumped off the horse with an angry face and spoke quietly with the children of his race. Adoriel and Gódi confirmed Shasta's story and endorsed it with another confirmation.

"A wagon passed by about two hours ago."

That was old news to Hans. He got that information as soon as they left and followed the trail to the village. The whistles indicated a transport coming back from the port. He didn't think that the information was important, but now he realized he had made a mistake. Tense, Hans Ranni Ramiro Roder spoke to the children sharply.

"We have been looking for you since this morning and not for three or four hours. What do you have to say?"

"We're sorry." they said in unison.

Big rat begins to whistle again and they hear the answers from afar.

"Did you hear what your parents said?"

"Oh! Yes, daddy."

"Now you will wait here. I will follow with these beings and I hope to return in a few days. Behave until then, or I will make a tambourine of your butts! Adoriel, you're the eldest and whistles higher than the baby. You know what to do?"

"Yes, sir. But it was Shasta…"

"It doesn't matter. Her blood speaks loud, but you're the eldest. Reserve the manners for the village, in the woods, the experience of the eldest prevails. Always!"

"Yes, daddy." he answered twisting his nose.

"And don't do that if you're not picking it." Hans ended the scolding and jumped expertly onto Dominescu's horse. Standing on the back of the saddle, he continued, "I will be watching from here and I want to hear you." Then, turning to the adventurers, "Let's go!"

Dominescu and Jupita stared at each other.

"Daddy!"

"No! It's not! I mean, they didn't mean "fa-ther". Meaning "father" so…"

"I see." the lady elf said.

"It's just a prank. The children of my people say that to every adult male."

Jupita held back her laughter and accelerated. Dominescu, realizing that his ride could fall, said:

"Are you going to continue standing?"

"Until I can't see my kids."

"Manner of speech also?"

"Well… May I ask you a question first?"

"Yes."

"Are you and the lady elf… Married?"

"No!"

"Engaged?"

"No!"

"Sweethearts?"

"No!"

"Lovers, maybe?"

"No!"

"Not even once in a while? You don't…"

"Now tell me, are they your children?"

"Two of them."

"Congratulations. And what are the names of the others?"

"You don't want to know."

"Why not?"

"I don't know!"

"The road is long."

"Right. Amyntas is the eldest, then comes Adelbar, Alberico, Odabal and Uriel, Livianor, Leni and Loreli, Reimar and Reimaria, Adelbar and… No! Hey, wait a minute, I already counted Adelbar. Then it would be: Amintas is the eldest, then comes Adelbar, Alberico, Odabal and Irmin, and Irimin and Irdain, no. Wait. Wait a minute. I lost myself, so let's see: Abner is the mother of Adelbar, Alberico and Amintas, who is the eldest. I only dated Ambrosiane, no offspring, but her skinny thighs sister, Romênia… Well… She gave birth to Eglantina, which I think belongs to her fiancé Eudóxio the club-foot. There are the tiny girls, Irimin, Irdain and Irmin. I confess I'm not sure if they're mine with Natéria."

"Little One, you really love confusion."

"Confusion? The master of confusion is Gábrio of a hundred leaves."

"Who?"

"A hundred leaves, Gábrio, Natéria's husband."

"Oh, I see…"

"The poor man thinks that Georgina, his lover, gave birth to Ellinor and Levi, but actually they are the daughters of her "chaste" sister. The rascal left her sister-in-law to raise them, because she was always ashamed of her romantic side. Now, with Myrka, Mitzi's mother, I had Terensis, Odabal and Uriel and ten years later, with Mitzi, came Livianor and Nicanor. Well… Am I forgetting anyone? Ah, yes. Mashisha gave me Leni and Loreli, Reimar and Reimaria, all twins and blows. How she liked to hit when… Well, but it was the young and sweet Samira, Adoriel's mother, who gave me little Gódi before she died during childbirth.

After talking so much, Hans stopped.

"You think that is a lot? You should see when my kids get together at grandma Nany and mingle with my sister's kids! Ouch, Ouch, Ouch! I spoke so much about myself, do you have children?"

"No!"

"Brothers?"

"Here." Jupita said. "We have arrived."

She reclined and jumped off the pinto back and tied the reins to a small tree before the slope, hiding the horse.

"I recommend that you do the same." imposed the lady elf.

They all reclined and looked at the slope below. Judging from the support barges on the beach and the distance of the docked ship, one could say that the waters of this "secret port" were shallow and the colorful vision of the corals evidenced why the ship was anchored at a distance.

The height of the hill, aided by bushes of thick and opened tops, walled and divided the coastline and the countryside.

Dominescu tried to understand how the Little Ones who came after that wagon didn't find the fat tattooed man. And Jupita in silence, kept to her thoughts.

The end of the road was a huge descent, wagons and goods would certainly fall if it wasn't for a great hillside pulley mechanism, used to raise and lower boxes and crates. "Nowadays? Useless." Anyone could quickly notice the frayed and greatly oxidized pulleys with an unreliable rope, stretching to the lowest point of the beach. The descent through the rocks and the mud ,caused by a recent rain, would be difficult and slow. A continuous zigzagging, stitching down the slope, was the most obvious option.

A metal grid crate, commonly used for small animals transportation, probably fallen from one of the wagons and, upon seeing the Little One, Hans Ranni using one of them as a step, Dominescu smiled with a bold plan. Thus, in a short time he appeared on the hill, bringing Jupita with her hands tied and the Little One locked in the cage. He whistled to the barge loaders while being careful not to roll down the hill of firm rocks and coarse sand all the way to the beach. At sea, a jaunty and a bit elongated ship, showed immense contempt for the high waves, resting its anchor on the reefs, it remained steady and fixed. In the distance he could see another vessel moving towards the horizon. Closer, the barges came and went carrying people and objects, but never in the same quantity. From the narrow port to the majestic vessel with dark sails. Dominescu's experience told him that they were preparing for a long trip. One to two months, maybe, until the next stop.

"Hold that barge, I want come aboard for business."

After noticing his approach over the coarse sand, the men looked at each other but because of the distance, he couldn't hear them. One of them, at the highest point of barge, signaled him to hurry up.

"What humiliation! Locked up like a dangerous animal." said the almost tearful Little One.

"The trail to the beach is steep, stony and treeless, Hans. There was no way surprise them. We have to rely on the hoax."

"Huh? Ah! I understand."

The Little One was trying to figure out whom or what was a hoax.

"You know, I still think that my idea is more…"

"You can forget the idea of me undressing and jumping and screaming to them!" exclaimed Jupita, enraged.

"Look…"

"Quiet, both of you! If Sartre is on that anchored ship, we will work it out." he said imperatively.

"Look…" Jupita, my dear, my little tied up present." Hans whispered. "and if he is already on board?"

"We will have to find out where they're going." Jupita added.

Hans tried to find Dominescu's eyes, hoping to convince them to get rid of this insane plan.

"Dominescu?"

"Yes."

"And if he is already on board?"

"We sail."

Sartre was not among those men. Dominescu sighed, however, he tried to keep a placid face. To continue the farce he pulled Jupita's ties with calculated strength, so the beautiful lady would trip. Next to the barge, he threw the crate with Hans to the men on board and to another, who pulled Jupita tautly, the other end of the rope. A third, gentler man, helps the "merchant" to climb aboard. Accommodated between those men, they were as silent as the sailors. The only sound heard were the oars hitting, sometimes soft, sometimes hard, the crystalline and slightly greenish waters of that sea.

It took almost two quarters of an hour to get to the ship. A really big and imposing ship. Dominescu had sailed in the past. However, the size of that vessel filled the eyes of even the most experienced seamen, a real floating village. Alongside the boat, thick and entwined ropes handled the boxes hoisting, as well as the cage with Hans.

"Look, he's the same race as that little girl. It was a shame we didn't catch her. The price of slightly intelligent mascots is high."

Hans angered immediately. They were talking about a child and he loved children. Running his eyes from top to bottom, he noticed the high boots Shasta had described.

Meanwhile, the tiny barge, compared to the great vessel, was hoisted by thick chains. Looking at the land, one can see the immense and dull black rock, that, due to its size, makes any imprint to determine the area as a port unnecessary as it can be seen from afar.

Dominescu watches one of the sailors near the central mast about to fly a black fabric in his hands. Immediately he recognizes the fabric as a pirate flag. The negotiation will be tense.

The cage containing Hans Ranni was put aside, along with boxes of supplies that exude a nauseating odor.

The clothes did not belong any specific country, judging by the lack of patches on the knees, elbows and groin, after all any good sailor could sew and those robes were new, recently purchased or stolen.

"Are you here to deal?"

"Yes. Call your captain."

"I'm the immediate superior."

Jupita's curly hair was pulled back.

"Tell me how much you want for the woman. Whatever it is, I want her."

"Hey! Without payment? No way. I came to trade her for something more useful."

"And what would that be?"

"I don't know, what do you have there?"

The men stared severely at each other. Dominescu knew that he was being analyzed, tested. Ahead, at the lowest and central point of the deck, he noticed a trap door being opened and two men were been placed there.

"What are you looking for? Men to serve you?"

"Prostitutes maybe, after all, women of this nation are hard to catch."

To her discomfort, Jupita was now seen as a commodity, a spoil of war.

"For this one I can give you a couple of girls. But I'm interested in that fluffy pet. Take what you want, Jones will accompany you."

"Uh… By the way. Who indicated you?"

"Darrel, who else?"

"Right…"

Dominescu expected a negative reaction at any moment. Jupita could never be left alone on a ship like this, the same goes for the Little One, who could be drowned just to overcome the boredom of the journey. Pirates, as well as sailors, surrendered easily to combat, since the waiting for favorable winds and tide in itself was an agony. Therefore, without nothing to eat or do, violence would became a diversion. That is why the captains kept everyone working, either cleaning the deck, scraping barnacles off the hull, or reinforcing the stitches of the sails when there was no wind.

"And what about…" the dealer's expression revealed distrust.

"Yuri Caleb?" interrupted Dominescu trying to be funny.

"I thought you would tell me something about him."

"He caught the flu. That is why I came in his place. They took the healer by mistake."

Dominescu noticed a sword being unsheathed.

"Bastard, liar."

Jupita then decided to end the hoax, using the slack in her favor and in a light and fast movement, she looped the rope around the neck of one of the sailors. The sword lands between her hands, she kicked him in the stomach, throwing him overboard. Without wasting time, Jupita attacked another sailor coming towards her, when she was pulled back abruptly by the rope on her wrists, making her fall. Dominescu held her, putting his foot firmly on her wrists. He reprimanded her with a glance.

Because his mate was thrown overboard, another sailor pulled a thin knife impregnated with poison, with clear intentions of stabbing the false slave. In two swift attacks, his nose was bleeding and he squirmed holding his face. Another one drew his sword, but Dominescu's sword was faster, as he locked it against the attacker's chin.

"Where's your Captain? Or would it be better to ask for your commander?"

"Bravo!" someone clapped. "relax men. He is who he says he is."

"Actually, he didn't say." the immediate superior said.

"So?" the captain asked lightly.

"Dominescu, if you insist on a name."

"Okay Dominescu, I'm sorry for this, they are a bit overzealous."

"And under your command, I suppose."

"I am Benedict I and gave strict orders that they react like that in case of spies."

"And what guarantees that I'm not?"

"Ordinary men can barely defend himself and are unaware of the good price of a woman of that race. "But…" and, with his finger between his lip and his nose. "Only highly qualified dealers wouldn't allow anyone to hurt such rare merchandise!"

He looked at everyone and then said to his subordinates:

"Hoist that rotten piece of man before the gods and demons of the sea think we're provoking them with such sad offering."

Everyone laughed and Benedict continued loudly:

"Take her away and tie her in sight. I want to appreciate her beauty occasionally." then he returned to Dominescu. "What did you bring in that cage?"

"A Little One."

"Congratulations! You are a great Hunter."

"When I was hired I was told that I could choose my payment."

"I see… Did you bring anything that supports your story? You will have to wait and meet with your employer."

"I can't."

"You don't have a choice."

Dominescu looked towards the land and realized they had moved away. The gigantic boat was sailing. When he looked at the wrists of the man he was speaking with, he noticed his thick bracelets.

"Does any of us?"

Benedict looked at him suspiciously, intrigued by the way he said it. But he decided to welcome back the wet man with a laugh and a firm handshake. Everyone laughs at him in a mild debauchery on how he was defeated by a female.

This soaked man looks at Jupita and pulls her to himself, stealing a kiss, causing her disgust and anger. And he says loudly:

"Thank you for the bath, darling." he smiled, showing rotting teeth between empty spaces.

The crew laughed.

"Next time I will bathe you in your own blood, you…"

He closes the smile and winked in subtle threat, then he turned his attention to a rude looking dwarf tied to the central mast. He was shirtless, showing rough and unusual muscles, even for a physical worker. The scars along with the pants and boots he wore were a set with the metal chest plate and helmet beside him. There was no doubt he was a warrior dressed for war. Most of the men who had nothing to do at that moment were there.

Another sailor approached the dwarf and stare at him firmly. The sailor shook his head negatively, while he scratched the few hairs on his chin and smiling maliciously, said:

"Piece of shit."

"Wow! If I'm this size and you call me a "piece of shit", I'm glad to hear that your intestines work well."

The seaman frowns and cowardly punches the chained man.

"Shit! On second thought, that maybe what you're best at" the muscular dwarf taunted.

Many more punches are delivered on the dwarf. His mouth, hidden somewhere beneath the thick mustache and beard, bleeds and drips.

"Wait, wait! Now I'm more concerned about the width of the exit. Are you constipated? I can help if you kneel down here."

The sailor loses his temper and punches the prisoner continuously, stopping only when he is windless. With a voice inflamed by hatred, he rages:

"And now, tough guy? Are you going to continue? What do you have to say to me with that rotting mouth?"

With so many blows to his head it takes him some time to find his balance, the cut and swollen lips, his stomach and ribs burned with every breathe. Struggling, he still says:

"I think I love you."

The beater's arm is crossed by Benedict, noticeably the strongest member of the vessel. His intervention completely ceased the sailor's hideous fun.

Behind him came the actual commander. And the evidence of his status were obvious based on two quick observations. First, how the crew looked at him, with a mix of respect, admiration and evident fear. Second, his expensive and barely worn clothes. The cuff ended in a kind of platted skirt with overlays.

"Mr. Morgrinald, what a pleasure to see you again!" he said with his soft and velvety voice.

"You again. I'd shake your hand or your throat if I could, but I'm a little busy trying to tear out the mast."

"I always liked to keep the company of distinguished and well influenced people."

"That's why you drugged my drink?"

The commander was a man with thin wavy and brushed back hair, when he smiled he arched even more his thin goatee.

"Can you tell me where is Astrias?"

"Who?"

"Maybe you could tell me about his damn brother?"

"Listen, do I happen to have a guitar, a flute or a tambour with me? Am I talking in rhymes and have that stupid smirk on my face?"

"We know you are friends."

"Or maybe you think I stand by the window expecting some spicy news to cheer my pointless life?"

"Some of these gentlemen can confirm your relationship with the merchant mage because you have crossed the sea with them on the same vessel."

"Wow… I never realized that a sea trip could make me friends with someone."

"Sorry, I assure you. The account provided by these perceptive collaborators refer to… Some trips for three years. I believe that can establish a bond. Yes, that is a sign of friendship for sure."

"I see. By the way, my axe wants to strike a deep a friendship with you."

"If I were you…"

"You would be more handsome." Morgrinald said, interrupting.

The commander stepped forward and, right next to his ear, said:

"Some of these men come from a land of weak soil and little food. And in the name of survival they practice heinous acts that turned into religion, they are ruthless with their enemies. Therefore, avoid angering them."

Life at sea was difficult. You could see sunken eyes and crazy mouths, dry by lack of water, tall gums due to lack of proper food to fill their flat bellies everywhere, when they were not fallen and weak.

"Don Victor Sapienza, I made an unforgivable mistake…"

"That's great! You are beginning to understand the danger of challenging people like these."

"That's not it. I only apologize for the day my axe slipped and only hit you with its broad side. Next time, I will make sure to hit with the sharp side."

"Benedict…" he says loud and clear, at the same time as his eyes locked with those of the man who was beating Morgrinald with such joy.

"Yes, commander."

"His skin is tough…" Saying that, he stole the carpenter mallet and stroke a blow to the middle of the prisoner's chest. "it must be well tenderized…" another blow. "But it is still eatable."

Incredibly the dwarf was still breathing, and in the midst of an insane smile that disturbed him, Victor handed the mallet to Benedict. The cruel look slowly reached each of the tied ones, aware of the endless horrors that they will have to endure. Then the leader paced in front of the prisoners. The boards of the deck echoed under the heel of his shoe, while the other leg dragged in an irritating symphony.

"Madame…" he said to Jupita, bowing in front of her.

"Sadist!"

"What are concerned about, exactly?"

"You…"

"Be careful! A flower loses its sweetness with ill-chosen words."

Jupita didn't have to say anything, her gaze was translucent. Frank. He approached and whispered in her ear:

"Have you ever seen a sea banquet, young lady?" his voice was sticky, low and sleek. "I once saw the putrid carcass of a sperm whale. Do you know what is that? A sperm whale? A whale? The dead creature attracted sea eaters and they started chewing, eating and eating and even satisfied, with bloated stomachs, they still chewed. In absurd ecstasy. Do you know why, my young lady?

They like to feel death close, have the sensation of murder. These foolish and dirty ones are not different and they love have something to pass the time… I can protect you during the trip. Until we sell you."

The idea was too sordid. The whole concept. Jupita spat in his face. Obviously it was the best answer. The commander didn't even look away and again he proposed:

"The dwarf will be flogged again and again until he stops being interesting, until they forget him. Then they might remember all of you! And you."

Jupita expected like a fool, hopefully, that Tarson would appear amid the wind and bring storm winds as reinforcements, but it was useless. When he realized what had happened, it would be too late, she would have already been swallowed by the horizon.

" … to reach our destination."

The lady elf was surprised, she didn't notice that she wandered off for a moment, which happened from time to time. The elven mind, as it aged, suffered increasing blackouts. She had to concentrate, avoid the blackouts. And so she did. She stared at the thin outlined mustache. Only then she heard his words again.

" …until then, not even the marrow bastard dwarf's bones will be left."

"I venture with the rest of those imprisoned."

"Very well, madam." Victor stood up a little more and said with a confused but deep expression, "As I said, the wind at sea is sometimes weak and sometimes nonexistent."

"There are also storms and typhoons." he answers by impulse.

"Let's see, then, how it will be. Remember… Sperm whale… Banquet. Lucky for you, we still have apples!"

With his arm braced, he toppled over the barrel showing mostly dark and rotten fruit. Without bending his left leg, injured by the dwarf in a recent episode, the commander picked up one of the apples.

"Damn! How things are…" he shrugged.

"I hope you enjoy the saffron and onions bathe."

"Gentlemen? I want to have something to eat early this evening."

Screams and cheers run through the deck in a rapt and vile concordance with their commander's sentence. As he departs, he places his hand on Dominescu's back, who nods slowly in agreement. So the "merchant" and him leave to discuss business.

CELEBRATION NIGHT

Once the fake negotiation was over, Dominescu was deeply relieved to get out of Victor Zaragoza's cabin.

How can you be so stupid? Now everyone was under a huge risk because of a foolish plan. He had to hold himself back when he spoke sales plans and about his contempt for life.

They were bound to Yellow city. How could such a place exist?

The city was as sick as its name suggested. The idea of throwing people against each other until only one is alive was… insane.

It was like the cockfights that Dobrovonski, his late brother; loved. Dominescu never saw fun or purpose in that. For him it was just bored people betting a few coins in a sport of fools.

The ship would meet the first island en route to another continent. The stop was only to resupply water and fruit. However, if they met with the bloody fat traitor Yuri Caleb, they would undoubtedly be killed.

And there was another way.

The inspiration hit him so fast that he took the necessary steps without blinking. The crew drank happily and like every bored group, they gambled. Some played craps, others, the dance of knives and a very active group was playing the Ouija board.

In the woods Dominescu had the habit of pelting acorns at his brother, even after Dobrovonski disappeared, the addiction remained. Discretely he took them from his pockets and shot one with his fingers on the back of a sailor and after the man complained, he alternated between targets. Without knowing who was hitting them, they accused each other, then Dominescu stopped. He took the bottle of one of the sailors and with a lascivious smile, hugged him and started singing a very popular song. Another one joins in and repeats the rhyme. Dominescu plunged the bottle into the barrel full of cider, sipped it and spat into the air for the owners of the winds as was the tradition.

He returned the bottle and the fool smiled, a perforated smile, then he repeated his gestures. So another one took his bottle, pushed him, drank, spat and was preceded by another, thus maintaining the motion and the rhythm of the singing.

The woodcutter prayed for another stupid plan to work.

In minutes, he was integrated with the crew of drunks and remained in a corner arm wrestling. Each loser took a swig. And Dominescu, facing weak and drunk opponents, loss only to those who were more drunk and pretended to take another swig.

And so the day went by, with games and small talk. Eventually, he shouted the peeing sailor song and headed for the bulwark. Isolated under the false pretense of relieving himself, without anyone watching, he went back to shooting acorns at his first targets and they began to push and blame each other. All it took was for Dominescu to head back and stumble on one of them for the one standing in front to punch him. So the fight had begun.

The fight slowly took the deck amid laughter, screams and swearing.

Hans, the big rat, without his sling or his twin daggers and still stuck in a small cage and weighed down, only hoped they forgot about him until the end of the fight that he didn't even see begin. Not that he cared about the fight, but it was like fire in tall grass. One of the apples that were tossed away, when the barrel tumbled, rolled in his direction due to the sea waves. "Food, at least," he thought, while trying a great deal to get it.

In the middle of the fight, although tied and beaten, Morgrinald, the dwarf, managed to knock down one of the sailors and as he felt close, he stepped on him with all his mighty strength breaking the sailor's ribs. At that moment he noticed a metallic glow from of the corner of his brown eyes and the thin and sharp sheet of a sword cut the air, digging into the wood, scratching his skin.

Without blinking or fading, Morgrinald fixed his eyes on the bearded man that had swung the sword. Suddenly he felt his lungs expand by the loosening of the rope cut by the bearded man's sword.

"If you are not their friend…" said his savior with a steady gaze. "I'm Dominescu and I think you know how to use this." he completed throwing him a sword.

"Morgrinald." he replied, slightly tilting his head at the same instant that he turned his body and punched a sailor that was running to alert the commander in his cabin. "Morgrinald, grandson of the honored Keldorn. And I'm dying to see shit fly."

In his fall, the sailor smashed a rotten apple and the pieces hit Hans.

"I hate apple puree." the Little One complained cleaning himself. However, he picked up another one rolling close to him. "I hope it's not rotten…" he prayed. "May it not be rotten… May it not be rotten."

In the center of the deck, Morgrinald ripped his double blade axe from a barrel just a few meters from him and dropped the sword. His agile axe movements with the adapted handle compensated for his race's short legs and arms. Accurate blows either broke the opponents' weapons, or sent them flying into the sea.

Jupita, in face of the difficulties, avoided the use of magic, preferring to use the sword. However, hard times demanded attitudes not philosophy. So she ran from the clash to the upper deck, to the helmsman. Because of the bad weather, that was approaching quickly, and because of the danger of reefs and sand banks, he would never leave the helm. The beautiful young lady needed only a moment to channel her magical energies.

Three of the sailors saw her and climbed on the barrels without using the lateral staircases, in order to gain time and have an easy fight with a mere woman. If they only knew how that thought itself was dangerous. The lady elf hands were shaking as she tensed her fingers until she closed them at once, when she pointed to two of them, the magical energy accumulated produced a loud crack and bright bluish sparks hit them. One was thrown against the bulwark and the other whirled falling unconscious on the lower deck.

Right on top of Hans' cage as he was struggling to get out, the Little One had his fingers squeezed against the grid and groaned, almost howled, even after he had pulled them.

A third sailor, moving toward the beautiful lady elf, changed his mind after seeing what happened because there would be no easy fight against her. Jupita looked over her shoulder and noticed the unexpected assailant. She turned around and punched the helmsman's face who was trying to hit her with a large loose pin from the helm.

"My nose! You broke my nose!" bleeding, the bastard dropped the peg.

Dominescu however had been dominated.

"Gentlemen?" the commander's voice had everyone's attention. "my knife is new and has never tasted blood. Drop your weapons before it falls in love."

They all lowered their weapons, except Morgrinald. He walked steadily toward the commander who, although holding a hostage was sweating, clearly despaired. Then, the dwarf released the axe, because in his blind fear, the scumbag certainly would not measure consequences.

So they were subdued again.

Jupita was gagged and had her hands and feet tied, and soon was she blindfolded also because of her fierce gaze. Dominescu and Morgrinald were locked in chains and led to the oars in the bowels of the vessel. Seated on the seats scrawled with fear of gods and anti-gods were a little more than twenty shackled. Men, women and adolescents either ragged or wearing minimal attire. And among them Dominescu identified the beaten and almost naked Sartre.

Suddenly, windows are opened with great excitement by the pirates.

"Unfurl the sail." Benedict screamed, somewhere on the deck.

The phrase had no sense for the chained ones. One of the men pelted himself down to the chained rowers deck and from the center aisle of captives, snapped his whip fiercely.

"To the oars, you bastards."

With his lively speech, the order was obeyed, so everyone moved the heavy wooden oars quickly from their laps to the outside.

"Row! Bunch of bastards! Row as if the devils were chasing you. Not by interest, but for meat and death wish.

That's what you are running from you useless bastards! Row! Or I will separate meat from bone with the whip."

Suddenly, violent bursts of rocks hitting the sea around, water invaded the starboard windows. It was easy to understand that the damn pirates were fleeing from another vessel.

"Row! Row! railed someone behind before hitting the huge drum, alternating between bawl and beat.

A new bang. The big, black three oars aside ship bowed to the right.

"Suspend to the right!"

"Stop the right!" shouted one of the pirates, slapping Dominescu's face and others who were on that side of the aisle.

"Everything and everyone ahead!"

Facing these flying stones, anxious for crushing their skulls, they all began to comply with more aplomb to the commands, even the pirates came down to the oars. They were like one on the oars, obeying outside eyes; they, the poor blind, were trying to escape death. A new and deafening sound reached some part of the deck. It didn't matter if it was one of the empire's ships, they were aboard a ship of thugs, whoever was pursuing them would rather sink them instead asking for explanations… They heard nothing more for a few moments. Except their heavy and brief breathing and the drum. Exhaustion knocked down one by one. There were no sounds outside, only the waves coming and going. The drummer silenced, the oars stopped. The shackled ones didn't even look at each other, they kept their eyes on the upper deck, speechless, waiting, just waiting. Maybe everyone on deck were already in shreds, or the vessel or vessels that pursued them had just boarded them. The fear and insecurity took the oarsmen in different ways. Urine and the crying produced from fear contrasted with the courage of a few others. The silence before the death, the silence of the predators before the strike…

All of a sudden there were shouts of celebration. Feet jumped on the wood deck.

"They gave up! They gave up! Triumph!" a toothless man screamed to the bowels of the ship.

The joy of retaining their life, even for one more day, ignited everyone's spirits. However, inexplicably, they asked to continue rowing. Half an hour later and at a lower speed, the drum sound ceased and the oars were collected over the chained ones' legs, but they were still alive.

The temperature of the water running off the oars told Dominescu that they were sailing in distant and deep waters.

The drummer, the whip man, and five others who helped on the oars also joined the celebration, abandoning the slaves in the dim light of the guts of the ship. Isolated, Dominescu told Sartre what had happened. And Morgrinald commented how he wished a chat with the one-legged bastard that challenged him.

"Victor? You are talking about Victor, right?" a toothless lady said.

Someone insisted on silence in a fearful wheeze, begging them to stop.

"Master Victor Sapienza, the bloodthirsty tool of another unspeakable." said a one-eyed man.

"Adopted son of evil." said another voice on the other side of the oars.

The dwarf just rolled his eyes. Cowardice was boring, but he planned to stay only a short time there. The bearded one, his liberator, looking at a rower beside him, asked incredulously:

"Who are they talking about?"

"Victor Sapienza." said the young lady behind him.

"Yes, the one with the knife smile." completed someone out of sight.

"With a cannon's look." whispered the same young lady.

"Only the captain challenged him, and it had to be that way." each of their words made the fear even more evident.

"So It's not the same captain?"

Dominescu asked but understood. If they don't learn to respect, the path was fear, because good men in charge could be easily killed, but mutiny? Mutiny was the vilest behavior on commercial and military ships. As its idealizers, these rowers deserved to be here. But what if they weren't? Such thought absorbed Dominescu without him noticing. If there had been an armed dispute between the captain and his commander and as both were equally feared, no one had done nothing. They thought it would continue all the same, because mutiny rarely changed the means of managing the ship. However it was a different time. Gradually, it was easy to conclude that the chained ones there joined the losing side and would love to rebel, free themselves of that condition, but they feared Victor as dry bush fears the sun. Dominescu blinked heavily, cutting the dense cloud of memories, trying to focus on what the bravest of all those cowards was saying .

"The captain was violent until scurvy, diphtheria or whatever killed him. Today, on deck, it's worse, in every place where there is at least a bit of silence, you can hear that fucking wooden leg. A grave and hollow toc."

As if taken by despair rooted with madness, an old man of about forty, with an aghast mouth and glassy gaze, invaded the conversation whispering quickly:

"That sound… that damn toc-toc. Actually it was Victor. Has always been. Laying in his hammock, delirious with fever he directed all the problems lightly until the captain was taken to the gallows. That's Victor."

"That's Victor." the others whispered, as a bizarre prayer.

"You know!" the one eyed blind old man was shaking his head while he continued his account without a breather, like someone about to drown in bad dreams or despair. "Master Victor Sapienza was a boatswain on another vessel and was forcibly 'added' to the crew. It was either that or swim for three months to find a piece of land. At the time, he arrived with a broken leg. I did everything I could. The herbs poultices only prevented the bleeding."

"You were there?" the young lady asked and was ignored.

"When gangrene took root and the fevers became frequent, I had to amputate from the knee down. Regulation said to give two glasses of a strong and distilled drink but he refused it vehemently. No one gave the order, except himself. And his soul went with the bad leg. He became dark, fearsome."

A storm of whispers about the cruelty of the punishments and how Master Vincent Zaragoza was regarded as an instrument of evil in the flesh.

"Cruel, but it he's a blessing." an old man confessed, shocking everyone bringing on another wave of murmurs but he kept talking without taking not of it. "Why? The ship was never required by the belly of the sea in the storms, was it? A devil yes, but a creature of the sea."

Dominescu analyzed the bitterness of that story, that kind of man should only fear the weapon that caused the fracture to his now dead leg and from what he heard from his dialogue with the dwarf, he suspected that the dwarf was the one behind the weapon.

On the deck, Hans made the men smile, the Little One was a curiosity. A cute pet. Very few had seen a Little One, not to mention the natives of the overseas lands. Therefore, he would be very lucrative.

So they worked happily dreaming of financial promises. The crew, although violent even among themselves, were effective and disciplined, taking care of the sails, anchor and helm. The others kept the deck dry so no one slipped on the slime and fell overboard. Although that was a little hard to happen due to the gunwales a meter height which itself avoided such misfortune.

Meals on plates and wooden spoons were soon served to sailors at their posts. Hans felt his stomach tighten, but he didn't dare ask for a piece, because the captain threatened to cook the troublemakers. He still saw the beautiful lady elf dumped in a corner. At least she is still alive, he thought. The hours dragged between tides and Hans didn't even feel them anymore, the only thing that bothered him was the lack of land. It was late at night when, already homesick, he began to whistle, looking at the moon with sadness. A sadness confused with light music as beautiful as a lullaby.

With this enchanting sound the other crew members, were getting drunker by the minute. Celebrating the battle victory. At some time, the brutal Benedict attention shifted towards Jupita's skin. After all, a beautiful woman, in minimal clothes, smelling like a little girl, and, with the drizzle smoothing the fabric, her breast became something irresistible for men thirsty for sin. Bonded and helpless, she ignores the first touches of the brute man with cesspool breath, his steady and maniacal hands open the young lady's legs. He kissed her free lap, while he abused her with his hands. Seeing herself without alternative, the lady elf became more accessible and surrendered to the caresses, returning the ardors with lust.

"No…"

A false negative given by who actually wants more, Benedict concluded in silence.

"Shut up!" he said, reticent, delirious with lust. "It has been a long time!"

His calloused hands traveled the female's waist and tighten her.

"No." the lady elf complains. "I want it slow."

Benedict bit his lower lip. Despite being a damn elf he could barely hold himself, a trophy he'd sing to everyone after relieving himself. Anyone could have easy women, but she had a different taste, she was the type who surrendered only by force and Benedict liked to use it. The elfish delight, being tied and blindfolded, would not even recognize him the next day, if the commander decided to free her.

However, unknown to him, Jupita was used with the darkness of the caves where she lived for some time and her elfish hearing was underestimated. He was there alone, and the voices of the others revealed either drunkenness or deep slumber. The thin drizzle of dawn would probably leave the wood deck slippery, an asset for her superior agility and a nuisance for the drunk and sleepy. Besides, the smell denounced a mist forming, great for hiding intentions.

Jupita embraced the daring one and among his heinous fondles she looped his neck with the rope that bonded her and applied a good kick in his groin, hitting more than skin and rather less than bone. When he fell, he rolled in mute pain.

When Benedict fell, Hans saw the twin daggers. And with the opportunity in range of his short and hairy arm, he stole them without being noticed and smiled between his crooked teeth. At the moment he remembered the nickname the lady elf had given him. So big rat hides them, thanking the gods for his luck so far. He easily unlocks the cage with the dagger blade. Amid the shadows and the distraction of the end of party, he quickly examined the resources offered on the vessel to help to free his friends. Climbing down the stares carefully, he was surprised and happy to see Sartre. Alive." He woke him with a fraternal hug.

"I never expected people like this still existed, willing to risk themselves for people they hardly know. That's heroism." Sartre said, moved.

The dialogue extended and as new phrases were added, the definition of age between them was lost. The roles of father and son reversed and blended. Their affection for each other had created this riddle… During the dialogue, Dominescu woke up.

"Hans? Here Hans."

The skillful big rat showed him a foolish smile and raised his hand, revealing a thin piece of metal.

"Little One?"

"You're lucky I came from B's house."

"What?"

"B! It's a nickname." as he spoke, his hands were moving up and down the padlocks of the thick chains. "So, I like discretion with married woman. I know, I know. But I'm hot and so is she. I love women with hairy backs, don't you?"

Dominescu was more interested in keeping his eyes on the access doors to the cellar.

"The crew may be here any…"

"Easy. This bolt, I created it after her husband got suspicious and started locking his wife and daughter when he left for the work. And it works fine, see!"

The chains next to the padlock made a sharp noise that disturbed Dominescu.

The other prisoners in that enclosure woke up, and the fear and the desire for freedom earned the tone of conversation during mutinies.

"I'm going back to my prison and entertain the drunks. If you hear the sound of a bird repeatedly, it is time, because everyone is asleep. We will easily take over this huge boat."

"You are well versed in the art of war, Little One! Dominescu said, with admiration.

"No. All I know is that an angry husband is more agile than a hungry tiger." winked the Little One. "Besides, after all of this, the lady elf will be grateful, and a welcome here, pleasantries there and…"

"Ha."

Big rat was surprised for making the serious bearded one almost laugh. However, he asked himself as he returned to his prison:

"Is he a boyfriend? Well, if it is, he should know it is better if…"

His thoughts were interrupted by a man who threw a small barrel of drink on top of the cage, squeezing his fingers again.

"Caught you." said a clearly intoxicated voice. "stay there little bug."

"Humph! Again… very nice."

A blackened heap in the sea caught a drunk's attention and made him run to the harpoon. As it was always loaded, he just turned it towards the target and, with some difficulty to aim, harpooned it.

"Yay! Ha, ha. I caught a big fish. August you fucker, we're free of your clam stew. From today until the end of the month we eat whale."

The thick chain ran across the deck of the ship, making a big bang rolling its links.

Dominescu heard little of the drunken speech, and by the subsequent noise, he concluded that the furry Little One was in trouble and could suffer worst. In his heroic exit, he inspired, without a war cry, the mutineers to follow him with bare hands.

On deck the drunks are no work for the ferocious mob.

Jupita was still trying to get rid of her ties while all this was going on. The commander opened, stupidity, the doors to his cabin. The light inside revealed a young lady cornered in the bed, in panic, trying to defend her innocence with bloody cloths. The vision of this scene infuriated the young lady elf raised by Darkay of Almokaryr. The ropes tied to fragile wrists are furiously ripped. The air around starts to crisp and electric flashes ran over the lady elf's skin, tiny rays grown through her body overflowing to the ground and from the ground to the sea. The lady elf inhaled and opened her arms like a cross and, kilometers above, the clouds meet creating lightning that in an instant snaked down the sky. In the vessel, the lightning on the face of the beautiful young woman reflected an immense and complete hate, the lightning stroke her opened arms then she closed them in a single clap. The clap resulted in thunder and a broad stupendous lightning that hit the commander's chest blackening the affected spot, his body now burned from inside out and not a sound came from him. After that, Jupita's legs, disciple of Darkay did not obey anymore, her body dropped to her knees.

Nearby, Dominescu realized the incessant grinding of wood and iron. The chain of the harpoon tensed slowly, his eyes bulged when he looked over the side.

"Careful!" he shouted and held on as he could.

After his warning, the thick chain of the harpoon caused a violent thud on the vessel and bent it to port. Unprepared to withstand such strain at its base, the secondary mast snapped and shattered on the counter weight. The black sails support log of the great vessel slammed into the deck, Jupita moved sideways dodging the heavy log that cleaved the deck causing cries of terror.

However, the lady elf's feet were still attached to the mast and, due to the blind fall of the mast on her restrains, it turned her body into the tip of a whip. Her beautiful body hit violently on the external side of the ship, and from the shock came unconsciousness. The weight on the free rope made the unconscious lady dive into the sea, like an anchor, in cold water.

"Jupita!"

Distressed, Dominescu jumped blindly into the sea, even though he was aware that he wouldn't have time to stop her from sinking. He resurfaced holding the rope attached to the lady elf, using it as a guide to reach her. He breathed quickly, filling his lungs, and plunged into the dark, there was no light, at least not at almost dawn. His feet moved frantically and his hands pulled the rope, suddenly his left hand misses the rope, then he stopped. No mistakes, he thought, he couldn't miss. The woodcutter groped around impatiently. In the water and unable to see, what should he do? This mild desperation made him lose some air. Noisy bubbles came from him running over his forehead. With that, he knew the way up.

He moved his hands recklessly and then he found the rope again. However, fearing to go in the wrong direction, he let out some more air and, making sure of the bubbles' direction, followed in the opposite way.

His neck veins bulged, his chest heaved its first seizure, his body begged for air, but Dominescu persisted, just a little more, he told himself. Just a little… He was grateful when his calloused hands reached Jupita. He was relieved, realizing that she was released with the impact. But there was no reaction when he touched her, she was unconscious. He untied the straps off the feet of the beautiful lady. Could she be dead? No! Of course not! Dominescu pushed away the thought and wrapped his weak arm behind her smooth neck.

The way back was slow out of weakness and necessity. He had learned long ago that he should resurface slowly from a dive or risk becoming stunned… Or he could die. It was horrible not knowing the his friend's current state, only the obvious came to mind… Take her out of the sea so she could breathe. The rope was lost, but blessings are granted when he noticed the slight glare of day above. With his head out of the water, he inhaled deeply and tried to find the vessel, it was close. He also noticed that one of the masts was severely bent to the other side. As a lumberjack he knew all too well that it would revert to his side and drop violently. He took another deep breath and dived deep with the unconscious lady to avoid the shock with the heavy mast.

Meanwhile, on board, Morgrinald, recently freed, fought as he could, although he was impaired, weak from hunger and wounds, he insisted in wasting time to put on his armor, using each combat pause to put on a piece.

"Hey. Here…" Big rat begged, trapped like a rabbit.

With a kick, Morgrinald removed the extra weight of the barrel from the Little One's prison.

"I know that the padlock won't be a problem for your skills."

"Of course not, but how did you know?"

"I was chained there."

"Oh, Yes? Okay, then. "Hey! Careful!"

Between punching and kicking his opponents, the muscular dwarf gradually dressed. The ship was listing, condemned. The fight was forgotten. The fight now was to save their lives. There was little time to do something, and few dinghies also. Then a new fight began, a terrifying fight of shoves and abuses, the purest and instinctive fight for survival. There was no good nor evil, only few boats…

With everything turning, the still lit night torches ignited the sails and the fire came dangerously close to the depot. Meanwhile, Sartre, Morgrinald and another of the rebels dropped the last boat and left. The condemned vessel begun to leak a black and viscous liquid from barrels that rolled down at random to the tide. Noticing it, Morgrinald took the oars and rowed as fast as he could.

Sartre saw, helplessly, several men, sailors and slaves, sinking in the sea and suddenly, when the burning sails touched the black liquid, a new nightmare began. The sea burned and the resulting toxic smoke asphyxiated quickly. The greasy liquid burned the poor men in the water as soon as it reached them. There were those who dived but their lungs couldn't resist very long and they returned to the surface to burn. Agony and despair for many. Survival seemed an unreachable gift to the a healer.

Sartre collapsed seeing such horrors. He squatted on the boat changing his hands between covering his eyes and ears.

Dominescu, farther away thanks to the tide, saw the ship overcome by fire and smoke. Between the waves a few boats went in another direction. Soon, the portentous ship would adorn the seabed. Screams of death or distress were heard everywhere but there was no way to help so many, so he surrendered saddened. Quietly, he dedicated a prayer to the souls of the dead and of the innocents that will soon follow.

"Cough! Cough!"

Dominescu turned around, relieved and perplexed. The lady elf was still breathing.

OF THE BLOOD OF KELDORN

Morgrinald and two others survived the shipwreck thanks to a small boat. Otherwise, the dwarf would have surely sunk with the weight of his armor, which he insisted on keeping. It was "an inheritance of the old ones". Actually, it was noticeably threadbare with its clasps losing taut. He really needed a new one.

Morgrinald imagined going back home, he thought of the waning long and extensive granite table. Sitting at it, with the family and the aggregates of his numerous clan. It was at that table that Keldorn, his grandfather, spoke about the war. The same table where Morgrinald would tell about his deeds, the news of the outside world and especially about his misadventures. The seawater wet his boots again and brought him back to reality. The puny man with small eyes still spoke. Shit, he thought. And, as this lad liked the sound of his own voice, his monologue was endless. Morgrinald sighed loudly, revealing his boredom. He saw him as a talking idiot. Trapped in the midst of so much water for two days with a madman who thought the gods cared for him and a retarded chatterbox with a thin voice. He was unable to sleep. It was dangerous and unwise to let these fools allow another boat to approach, after all, they may be the only ones with food and water. And that wasn't luck or coincidence. Morgrinald called it fate. In the face of danger, he, grandson of Keldorn owned a admirable coolness; even legendary; And calmly, Morgrinald collected a barrel of water and supplies before the slave ship sank.

"What a shitty fate." mumbled the hardened dwarf.

After saying that, he compared himself with his grandfather, old Keldorn. He had a raspy voice because he had lived a long time with the king of a great human city and Morgrinald remembered well the beautiful sentence about fate that he used to quote:

"Fate works beautifully," he repeated, plagiarizing his grandfather's habit of winding his beard. "polishing the paths while carving the face of all travelers, transforming the weight of the years into wisdom."

Of the two humans who shared the small boat with him, one was a healer. Someone called Sartre. There's someone important to have around at moments like this, he thought to himself and at the healer's side, Hellsing, the talker. He had been talking well over two hours and wasn't tired yet. The idiot talked about men, horses, birds, worms, foods, kingdoms. He spoke of his experiences, of people he lived with, people he talked to, what he said about people and what people said about him.

Morgrinald saw the waves coming and going but nothing around. I wonder if that bastard Victor survived. He hadn't seen him, so there was still a possibility. If the drunk that caused the ruin of the ship survived, he surely would die from a beating or any other death the crew could think of. Even during the pause between his long and entertaining thoughts, the fellow, now behind him, was still talking, so he tried to get some sleep. He urgently needed earth under his feet, the sea always made him apprehensive and listening to that brandy pudding of a thousand tongues speaking as if it was a pleasure cruise, didn't help.

"No… So allow me to tell the details…"

"Fuck!" Morgrinald could not hold back his irritation.

That voice, that pitch, between drunk and cheerful, between comic and shrill, slowly became unbearable. Even the sea seemed tired of him.

Fortunately, the connection with earth, stone and dust had always been strong in him and so he easily saw the signs of land in the distance. The healer would have also seen if he wasn't paying attention, or worse, if he wasn't hostage of the endless speaker. Could it be an island? Were they back to the mainland? Could it be some dumb isle?

Half an hour later and the place seemed to drag itself towards them. Coral reefs, sandbanks, maybe both. The weakness from hunger and thirst combined with the incessant talking of the skinny fellow, overcame reason. By no way Morgrinald envied Hellsing's experiences. Maybe they weren't even real experiences. But what choice did he have? Surrender or talk about yourself with the same enthusiasm? Did humans understand the density of his culture? That they all read and wrote in more than one language? That he, Keldorn's grandson, knew the secrets of metal and the best way to forge them? And, above all, a noble of his family could…

"Noble comrade, allow me to remind you what I said earlier…"

However, Morgrinald, Keldorn's blood, had inherited the subtlety and foul mouth of his mother.

"Shitty pomposity." he said angrily as he spat inside the boat "besides talking like a woman and enjoy singing, what kind of use can a bard like yourself have?

Hellsing looked at him shocked by such abrupt interruption of his lively conversation with the healer.

"Boy?" Sartre tried to manage the situation "don't be intransigent…"

"Answer, scrawny."

"In times of peace or war? We are sent into the world to tell about the events between the kingdoms. We like to sing the feats of the world."

"Besides gossiping, talking like a woman, enjoy singing and busting my balls… What fucking use can these useless, worthless bards like you can have?"

"Gentlemen, stop it…"

"We talk of feelings, acts of great heroes."

"I see… So aside from talking like a woman, like singing and gossiping, and story teller, what fucking purpose has these useless, worthless ass kissers bards, can have?"

"We are literate, we can read and write enough so that we can take written words from one kingdom to another, from the humblest to the blessed that inhabit the most sumptuous palaces."

"Sumptuous? Come on… Okay, then. A stupid bard, talker, ham actor, drooler with an inverted smile, as I understand it, is a parasite bum who takes advantage of the lack of education of some people, gets paid for this and assumes the role of a damn carrier pigeon. Besides, loves talking like a woman and enjoys singing. And not the useless boot licker who speaks for more than two hours about nothing."

The extremely thin man squinted his eyes even more.

Sartre, between them, expect the worst.

The dwarf wondered if the skinny fellow could talk underwater.

In the meantime, a soft and lyrical singing was heard, soothing their souls.

"Who's voice is that?" Hellsing smiled.

"Must be on the other side of the rocks, next to the beach." Sartre said gaping.

Morgrinald gritted his teeth, looked around, put his fingers in his ears, tried not to lose his mind, not be charmed.

Suddenly, the agonizing cry of Hellsing, being devoured by the mermaid with dirty, seaweed matted hair brought them back to reality. The boat had suffered damages and a fissure bubbled water inside, therefore, the boat would float for uncertain time. Morgrinald grabbed his double broad-bladed axe and quickly used it as an oar to escape the beast. Sartre, taken by terror, struggled to keep his senses. He couldn't look away, not even close his eyes on the grotesque scene. Life abandoned Hellsing among the horrible sounds of bones breaking.

"Row! Wake up old man, and row to shore."

"Gods!"

"No praying. Row you worthless creature, before I send you in as dessert."

"And…"

"Minus one."

"Heartless!"

"Better that than dead. The talker is gone. He's dead, gone, ended. Lets take care of the living. This isn't over, row!"

"The beast is coming."

"And we're going. We won't be able to fight in the water! She has the advantage there!"

Close to the beach Sartre jumped off the boat and swam until his feet touched the sand. Only then he searched for Morgrinald.

Compensating the waves motion as he could, Morgrinald, Keldorn's blood, of the brave clan of the Battle Hammers, looked at the rows of razors in the jaws of the creature and thought if they would work better on a meat hammer or as a bunion file.

"Shit! I Need both of them. Hey! Ugly, stand still while I kill you."

The mermaid wasn't interested in the dwarf, wearing all that armor, he could easily be an enchanted machine. She wanted the other one's meat, the one who swam unprotected, and with her impressive speed and agility in the water she dodged the dwarf one easily.

"Son of a…" said the frustrated midget lowering his weapon. "Shit. The old man is going to lose his legs." There was nothing to do, he thought. Anyone knew that, however… "Keldorn's grandson is not anyone!"

In the dwarf's logic, even if the old man escaped, he was still in the water. He looked at the axe and sighed. A single bet. If he missed he would certainly have to deal with the creature bare handed.

"Maybe it's time to discard it anyway…" he completed echoing his thoughts.

Suddenly other shapes passed under the boat. "They are following their leader," he concluded.

There wasn't much time to aim. The mermaid resurfaced in the shallow water, raising a spray of water and the dwarf hurled his weapon, but the predator was hit sideways by a gray shape and because of this, his axe only grazed her scaly skin, then she disappeared in the water. The other creatures, that resembled large fishes, appeared beside the first one jumping out of the water, surrounding it. The filthy and hungry female got angry and swam quickly toward the rocky beach area, where she disappeared, to the relief of the castaways.

The big smooth and scale less fish seemed to laugh in triumph, and two of them gently pushed Morgrinald and his boat to the shallows. Happy about the battle and the escape of the hideous monster, the fish jumped over the water with flips and galloping laughter and returned to the depths from whence they came.

Sartre and Morgrinald are safe. But where?

THE DAUGHTER OF THE WIND AND THE WOODCUTTER

Although salty, the fresh water woke Jupita. Dominescu smiled, relieved.

"What happened?"

"The ship is gone."

"And Hans?"

"The Little One is a hero."

"Tell me."

"After our arrival and after everything happened, I was taken to the oars and there I found Sartre…"

"Alive?" Although still groggy her perplexity worked as a tonic.

"Yes. Weak and chained to a rowing bench like the others. Humiliated, like all of us. Hans proved to be a… Big rat indeed. He got out of the cage, sneaked through the ship and freed us. He saved us Jupita. That's how I ended up leading the mutineers. And before that, he delighted the men with his whistling, and turned them over to drunkenness. Honestly, I think he harpooned that rock on a sandbank and caused the confusion. That agitated everyone. A genius."

Jupita couldn't contain the tears that rolled slowly down her beautiful golden face and joined the ocean. Saddened, she embraced her friend, ashamed and angry at herself for not having deposited the respect and value the Little One, Hans Ranni Ramiro Roder deserved.

"He was very fond of you." the bearded man whispered to his shaken friend.

In response she laughed shortly.

"Despite the obscene remarks?" she added drying her eyes.

"He may still be alive. Don't be like that."

"What do you mean?"

"After the wreck I saw some boats at sea. Boats like those that took us to the ship, circulating adrift like us."

Amazed at the new hope, she asks:

"And where are they? Sartre and our big rat may still be alive. They must be alive yes!"

"Jupita, the sea is always moving… I haven't seen them for hours. There are no guarantees."

Gradually a tragic silence invaded the sandy environment, and with the passing minutes or hours, boredom gave way to hopelessness.

"I wonder what happened with Tarson?" Sitting, Jupita just hugged her legs reflecting. Distressed for not knowing and relieved that he didn't go through what they had just experienced.

Dominescu slanted his gaze.

Silence wore them. An invisible wall. But… Despite the current conditions, they were triumphant.

The woodcutter had swam for hours, he felt weak, exhausted. Momentarily, he ended up staring at the lady elf with her wet hair, lightly curled, her golden skin and her firm sensual face. It was hard to ignore her beauty and because of that, he concluded that the charm was also a curse, because it surely caused a lot of trouble. And despite the short time beside her, he learned to read her face like a letter.

"Sad?"

"Yes, we're lost."

Dominescu noticed a defensive reaction.

"When I saw you; I mean… you and the elf, I suspected your abilities."

"Seriously?" Jupita asked, beginning to show interest. But it was the human's pretext to move to another subject.

"I went back there when… Well… When we met my brother."

"Look Dom, about that…"

"There's nothing to say. He sought to die on his own terms. I have to respect that. And, if so, Jupita…"

"Forget it. Your death won't be like that. Neither mine." Jupita, actually didn't know. Her friend was human, and that alone made it easy to predict who would have a better chance of survival. Vigor was an inherent ability to humans.

"Tired?"

"No. You?"

The young woodsman was more used to bareback riding than swimming.

"No…"

Another moment of silence. The weather was overcast with no rain nor sun definition. For Dominescu, the woodcutter and blacksmith, Jupita eyes reflected how much she was lost in thought. He smiled briefly, and breaking the pause, said:

"Sonya, my mother, got like you sometimes. Staring at the horizon… Immersed in loneliness… Don't get like that, the blushing doesn't suit you. I never told you anything about myself, right? They only know that I was a lumberjack. It was a simple life and I liked it. I still do.

I lived between the village and the north woods, with my father, mother, my brother and Kayla. Father adopted her as a child, before the reptilian invasions and…"

Jupita raises her eyes to meet Dominescu's, and devotes her full attention.

"We were numerous in the city. The sum of the families made the difference and that's why we defeated them, about one-fifth of them left alive, fled to the southeast.

At a glance she revived her traumas and, almost at the mercy of a trance, she corrects:

"South. They deviated, followed south, following the course of the river. They caught us by surprise, invaded and slaughtered all the villages on the riverbed. It looked more like a green marching wave. Parry-Sharran was one of them."

"Parry-Sharran was a city?"

"No, a memory…" a very painful one for her.

"Cities and ports suffered greatly with the sea thieves, terrorizing seas and coastal cities." Dominescu was talking and scanning the horizon, and he didn't see tufts of herbs floating in sight and in the sky, no albatross or frigates. Therefore, they were far from land.

"Men like those on the ship?"

"The same… worse… My brothers and I lost part of our youth defending the neighboring families and our homes. But the best part was always coming back and finding my mother at the window."

Jupita lowered her gaze, fearing to give away her thoughts.

"Look…" I have to tell you…"

Suddenly Dominescu was pulled violently into the water. Jupita widened her eyes unbelieving such a swift snatch. The lady elf immediately raised her aura and the bluish glow surfaced in a flash. And soon she began to glide in the air. She didn't completely dominate the technique, so she remained just above the waves. The transparency of the water at that spot was surprising, but she couldn't understand what had attacked him. Jupita was desperate because although she spoke three languages and mastered her sword, what did it matter? What good were the lessons of her master, Darkay, in the darkness of the caves and worst... What good was a sword now?

"Have you ever seen a sea banquet, young lady?" The low and insinuating voice of the vessel's commander came to mind in a flash. She wanted and had to do something, it was her duty to save him, but how, if she never learned to swim?

The movements of Dominescu's body and the immense white fish were tangled between air bubbles, a thick red spot spread in the water until it was impossible to see anything else.

Jupita gasped with her thoughts, her tears fogged her sight and she heard nothing but silence. Suddenly, bubbles of air and a huge mouth full of teeth emerged, but there is no life in those harsh eyes. However, where could Dominescu be? Jupita looked everywhere but nothing.

Until she saw a body returning to the surface. Tired and weak, she risked her wellbeing casting another spell, one that suspended the woodcutter's body, bringing him close to her and to the same height.

However, it was late, he had stopped breathing.

Jupita grieved, she couldn't even whisper the name of the brave man who stood beside her that week, she had never connected so fast with someone…

Suddenly, the corpse twisted and spat the salt water. Jupita was wrong about his condition and she was never happier about being wrong.

"Dominescu? Dominescu, are you okay? How do you feel?"

"Alive."

Jupita held back her tears of joy while she laughed.

"You can fly?" he asked astonished, breathing rapidly.

"No." embarrassment ran over her cheeks. "I can only glide for awhile."

"Then save your strength, instead of me…" saying that, he threw himself back into the sea and swam to the body of the immense dead shark and removed a piece of its flesh with his knife.

"We need food. I will go back to the trunk of our makeshift boat."

"Dom… Hold my hand, I can't hover forever." she said, aware of the limits of the spell.

Instead of offering his hand, he threw a strip of the sail from the mast from the wreckage that surrounded them and they used it as a rope. The wind was nothing more than a tired breeze dragging them through the oceanic waves. Sometimes Jupita kept close to the water. If anyone saw her floating above the sea, they would be under the impression that the waves wanted to snatch her.

The stench of dead fish now stifled even the air itself. Soon carrion beasts and several types and size of fish appeared, forming a grim feast of the flesh of their defeated cousin.

"So Many!"

Jupita was perplexed. She immediately remembered the commander talking about sea eaters. Without a doubt, with no doubt at all, it was her turn to witness the grim banquet.

"The blood in the water awoke their hunger."

"To think that it could have been you…"

He contemplated silently, wiped his wet beard and settled in better, keeping his feet out of the water then suddenly, he changed the course of that conversation.

"Jupita, you will find the noble Tarson again, and I think you have to tell him how you feel."

"But…"

"Say no more. When I left my home and my business, it wasn't only to find my brother. I wanted to apologize. I fell in love with Kayla, and she corresponded. I love my foster sister as a woman. He left to find another job because he didn't want to work with me, he couldn't stand the idea of looking at me. He thought I had taken advantage of her innocence and he only didn't tell our parents because they are old and he feared their reaction.

She looked at him with depth and candor, and for the first time, she found his soul. Dominescu was not a serious man, but a sad one.

"Jupita…"

"Just row my friend, land is to your right."

Dominescu turned and raised his eyebrows to glimpse the close by land. From there it was possible to contemplate a wide beach that ended northwest in a rugged and rocky massive mount.

"And… Dominescu?"

"Yes?"

Jupita pulled the thin rope to get closer, and, already close, she kissed his bearded face.

"Thank you."

Already on the beach, they both dropped exhausted on the sand, amazed at how lucky they were to be alive. When he sat, the former sailor Dominescu saw some broken boats on that bay, therefore, there were corals and underwater rocks there. And, scanning the entire length of the sand strip, he was stupefied with the improbable.

"No! It's not possible!"

Saying those words, he got up and ran toward the Little One, Hans Ranni Ramiro Roder, the big rat, who mysteriously appeared floating on top of his cage, using it as a raft, but rowing in circles. Once on dry land, the Little One jumped from his makeshift vessel without uttering a word. His exhaustion was patent, he staggered, raised his hand, as if remembering something, turned back and plunged part of his body in his "raft " and raises, with both hands, a pair of human boots.

Jupita went to them. The lady elf could not contain herself to learn that Hans Ranni Ramiro Roder, the smallest of heroes, was still breathing…

Hans became serious and quickly motioned her to wait. Jupita stopped sad before him, thinking how much she had been cold and distant. And to whom, from the beginning, decided to help unreservedly.

"What is it, Hans?" the woodsman wished to know.

Hans grinned, then threw up inside the boot. Jupita writhed in disgust. The sick one wiped his mouth with his sleeve, threw the boot aside and said:

"Now then. My dear, you may save me."

And then he collapsed exhausted.

LAND

The sun fell tired on the horizon, soon it would be night and the Little One was still groggy walking the sand in twisted lines. After the wreckage, the idea of returning to the sea was undesirable, but maybe necessary. However, making a boat for that kind of sea was crazy. And without drinking water, it would be suicide. Besides, had they reached an island or some southernmost part of the continent?

All of a sudden, right before their eyes, they saw a huge humanoid emerge from the water. He straightened his hair and raised a net with fish of various sizes.

Dominescu and Jupita looked at each other and, instinctively, drew their swords.

"No weapons." the giant said. "I will give you the fish."

"Back, sea creature. No tricks" Dominescu imposed raising his sword.

"Sea creature? Ha, ha, ha… If you can speak, you can't be dead right? Forget the hostility and help me with the fish. A week ago I found a bell that can be used as a cauldron. We can have baked fish or fish broth with herbs."

"Who and what are you?" Jupita inquired unsure.

"A castaway like yourself. I'm Iurik, beloved son of the house of Koth, if that makes any difference here."

Iurik was immense. He had a thorax as wide as the fishermen of the islands and almost the measure of two men. When he approached, Jupita raised her sword aggressively.

"Ok. Suit yourself, but the Little One looks haggard. He needs to eat the roots of that plant to the his right or he is going to vomit all day. That way! A couple of kilometers inland, there is drinking water and, if you want, you can find my home to the southeast."

The woodcutter and his people have had some bad experiences with giants. On the other hand, that figure was only two-thirds the size of one, so the term giant was inappropriate, maybe he was just a man, one of the biggest he ever met.

The splendid sized man slowly walked away from them, through the beach and then disappearing behind the dunes and sparse vegetation.

Jupita, afraid, remained on guard. She wanted to ensure that he wouldn't come back and capture them with the net.

But they were exhausted and Hans unconscious. The lady elf and the woodsman kept vigil for as long as their bodies were able to sustain them. Jupita was the first to fall. The sound of the waves breaking in the sea was violent. It hurt the ears and even so, Dominescu also collapsed. Nightmares and incomplete dreams merged until the heat of the sun on Dominescu's eyelids woke him completely. As soon as his mind revealed where they were, he covered his eyes with the back of his hand and saw only the boots Hans had vomited in, but he didn't see him nor Jupita. He turned over and saw the beautiful lady elf.

"Good morning, my friend."

"Good morning. Well… is everything okay?"

"Hans is still vomiting, but he has improved a lot since eating the roots."

"Jupita, do you think the roots are indicated?"

"Damn! I hate it when you talk as if I wasn't here." Hans said, coming from a small foliage.

Suddenly, a shadow came up behind the Little One. Dominescu could barely stand up.

"Have you met Iurik? He recommended the roots. With his knowledge of plants, he could well be a Little One.

The giant looked at Dominescu and before he uttered a word, said:

"Look, I'll go back. Apparently someone here still needs some time."

"Iurik, wait. No! Hey, wait!" Jupita insisted sweetly.

"Right. He's gentle. Hans completed chewing. "He brought the fruits. He doesn't bite."

Dominescu was skeptical, he and his people were taught to hate giants.

"Bite? Ha-Ha-Ha!" the giant laughed as he walked away. "Old Dainthgorn doesn't even eat nails…"

"Dainthgorn? Impossible, Iurik Dainthgorn died. He disappeared… At sea…"

Several thoughts invaded Dominescu. Could it be that the half giant found the king's son and devoured him? It was the only explanation for him knowing that name. Many certainly knew the name of their own king, but the name of an heir is less likely. A prince was just the king's son and his name, a mystery of little curiosity. Dominescu ran to him, yelling imperatively:

"Giant!"

The giant stopped immediately with a placid expression, totally calm.

"Where is the one you mentioned? How did you find him?"

"Oh, you know him, there's a interesting recognition. And partial."

The lumberman of the kingdom of Dainthgorn pointed his sword and insisted angrily:

"Tell me what happened to Iurik!"

Motionless, the gigantic man stared at Dominescu for awhile, and suddenly his pinkish face lost all expression.

"Humph! Alright. Moved by the most visceral of impulses for adventure, he set to sea with twelve vessels. He took his entourage to a remote corner of the world. They brought with them, besides the servants, vassals and the bodyguard, assorted items to trade. They were attacked by rough seas and many lives and ships were lost. After the greatest of the storms, his ship was separated from the fleet. He found one of them adrift, during a morning fog. On the deck, there were several dead and two sailors tying the body of a dead person and tossing them one by one into the sea from the plank. Our ship's crew noticed other corpses in the water and fearfully mentioned some curse and there was no way to persuade the wretches to help their countrymen.

The giant's face fell as he continued.

"The touch of a dead person on a ship was regarded as cursed also, it was bad luck… The dead were tied with stones and released from the plank to prevent them from coming back up and demanding their place back or even revenge."

"So that was it?" Dominescu was impatient, bitter after seeing so many deaths and hearing of more. His brother, the villagers, the pirates and now more.

"Well… The following day another ship, sailing aimlessly like the first one. Secretly, Iurik sent off five trustworthy vassals in a dinghy. The survivors claimed they were attacked without warning by their own comrades."

The giant seemed affected by the story.

"Vengeful ships." Dominescu said almost in a whisper.

"What?" Hans thought of something ridiculous but he considered that it didn't even deserve credit.

"Ships attacked by pirates that can't be repaired are sunk with everyone on board, including the crew." the lumberjack commented with the Little One. "Mostly, they would only remove some wood for repairs. Hence the legend of vengeful ships filled with ghosts. Pirates and sailors alike are scared of this myth. That is why ships adrift are always avoided."

"I didn't know that… Iurik, the stupid prince, was unaware of this and instead of ghosts, he brought disease to his ship. The disease spread and killed everyone… In the basement, food and water shared space with weak sailors, vomiting a lot… In the middle of a night, I noticed I was the only one still breathing. I threw all the bodies overboard to avoid the stench and the proliferation of rats and roaches, however, sooner or later they would take over the ship completely. The act of throwing so many bodies overboard attracted sharks and other sea scavengers, the funeral procession turned into a banquet."

"That explains only how the boats sank. What does this have to do with Iurik's fate? You didn't answer my question."

"Actually, I am answering. He died the same day he realized that his useless life of etiquette was worthless against the treacherous sea. He had to watch, terrified, his vessel adrift colliding with another ship, sinking both. Blind and wounded, he died in a cyclops' cave. I'm just Iurik, the only survivor of the one-eyed monster lair."

Dominescu lowered his guard and his face. He was dazed with so many tragedies.

"I apologize. And thank you for helping us."

The giant just nodded and moved on. And on his way he thought. How could he, Iurik Dainthgorn, tell them about the creature that, initially, sheltered him? How could he talk about the cyclops? In fact, shortly after the shipwreck, Iurik was weak, impaired, only the gods knew well that it wasn't from the same disease that affected the sailors and the rest of the vessel. Sick, weak, he saw a stubby person with a silly face, one-eye, fitted with a thick brow and ugly like the rest of himself, a fellow who fed him while talking nonsense.

He wasn't strong enough to mention that he had been forced to eat human flesh. The flesh of his subjects. What kind of prince eats his own people? On the day that notion finally settled in, he saw the environment around him, felt the smell of burning flesh and realized what had happened. He experienced severe dizziness when he got up and stood face to face with the one-eyed pariah; with the abject monster of filthy habits; who, in the end, was not one-eyed. No, not at all. The line on the monster's face was an old scar where there should have been another eye, or its empty socket. He had only a single central eye, the scar just slanted even more his foolish face. The creature, with vague human recollection, smiled at Iurik, glad to see him on his feet. He smiled with his crooked, rotten teeth, from which ran a lousy color, between copper from the lack of hygiene and yellow pustules of infection. The single central eyed idiot brute had just ate.

Then Iurik felt a taste of meat in his mouth, his heart went wild while his body seized up, stunned. Around him, he saw the remains and clothes that terribly proved his bitter suspicions. A fiery fury pelted the prince's hands forward, reaching for the creature's throat, trying to strangle it. The smell of blood, feces, meat and rot impregnated in this place of insanity was nothing compared to the taste of flesh and blood on his tongue. Involved by this hideous sensation, his hands trembled in terror. His body, unaccustomed with its own weight, lost its balance and was easily thrown to the ground by the monster. Reason itself cried, his crushed heart screamed. He noticed little cages close to them, full of tiny humanoids. And, even without believing in their tininess and existence, Iurik opened the door in a haste to free them. One of them bit him in a clear and desperate attempt to defend itself and the rest ran and jumped away like the one that bit him. The corpulent and gigantic monster watched. Disgruntled, he spoke about Iurik's ungratefulness because the dinner he freed was also his. The beast even spoke his language. Wroth and enraged, the cyclops kicked him and dragged him by his hair out of the lair and abandoned him.

Much later, when his strength returned and he managed to stop crying and vomiting, Iurik began to wander away tearful and tottering. Aimlessly, wanting only to get away from all that nonsense. On his way, he saw huge reptiles tasting the flesh of some of the tiny beings from earlier and others he didn't know or even want to understand what they were. Knowing or remembering at that moment was a most undesirable burden, he preferred the balsam of oblivion. And found himself having to watch his wits, because he could still hear bones being crushed and blood staining yellow and dirty teeth. That was the day that prince Iurik Dainthgorn, of the estimated house of Koth, died.

A few hours later, Jupita, Dominescu and Hans were standing in front of the place Iurik used as residence. Actually, it was no more than a crack in a mount that could not be regarded as a cave for the lack of a ceiling, a mini volcano partially cracked on its side, a so-called volcanic cone.

At one point, they hear sounds, sometimes high, sometimes low, and then few periods of silence.

"That hammering, what is it?"

"A continuous nuisance, and I can't do anything. They are pests! That's what they are."

"You mean they are animals?"

"If I knew how to build a hovel, I would have left long ago. Soon it will be rainy season and you can't enter the sea, the fish keep away. I have to live on fruits and roots and with so many cavities, this place is perfect to stock supplies.

Looking around, Jupita, Dominescu and Hans noted that his residence had parts of ships, possibly collected from the beach and used to improve his home.

"I have no peace, even at night because they are always hammering and digging in the walls. All I really wanted was to rest, so I could have the time and patience to solve my problem. Forgive me for ranting. I don't even know if you're willing to share a roof with a stranger, so take whatever you want. I will leave you in peace. I hope you're a better neighbor than they are." he said pointing at the walls.

"Hey, big fellow, " Hans said. "I think I know what are those. And I think I can help."

Saying that, he ran and jumped with great mastery into the collected boat remains and went into one of the cavities.

"Hans… No!" Dominescu screamed, without being answered.

"I also think I know what they are. They seem to be gnomes." Jupita crouched and examined one of the cavities near the ground. "they always risk themselves when they suspect or are sure there is gold or precious stones encrusted in the walls."

Suddenly, she entered the narrow cavity too small for the large lumberjack.

"Be careful!"

Meanwhile, the shadows eliminated the Little One's certainty about what could be in those tunnels. Suddenly, there is a strange and loud roar. An unknown threat. And Hans began to run. And between the curves and recesses, something grabbed him.

"AAAIIIEEE!!!" it was the end, Hans would be devoured.

When the Little One opened his eyes, he found himself in a bright place with no sun or moon and beside him, the dwarf from the ship.

"Shit. I died, right? You died first and I was devoured." Hans held back the tears.

"You coward. You passed out right after I found you."

"Liar! You only want to cheer me up… I know that I died, I fought hard, you know, but…"

"Oh you tricky pet. What's your name, Oh, hairy one?"

"Hans, my name was Hans Ranni Ramiro Roder. Ranni was my mother and Ramiro was the leaf collector, my beloved and lost to the world father."

"So… Hans of Roder…"

"Actually, Roder was just for show, and it don't mean anything."

"Okay. Then Hans of surname, just for show, Roder, fought with a great evil and was eaten?"

"Okay, I ran so what? It doesn't make any difference. Hey! So this is the land of the dead?"

"If you keep talking shit, then I'm going to send you there."

"Poor man. You're suffering, right? You don't even know you died. Who were you, anyway?"

"If so, how do I know you entered, I don't know why, in a hole, and, by the way you ran blindly through the cavities, heard the "machine" and, being a pussy, you thought it was a monster. When I found and held you, so you wouldn't fall in the abyss to your left, you had a fit and fainted."

"So, I'm not dead?"

"How did you get here?"

"I'm not dead?"

"Has your hairs entered your brain?" tired of that, Morgrinald rose from the floor, holding the Little One firmly by his balls and smashed him into the wall. "Listen to me, if you were dead could you feel that?"

"Ouch!" He said with a hoarse voice of pain. "Weeell… I guess not." and then in a squeak . "I'm sorry then."

The dwarf dropped the Little One.

"The only monster that threatens this place, according to the gnomes…"

"Gnomes? I Was Right! YES!"

"Quiet, hairy one. The gnomes mentioned a giant. A flesh eating giant."

"I see… Listen, would you take me with you? I want to meet the gnomes."

"Where did you come from?"

"Honestly? I don't know."

"Imbecile."

"You are you saying that because you can't remember my name, right? Listen, what was yours? What is yours, what is yours?" he said protecting the groin. "Sorry… Bad habit right?"

The dwarf breathed trying to be patient. He frowned, hit the chest of the old armor and spoke with pride:

"Morgrinald of the blood of the Keldorn clan of the Battle Hammers."

Suddenly, Hans heard the same sound as before, and the smell was odd. Morgrinald pulled the little one behind without dropping him.

Morgrinald stared at the darkness. And the Little One felt the air warm around them and without understanding what was happening and fearing what made the strong and heavyset dwarf shut up, decided not to move.

Morgrinald dropped Hans and, to his surprise, the place was slightly lit by a reddish light that soon faded. The dwarf positioned himself. It was a metallic sound and for a moment, it seemed to move away, but the experienced warrior would never fall for this trick. He just stood there and the metallic noise and covered the sound of his footsteps. Morgrinald realized, by the talents of his race, that distance was shortened. That's great, the dwarf thought. The creature was foolish because it was coming in his direction. Finally something with the taste of earth to eat.

However, the experienced mountain dwarf noticed it was a light bipedal with a meandering stride, and besides being larger than him, it was above all, cautious. Morgrinald stepped slowly, keeping one hand in front. He planned to stop it. Suddenly, the sound died down. He expected Hans Ranni "whatever" to scream or say something silly. He was still there right next to him, protecting himself. Away from danger, but close to his defender. In other words, a coward. He was still, however, breathing too loud, too fast. The idiot was desperate. Morgrinald pushed him away, he needed space.

The clear and crisp sound of metal coming out of a sheath reached his ears. Thant's it: now is the moment. His attack was quick. The dwarf used a loose stone to defend himself. The metal scratched and raced over the stone, and from the friction sound, it was a medium size sword. Morgrinald was unsure. Axe or hammer? Both then. Running steps, there was no time for both. In a slight and swift move, the wide plate of the sharp axe that he kept on his back stopped the blow and acted as a shield. Keldorn's grandson smiled behind the axe, glad for rescuing it from the water during the low tide. Marine beasts did not dwell in caves so what was it? The opponent was good and he was enjoying the fight. However, now it was his turn. Morgrinald spun his body so his left-hand could reach the anxious hammer, while his feet turned in the opposite direction and, with this arc movement, the hammer gained momentum, but found nothing. What happened? Where was he? Then…

His eyes pierced the dark. This ability, luminescence, was a gift from a god to his kind. So he used it briefly, he wanted to see his opponent, and, above all, he wanted to be seen, as doing this made his eyes shine also. However, when he did it, he saw a the blade of a ruby laid dagger reach for his neck.

"Drop it!" someone said.

Morgrinald, the bravest of his caste knew:

"It's over."

"YES! So it seems… Sorry."

"The pointed ears lady from the boat?"

"You shouldn't talk like that to someone who has the upper hand." Jupita said.

"Um!" the dwarf smiled with his eyes.

Only then Jupita felt, on her belly, the cold and sharp metal of the double blade axe. Its blade touched her, without even brushing her leather jacket, going straight for the undone stitched point.

"Truce?"

"Sure."

The disciple of Darkay let the magical energy in her body flow. Without restrain it, her body was glowing a subtle bluish-white light and little by little the surrounding was illuminated. The dwarf squinted a little bit as it was not good to use his sight in the light soon after using the luminescence.

"What… What… Good… Understanding is good." Hans stuttered on the floor, holding the sword of his beloved elf with his bare feet. The sharp tip was held very close to where it really hurts. Almost chopping off his pride, his manhood. Breathing deeply, he said without stutter, "look, guys, I'll be right back." saying that, Hans fainted.

"The little shit needs air." Morgrinald said, almost laughing "Do you know the way back?"

Jupita made the way back easily. Even without using magic, without light. It was a short walk. Two or three forks in the path and they arrived. A beam of light cutting through the middle of the corridor marked the narrow access. There was no more need for magic.

Iurik and Dominescu saw that Jupita was the first to return from the hole. Then the fainted Little One dragged by her.

"What happened? Is he well?" Dominescu asked, coming to their rescue.

Morgrinald scraped his armor on the walls of the small exit. He cursed a lot in his tongue.

"You brought one of the little pests with you!" said the alarmed and awed giant Iurik.

"Pest?" the dwarf wroth with the reception. He hadn't looked up, so he left of the hole and quickly drew his hammer.

"So this piece of shit is the killer giant?"

"Wait!" Dominescu asked, amazed at what he saw. "Morgrinald? The warrior from the ship? Please, take it easy. There has to be a reasonable explanation."

"Dominescu, be careful: they told me that long leg here is a gnome eater!" he replied without taking his eyes off the giant.

"Gnomes? As I suspected." Jupita said while trying to revive the Little One, forgetting for now the new impasse.

"Aha! I was right!" said the naughty little Hans, in Jupita's lap.

"Why, you little cretin! Are you okay?"

"I am now, my dear."

"Then get off my lap."

The young man was shoved away. Right between the dwarf and the giant. To be exact, on the floor, looking at both of them. They faced each other fiercely, like they were waiting for the other to do something, a movement was enough to start the fight. Dominescu scratched his beard with both hands, then placed them at his waist and said:

"Well… Ladies and gentlemen, on this side, Iurik, the giant, devourer of roots, crabs and fish, and on the other, Morgrinald, the blood of Keldorn, from the grand clan of the Battle Hammers.

"A dwarf of the mountains!" Iurik, with a long and revered movement, knelt on his right knee, and with his right hand closed on his chest said, as most respectful as he could in the language of the dwarves. "Except for the day I no longer exist, I will keep a pure heart and the axe sharp."

Such words take Morgrinald away on memory lane, the axe returned to its resting place. The giant straitened his hair and humbly spoke in the easy and common language of humans:

"I hope my accent didn't bother you."

"It just made me curious." he continued in his language that resembled heavy rocks falling.

"What do you mean with 'of the blood of Keldorn' "?

"I'm his grandson." he answered promptly and continued, without thinking, to speak the language of his race. "is it true what they say? You eat flesh?"

In both languages, it was a dubious question, but to Iurik, the situation didn't ask for details, but straight answers. Because if Keldorn's grandson was capable of half of his legendary grandfather deeds, his head would not stand for long on his body.

"There is some truth, I love fish and crab."

"I'm Jupita" the elf lady interceded, in the easy tongue of men.

"Jupita." he bowed his head slightly without lowering his gaze.

The dwarf recognized the name:

"Sartre speaks highly of you."

"He…"

"Yes, he is, on the other side, somewhere south of here. He stayed with the gnomes. And that's about it… They told me that they opted for digging tunnels to avoid encountering the giant and to make a path to the forest on the other side of the island to get food."

"Island?"

"Affirmative." said Dominescu, with an askance look at the elf.

"Island? There was a cave-in, and they blame this big fellow here."

"Huh?"

"They say you punch the walls just to see if food would fall out…"

"Those pests don't stop, even at night. The noise is unbearable and…"

"So I hit on the walls."

"Once… It had been a hard day, I was running a fever. If I hit the walls, I did it in my sleep. But they are considering me way too strong don't you think?"

"Are there others like you?"

"If I was able to move the earth I would have already ripped off a piece of the rock to the north and would have used it as an oar. Then I would take the damn island with me and go home."

"It was like you were trying to make them roll out of the tunnels."

"Nonsense!"

"You actually wanted to destroy them and cause it to collapse, isn't it?" the dwarf beset.

"You're not helping." Dominescu said firmly,.

Jupita thought of something from her past, which she soon abandoned and then turned to the dwarf:

"Take us to Sartre and the gnomes."

"Oh! So now I'm a guide."

"Then stay here with your insolence and the others and I will go find them."

"With the giant? They will think I betrayed them. Then they enter these tunnels that may well have kilometers and you will never see the old man again.

"Wait! He has a point. I'm going to stay. There aren't many places to go on the island anyway."

In Morgrinald's eyes, the discussion was futile. Iurik was no giant, only an overdeveloped human, that's all, almost three times his size. However the "giant" recited a verse of a poem of his grandfather or was it from one of his grandfather's partners? Whatever. It would be interesting to hear the exploits of his grandfather from his mouth. Hear about the past, he had issues to solve and wanted to remember others, so he said firmly:

"I'll stay."

"You can't. The gnomes know only you."

To Morgrinald, the elf's authority was already getting out of hand.

"You should go, no problems." Iurik added. "Like I said, there aren't many places to go."

"And neither to hide." replied the dwarf, mocking Iurik's size.

The gigantic human sighed with an air of disdain, and humor. He sat quietly and with a branch, went on to draw in the sand while the others left.

The journey was full of poisonous animals, but the experience and the agility of Hans; the young big rat; surprised even those whose job is to surprise. Finally, they arrived at an illuminated entrance on a short, ugly beach, full of wood scraps. At the end there was a small stream that poured its brownish waters into the sea , along with rejects and inventions remains. That was where the gnomes lived.

Certainly they have been housed there for generations. Nearby, in the middle of the tall and punctured hill, they could see square windows and doors of various sizes in all the cavities. From them, from time to time, a gnome came out. Some, more curious than others, began to point at the newcomers and others showed their face through those same windows. But soon their curiosity seemed to end and they went back into the holes and windows.

Hans, Morgrinald, Jupita and Dominescu walked by the strip of sand bordering the hill and soon they saw on the beach ahead, a wrecked galleon. Like the opened entrails of a fish. It was clear that it was the home of other gnomes. As much of the side of the hull was gone, they could see the gnomes doing their daily chores. About ten or twelve onlookers joined the newcomers and began to touch and harass them with many questions. Gnomes were short, somewhere between the height of the dwarf and the Little One, however while Morgrinald had a prominent chest and leaked muscles from every angle, the gnomes' arms were slender although still meaty . And they now acted, with the visitors, like orphans recently abandoned in a city market. All Gnomes, without exception, were dirty and dusty and wore raw cotton overalls. The few colors existed in the pockets of various shapes and sizes. Such pockets and bags held tools and some useless items that showed now and again.

"Why so many holes in that hill? Hans asked.

The answer came in form of another question.

"Where did you come from?"

"Huh? From the west."

Dominescu noticed that parts of the ship were disassembled and the wood may have been used to make bonfires, on cold days. But he wasn't oblivious to the questions.

"Actually we don't know much. We were victims of a sad shipwreck. At sea you lose your references, so… We ended up here."

"From the east lands of the Great Kingdom. added Jupita, staring around very curious. "You live there too?"

"Are you hungry? Thirsty?" said a gnome grinning so hard that his eyes almost disappeared in his cheeks. "We have food. I hope you like vegetables, because that's all we have for now…" then he noticed Dominescu."Hey! You're strong, can you help with the trawl?"

"Sure."

Dominescu had been a sailor, but not a fisherman. Back then, some of the men often spoke of this method of fishing with trawl.

When he saw it, he doubted that such small people were able to handle it.

"Hey. Cousin, do you have beans here also? Green beans maybe? Do you? You know, my tummy is anxious for a nice stuffing… Hello, people of the hill!" Hans yelled, waving to the gnomes busy with their work.

Morgrinald realized that they waved only politely and returned to their duties. Hans something didn't lose his pose, they may not have noticed, and in an outburst, the wild Little Ones bellowed at the top of his lungs:

"WOOOOW! Look at the size of that lettuce! Sunflower seeds! Spinach! Wow! Even a cricket."

"This guy is irritating."

"No! No, it's not. If you fry them in fat, well fried…

"Argh! That's disgusting!" the elf complained.

"Disgusting? Er… You're right. Don't do that with crickets, yuck! They are disgusting." but, from the corner of his mouth, he whispered to the gnomes. "Well fried, with a little dried herb, or have them wrapped in lettuce leaf with some corn…"

"HANS!"

"Huh? What?" Hans glanced around quickly and masterfully remedies his mistake with his "hottie". "I was just praising their plantation, little princess, it is obvious that the grains and vegetables were brought in from outside."

"How can you be sure of that?"

"Are you kidding? Have you ever seen plants like these on the coast? Are they eating monkey leaves by any chance?"

"The others I brought them from afar." said one who had just arrived mounted on a mechanism resembling a crab's legs and body. The contraption made of wood, chipped stone and braided rope, walked oddly because of some sorcery and caused awe and fascination to the creativity of the gnomes. "And you came from the shipwreck just like "Morinalk".

"Morgrinald." the dwarf corrected squinting his left eye in an almost hidden disapproval.

"I have trouble following your thoughts, 'Morginalk'…" saying that, he moved one of his tied hands and, thus, raised the shovel shaped stone clip attached to one of the contraptions' tips.

"Moorr-grrri-nald."

Again the dusty and earth stained gnome, from the top of that contraption, started moving his hands, and the clamps followed his movements like they were a single organism.

"I am referring to your… vigorous reaction, when you learned about the threat to our people." the movements of the apparatus, made by the gnome, seemed natural, but in his voice, there was arrogance towards the dwarf. "And during the conversation with my peers you intervened. Rather, you proposed to find out the nature of the threat we told you about. Although evidently with less eloquence."

To Jupita and Dominescu, whoever was that gnome mounted on that contraption, he was someone who commanded respect. If he wasn't the leader, he was surely one of them. That's what the elf and the woodcutter thought, Hans however…

"I never understand anything that they say… What about you friend?" Hans asked, covering his mouth so he wasn't heard.

But he soon becomes embarrassed when he realizes that, distractedly, he said that the another gnome.

"Our colleague replicated what the dwarf had said during his meeting with us. That he would not only examine the reason for our suffering, but he also proposed, immediately, to get rid of the freakish and despotic biped. And he said all of that with clear signs of pride and determination."

The other gnome, that had initiated the conversation continued:

"Therefore, and, as exposed by our colleague, should I believe you have failed or qualify you as inadequate for the task entrusted to you?"

Morgrinald grew tired of the provocations and holding and lifting both front calipers of the mechanical apparatus, advanced quickly, pushing it back until they hit a small rock where he pressed his forearm on the arrogant gnome's throat and, without dropping the pincers, he looked deeply into the gnome's soul, then, the grandson of Keldorn asked slowly but loud enough to be heard:

"And who said I was finished? You?"

"Actually…" shouted a voice from afar, a voice well-known by Hans. "I have always been told that there are two types of men in the world, those who build and those who destroy."

"Old man, I would rather say that there are two types of beings, the ones I tolerate…" during the pause, he twisted one of the pincers and making the gnome moan due to the resulting pressure on his fingers. And those who were beings until they met my axe.

With that, he released the apparatus and stepped back, making it spring back to its initial position causing the gnome to fall forward, kicking the wind out of his lungs.

Everyone looks for the owner of the voice. Until they see someone coming from behind a rock and in a simple leap to the sand, the face of a middle-aged man gained a name again.

"Sartre?" Jupita could not believe her eyes.

"Sartre" This man has a thousand lives. Old man, son of a…" Hans looked at Jupita and then shrugged. "You bum, son of a chinless bitch! How?"

With a tired smile of bad memories and for the lives that were lost on the way there, he started his account.

SECRETS IN THE AIR

From above, the grass ran beneath his feet, Tarson-Romanei was flying, but unstable. He faltered here and there in a vertigo that evidenced his illness, it was hard to remain calm and aloof. Even all the detachment practiced in the halls of Ice Crystals and the deep scar in his soul, caused by the loss of so many loved ones during the week of the reptilian attack, nothing had ever shaken him so much. There was no comparison nor scale. Not even the most terrible experiences during the time of the war of the races could peak the horror he now felt. Without masks or fantasies.

And everything happened as soon as he left the presence of his beloved friends ones and the woodsman.

There, in the middle of the clouds, while he fled the huge dragon. Neither it or its roar of anger and frustration managed to break through the wall of clouds. Flames made the cloud scarlet, but that was all.

Close to the ground, panting after such terrible vision, a fine and lively mist involved the area. The sensation and certainty in his bones that it was something old and it was hard to establish its origin, without venturing into the extraordinary. Parts of its essence accumulated in certain places, generating a form with such refinement that now and again it framed his face expressions with thin clear air rags, moisture, light and dust. This "shape" was headless, but the entire shape could reach a cube of kilometers. For Tarson they were neither masks nor illusions. He could clearly see the shreds connecting and moving as the puppet master's fingers. Being stunned before such fantastic and rare presence quickly transpired in Tarson. Questions and more questions accumulated in his mouth wanting to ride off the tongue locking his light language.

"Shut up, now, elf. Know by my voice what happened with the patriarchs of your kind. For I speak on behalf of all and I will not be contained nor ignored. Long ago, in the venerable world of pure air, everything followed the gods' plan, my world, just like this in which you live, is one among many. So that you understand what I'm talking about, I will make the simplest comparison that comes to mind. Everything that exists is overlaid, like the layers of an onion from your world. And, between them, there are cracks that give passage to a bit from another world to nurture it, change it or to bring forth renewal."

"I have no intention to ridicule." Tarson commented carefully. "I know the legend of the eternal ones and the worlds placed between them, so that they, the brothers, couldn't destroy everything in this world. Skip the details, I beg you! What happened with the patriarchs?"

The pause accentuated the expectation, Tarson sensed something terrible.

"If you know that, then my task is less painful." the voice said in a jolt. "I bring news of the end. Facilitators, devout beings, thirsty for reward or of unwarranted and lethal curiosity, opened a portal. The result, in the long run, was the passage of ZHI, the demon… the plane of fire was the first to fall, followed by the planes of earth, water and finally the plane of air."

The elf choked in fear. The words stuck on their way out and only incomprehensible sounds came through. The one in front of and around him seemed to be made of word, a relentless voice and not light air.

"Much of the demonic army fell in each passage and most ceased to exist in the august plane of air yet… Winged beings…

"Dragons?"

The vague silence established the agreement with the name and the voice continued:

"In flock, and multiplying in the clouds, amassing their armies, until the day when there was a massive attack, as the fierce and fiery storm. The winged ones had the nefarious mission to destroy several beings of this world. I am Sargauss, I wasn't that good to be the gatekeeper between worlds, and by being squeezed near the passage, I, Sargauss chose to warn the inhabitants of the material world, but it took me years to reach my goal. Given that, my body and soul; my substance; nothing was beyond a brief gust of wind, an invisible being to the natural inhabitants of this plane. And, what's worst. Without knowing how to express myself and speak any language… It took me awhile until I learned to speak the language of the children of the fire, the wind's children, like yourself. And following Sartre, I learned the easy language of men."

"I met him. You speak of the village healer?"

"Yes. I, Sargauss, helped him whenever I could. Back then, Sartre was a farmer. And, like I, Sargauss, he knew how to drag the clouds. I planned to make a rain blanket so he could see my shape and body, that's how I got his attention and amazement. At the time he thought it was the shadow of his son, killed son by madness from wheat fungus. The months were gone with the old days and the prosperity of his land was noticed, other poor farmers settled their homes there."

While Sargauss was speaking, Tarson regressed to that place inside himself. Reflecting on the flow of events. It was due to the direct intervention of this splendid being on the flow of the rains that the land became more fertile. The news of this fertility spread among the poorest resulting in a rapid and massive emigration. Obviously the economy of the place grew from a trading post to a settlement and the settlement soon became a village.

"Should I continue? I know the immersion ability of your race."

"I'm sorry, I ask that you continue."

"However, before I, Sargauss, gathered courage to teach Sartre about the reason of my arrival, I noticed the presence of other beings. The children of the forest, called disdainfully as 'Little Ones', settled on the outskirts. And the humans ended up building their houses upon the gate passage and around it. An excellent hold by the variety of elements. Then, months became years and the place got the name of settlement and village. But all this happened too late, because the servants of ZHI, the demon, were already present among the humans. Then I, Sargauss, left them to find defenders among the worlds and bring reinforcements and allies from all places. And only now I learned about Sartre."

"The farmer and healer?"

"Blessed by the gods. He is the key link of the entire community."

"Are you asking me to rescue Sartre?"

"Something so terrible is not, in itself, something to be avoided?"

"Don't judge me by a bad worded question. You are an ancestor of my race; being in your presence is an honor . No to mention, to hear you. Serving you is my duty, I couldn't refuse. I beg your pardon. I'm just baffled by the unexpected honor you grant me."

Then Tarson silenced with the arrival of those disturbing thoughts and Sargauss, as if he could read them, said:

"If Sartre dies, the village dies and the gate can be opened."

"What about the dragon I saw?"

"It's lost in the labyrinth of clouds I created."

"And… is it safe?"

"It's not my greatest concern, but certainly we must prevent their proliferation on these shores, as the burning of crops may open a slit between this world and the world of fire."

"And ZHI would win."

"Yes."

"Not with us." said a warm voice coming from a mist that when he approached it, he saw that it was Ypsallu Khernel, the famous bard, owner of thirty voices.

When he approached, he revealed the others, although Tarson had already heard them. They were the other allies that Sargauss summoned while he was away from the village of Miller. They kept a respectful distance while they talked.

"Do you understand the need for secrecy about the village's condition, Tarson Romanei?" Sargauss cried, filling every corner of Tarson's being.

"Yes, and I will be silent."

The promise of silence tied big names in a single journey. Tarson immediately recognized, among them, Hanoo, lord of the staff, and renowned mercenaries like Vapsi Rastrielli; aka White Bear, the elf archer, Hagane, and Maurak, the scout. And reading a long scroll, the most illustrious of the entire company… Lord Talassas, the first Knight of the air. Besides them, there were others that the noble Tarson-Romanei did not know, but certainly they would earn their due importance, writing their names with their own nails on the wall of glory.

"Dearest friends, we still lack transport." Ypsallu argued while he picked a strange flute.

"Not anymore." said a man leaving the foolish hideout that concealed him. "You know all too well my toy on the water."

Tarson was surprised to recognize that man.

"Darrell?"

"Once again at your service. Would you all please come through here."

Passing the small grass and thickets, they saw a small beach where, on the sand, a prodigious vessel was grounded.

"The seas rise every eight years to clear my…"

"You mean we have to push it." despite the impossible mission, White Bear was already climbing down the slope of stones to the short beach that had almost no sand strip.

And so they went down to better evaluate the situation.

Then, the great essence that was Sargauss passed through them. The first sign, to common eyes, of Sargauss's arrival, was the breeze like a soft, almost inaudible chant. He went up the vessel, paced over the thick fabrics and made the knots of the ropes tied to the wood moan, as well as the support trunks and the masts. Suddenly, they could see clearly that the whole ship shook. On the sails, his subtly shape filled the fabric and sometimes hands, torso or face were seen. The vessel spun from one side to another, but no one knew what he wanted to do with it. The presence of Sargauss alone, considered a mythological being, was amazing. And all human understanding of him would be actually, incorrect, inappropriate, or merely inaccurate.

Tarson-Romanei, benefited by the power inherent to his kind to see and understand such unusual things, noticed promptly that this was no joke and through his jumbled movement, he achieved precisely his purpose. Sargauss was adapting the fluidity of his essence into the boat, he was joining parts of himself. Very subtle parts condensed themselves. Like fine fabrics of a light web flowing down and into the recesses and accommodations of the vessel. Taking care not to implode such a fragile structure with the immensity of his being.

Suddenly, all the movement ceased, then the ballast water spurted through cracks and minor disruptions on the wood while the whole vessel was raised out of the sand into the air. Sargauss and the rich ship become one.

Everyone's perplexity was equal to the magnitude of that moment of the past. And suddenly Tarson thought. All this happened four or would it be seven months ago?

"Jupita…"

REVERIES AND REFLECTIONS

"From this condition I understand that you are very unhappy to accept this as plausible probability."

"I strongly disagree, considering that, in determining patterns of innocence in a spite doesn't mean that it's ignorance. Would there be surviving laws if so?"

The gnomes discussion on duties and responsibilities made Sartre promptly remember his beloved home. His fears replicated in the volume of their voices and the speed of the sentences. From everything he had heard up to that point made him realize that it was the same essence of the previous kind of fear. The amalgamating kind; it merges all your fears in a larger and more primal one. The same kind of fear from his villager friends when the disappearances begun, when they stopped thinking of the attackers as normal bests, although hungry, to imagine them as hideous monsters hidden in the dark bosom of the forest. The farmer observed everything with the detachment of a dream and the dark ardors of a nightmare. And despite the time spent up to here, the questions weren't dead to Sartre. Did the village still exist? Did they get help? From the noblemen? Unlikely. Who should take the lead in defending the 'no man's land'? Who would have been entitled to the land were the village of Miller was? They were in the middle, hence the name 'no man's land '. The refusal of the noblemen could be caused by fear of a war between them? Did their fellow noblemen understood that to come to their rescue declared that they had other interests on such land? Why not interpret it solely as a noble and honorable help to those in need? The concept of noble was also of loftiness, of benevolence, of charity, right? What was so shameful in that? He would br rewarded for his solicitude.

Celebrated at the mere sight of his coat of arms, cheered with joyful tears. His action eternalized by bards, poets and speakers. Ladies and women of all classes and races would sigh at the mention of his name. Brave men and people would follow them until the end of the world and beyond. And, above all, he would be knighted by the queen and the mother of all men, the kind-hearted and virtuous queen Cecil and graced with blessings from the powerful and magnanimous king.

However, what if no nobleman was moved by the suffering of the poor people? Was something done? Hard to believe… Help directly from the king? Maybe. How many days more would they have?

What is the real problem to help them? Why the noblemen resisted? Could it be problems and completely divergent opinions? Or was there some obscurity in the rapid denial of the knight of Kleitos, Sir Plézoun Raymovick?

At the time that Sartre had been at his home they talked a little bit about everything and maybe that's the problem… Disease was still a possibility for the disappearances. Now, on second thought Sartre clearly understood the real terror on the face of the nobleman, not from illness but the extent of an epidemic. Of its extent and madness. The noble and valiant knight of Kleitos limited himself to gather information about how much time he would have to escape, and if he would have that time. Unfortunately at some point everything went amiss and they became interested in discussing experiences and intellectuality. A war of fools.

If he had sought Father Cyrus, owner of the south lands first, would he have reached another outcome? Would he have less stormy reactions? Or would he consider diseases as curses? Who knows?

With the first gentleman, Sartre had been clamoring for common sense, for everyone's sake. A spoonful of wisdom for each dose of idiocy… That was what the noble Plézoun had said then. He said he favored the death of ignorance through finding the initial cause, but he still wanted to keep himself safe from diseases, plagues. Far and away, with his people, or rather, with his vassals and aggregates. In short, contrary to what he defended and stood for. He declared himself owner of the truth! He didn't even entertain the probability that a mere farmer and healer or someone else who wasn't a soldier or a noble could be right.

"Who knew! Neither I nor he." the sentence snuck out of his thoughts.

Before the turn of a season the villagers were more lost than newborns. And some of those missing he helped bring out of the womb of their mothers. Lucretia, Djamir and Ektor, son of dear Moriel, Hadish, son of Haskam, Iago and Klei. What was it? Tens? More? The point was that he knew every one of them and Sartre didn't even suspect that wild animals were far more savage, and were called "traders". These beasts had simple people as feed and, as their grater god, money.

And today, being there, in that situation, isolated from his old friends, gave him the opportunity to clear his head and understand that he would never go back home… The others were not yet willing to consider that possibility.

Morgrinald, in the healer's eyes, and whoever was watching, was digging his large nose and seemed interested in nothing else. He examined it and wiped it off on his other hand, cleaning his finger carefully. Then, he hunted more from the other nostril. After finishing the grotesque grooming demonstration, he rubbed his hands. While two gnomes went by him, the scoundrel took two fruits from the stretcher they carried and began to eat them.

"Useless parasite"… Sartre whispered disgusted.

The healer never liked him. And why should he? In the dinghy, right after the shipwrecked, he kicked the desperate ones trying to save themselves. He pushed away enemies and former prisoners like them. I wonder if he couldn't distinguish anyone in that chaos?

Then there was that hateful reaction regarding the death of Hellsing and even before, while they were talking to pass the time, he showed his obnoxious temperament. Everything in him had a bitter edge. Contrary to all the values that Sartre held dear.

Suddenly, his mind darted to a disturbing question. Who were those who initially came to rescue him and the others? What did he know about them? They arrived without warning as the result of a silent prayer, a prayer of many minds.

Elves! And what did he actually know about elves? Elves descended from the venerable air race. The air ones. He knew a lot more than others through his friend Sargauss, an ancestor of that race. With Sargauss the high slopes morning fogs danced around him as a welcome greeting. He saw rays being used as powerful weapons. Winds used as transportation and clouds dragged like dry hay bales. Sargauss never said nothing specific about his kind, but Sartre understood his fears of high longevity from the beginning. When they spoke about the dreaded death, he said that it was possible to hear the gale run crying and if the soul is weak or confused it could spin until it found its place in the slots of the sky, dragging everything from the ground like the swirling winds formed at sea that swept coastlines with fury like tavern man Darrell had mentioned once with terror in his eyes. About the elf lady, even during the past months, he concluded that she must be sad for being separated from her friend, brother, lover or partner. Tarson, that was a name that he memorized quickly without even knowing why. Tarson-Romanei. Perhaps because of the noble and dignified presence that emanated from him. What was he doing now after seeking Phillip Darrell? Had he killed him for being part of the cads' plan?

And where would his friend Sargauss be, whom vanished a long time ago? Well, considering what he knew of his friend, and his experience with Jupita, he would say that the people of the air were a caring people, diverging drastically from popular opinion, according to which, the air one were very vain.

Jupita said that with them there was, believe it or not, a devotee of the god of war. The eyes of the elf lady sweeten when describing her lady friend of intense temperament. A committed woman who, in life, did everything to help the people of that village. Of his village. Hans Ranni later whispered about her recuperation fearing what he called the plague, hoping that they buried her quickly.

Hans Ranni Ramiro Roder, the Little One of brave appetite that always stole from his silo, came as a guide. He had said that he had come for the thrill of the rescue. Untruth. A farce that he will never confess to. The healer knew him and liked the truth. Little Ones are cowards, they always live in groups and the courage came from the group. He never saw one of them alone for more than a day. Their families and relatives also began to disappear, but his mission ended at the end of the trail. Hans risked his life for a friend. Certainly, he missed vast family. A fact that made him think of the last member of the rescue team…

Dominescu, from the mountains and resident of the village of Miller, where its residents called it home. Sartre knew his family. Good parents, devoted to a simple life. They had two children, Dobrovonski, the oldest, and Dominescu. There was also Kayla, a beautiful girl with a shy and hidden smile, adopted by love and charity by Sonya and Enzo. Gossipers mentioned the love between Dominescu and Kayla, but unlike the evil expected from these gossips, the speakers were actually a sympathetic crowd. Obviously only the young woodsman thought his heart and face were illegible. A torrent of heavy feelings probably burdened them in sleep or awake.

The healer raised his eyes and his back that for the past few years had begun to pinch harder and longer. This sudden throbbing marked and reminded him even more of his age. He saw strangers around him. New people, although he was the new element. Behind him, a wrecked vessel, grounded in the sand. Broken dreams. However, these people continued their lives in a simple way, they began to dig into the hill and the rock close to the strip of sand. Maybe that's what the villagers are doing… Trying to rebuild elsewhere.

Sartre went to the stream and collected water with his hands.

“What do they gain by not acting?” Sartre reinforced his thoughts with words, an old habit of who lives alone. “Well… at the very least ,it stays as it is.”

This internal dialogue was not the type that silenced quickly and he sat making small mounds in the soft sand.

“The village vanishes the same way it began… From nothing.” the healer smoothed the hills thoughtfully. “Maybe that's the issue.”

“Why save something from which you can gain nothing? What? A handful of souls? There must be something more! The territory is far from good.”

Seeing the hills carved and ruined he saw himself as a bird watching the terrain of the village. It was close to that, a lean land like a patch of land painted with vegetables full of insects as hungry as its people. A people who just blew them away and ate the leftovers of this land rich with dust and swamp mud.

"Do you, o, bird high up, see what and how many we buried?"

Suddenly the thought closed his face and his smile was excised by embarrassment. He blushed and froze with things that an old man knew, and others more that his ears heard.

A silence took him so deeply that not even thoughts or memories dared to be in this barren place. His body seized completely. What he learned from Sargauss was something dangerous, whether it was true or not. Although he knew the answer in his heart. His body was sweating cold, his heart shook him with strands of blood, urging him to escape, but escape to where? How to walk away from this? And, as the facts tend to be what they are, his entire being was anesthetized and the mind played its part, trying, strongly, to bring his memory to moments before this dangerous awareness, this terrible knowledge. Exactly when he decided to start over in this place. At a time that he did nothing but moan the rocky land and bring humus from the placid lake, on his back, form the stone shores.

"It was months of struggle."

Every villager had his calvary. The barkeeper, Phillip Darrell, Raquel and Juna and even old lady Miller, who lent her name to the village.

How many friends, and especially how much sadness overwhelmed the joy. Imagine how much Dominescu and his family suffered. Close brothers separated. The eldest son gone, like so many before him, and now his brother.

Lost children. A suffering that Sartre knew all too well. One, two, a thousand children… the number can never be measured. There is no bigger or smaller suffering, only the importance we give them. Mankind, from the beginning of its existence, named everything: dog, chair, knife, food, shelter, as well as the immaterial, the intangible; like the wind, love, loneliness, hatred and hope. He created important titles, revering the undeniable importance in every fraternal or social bond. So he named who inserted life, as "father" and who conceived it, as "mother", and the fruits of that relationship were called sons and daughters. Those who had the same parents as brothers. However, due to the bewilderment, man never gave a name to the father who lost his son, a name to the mother with no more tears to cry. Sartre knew the pain, the grip, the void and the roots of the old tree canopy where he buried his boy.

From one moment to another, he pushed away the pain of homesickness to attract the needles of doubt on another issue. Thus, without reaching a conclusive opinion, he asked himself:

"What noblemen gain without acting? What is the bonus of this indifference?"

The answer would never come. Then he turned his attention to the gnome conclave.

The gnomes were a short people, with exaggerated facial features, a people excluded from the known world. And these gnomes were mindful of others in the center of the group. The maintainers of order… Like ministers, judges of their peers. And those gnomes held such a degree of respect that others avoided interrupting the debate, and obviously neither did foreigners like him and the others. But that world and the other wider one of his thoughts fought for his attention.

"Master Sartre, where are you from?" He remembered well the question made by the noble Plézoun and, above all, the end of that conversation. "Certainly the fable of the three wishes made to a genie is known there, isn't it?" "Could it be that master Raymovick really made a bad choice of words?" "That one that brings on the war? "

At the present time, although far from his beloved village and immersed in such different cultures and traditions, could he be witnessing the beginning of a local war? Gnomes against a huge opponent? There was an almost poetic comparison with the villagers and the abductions monster…

Suddenly, a fat and clumsy beetle zoomed loudly and slammed into a web made in the undergrowth. The spider acted quickly and moved towards the huge intruder. She moved back forward, waiting… But always moving forward. The beetle struggled noisily, but got tired, so the minute spider won.

IMPASSES OR WHIMS?

Anyway, the deadlock lasted weeks after this first clash of ideas. Certainly the gnomes were intelligent, but proved to be too suspicious, almost to the point of anarchy. All the time, they spoke or quoted a certain Master Rolker with pride and feeling. This fellow was the leader in what was called 'contraptionic', a creative inventor and, curiously, a self-taught researcher of new cures based on herbs, roots and vegetables. A person with an extensive resume. Each of the shipwreck survivors were interested in one or another aspect of this gnome leader. However, this person never appeared. Everything was done through intermediaries and emissaries. When asked or insisted about him they were faced with an insurmountable wall of defenders. The less idolized version came from a serious and family dedicated gnome.

And again, the gnome community gathered for yet another day. A consensus was about to be determined.

The permanence of the shipwreck survivors in the village was never the issue. The gnomes tolerated their extreme curiosity, an ostracism that time would fix. Being honorable and civilized, gradually they learned their customs. So what would be the big question being addressed, that took the obsessed gnomes out of their routine? As other gnomes arrived, it was visible that the total number of that community, unlike what was initially thought, was never that big. Twenty, perhaps twenty-five percent more than those seen in everyday life. When those almost always submerged realized the presence of the castaways, they weren't even surprised, for surely they had heard the news from the surface. These gnomes seemed indivisible from the land in which they wallowed.

The community had a tight deadline for the construction of other houses. They wanted to leave the ship they used as a temporary home soon. And for a simple reason. The ship was listing increasingly, due to its weight and by the insistence of the tides. Sooner or later it would collapse.

Jupita imagined that one of them could be Master Rolker, however this illustrious being never introduced himself, thus, the mystery remained. While another one becomes clear. Amid murmurs and conversations, there was a great surprise, the excavations found promising galleries, some even went around the giant's home. The first order of their tunnel investment so close to the immense and 'deadly ' creature, was to measure the integrity and soundness of the galleries and, secondly, observe from time to time the actions of their giant neighbor, such as diet and habits. By precaution, they made the necessary changes at night, when the beast was resting its vileness. Even while asleep, the giant proved to be dangerous because when he punched the walls in his sleep, he could compromise the structure of galleries and adjacencies. At this point of the story, some went into a visible disarray, raising their voices with brief outbursts about it "being the attitude of a killer" and about "trying to smash them in the tunnels". Besides, hearing another effusive one saying things like "I was there", accompanied by others with saying "I felt it also". Suddenly it reached a dizzying vortex, when others concluded, in sheer xenophobia, that in fact the action of the giant revealed an evil intelligence as he planned to evict them from the galleries and that would leave them in the open and, thus, powerless victims of his brutal appetite. Hysteria flourished in every comma or breath. Dominescu, Jupita and even Hans tried to act as judges and diplomats, but it was a territory of thin shells and lost ways. But it was Morgrinald who succeeded. The gnomes' eloquent, fast and prolific speech found its match in the dwarf's attitudes and language. And, in the end, all the yeses, noes and howevers subsided into an agreement.

"Ok! That's fair." Morgrinald shouted closing the discussion dramatically for he could no longer stand them repeating the terms. "Within a week, when the rainy season is over, the gnomes will use the digging machine. The one that looks like a crab, like this one. They will build tunnels where they will be free to do soil research and build roads for quick access to vegetation and houses in the cavities of the hill, as long as it is done during the day."

"And how do we know that the day is gone?"

Morgrinald realized that the problem was bigger than he imagined, so he replied with his usual delicacy:

"I will ask the sun to remain longer in the sky."

However, they looked at each other without understanding the sarcasm. And before they could ask how it would be possible, he bellowed:

"You piece of shit! Just put someone outside the excavation area! I'm happy, so you should be happy." he said, staring at the gnomes faces, who seemed wary of secret intentions and connections with the giant. "Or am I mistaken?"

"A ground drainage system and a framework for rain water storage, in order to shelter the aforementioned individual." a gnome named Frederico Hágar-Minus said. "Will the agreement ensure us free circulation through the passages, without any hassles or threats of violence, direct or indirect, against any members of our community, even when they need new tunnels or vent ducts, ensuring free research rights, outlet and extraction?" This gnome was one of those who scribbled in the air so he didn't lose track of his ideas. He babbled scribbling in the sand. "It's a deal. I warn you in advance: after the drawing of the local plans, we will study three or four means of obtaining the best result and harnessing both the material to be used as the area that…"

"Little gnome, you're pushing your luck, I will punch that swollen nose of yours until it's flat…" Morgrinald smiled as he threated the gnome because he could see himself doing it. But he controlled himself and turned to the other gnomes. "You! You little shits in overalls! You will build the drainage tunnels in the walls of Iurik's immense home. And the latter accepts to live there only during the rainy season. When you install a roof for him."

"Phew! I thought we would we have a short deadline. So will still have twelve days. Good, good and very good." Frederico hugged himself, satisfied.

THE FLOODED CEMETERY

With nothing to do and hoping to get out of that place, the castaways formed a vigil. However, the first week of watch was fruitless: no vessels passed close there. So Dominescu went on to swim in the wild sea and investigate the sunk and wave battered ships in search of answers. They weren't exactly ships nor "ships". This simplistic designation was a right reserved only to the lay, but it represented all types of sea vessels. The former mariner identified triremes, galleons, frigates and ships with triangular sails capable of facing headwinds. And at the bottom of those clear waters others that were maybe fragments of the visible ones, so the final number was unclear. The lovable giant said once that they exceeded his coming into this forgotten world.

And according to the gnomes, there were no external contacts, which reinforced the idea that everyone there were the children and grandchildren of the first castaways. But, despite the testimonies, the stories didn't convince him. Dominescu had his own ideas about these boats that sticked out of the water like gravestones; as huge mausoleums buried in the sandbanks and corals. In this dangerous and fatal port, there could be weapons, cloth for making clothes, tallow candles, among other things in those debris. Evidently, he did also consider treasures, but there, in that place of water and sand, what mattered was not the value, but its usefulness.

Therefore, he had to convince the others about this endeavor. Sartre, the old healer, excused himself saying he had a lot to do as many of gnomes, who worked in the tunnels, had a strange skin disease and he thought it was his duty to take care of them. Hans bristled just at the thought of sea water and said with a trembling voice that he would be more useful helping Sartre, because he knew well the plants, herbs and roots; Besides, he had promised someone else that he would take care of the man.

Morgrinald slyly said:

"Go into the water to pick up junk? Not for you, nor a hooker nor a king. Forget it!"

"You find the gnome village familiar." Dominescu commented.

"Very. I'd rather not lose sight of them."

The woodcutter padded his friend on the shoulder.

"You're too paranoid."

"Paranoids live longer."

"Turtles also." he jested and walk away. "Maybe there are equipment, clothing and tools there."

"Actually, I don't care what you find."

"Wine…"

Although the woodsman now insisted with a good argument, the dwarf shrugged. Morgrinald reflected on the hallway he found shortly after arriving on the island. He had found it when Hans had fainted in the galleries. Nothing in the world could have prepared him for such an event. It was a stunningly decorated hall with huge panels painted on the walls with everyday scenes depicting the gnomes trading with other peoples. Barrels filled with a viscous black oil fed high flames, and these lit up a much larger and more impressive scene. In that rich hall there were several statues of gnomes. Perhaps generations… a cemetery. Gnomes and dwarfs descended from the same family and as they age, they eat less and less, and develop a rigid layer of skin which gradually hardens enough to severely restrict their movements. With the extra weight of the rigid skin, muscles hurt and the exhaustion of a simple stroll can be fatal. Morgrinald buried himself in thoughts and memories.

Dominescu realized that there was something wrong with the dwarf. But would he ever open up? Well… Now, there was only Jupita.

All it took was a few arguments for her to accept. She was always keen and fully supported him, therefore she became an active part of the expeditions. However, Jupita couldn't swim, but they solved the problem by tying a thin and short length of rope to their waists. Floating magically through the air, the elf became a kind of human bouy. And the human became her heavy anchor against the strong and sudden winds. One an exceptionally cold morning they decided they would go to the reddish galleon and make three stops. One for each vessel previously investigated. The journey was long and the waves were irritating like guardians of secrets and a rain blackened the sky halfway.

"Let's go back!" Dominescu said, with clear concern in his voice.

"Between coming and going, either way works for me. We are halfway there."

"Rain brings wind, and what's worse: it brings lightning."

"Lightning and winds are friends of my race, my only concern are the waves."

"It's your friends who makes the waves swell."

Thunder and lightning hit the surroundings. Jupita squeezed her eyes, trying to beat the rain water thrown in her face. Lightning cut the gray day, and its brightness formed an image. A tenuous body appeared and fled quickly. That worried her because it could be delirium caused by fatigue.

Twenty more minutes were enough to finally reach the sunken galleon. This one, unlike the others, had a hole in the hull, a hole with darkened extremities.

"It was sunk on purpose, Jupita."

"Pirates? Warship?"

"Something worse… Both! Pirates usually loot ships and add them to their fleet. Warships are not that different. In both cases, they avoid doing this kind of thing. Unless they had another reason."

"Accident maybe?"

"Or premeditation? Jupita, promise you will be careful dealing with the the coast inhabitants."

"You think they had something to do with this?"

"I hope not."

"Dom, you drunk a lot of seawater." She joked. "There are several ships. There are five very different ships in sight, even I, a layperson, I can see. Imagine then the ones that are fully submerged."

"Yes. But for now, prudence is the best strategy. Jupita, don't say anything to them, ok?"

"Ha, ha. Creatures that small subjugating ships this size? Ha, ha."

Given the beautiful elf prompt disbelief, the woodcutter decided to keep his thoughts safe from unnecessary hysteria and surely more mockery. After all, they already had the concern of getting back home. Speculating on the existence of a pirate refuge around, that served as means of getting rid of unwanted material, would not be suitable without being sure.

There was only one certainty, that the inhabitants there were castaways from those, or maybe even older vessels, including obviously, the ship that brought Iurik.

Already close to their goal, they immediately noticed the rounder hull. Inside, grilled potholes marked the interior with dim light, although enough to identify the benches where the rowers did their job in the absence of wind. The two investigators had distinct impressions. Was there an obvious concern with comfort or the hull was wide to accommodate heavy commodities?

Drawing closer, the waves near the galleon were almost non-existent, as well as the wind. The broken thick wood boom in the water, served as an access point. On its fallen and worn flag there was a thick layer of silt, which concealed forever its age and nationality, but pointed how long it had been there. The deck was slippery and falling there would never be funny because the mollusks encrusted here and there in the wood could cut and infect the wound. And, without the appropriate ointment or salve, such wounds became serious and permanent scars to say the least. In the long run, it could cause amputations and death. Besides that, the danger of loose floorboards could make them fall to another level and mortally injure themselves. By instinct, prudence or certainty of accidents, they stood in several sleeping hammocks. These hammocks weren't for the choice of sleeping under the stars, but for the lack of space. The covered area, as well as the lower levels, were really dedicated to goods, the good old-fashioned trader way to expand cargo space. Even there on the deck, there were a lot of riches exposed, you just had to know what to look for beyond the glare of metal and stones.

Ostentaticious. In the carved wood support beams, on doors and doorstops, or in marble statues of haughty and imperious creatures. Besides these, there were tied boxes and barrels that deserved further examination later. But at that moment, they wanted to investigate every corner. The access door to the captain's cabin was twisted and bloated. On it, several minute crabs stung everything in their path. Crustaceans inhabited the cavities and appeared to be feeding on something. A little closer they noticed, disgusted, a cadaver with its face eaten. After the initial sickness caused by the gruesome scene, Dominescu explained to his partner the role of these scavengers, making the elf's stomach revolt.

Suddenly her ears picked up muffled sounds and moans. Wasting no time, she went to the cargo bay doors.

"Dominescu! There are people here. Many! And they are injured.

Impulsively she removed the loose floor plank that sealed the doors. The links were pulled rude and hastily, so the wounded were freed.

"Jupita no! They are not injured, they're dead!"

"What?"

Jupita pulled back her arm just a moment before being bitten. She recoiled trembling and horrified.

The man in front of her barely had skin on his cheek and he lacked an eye. The others whispered in a sick chorus pelting themselves towards the adventurers. A violent and insane struggle ensured, in which many of the undead hit each other. A whispered voice from behind warn them about the sail of the mast. Dominescu decided to give the voice credit and lunged for the sail controls. The knot, although complex, undid easily and the released sail descended heavily, hitting fiercely the demented zombies, crushing some and hurling others out to sea. With their numbers reduced, Dominescu fought with a curved rusty sword and another one with a grip thin as a needle and mutilated their dying bodies that whispered, asking for something like food and mercy. And when they finally stopped moving, Dominescu sat almost breathless.

"Did you find what you were looking for in the last sunken ship you visited?" mentioned fine velvety, almost between a whisper and a moan, voice from somewhere.

"A ghost!" Jupita said, startled.

Dominescu rolled to the side, getting into a fighting stance trying to see what could not be seen.

"Yes. And a most thankful one for granting mercy to the suffering of these sailors and crew." the slightly luminous apparition said a little louder.

Dominescu tried to control the thudding of his heart. In his mind when superstition becomes reality, everything must be reviewed carefully, because fear without control can be converted into weakness, and therefore, helplessness. Thus, he squinted his eyes to see it better, and, from the little he saw, he noticed its old shape, the translucent spectrum revealed a grateful face that said:

"In the ship before this one there are weapons in boxes, and I suspect they're still in great shape. Although I'm a ghost, as you rightly said, the reality of earthly things are blurred to me. Therefore, it is difficult to distinguish good weapons from those dull or useless due to time and lack of use.

"Can you read minds?" Jupita inquired, between fear and curiosity.

"I could hear your moans during the days you approached here."

"Why couldn't we see you before?"

"The absence of light helped me stand out. My essence thins each day, one day I will cease to exist altogether."

A sad gloom emanated from the ghost.

"And what holds you to this world?" the elf inquired, still scared about whole thing.

"My body is holy by the obligation bestowed on me, and it was not given a proper burial."

"And where is it?"

"Almost submerged in a chamber beneath your feet."

"Say, spirit, what should we do to give you peace." Dominescu said serenely.

"It is not your obligation."

Dominescu looked around. The entrance to the interior of the cabins was blocked. A few meters away he saw the secondary mast in terrible shape and, picking up a thick and heavy axe from the remains of one of the undead, he positioned himself, and after two initial swings, he began to chop the wood. With four powerful blows, half of the mast shattered away. Dominescu abandoned the weapon and began to push the mast vigorously, however the weight of the mast brought it quickly towards him and with his expertise, the woodsman took advantage of its movement and converted it into a swing.

"Get out of there!" Dominescu shouted with difficulty, given the effort he was doing.

The shout brought Jupita back from a light trance. The wood of the mast was almost as wide as a horse's chest and its weight ripped the deck scattering splints and pieces of wood everywehre. The elf contracted her body and before the debris hit her, the ghost stood in front of her in a foolish attempt to stop the splinters. Fortunately the flying splinters and small pieces of wood weren't big enough to cause injury.

The elf noted the sincere effort of the sad soul. It was a nice gesture, and now calmer, she said with all sincerity:

"Thank you."

The woodcutter moved back being careful not to fall into the hole he made in the deck. There, in that unusual access, the light entered into dark spaces and revealed the intact body of a handsome young man. Dominescu jumped to the lower floor, but as the planks shrieked under his weight, he walked slowly. Besides, the roar of the deck floor suggested that the weight of the large mast was not yet set. He had to act with speed and accuracy. If not the mast, something else could hit him. Probably the next level was fully submerged and quite possibly, there would be other zombies.

"I hope they remain drowned." Dominescu prayed in a whisper.

The clothes suggested simplicity, and the corpse's pose, with a knee on the floor and hands crossed over a sword, seemed to pray in sacred silence.

Suddenly, the bright image formed beside Dominescu and. The fear was gone, thus, he took a closer look and the resemblance of the ghost's face with the corpse of the young noble cleared any doubts about his identity.

"Yes, this is me. Luckian Bragado, outcast son of the Alina Marcel house. Here… Let me see it once more."

The broad-bladed and porous sword showed points of rust and oxidation throughout its length. The handle had a long cloth ribbon, with worn symbols and writing, over which Dominescu ran his fingers with interest.

"You recognize the words?"

"No. I can only read runes and brands like every poor man."

"And the ribbon?"

Dominescu had been a sailor but that didn't mean that he knew or even that he remembered everything, except of course the on-board routine. Strips determined profession and function, something very practical for those who don't want bodies abandoned with unowned weapons. However, the braided ribbon denoted the complexity of a rigid discipline and mastery in the kind of knot used, but it said nothing about the dead.

"I would be happy if you took the sword from here." Luckian, the ghost, whispered. "Because for me there is no more sense in keeping it."

"Listen. I'm just trying to offer you a proper burial."

"And you will if you accept the last will of a dead man."

"I may not be a good guardian for it."

"If you say so, so be it. But take it away. A plow without an ox can be used, though not to its full capacity. A sword in a dead man's sheath would not have similar use?"

Dominescu can't resist to wield it. The woodcutter who also learned the craft of forging notices, surprised, the extreme lightness of the sword. It just under half of the estimated weight for its size. Curious, he exams it thoroughly.

"The blade is not that thin to be so light... What spells are trapped in it? I've heard songs about it. Its enchanted, isn't it? That's the only way it could be so light."

"Spells? No. It is an extension of the air world. In my current state I can no longer wield it. Take it but use it only when in need. The ribbon must be attached to your wrist because the weight of its greatness may be too strong for you. That is the only way to wield it… Guardian.”

Dominescu remembered the stories about the worlds. An old and known story. Overlapping worlds. Worlds that separate gods from demons. The guardians were those who guard the passage from one world to another. In a heavy sigh, he replied:

“No.” Dominescu frowned and vigorously shook his head negatively. His eyes watched the beautifully finished sword. “It’s too great a responsibility.”

Luckian smiled.

“I'm only providing a tool that no longer fits me.” the ghost reached out and gently ran his hand over the length of the blade.

“Dominescu. That is your name, isn't it? The choice isn’t only yours. If what you say is true, fate will have the sword find another owner. You will serve it as much as it will serve you. Believe Me. Everything must have a use.”

The words impregnated of truth and wisdom convinced him. Thereby, he finally took the sword, still surprised for it being lighter than its size suggested.

“The sword of the winds is dull and needs a careful guide for its miracles.”

“What? How?” Jupita said as she approached them. Floating and stopping with her feet slightly above the fragile wood floor.

The spirit stared at her and although the gaze was placid, Jupita thet the air was impregnated with a bitter and heavy sorrow.

“I'm one of the guardians and…”

"… The fate of my soul is not as important as the sword." Jupita interrupted and completed almost in trance. Jupita's mind was far and fogged with ancient and powerful stories. "The sword of…"

"Yes. The sword I held when I was alive is the same of the guardian before me. The faithful sword sensed my death and, eager to find other hands to serve, caused a lot of things on its own."

"Storms. Gusts and more."

"It was an appeal!"

"Yes. You understand, then."

"You want to go."

Luckian closed his eyes in deep agreement.

Jupita, Tarson, every elf, each being of that august race knew what to do. The difference was whether she was brave enough to do it, to go so far and suddenly not return, die in her choice. Choices, in the end, it all boiled down to them, and the sword had chosen.

Her skin, between white and a soft blue, now gained a more intense and darker tone of blue. Jupita, the most beautiful among the beauties of Almokaryr, disciple of the great Darkay, was evoking the high magic. And with a gesture she dissipated the clouds above them, revealing the sky. Arteries and veins were the most obvious point of the force sucked from her effort. In another gesture to the clouds fit to focus sunlight on the dead body of the former guardian. The light, intensified with high magic, incinerated the corpse and quickly turned it into light ashes. The disciple of Darkay rocked from the excruciating pain. She blew with all the strength of her lungs and the ashes involved the spirit of Luckian, thereby allowing the perplexed Dominescu to see him in detail.

Gradually the ashes gained a golden glow. The brave and noble Luckian, after one hundred and eighty months, finally sighed relieved. Feeling liberated from his obligation. Looking tenderly to the sky he noticed the dizzying vortex made of clouds around the sun. He was finally freed from existence.

At the same moment, his golden luminescence dimmed down to a soft silver tone and finally… emptiness filled the space.

"Go in peace." Jupita said, visibly taken. And then fainted. The high magic stole all her strength. She heard Dominescu calling from somewhere behind the realm of dreams. The evoked magic guided the spirit to another plane of existence, and almost went with him. Darkay, her master and tutor was there in her dreams:

"You risked yourself too much. You're not ready for the high magic. The gesture was foolish, although the intent is noble."

"Darkay! Darkay…" She raved out loud, frightening Dominescu.

"Wake up, girl."

Seeing be that his slaps and shaking were useless, Dominescu laid his friend's head in his lap. He also was tired, as much from the swimming as from the fighting. So he removed his boots, cursing himself for the silly idea of swimming with them.

"Damn habit! Dobrovonski is not here to steal them, fool."

The woodcutter's eyes fell along with his quick and muffled laugh. Behind the lame name of his older brother, was a simple person, easily amused. The night came slowly, slow enough to add one by one the memories of his brother and the hate of the elaborate process of fate, the ever partying fate. And in an instant his dreaminess took him to the future, seeing and feeling the grief caused by the disappearance of children to their parents. What kind of heart could resist such bitterness?

Frustration stole fickle sighs from him… He lost his friend and brother to death; and the love of his life in life. Could there be greater frustration? Dominescu looked somewhere on the damp wood of the deck, and beyond the bulwark, waves hit the galleon continuously and from the beating, high, unpredictable and insane sprays of thin water exploded loudly.

Suddenly, his eyebrows raised from what he saw. From an opening in the hull he saw something alive, half fish and half something else… climbing the crest of the high waves and disappearing. He squeezed his eyes and without seeing it again, he could only ignore it because it was surely another dead body in this bay of graves. On the other hand, could it be a 'standing dead'? An undead like the ones earlier?

He was exhausted and Jupita was passed out. Given the physical condition of both, the thoughts and possibilities of a siege were glaring. His eyes ran in panic to other side, like wanting to escape those thoughts, or identify where the rotting flesh and dead heart would come from.

The mast groaned, stealing his attention for a moment. Nothing there. His eyes then swept the surroundings in search of threats. Reverie of an exhausted mind? Whatever it was, his mind retreated in time. He visited his home again… And what was happening there? His father had a heavy look behind his mother, while she stood at the window. Waiting. Gradually the his parents vanished and suddenly the house was emptier. Kayla was now absolutely alone. Would she find a husband? Forget him? However the dream continued and, like a worm eating through leather; madness came and took residence in the bones of his beloved sparrow. Too much weight for someone so young.

Memories were sometimes a balm, until horrific ones as these. It was body's attempt to tame the horror and focus on perseverance. This nightmare should never come true. However, the exhaustion was severe and the woodsman's body, although young gave in languidly. Dominescu shook his head like a dog drying itself. He turned his attention back to the surroundings. He tried to pick up sounds that stood out. He had to be sure. He tried to wake his friend again. But nothing happens… Slowly, the idea of the dead on the waves became a perverse fantasy of his mind. Thus, gradually he lowered his awareness and tried to convince himself that it was an illusion brought on by tiredness. A legitimate exhaustion after so much activity, after all the swimming and fighting.

Dominescu had his naps blasted to pieces by his eyes flapping without strength, to a debile, sloppy vigil. Jupita coughed sleeping, and woke him up to a new and clumsy guard that did not last. The elf lady was still out, breathing deeply. Then he finally understood the futility of the vigil. He was exhausted and whatever he had seen on the crest of the wave was a mistake from his exhaustion. And if there was something out there, it certainly was one of those who he had killed. In the distant sky, the moon was nothing but a mild scratch, a smile with a hint of sweetness and provocation, a moon that might be in collusion with fate.

"What do you plan for me, now, huh?" the question of the exhausted one was legitimate. However, the lack of moonlight turned the horizon, the sea, the beach and the sky into a single mass and Dominescu, exhausted, relinquished to sleep without waiting for his answer.

The day came and the squawk of an albatross woke him up. Seeing the top of the bent mast and hearing the sound of water, he remembered where he was. He rubbed his eyes and scratched his chest lazily, and he jolted in horror when he felt the smell of sour milk, not from fish but a smell dreaded among sailors. Right beside him, two reptilian eyes widely opened, peered through dirty hair, smudged with algae and fat. The fish tail of the creature stirred slowly while it crawled, belly down, on the deck. It was very close to the elf, and Dominescu prayed that she wouldn't wake up now. Maybe it was just curious about the rare race of the air. Serenity and moderate movements were the best option, avoid fright and strike. An obvious priority.

To the beast, Dominescu and Jupita were a sumptuous find, that was clear by the wild joy with witch it stared at them. The thing smiled with its big mouth opened, in which tapered teeth, common to snakes and lizards, bit its lower lip with lust. A mermaid. A creature of diurnal habits and violent by nature and passion. And even so close, it kept squinting between the strange eyelids demonstrating that it was clearly shortsighted. The legend, told tirelessly by sailors, didn't match what he saw, neither the thick, smooth and dark downy covering its grayish skin with shapeless stains, or patches burned or aggravated by the sun. Such creatures, wild creatures of the water passed to adulthood in a matter of years. Grimlik, the snail, was who told him those things. The sailor, with a curved body and a crippled leg said, before old age warped his mouth and left him silly, that, out of nowhere, tens, sometimes hundreds, emerged from the water, attacking all warm-blooded beings and that, at the height of the frenzy, the victims who survived were taken away and have the creatures' larvae injected into them through long stingers. The larvae became adults in just one season and they devoured their former hosts. A cruel way to die. Dominescu could see the stinger on the creatures' forearms. Like broken arms with bones sticking out. An ivory limb with a fine tip, and a bony spur. His sailor friend spoke about everything and many said that his lies were good for sleeping. Come back after the fifth bottle, they would joke. From now on, if he ever saw him again, he would apologize for laughing at his stories.

"Um… What do we have here?" the monster hissed.

Up to then, Dominescu had controlled his breathing almost to the point of stopping it completely. But, faced with the execrated words of the beast, fear grabbed his abdomen making him grunt lowly. Beneath the thick beard his lips trembled.

"One sssstill breathessss." the odious creature said that as if it was the woodsman's name. "Thissss morsssel of food issss yourssssss?"

The bizarre creatures spoke about Jupita.

"Yes." he didn't even know why he had replied like that.

"Hungry too…"

"Get away." Dominescu almost spelled out what he said. And while he was talking, he slowly stretched his fingers to his boots and gloves and put them on. His elf friend was one step away from oblivion. Would she survive if the mermaid bit her? Maybe. But what could he do? She was still unconscious and still in his lap. There was no way to get up without hurting the elf and what's worse, maybe ti bit them both…

The panting of the beast made a reptile noise, almost a phelgm. The shallow lips were insufficient to cover its big mouth, soon the monster drooled constantly. Its "V" shaped nostrils opened and closed and, judging by the raising and lowering of its chin, the marine imp was sniffing the elf without losing sight of her. Translucent eyelids like sea caravels flashed idly making a wet fabric sound. On its throat, sealed gills prevent air from getting in.

"Niccce ssssmell." When the creature spoke, a slight drip of water and saliva escaped it along with a heavy breath of rotten fish. "Unlike you." it completed with a jagged grin.

Hirrofied, Dominescu noticed its blank stare on Jupita and soon it made an impossible proposal:

"I'll take just one leg!"

"Not! The prey is mine!" It was despair. Dominescu walked into that craziness trying get the best outcome. After all, as long as it was talking, it wasn't biting. It won't be able to eat if I keep it talking.

"Offer meeee."

"No."

"Oferrrrr."

"Stubborn creature. The is not enough meat."

"When hunger leavesss you..." she flinched and threw up some water. "I will keep what's left."

"You can't. I'm going to eat everything."

"I like meat, but I alssssso like bonessss and hair. Give them to me then."

The kind of meal appreciated by that marine demon was almost impossible to bear. His stomach stirred endlessly. But control was vital at the moment.

"What do you want for her?"

Dominescu failed to say anything. Gripped by the horrors of such vileness, he only shook his head negatively.

"Yesss you do!"

The beast smiled lightly with its eyes. Its breath reminded him of fish entrails, the acrid stench made him gag.

"Do you think you have something to offer?" Dominescu felt bad, shaken. What if this was the final moment, his only chance of survival? What right did he have to prevent his parents from seeing him back? He had to escape. At least him. Immunity. He wanted to escape… and there was a price. Brutal, but still, a price. Could he turn the elf over? Now he knew what to do. The woodcutter let his eyes smile.

The marine beast focused on the bargained meat licking the air around, as if it could to savor the elf's taste. It munched its teeth in anticipation, desire… The mermaid faked a touch and a cut with its ring finger, studying the best use of the delicacy and then retracted her arm, hugging herself expressing something between depravity and savagery. Then suddenly she said:

"Asssk."

THE BITTERNESS, BOREDOM AND THE WINE

On the beach, Morgrinald was in a corner, leaning on a big and large stone, splitting his attention between the gnomes and the sea front, where the elf and the hero ventured daily. Damn hope, he thought. The woodcutter had contaminated the elf's weak mind with nonsense. And every day they stayed a little longer. Searching, mining treasures or other nonsense. Namely, a daily uselessness as a hobby. Even if a vessel came through there, not even the most insane captain would risk approaching a beach where ruined ships boats marked each sandbank and coral.

The dwarf took a swig at the wine he found in the destroyed vessel on the beach. A whole crate of wine untouched by the gnomes, cousins of his kind. They were quite different when it came to driking. But for the rest, it was amazing how much the two races were alike… The hollowed hill, now home of his cousins, resembled the muddy and crowded streets of his people. In the distance, who watched from the outside, could call them ant-people, from the frenzied queues going and coming from inside the earth. The dwarf's mind, Keldorn's grandson, closed on heavy memories and his rare smile was gone immediately.

Hans Ranni, suddenly arrived and a jumped, easily sating at the top of the stone, saying:

"Can I talk to you?"

"What do you want, hairy?"

"I brought fish."

"Thanks."

"Morgrinald."

"Spill it shorty."

"We're going to stay here forever, right?"

"Says who?"

"We are, right?"

"I have always faced difficulties."

"I see…"

"Little One, look up. What do you see?"

"Nothing."

"Humph! That's how I lived for some time: inside the earth, in the depth of the abyss. It was an accident of fate, damn destiny wanted it to be that way. I fell and ended up in the deep. And where I landed I saw many points of light, like these here. There were others of my people working, strolling and…"

"How did you survive?"

"The question is: for what!"

Morgrinald paused and bit a piece of fish. He continued talking while eating at the same time.

"I starved, I was thirsty, angry, remorseful…"

"And you didn't ask for help!?"

"I couldn't…" Morgrinald passed the wine gallon to Hans, and took another bite of the white roasted meat.

Hans stopped, sniffed, dropped a bit in his hand and licked a little bit and before taking a nice gulp, he inquired seriously:

"Proud, huh?"

"Pride my ass! One thing you have to understand, your little fur ball: a scream in a cave can cause it to collapse. If it doesn't attract something worse, like predators that love to eat you bit by bit.

"Stubbbbboooornnn…"

The dwarf turned and tried to catch the Little One, who dodged him. Even so, he still tried two or three more times.

"Stop jumping you piece of shit…" Morgrinald returned to the rock and crossed his legs.

The sudden stop and silence indicated the obvious, Keldorn's grandson didn't have to say it, but he did.

"Don't make me say it, son of Ranni and Ramiro…"

Hans sighed, lamenting for having gone too far, then he slowly returned and leaned back looking at the big bottle next to the dwarf.

"You're going to drink alone?"

Morgrinald raised his clenched fist and stopped it midair close to the Little One's face. Slowly, he pushed his friend's hairy chin. And then he passed the wine to him.

THE ROCK

Jupita woke up lazy and dizzy, she felt water on her face, but it took her awhile to figure out where she was. She failed to rise, her hurt body evidenced and reminded her of her deed. The sky moved and she could hear the sound of the waves crashing. She was alone in the dinghy. Did Dominescu…

A calloused hand grabbed the wood at her side. A muffled thud woke her completely. Dry land. Another thud and Dominescu's face appeared.

"It's about time."

"Mmmmm… Happened?"

"You're still sleepy?"

"Somewhat…"

"You talked a lot last night."

"Sorry."

"No problem." with those words, he stretched his hand to the elf, who, with some difficulty, stepped onto the sand.

"Wow, I even dreamt!"

"And in your language, I couldn't understand a thing."

"Really?"

"You repeated some words a lot. Look." he said, pointing with his eyes.

A trail of bottles led Morgrinald and big rat that were spent and deeply asleep. The dwarf was barefoot and who knew were his boots were. Hans's legs were hugging the bottle and from his silly smile, it was easy to imagine who and what he was dreaming of.

The woodsman vigorously lifted the boat above his head and took it away from the water, beyond the sand hills created by the waves. Jupita who staggered about with crooked and faltering steps, followed Dominescu, then leaned back on the boat.

"You're still in bad shape."

"Magic is like blood. The greater the power or time used in its execution, more you lose."

"Translation: that means that you have to take it easy for awhile." Morgrinald said suddenly, still with reddish eyes typical of drunks "Hey, boy! Come here."

Dominescu, intrigued, came to him. The drunk nudged his nose with his little finger and asked:

"Ditch ya u know that thish piece of shit here hash a bunch of kids?"

From the level of inebriation, Dominescu calculated that he would be like that for a few hours. He looked back at the elf and she had fallen asleep again. And from the thud close to him, so did the dwarf. Dominescu turned the dwarf over so he won't suffocate in the sand and went on to ask himself about the things that he had seen. He had dangerous ideas that wouldn't leave him. Ideas that latched on like vines on branches and mushrooms on stumps.

He turned around calmly, examining everything closely. That was one of the most miserable lands he had ever stumbled on. From where they were it was impossible to describe the site as an island or a continent. Everything behind him was just an immense beach that dwindled to the south and followed suddenly southeast where it ended in rocks immersed in water, like fingers and nails of a colossal fallen creature. Beside him, there was only sand dotted with lean trees and ahead, about half an hour, a huge vertical rock with thorns on its uppermost point concealing the north altogether, like a giant lying down.

"Sir! Sir!" a gnome with smooth and curled black hair waved his cap with a broad smile. "I'm here this early, not only to wish you a good day, but also, additionally, bring to you… Ops! I'm sorry. I thought that, seeing you from thirty-four and a half meters away, you were all already awake."

"No need to apologize. You couldn't have guessed."

"No guessing. Gnomes calculate not guess. However, I ignored the likelihood of this occurring, although it was a small probability."

"Gnome…"

"I know, I know… Never ignore any odds. If it exists, it is likely."

"Actually. I was going to ask your name."

"Frederico, inventor, concepts designer, cook, singer, dancer and instrument player. Terrible singer-poet they say… Although I think my weakness is the verse and not to scale."

"So… Frederico. We're on an island, right?"

"The answer to your question is simple and positive, given that there is not enough width in its extension to be called otherwise. There is neither another one visible so I presume therefore that its single and not part of an archipelago."

"Archipelago?"

"A set of Islands grouped and separated by the ocean. I mean for the whole set of islands, islets and large islands."

"And what's beyond that rock?"

"Another strip of sand."

"And…"

"No, no. That place has many dangers, the place is inhospitable to life."

"Okay. What's in the basket?"

"Fresh vegetables."

"Could you bring some more? It's enough for the elf, the dwarf and myself, but the Little One is a glutton."

"I'm sorry again. This element was really incalculable. The gnomes hospitality shall not be questioned for so little. I will be back in three quarters of an hour and I am sure of this. The margin of error this is minimal and I increased it, so… I will be right back."

"Thanks."

Dominescu was sure. Something about the way the gnome talked and acted, led him to suspect excuses and lies. There was something else after the giant lying rock. The only way there was through the beach. He waited a little, until the gnome disappeared. The others were in terrible shape, besides he didn't want to scare them with his deductions and ideas. If he was right, somewhere on the other side there could be a pirate port. Or a place where they could land and replenish with fresh water. Then, he took a deep breath and began his journey.

From a certain distance of the rocky seawall he could already see the hardened lava, forming concentric rays in certain places. Suddenly he remembered his father's wrinkled skin and he prayed silently, to whomever heard him, to protect his parents against the misfortunes of life. Protection against the emptiness they may feel for their missing children. Dominescu had no idea how he would tell them about the death of his brother Dobrovonski.

Much less how to speak of the love of man for his sister. Would mother approve? This was a recurring thought. He wished to marry Kayla, but there was still the matter of the Lord of the land. He would have to ask his permission to get married. He prayed, hoping for the gods' mercy… And the opportunity.

His leg began to itch a lot. He opened his eyes. In front of him, both the thorns and the height of the rock discouraged, a lot, any idea of overcoming the natural wall.

Would he be able to climb it? He was uncertain, but he knew he had to do it… The itching insisted on not letting go.

In a few hours he arrived at the foot of the black and greenish rock where he saw grooves forming bizarre symbols, gigantic monsters, bloodthirsty animals and other atrocities. Too uncertain to draw any conclusion…

"A warning or a farce?" he asked himself.

In the days that followed the wreck, from the information gathered from the inhabitants, he learned of legends, and the strange disease that affected those who dared to touch the wall and there, on the rock, the painting suggested the existence of several monsters. Each time they repeated such stories, they made the tragedies bigger, with only one consistency, their size. But there, in front of the imprints made on the wall, he had a glimpse of where came the inspiration about the size of those terrible beasts.

"Like the giant Iurik."

He looked back and thought of his friends. From there he could see many sunken ships throughout the region. As the tide made the waves break to the right, Dominescu assumed that on the other side, the sea would smoother, and, perhaps, he would actually find a quiet harbor and a ride back home. No vessel denied help. That was part of the sailors code and even pirates respected "The Code".

He had to risk it, so he could sooth the homesickness he felt, the emptiness of missing his parents and he needed pay the rites of death to Dobrovonski and especially… take a chance to go back to Kayla.

The water and the rock had fought each other for centuries and in this fight, the water left deep wounds on the rock. He imagined that, at some point, such cracks would meet the other side forming a passage that would make climbing unnecessary.

But there were no guarantees, maybe he was on the only beach or who knows, the other side is hours or days away, as he waited for the low tide, the former sailor begun to scratch himself again.

And after hours, when the tide finally relents, the expected the cracks in the rock to become evident. Without wasting time, he ran and swam to examine them. He even entered one of them but soon returned frustrated, seeing only incomplete passages.

Until one of them brought bigger surprises. A strong smell of feces, obviously a den. However, he saw shimmering lights in the back and that reanimated him. The crossing was difficult, but inevitable, after all he was going through a lair. In certain points he had to kneel and crawl to progress. Several times, the lights came from the ceiling, through the so-called "skylights". He learned this word from Jupita and Tarson when they entered the abandoned temple that fused the caves. Dominescu ignored the memory. He had to stay focused not to fall and hurt himself on the thin, sharp as blades rocks. In the second quarter of an hour discomfort hugged his body, squeezed him on the wet walls. The rock seemed happy to suffocate him. Suddenly, he noticed moisture in the sand and began to walk faster. He had taken too long and the tide was rising again. His feet sank briefly in the damp sand. There was a fork in the path ahead of him and little time to decide. He wished Jupita was there. With no time to think, he followed left to where the light was stronger, the cavity went up. However, shoulders, elbows and knees started to graze the passage, although fresh air indicated a way out. So he persisted.

The stretch was too narrow and worse.... It became steeper every meter, and climbing became almost impossible. Slipping now would mean scraping himself for meters or cut himself, or worse, break something. In other words, he would have to go back.

Returning, backwards, without seeing, was dangerous, but inevitable. It was a new agony when he reached the ramification. Now the water had taken him, so the rest of the way was completely submerged. He dived and moved quickly to the right hoping it wasn't more slanted and slippery than the previous one, and that there was a way out, otherwise he would drown.

Suddenly there was air, but the water still rose. This tunnel, unlike the first one, was open, allowing Dominescu to increase his stride. Until he tripped and fell into the cold water, which covered him completely. The high salt content reacted with his injuries and made him scream in pain. He controlled himself and tried to come up for air. He floated for a while and then swam with strong strokes and climbed onto a drier part. However, a sudden and noisy wave submerged and spun him. The light saw there formed a graceful flower with petals made of multicolored lightning. Dominescu swam vigorously, but the tide rose to the beach again. The water went back the way it came, taking him with it. Without surrendering, he held on to a long hanging root hoping to anchor his position. His plan worked. So he breathed roughly, almost breathless and, without wasting any more time, climbed the thick and flexible root. The waves beating on his back seemed to greet him for his feat. Dominescu tried to ignore the pain and, grabbing other roots, headed to land. When he stopped on a small platform, he saw that he could pass over the water, but the sea was rough.

Swimming there would be certain death, so he chose to climb the rock and follow carefully through the bramble at the top. Returning was obviously impossible. He took awhile to reach the top and, once there, lay down to rest. The effort had been extensive. However, he was overwhelmed.

The sight there was exuberant.

Trees well spaced between each other proudly reigned over minor thickets and tall grass. That side of the beach contrasted heavily with the place he came from.

And another hour passed when finally he jumped to the sand with his leather boots.

DECISIONS

The wind was mild, slightly moist and the constant waves easily erased any thoughts, inviting the mind to relax, to forgetfulness. And opposing this tranquility, the Little One's jaw worked furiously. His hands still held his future and brief victims. Several types of greens, vegetables and roots, aromas and flavors. Shattered, torn at the base, through the shell or in the center until his cheeks were swollen. Watching his long and crooked front teeth and listening to the long, gasping breaths followed by sighs and other sounds was a hideous spectacle.

Jupita was still very drowsy, between sleep and awakening. Despite the placidity of her beautiful face, even for the ravenous Little One her discontent was clear.

"My beautiful, I'm sorry to say, but..." he stopped chewing the root still in his mouth.

"I also think we should go after him." Jupita said.

"No, it's just..." big rat spat the excess from his cheeks to speak freely, but Jupita was already standing and sheathing her sword. It was useless to argue with determined women. Hans, the big rat, was sure, because two of his wives were like that. "All right, all right. Let's go."

"Where?" Morgrinald shouted with a scratchy voice.

"The woodsman went alone to the north of the island."

"Who?"

"Dominescu! The bearded serious guy. The human..."

"North?" asked a young inhabitant of the island. "But that place is infested with animals."

"Dominescu must be looking for good wood. At the very least."

"He can't." said the young man. "The north rift is at the highest point of the rock and it would be very hard to pass the cut wood."

Morgrinald pulled the young man by the arm.

"Elf!" yelled Keldorn's grandson. "I found a guide."

"No. Who said I know the place?"

"You."

"No, no. The rift has been inhabited by predators for a year."

"Did you hear?" The dwarf asked.

"I did." Jupita replied while she examined the footprints left by Dominescu's boots. She turned and looked at the gnome. "What did you say was your name?"

"Frederico… Frederico Hágar-Minus, but everyone calls me Lefty.

"Are you brave, Lefty?"

"Yes…" he replied hesitantly.

"But I wonder what motivated Dominescu? Curiosity?" Big rat asked, not expecting a "Yes".

The word; his "yes"; translated well the adventurous spirit, the desire, the hidden trailblazer waiting to be revealed. However, this word didn't connect easily to Dominescu, it didn't become him because he was cautious and reserved.

"I'd bet on idleness." Morgrinald replied, with some disdain in his voice.

Jupita stared at Morgrinald deeply:

"This side was awaken by other reasons…" She flinched a little, because Dominescu and her spoke so much when they were lost at sea, they seemed to exchange confessions and secrets.

However, the situation called for new opinions and not secrets, so she continued:

"Dominescu, the woodcutter, is poor. His family, as well as the neighboring families live thanks to the lord's and land owner's grace.

"Dominescu looking for riches?"

"Riches that would rid many people of the yoke and spite of the noble. So…" Jupita turned, walked widely towards the young Lefty and, with a knee on the ground and a hand landed on the gnome's shoulders, "Frederico! Known among your peers as "Lefty", I'm going to ask you again. Are you brave enough to help the man who saved my life from sharks and, earlier, from drowning? Actually no. I beg for your help!"

The young man blinked, not believing the elf's devoted gesture. Especially from such a proud and self-sufficient people. The dwarf touched the elf's arm and she moved away, then Lefty turned and noticed that the dwarf had his eyes and head turned to the ground. It was another request. Suddenly he raised his eyes and said determinately:

"You don't have to go through the crevice. Just guide us there."

"Su… Sure. Follow the beach. I will meet you in awhile. I need to get some equipment. And, please, don't go in the fissure from the sea-side. There are carnivorous mermaids there and in the remote probability that you leave unharmed, you will drown on the way out on the other side. Many have died there."

Morgrinald felt a shiver remembering the bard being devoured by that sea creature.

"I will meet you in half an hour." with that, Frederico, the Lefty, walked quickly toward the village and before he disappeared, he turned and warned again: "Heroes, I beg you. Wait for me. Don't go in without me, the place is tricky. I know another way, the hiking is heavier, but safer. We might just even get there before your precious and brave friend."

Saying that, he ran, stopping several times to gesticulate for calm and patience.

"Well… Can I ask you something?" Hans whispered with Morgrinald.

"Spit it out, hairy."

"How did you find out the kid had been there?"

"I deduced."

"Deduced? How? He never said that he had been there. Or did he?"

"No."

"So?"

"I saw no trees here and the houses, their utensils and that weird machine."

"All made of wood. I understand. But don't you think that the wood could have come from the sunken ships."

"Maybe."

"I Think? Wait a minute…"

"I bluffed, so what, bucktooth?"

"Nothing." big rat said, afraid to be nabbed, but with a smirk on his face.

Jupita kept quiet. Most of Dominescu's tracks vanished at tide rise, so the evidence of his route or whereabouts were gone. If he had climbed the high wall of rocks, could they see it from there? However, the path to the summit was difficult even for skilled climbers and Dominescu was a swimmer.

"Look! The cracks!"

From the tone of his beloved, big rat sensed the worst:

"Sweetie, you can't go through there… Did you hear your fellow here?"

She unbuckled the heavy sheath belt and dropped it on the sand.

"Holes, just holes." Morgrinald said.

"And they can open wider and make a passage." Jupita replied. "The water is strong and can carve the rocks easily. I'm going."

"Don't be ridiculous!" Morgrinald emphasized. "the caves are covered with water."

"Listen, since a violent invasion on my hometown, my master Darkay and I live in caves. I know my way around them."

"Elves in a cave? Elves in a bucket, fuck it. Listen pointy ears, besides that ridiculous statement, so what? If they lived, it was on the surface, at the edge of the cave like bears and bats. At the very edge. My people are made of rock and fire, our cities have always been embedded in the rocks. When not inside massive rock. The water can make cracks, but most passages are incomplete."

"Most."

"Oh shit! Listen busty, its volcanic, and quite recent I would say. Different from the small dead volcano were that…"

"Iurik."

"Right. That creature lives in an ancient summit, the entire region doesn't have much green, why? Let me tell you why. Because this whole area is subject to disasters and life almost went to shit here." Morgrinald saw what he was being clearly ignored and then kicked the sand. "Shit! This is ridiculous. I'm wasting my time arguing with a female and on top of that, a female elf."

"I'm not going to argue. I Never met others of your race, never been with your people. Actually…" Jupita turned her back to the angry dwarf. "Never mind."

"You bit…"

"What matters," Jupita said sharply. "is that my friend is somewhere and have you wondered if Dominescu knows what you know? While you fight to be right, he may be drowning. And that, in my opinion, is what's ridiculous."

Saying that, she went to sea and was soon in the water, defying the waves and swimming like her friend had taught her a while ago. With that in mind, she inflated her lungs and employed powerful strokes until she reached the stone complex, full of slime and corals and very close to the rocky giant. From there she went towards the almost submerged cracks.

Under his thick beard, the dwarf felt his face burn with hatred. He crunched his teeth and roared lowly, then said out loud:

"I'm going to rip off that bitch's ears!" uttering those words, he marched fully armored into the water.

"Hey. Morgrinald? Come back here, don't do that! Hey…"

The waves beat on the breastplate of the raging dwarf and spread sideways until the distance from the beach increased the depth and he was engulfed altogether. In the distance he could see Jupita swimming against waves and coming dangerously close to the rocks, where the waves beat the great wall.

"Oh mother…" Hans ran from one side to the other, and almost yelped with concern. "Now the soup is going to boil over. One missing and two drowned." and with that, he went off chasing the gnome.

THE DAMN WATER ON THE ROCKS

Few were the times in which he was taken by water that way. Keldorn's grandson Morgrinald hated her and she, the water, seemed to know it. Every time he crossed the sea he felt it teasing him, shaking the vessel, mocking him. And during the last shipwreck, the water almost managed to beat him. That's why he felt stupid to follow the elf. A damn elf. Letting her out of his sight was never an option and stop beating on her face until her eyes met the neck wasn't the case also. She shouldn't drown, the sea couldn't take that caustic pleasure away from him. On the other hand, they were in this together, as well as Hans, Sartre and Dominescu. The image of the brave human who she clung to emerged in front of him and then he suddenly realized he was totally immersed in the damn water. Standing at the bottom, and inside it. A thick foam covered his sight and by the dull thud, the large rock was to his right. It was impossible to follow the elf now. He was on his own. Nothing to do. Nothing at all. Was it his fault if she drowned herself? His brow blinked and the side of his eyes smiled discreetly in a thought that soon went away. Now the sea had begun with its antics, its annoying habit of coming and going. Certainly it intended to smash him on the wall. It wanted to hurt stone with stone, very funny. The tide was working its way to pick him up off the ground and throw him. Morgrinald rolled his eyes at the simplicity of the plan. It will never work. Knowing the next step was a military obligation and being aware of next two steps, was a very efficient method to survive. The coming and going only varied its rhythm. Therefore he only had to worry about the speed bursts. However, to 'The Water'; that is, water as a 'Being'; It didn't matter if it was present as sweat, saliva, drops, puddle or sea, it always ran after its objectives with unusual calmness.

Sooner or later, "the patient one" would find a way to kill him.

Morgrinald opened his toes and his thick, uncut nails. He began to dig the sandy soil full of shells and sea animals remains. The dwarf's massive and compact weight made him sink slowly into the ground of water and sand. He felt safer having the ground back under his feet. No matter the shortness of breath, not for his race. And by contact of his feet with the ground, despite his yearning, the unique powers of his race their race arose. Under his feet was a plantation of shells, pebbles and shards of coral but now he knew the safe direction to follow up the cliff.

The water was not only salty, but also bitter in the mouth with an unusual acidity. In Morgrinald's mind, theory and practice had always been bickering sisters. But they shared a common lover. Doubt. And doubt began to bleed his short patience. Either the rock was or would be… He didn't mind to finish. He focused on what his feet told him and not his mind, thus found easily the recesses on the rocks, a hidden path. If the elf lady was aware of that, or was lucky, he couldn't say. Alive? The bitch succeeded? However, light bodies like the elves would have low or zero resistance to the insane water and following this sinister understanding, suddenly Morgrinald felt the weight of what seemed the right possibility. Jupita something or whatever her name, had died. She had her confused head hurtled by the damn water against the rocks.

As soon as he deepened into the hidden path, the light disappeared, reminding him of Lefty's words about the mermaids den, he drew his axe and for a moment was surprised to see that there was still bit of an emerald glow at the edge. The glow came from a sticky paste made of the cave fungi extract. A time when his weapon was treated to glow upon the amount of hits, while wagerers in that underground arena grunted, saluting and cursing the gladiators. He remembered another experience, an earlier one, and the memory seized the moment. One in which Morgrinald was in command of a small group against a minotaur. His group, properly armed to defeat the monster, the hated creature. And this creature, that had never been taken to meet the light, was clearly disoriented and judging by its arched posture and dry abdomen, far from top shape. However, the public saw only appearance, size and prejudice. A coward, wimpy prejudice. The minotaur was docile, gentle, and spent two weeks with them, the caged ones. Morgrinald had never met such a kind being... even so, he killed him. Morgrinald and his team killed him. With no mercy. Without remorse. Was he good? One must never arch his face with this doubt. Never! Not now. And in the days of the arena, the only way to remain sane, was to be oblivious to it, but stay alert to the maneuvers shouted by the audience, that, in one way or another, helped sometimes. Surely only the cold-blooded, the murderers and the survivors of the horrors of war would have enhanced ears to discern these mournful cries from the yelling for crippling, insanity and death. Morgrinald remembered his suited cell. A form of gratification for the beautiful performance of the most acclaimed gladiator, the most powerful of the lords of murder. Standing at the top of that position, he had privileges and favors in the enclosed space of his private cell, which included health care delivered with aplomb. Literally, anything to quench his desires so he would keep on killing. They would bring anything you wanted, men, women, food, good liquor, sweets and pies. He would have everything except freedom. A circle of elite betters of the community, including some linked to the court and/or nobility therefore, knew that the chance of freedom narrowed quickly, considering that the pockets of those gamblers represented a high revenue to the city. And although his ascension was clear in that circus of horrors, the guard who locked his cell, revealed that the distinguished treatment was thanks to the influence of an unknown godfather and spat disgustingly in his face. Only later he discovered that the godfather had been Astrias. And he had to sail with him for three long years.

"Was it out of kindness?" he asked himself. "We're all good people... the leader, dictator would say. And both kill..."

BATTLE AND TRAGEDY

On land and unaware of such terrible things taking place far away, Sartre scratched the ground absentmindedly, it was an old habit. The gnome in front of him looked like a dirty and abandoned statue after he asked a question. He was thinking before he asked foolishly, because sloppy answers tend to be killed at their root with more questions, and that's what he was trying to do. In other words, reduce the proliferation of new questions. While he waited, Sartre thought about the gnome society. And how much he had learned since he arrived. Unique societies like that had protection as their first priority. Protection of the only thing that was worth more than money in that place. Privacy. Sartre sighed amused, he knew that kind of situation, exactly the same elusion as the nobles.

"Listen…"

"Phew! You're finally moving again." the healer joked.

"Denying the question that writhes your facial muscles would be offensive, stupid, but if you allow a brief study of the general situation you will clearly see the irritability of the issue, the vicious addiction… A fault that befalls the victim, moving from cause to consequence of your initial act and/or its reagent."

"AND?" The "other question" came out foolishly of his mouth, maybe that was the mistake. A typical plaything of children who lend inadequate attention to the master.

"AND?" the gnome, visibly shocked by such amendment, didn't waste time and answered promptly. "Yes. Maybe. Maybe it's who do you think it is…"

With no time to enjoy the brief victory over the gnome's intellect, Hans emerged suddenly jumping on a tree that bent and launched the Little One up in a double and confused flip on his back, while on the ground, a gnome came running. They were both desperate and had appalling news. Amazing how life repeated itself... He saw himself reflected on the young gnome when he argued:

"Should I find someone else to mediate the situation?"

That was what Sartre had asked Marin Bey, the Saint, but only now, far from everything, he understood the subtle response of that astute woman. "I like roses. They are simple and like water. And all it takes is just a little sun for them to thrive". She had contrasted the simple roses with simple people. "Some time ago the roses ended up here. I didn't even notice them, at least not at first, I think. After all, who would notice a dot in the middle of nowhere?" And she was right, after all who would notice a small village compared to kingdoms and cities?

"It certainly lacks a name that takes the responsibility for these events." said a gnome lady.

"Are they your problem?" The saint's voice repeated in his ears.

Sartre understood. They also didn't hear them. Funny how fate always found a way to give him a second chance. Now he understood, he should be the one to act. As well as the villagers. They were all were part of the charade, thus, part of the answer.

"There has to be someone who can help!" the gnome insisted.

"And there is!" Sartre puffed out his chest and went with them.

On the way back, they rushed by Iurik, who fished with his wide and thick trawl. The giant nodded sympathetically and given the urgency of the situation, he received only a subtle response. Sartre wouldn't plea, he would act.

To Iurik the gesture was so subtle that he seemed to have been ignored, so he was going to shrug it off and finish dragging the net when he noticed a large group of decided gnomes following him. All of a sudden some stopped in front of the giant and asked for his aid, a surprise but answered with a satisfied smile.

At the site where they were, Hans had captured the elf's heavy belt and it took only a moment to realize that they hadn't returned. He went running and jumping over stones and rocks scattered randomly on the way already placed on the rock mass. Lefty was also fast and reached Hans quickly. And, competitive as boys, they ran one of the fastest and curious races. Iurik was already falling behind because the loose stones and scattered rocks showed that size was a disadvantage there.

Suddenly, a rock fell and blocked the gnome and the Little One's passage. At that moment, a giant about five wolves taller than them and wearing tatters made of fur and leather, came down from the high rocks to that narrow passage, rubbing his hands, talking culinary nonsense and profanities. On the fat head, full of lumps and spread lints of hair, a central, and completely disproportional, opened eye. Obviously its sight was weak and lazy, because he didn't even notice some gnomes coming up shortly behind and stopped, froze by panic.

The huge monster leaned closer to look at what he had caught and was surprised by showers of stones. And fired by Hans Ranni Ramiro and Roder, stone throwing champion of the lake. The cyclops however, merely smiled instead of protecting himself:

"So there you are! Come. Me won't hurt you…"

The brave gnome Frederico Hagár-Minus, nicknamed "Lefty" threw a pile of rocks at once and one of them struck his single eye. "Just like you didn't hurt the others?"

The "one-eyed", frowned in disapproval, scratching his eye as if hit by a speck.

"Run, relatives, save yourselves."

Quickly, the gnomes ran, passing between the giant's legs. The Little One and the gnome looked at each other and had no doubt, they continued throwing stones which hit him in several places, but even so, he progressed. Until he was hit in the eye and began to walk slower. Hans smiled at Lefty and turned that into a silent dispute over who was more accurate, and who was the bravest. Although the gigantic opponent gradually reduced the distance to the irritating resistance.

"I never seen food resist this much." mumbled the monster.

"Fucking cyclops!" a strong and imposing voice shouted from behind him.

Surprised, his deformed and opened ears stood up in the air, and as he lowered the hand that protected his from the stones, he was hit once more.

"See. There, there. I'm good, am I not?"

"Hans!"

"Admit it."

The giant lowered his body, he was close enough to catch them.

"Hans?"

"Admit that I'm great, Am I not wonderful?"

"Yes, but run!" Lefty screamed started running.

"Caught you." said the titan, with a silly smile.

His hand was big enough to envelop the Little One's head, and with the other had he caught the gnome by the bottom of his jumpsuit.

"Meat is tender when beg, I happy. But this… too much fur."

"Hair." corrected Hans, with a smothered voice between the fingers of that hideous hand, that had a strong smell of dead flesh and blood.

"Get your hands off of them!" a voice close to them said imperiously.

Suddenly Hans and Frederick were hurled forward. Loose again, and taking the opportunity, they fled the carnivore. When they reached a distance they thought to be safe, they looked back. Perplexed, they watched a fight of giants in fury: Iurik and the cyclops unleashing severe blows at each other.

Despite the ferocity of Iurik's surprise attack, the beast exceeded him in size and strength and threw him against the wall of rocks and thence to the ground.

Hans and Lefty didn't stay to watch.

"Ungrateful bastard!" the beast mumbled. "Now you want to steal food."

It began to lift a heavy rock to throw at Iurik. It would be the final blow. However, at a glance, before his rival raised the enormous weight above his head, Iurik stood up and punched the cyclops in his kidney, making him lose his footing, however, both plummeted from the top of where they were to a lower point of the passage. And the rock ended up falling and crushing the cyclops's chest. Iurik was surprised. Not by the terrifying vision of growing red sludge entering the recesses of the rocks. He was standing, inert, because he finally felt that he had rescued his honor. And to live again, he had to kill: now, that's an odd way to come back to life. Not weird... Horrific, obscene.

And so it was... There was the fallen opponent, broke, life draining from his pores. It was hard to express how he felt, he devoted much time to hating him and that clouded everything. Seeing the cyclops lying there on the floor without any expression but dead. That suddenly caused him an empty, a growing sense of emptiness, swollen, nothing.

Iurik Dainthgorn; son of the king; the heir to the throne, in a setback went from prince to a mere survivor, considered lost at sea, and again he felt lost. It was like before, at sea. I didn't feel the scrapes, bruises, neither the body nor the very soul. There was no meaning there. In his wobbly walk, he found gnomes frozen in fear, shoved in a corner.

Slowly, they broke free from each other, the gaze of the gnomes told him everything. The reason of his life. The he smiled and fainted...

On the beach the Little One and the gnome have another vision which increased even more their dread. Right there, on the beach, a huge reptile was getting very close to the fallen body of the one they came to rescue. Dominescu seemed unconscious, perhaps dead. They ran to him, and fortunately the reptile was scared and ran away.

"Wow! What a coward!"

"You think so?" the Little One asked, scared.

Lefty finally identified what was coming through the grass and scared Hans and was also disturbed:

"Damn! You had to open your mouth?"

Automatically they dipped their hands in the ground, but there were no stones to shoot, just sand and shells. Small and light shells. They were helpless. There were three reptiles, different from the first one. From their tongue hisses and the guttural roar of their throats, they understood why the first one had fled.

"Wake up, woodsman." despair made Hans slap his friend's face strongly. "Or we will be a treat for each one of them."

The bared teeth and dense leather reptiles walked slowly, analyzing and surrounding.

"Wake Up!"

It was too late now, they were lost and knew…

The three heavy beasts with yellow and furious pupils, progressed slowly, a step away from striking. Suddenly, one of them claimed the right of the first bite, by clicking its powerful jaw in the air, towards its hungry friends. Conceding the lead, the other two let it pass.

"Can you swim?" the gnome asked.

"In the water?" the Little One's terror of getting wet overcame reason.

Suddenly the sands around the three are agitated savagely. The sight of the reptilian menace became blurry because of a fierce wind that whipped around. A barrier of sand, wind and shells spinning quickly preventing the success of the hunt. The reptiles tried, but failed to overcome it.

"I'm glad you know some magic tricks." Hans shouted, as it was impossible to talk over the roar of the wind.

"Gnomes with magic? That's horrible."

The speed of the wind was so high that in a few moments they couldn't see nothing except for a creature coming out of the water.

"Love? Jupita my beautiful! Jupita my sweetie!"

"Elves may have magic."

"Ha, ha! That's my girl. Hit them Jupita! She came to rescue her lover here. Golly, she loves me! She loves me!"

Jupita had taken far longer than she wanted to bypass the rock and it had been a close call. When the wave was about to throw her on the rock, she floated and barely escaped hitting the stones. She noticed that hovering no longer demanded so much of her body. Swimming with Dominescu ended up being a good workout. However, taming the wind at a distance like that while floating was horrible and all it took was a slight gust of wind to lose her balance and dive into the water. The high salt content in the water had made her chest burn, but it lasted only a second. Floating above the water, she coughed to expel the salt water, but soon sank again because of a wave breaking on her back.

On the beach, Dominescu began showing signs of consciousness. Hans rejoiced and hugged him without seeing the predicament of his beloved.

Lefty, gazed at the wind and sand barrier in front of him, but he could see very little beyond it. But he knew that a new battle was about to begin, some other fantastic creature had arrived.

"The flesh-eating giant, the cyclops, is here too!"

"Great." Hans replied still hugging his bearded friend. "So they have each other to play with and we can get out of here!"

The walls of wind fell gradually providing a sight to the another show. It wasn't the cyclops but Morgrinald, grandson of the powerful and honorable Keldorn of the Battle Hammers clan, was fighting the beasts. One of the opponents struck a fast bite locking Keldorn's grandson muscular armored arm. The second opponent of the trio of beasts realized that the dwarf's weapon was stuck. The hammer, his reserve weapon. Precisely the weapon that over a year ago he decided to not use on just any enemy.

"Ah! Son of a…" the dwarf was outraged for being caught so easily. The weapon forged in fires of a volcano was now covered in a viscous sticky drool. "Look at that. You break a promise and this is what happens."

The two other beasts lowered their heads and moved slowly to devour the intruder. And they seemed to relish at the sight of the immobilized prey. The animals, covered with wrinkled, thick and lumpy leather moved with a wicked coolness.

Morgrinald, with his eyes widened and open nostrils, thought about his weapon. The beauty of its swing the glare. And now locked in the fetid mouth of an animal.

The hungry creatures snarled gutturally. The hammer and the name of the warrior were one.

He could lose his arm, but never his hammer, after all "War Hammer" was also his family's given name. Keldorn's grandfather received the hammer hands Nigellus and remain there imprisoned in that reptilian arch was the largest of the offense.

No further step separated prey and predators.

With a punch and a kick, he pushed away the other two at the same speed of the bite they tried to give him. It was true that they faced only one opponent, however, it can be clearly said that in this battle, numbers were a disadvantage.

With a fierce look, he shoved his fingers into the nostrils of the one that held him, making it release the bite shaking its monstrous head.

"There was snot, sorry."

Now free, the dwarf; Morgrinald; the blood of Keldorn of the Battle Hammers clan removed his axe and swung his vigorous arms in an arc. At the sight of death, he always smiled, but he smiled knowing that once again it wouldn't be his own. Then he attacked, turning, twisting his hips, moving. A fight against animals was unpredictable because for them it was just timing between attack and defense. However, those reptiles acted alone. The dwarf grinned, railed, roared and laughed loudly between powerful blows and impossible spins. It was a confused dance, accompanied by a sinister music propagated by biting snaps into the void and the axe slashing flesh and the hammer crushing bones. One of them lost a leg and started to flee followed by its two companions. The weight of the axe doubled in the warrior's expert hands and with a straight frontal slash, Morgrinald, Keldorn's blood, cracked the skull and jaw of the creature. In such a brutal way that it didn't even seized. It just died.

"Ha, ha, ha…" Morgrinald laughed happy as a prince on a ride.

Lefty, on the other hand, breathed deeply and quickly. That was unique. Of course it was not because of the danger or close death, but because of the dwarf who fought so quickly in front of him.

For many, dwarfs were just gnomes that have similar physical structure to human dwarfs, but without the atrophied or disproportionate members. Among the gnomes there is a legend about an ancient ancestor that recovered his youth by laying on lava. Another story said that the common ancestor of gnomes and dwarfs had made a deal with a legendary and evil people of the underground and even that dwarfs descend from these. Thus, the gnomes had conflicting emotions seeing a dwarf like Morgrinald. Therefore, a dwarf must show his value on his own. He would either be a fool puffed with glories or be as Morgrinald was. Frederico Hágar-Minus was perplexed, utterly amazed for witnessing history unfold in plain sight. He wished he had a feather or a chisel to immortalize the scene in the same way he did throughout the large rock… with everything he saw.

"Jupita? JUPITAAA!

Hans bleats evidenced how crushed his chest was with concern and even submerged, with so many air bubbles around the elf could hear him. Her chest was burning and she was beginning to drown. She let herself go, her body began to sink, she raised her hand to the distant sky, her thin fingers covering part of the sunlight. She remembered everything she had done, her master, her beloved, her friends. Life seemed run out along with the the air.

"JUPITAAA!"

Morgrinald held Hans, there was nothing they could from that distance. It hurt too much to tell the Little One, but he said:

"She's on her own. There is no hope, she is gone, hairy."

"NNNOOOOO!" he slapped the dwarf and tried in vain to get rid of the grip around his waist.

"The sea takes another one." Lefty regretted removing his ragged cap and placing it on his chest.

"Ju?"

Everyone noticed that the Little One was staring and at that point, the sea lost its greenish coloration and gained a bright and strong shade of blue. Gradually, Jupita left the water. Emerging magnanimously from the water into the air, taken by a mild wind to the beach with arms outstretched and palms turned upward.

"Nice Ju! Very nice Ju! Yes!" Hans sang, passing from despair to an unbearable happiness, he danced and wriggled hugging the dwarf's chest, who quickly threw him to the ground.

Morgrinald was impressed, but he wasn't about to admit it anytime soon. Besides, there was someone more important there. He reclined and held Dominescu's head on his lap while the woodsman gradually regained consciousness.

"Morgrinald?"

"You wanted to enjoy yourself alone, you selfish."

"Apparently I missed the best part." Dominescu said looking at the big reptile with the dwarf's battle axe driven into its skull. Other than that, the woodsman took a while to take in the rest and, when he realized the tall and winding shadow above him, he recognized his elf friend, while she herself was held by Hans and the courageous Lefty. Exhausted, she did little more than pant and smile. Her skin lost its color gradually.

Then they all talked for awhile, trying to understand why Dominescu risked so much alone, but soon the attention converged silently to where the pair of titans were and they noticed Iurik's big eyes staring at nothing and… Forever. Undoubtedly dead.

Sartre had just arrived and saw nothing of the fight, only the bruises on the gnomes' thick skin. The trail amid the thorny plants, although painful, had been quick, but on the beach, on the other side of the rock, he ran towards the cyclops thinking it was Iurik, it was a double surprise. Legends were real, yes and apparently, a few nightmares too. A huge crocodile lay dead ahead and farther, the ones he come to help.

"Thank the gods!" but he thanked too early, it only took a glimpse to notice, in Iurik's wounds and injuries, the purplish black streaks of poison. The outcast used poison on the spikes of his club.

On the neck, beneath the long and thick beard that the years spent there in solitude gave him, Dominescu saw the royal symbol, the only proof of his true identity. Iurik lived there ignored, hated and now, only now, with no life in his lungs, he was respected. The woodsman, despite the abuses of the lord of the land in which he lived, had always been faithful to the king and he could hardly believe the privilege of having lived close to the king's son. And this man, a humble giant, lived his life as a commoner, but without doubt... Died a hero. Pure of heart, unscathed, without his title and royal position, but certainly, he earned his own titles.

"Fool! You should have saved yourself." Dominescu said and punched the giant weakly while he stole the royal medal.

"Dominescu, don't blame yourself. It was the poison, not you. Do you see the flowers of death? The purplish black veins? If he was touched only once, given his size, he might had survived. With sequela yes but... The poison... Dominescu, my son, death owns the most heinous whims."

"Instead of talking, Sartre, let's move him." Dominescu said resolutely.

So they all left, elf, dwarf, Little One, gnomes and the faithful woodsman of the Great Empire in an entourage carrying Iurik's body to the top of the rock.

And from the time spent between the arrival at the top of the large rock and assembling the pyre, Iurik was sitting on a throne of small trunks, piled and entwined by Dominescu of the Great Empire. The woodsman found a worthy way to enrich the burial of a secret prince, hero of the gnome people sincere friend of Hans and Jupita and respected by the distant Morgrinald.

"Well done son." Sartre added carefully, in mourning, he felt the emptiness of so many lost lives in the village and it also reminded him of his dead son.

Only something so grand could be the resting place of another magnificent being. Dominescu said seriously.

Tears and sadness covered many faces. Jupita, by nature of her kind, seeing the dense smoke ascending into the clouds, could see the soul of the giant walking that gray and white road to new places, shortly before the end.

The flames were fed continuously for three days and three nights. A good vigil, as tradition required. The high flames weakened the night, and remembered the gnomes of the chance they had lost to have a good neighbor; while the others thought how lucky they were to have known a hero.

And Dominescu among the others was by far the most meditative.

THE SOLAR ECLIPSE

The reflection in the vat received the Sartre's calloused hands and washed his forehead's deep and permanent grooves gained from two pasts, a longing past and an unhappy one. His mind always revisited villager friends from the village of Miller. Disappearances, despair and no answer. He had aged a lot and it didn't matter, because someday those tired eyes would rest forever. Did someone else die? Now he knew every details, from the slavers to the underground creatures. And Sargauss? Was he found? Was he alive? Was his divine mission completed? And there was something else, an idea grinding in his head and that he was doing everything to ignore such chain of thoughts, but today was one of those days where his perseverance lost. Why didn't the gods intervened?

"Not intervened..." his mouth echoed stating the terrible obviousness.

Sartre had his opinions, his ideas and especially... about the imminent arrival of the army of ZHI. the mere act of keeping that knowledge to himself made him one of the Guardians of Sin.

The saliva thickened, but it did go down his throat. He was afraid to look at the ground, up and to any other side, then he closed his eyes tightly as if it was possible to pinch with his eyelids, hurt the thoughts and keep them... Oppressed. However, the facts excelled and attested. The brother gods were gone...

They, once magnanimous and perfect in their spheres of power. They, who dominated the world with the force of hurricanes and making the earth shake beneath their feet. If anything displeased them, water reversed from the sea to the source salting the rivers to later dry them. Fires were created from their fury until the flames bit the ashes, plants dried out at a mere glance. And sweet fruit rolled rotten simply if these gods became bitter.

Sartre's mouth was dry, his heart pounded. The water in the vat still carried that sad and tired coming and going that gradually ceased, dying movement. At some point it would end. As was with them too… For a moment, at the most critical and somber moment, some of the beings of this world grew tired of their oscillating moods and dependency.

His forehead sweat continuous icy drops. His body hair stood up in an increasing horror. For knowing and keeping was a sin so severe as inaction and indifference. Maybe the nobles suffered similarly. Surely they knew of things that they could never confess, what made them, like himself, one of the Guardians of Sin, although of course, they were on a lower level. His secret, his knowledge was far heavier, more disastrous and lethal in every way.

However, laughter and cheers rescued the healer's wounded mind from the terrible evil of knowledge. Lefty's remarkable voice stood out above the others. A quick translation of the gnome language said that he was talking of Jupita's power growth which, according to him, exceeded the subtle evidence and went on to reference. He continued, now speaking of Morgrinald and his dance of death against the crocodiles, which in his story were called huge lizards, even Hans got a few lines. Lefty's words continued relentlessly in a poem full of big and rarely used words. Obviously it was an easy language for his comrades and slightly intrinsic to the human standard. Hans, nicknamed big rat by the elf lady had adopted it as a second name, it lent more excitement and life to the tale with his dramatic comments and intense theatrical gestures addition.

Sartre could see and hear the comments and smiles and slight head nods of the attentive gnomes about Morgrinald's bravery. A murderer for denying aid to those who were in the water, fearing the boat would capsize. And for always wearing his armor. A warrior always ready for the clash. Thus, fighting saltwater crocodiles was just fun. A means of distraction. To see and taste blood once again, generally something completely different of what others thought. Sartre saw him as a warrior also although in the rotten version of its meaning. However, truth be told, as soon as he heard that Dominescu, his rescuer, had gone north, he followed hastily, without asking for help. Now, was his attitude out of legitimate concern or to pay off his debt? Or, and this thought sent a shiver down his neck, the debt was so unbearable it would be the opportunity to get rid of it. Because if this was right, the mere presence of the woodman was an undeniable reminder of the fragility of the dwarf. Wounded egos were always worse than swollen egos.

Anyway, the debt had been paid.

"Was it?" the water in the vat settled, in the reflection, the man full of questions dipped a cloth and swept the feverish sweat from Dominescu. Despite the knowledge that he was beyond cure, voraciously delirious and will be so until death finds him. According to popular myth, the agony was the song that guided the coming of the calm god of death to the body anxious for the rest of its torments.

Because of Dominescu's injuries the return by litter was made very slowly. With breaks stipulated by the healer. The delusional man expressed himself in a not articulated language; a dying prayer; a chat with the other world.

Suddenly the sun was covered by something denser than clouds. And the Little One, concerned for having eaten bad cooked fish envisioned in his simplicity that the spirit of the resentful fish had come to curse him for his disrespect. Sartre peed himself in fear and shrunk in horror. An eclipse was a harbinger of the end.

Henceforth, Jupita was the first to face the situation, looking up, she had to see, but above all, hear.

"No!" said the elf lady, transfixed.

"I agree, my darling," said Hans, smoothing his swollen belly.

"So..."

"That's it!" he said, holding a burp. "Sorry."

"How can this be?"

"I'm sorry, I shouldn't have eaten so fast."

"What?" only then they realized that they were talking about different things.

Morgrinald didn't even notice because he was busy trying to understand where the ocher stench was coming from, the experienced dwarf reeked of blood and sweat and regretted having the habit of cleaning his weapons and not himself.

When he walked into the gnome in front of him, he turned his eyes to what was not an eclipse, gaping, he dropped his weapon on sand due to the impossibility of what he saw.

That wasn't an eclipse but a ship floating gently above them. Despite the fever, Dominescu promptly realized it was a caravel. He estimated about twenty meters between stern and bow. Installed at the bow, a metal spur ready to chop enemies. This spearhead, six or seven meters long, was common on warships. Is she one of those? Anyway she was amazing: 45 meters up to the top of the main mast. The sails covered a whole block of a village, close to thousand square meters. He calculated roughly 700 beautiful portentous trees were toppled to build this marvel. On the almost dry hull, barnacles lent it a rough beard, evidencing that, in addition to flying, she sailed well and had been for some time now.

A wide rope and wooden ladder rolled out, dropping precipitously until its end snapped the air. Soon after, an elderly gentleman with long and snow white beard came down with difficulty taking a few minutes to do so, along with everyone else's anxiety. Each one reacted in their own way in face of the novelty, the hope and the threat that seemed to be that flying marvel. If he waited a bit more, the old man wouldn't even have climb down for the vessel came down until it stopped between three and five meters above the sand. A thick and thunderous anchor came down into the shallow water near the beach, scattering wet sand and water everywhere.

"Too much anxiety, lord Talassas!" the single tone, serene voice came from the figure floating down slowly, almost weightless to land his feet, gently, on the sand.

The vision of that man sped Jupita's heart. Could it be? The elf lady ran to them, and hearing the hiss of the wind warning of the impending approach of someone else, the figure turned around and was surprised by the immersed hug from Darkay's disciple as she reencountered Tarson Romanei.

Questions, doubts and judgments were made and answers, clarifications and theses were defended. After a short time, it was easy to agree to leave the island together.

However, Hans offered huge resistance and not even Sartre nor Dominescu convinced him to board.

"He's probably afraid of sinking." Dominescu said, climbing the ropes, with great difficulty.

"Afraid? I'm terrified! Can you imagine if this thing falls?"

"There is water beneath…" Sartre teased.

"Yes and it might sink immediately!" the Little One walked in small circles and scratched himself restless.

"That's enough!" Morgrinald said running after him. Hans didn't make it up the grove before being caught and dragged away unkindly.

"I'm not going, I'm not."

"Your hairy piece of shit, you will go and that's it."

"I don't want to, I can't fly!" big rat yelled desperately "Do you see wings? No wings, no beak, I'm hairy! I'm hairy! Hair, understand?"

With the last tug, the grove broke and before hitting the ground Hans rolled through the sand and fled to another tree. Angry, Morgrinald shrugged and followed to the boat.

"The little guy insisted on staying and convinced me."

"Are these the only ones coming with us?" Tarson asked.

The long bearded elder, called Talassas had climbed down anxious to speak with the gnomes and as he spoke well, he was quickly surrounded by the immensely interested gnomes. Suddenly he turned his head back as far as the neck allowed, and answered with joyfully:

"Yes, the others share the same opinion about Hans. This place has its charm and I can't deny that these fellows really interest me too."

And that turned out to be the purest truth, nearly all gnomes had already left the beach, while the others said farewell:

"Goodbye, Jupita, Dominescu, Morkrinal…"

"IT'S MORGRINALD, YOU MORON!"

The vessel slowly gained distance and speed until the morning mist turned the island into a memory behind a veil.

"Something here does not convince me." Sartre said looking from the bulwark and everyone else who were also saying goodbye to the island turned to face the old healer.

"As they are all castaways, why didn't they want to come with us?"

"The answer is simple." Morgrinald said, looking at the north wall, where they almost lost their lives recently. "The precious stones here charmed them, they don't want to leave without digging up enough, they prefer to stay."

The others looked in disbelief.

"Ops!" Keldorn's grandson got angry with their ignorance. "Nobody noticed that after they helped us, they went back to work?"

"A mine, and you knew all the time?" Dominescu said controlling the pain.

"Didn't you? Gnomes have a festive nature, the little shits smile at anything. Surely they were hiding something."

"Do they trade with someone?" Sartre said, already thinking about the answer.

"Why don't you ask "who"?"

"Caleb!" the healer shouted touching Dominescu as if to share his understanding. "Yuri Caleb?"

"I'm not sure…" pain bit into him. "But it is possible."

Jupita, on the other side of the large vessel was oblivious to the conversation, and immediately asked Tarson, with a broad smile:

"Okay. How did you find me?"

"I knew exactly where to look. I had good sources."

"The boy found you!"

"Of course, he said that I would give him two coins for the message."

"Two? That cheeky bastard…"

"Forget him, besides, we concluded that you would be in this direction, one of the villagers held two huge pots of gum. It was the kind of gum for sealing boats."

"That doesn't prove anything."

"Yes and no. Well, I pressed some people along the way, and… Look up there, the guy at the helm."

"That son of a…" Jupita recognized him immediately.

Anticipating her next move, Tarson held her arm.

"Wait, you don't know the whole story."

"But?" Jupita tried to argue and was interrupted by her friend.

"Darrell was a pirate, a mercenary sailor."

"Tarson, that much I know."

"Do you also know how many months you were gone and how many months he looked for you by my side without fading?"

Months? As an elf, Jupita didn't remember the humans measure of time. Cutting the time in small parts, indeed it was months, because the Sun was far more distant, it was the end of a season and only now she reflected on how many years and so many more seasons she and him lived among the humans. It had been so long that Tarson counted the time like they did.

"But what made me find you was that huge fire." Tarson pointed.

"Fire?" she said loudly, without noticing the pitch of her voice.

Morgrinald, perched on the ledge, turned his head and, in the same tone, said pointing with his chin without unfolding his arms crossed:

"Busty! Do you mean that smoke over there?"

"It seems to be coming from that mountain peak." Jupita said paying no attention to his remark.

"And it is not from a volcano." he completed smiling beneath the thick beard that in that wind whipped his face.

"Could it will be a fire?" Sartre worried. "Maybe we should go back."

"No. They must be melting the metal in huge forges, exactly where we never went… The inner part of the island."

"Didn't you didn't say something about gems?" Sartre became confused.

"So every once in a while you should pay attention. They may have found more things inland."

"The barkeeper spoke about overseas mines." Jupita told her friend. "But it was salt."

"The gnomes mines can be much more than salt mines." Tarson replied.

"Humph!" Morgrinald closed one eye and shook his head negatively while approaching the elves. "If they said there were precious stones or metals, it could raise hopes of conquest by other forces and kingdoms. If it were me, I would certainly act like that… In silence." saying that, he pressed his lips as if to taste his thoughts "but surely they would prefer to use slave labor. Screw them. Many kingdoms do that. Forced labor or death."

"I know very little about your story sir. Should I call you tavern keeper? Sailor? Or just liar?"

"I understand your outrage, but I thought I had killed this disagreement. Well, ok. Yuri Caleb and Maqui Bone Breaker should have ignored their past, that was their chance to follow another path but, as we say at sea: no matter how much they bite, a dog gets used to his own fleas. I was sure there was something wrong when they occupied themselves with other activities outside the bar we bought. But you know how it is… Keeping away from it was the easy way." Darrell said, flatly, but soon dropped his eyes.

"The cowardly way."

"Jupita!"

"Captain, forget it. She's right. I wanted to avoid trouble and found new ones."

"Captain?" Jupita was skeptical. There were too many surprises, she really had spent too much time away from her beloved.

The barkeeper, now helmsman, closed his eyes and staring at the empty sky, remembered things: wounds which he hoped were healed. He held it until he couldn't stand it another minute, then fired:

"Please… Believe Me! The ship is my vow of goodwill and also the means to redeem myself by omission. It's just that everything…"

Looking closer, it was possible to see the strength of Darrell's hands twisting the nodes of the wooden wheel.

Jupita, the girl and now woman, knew the no man's land that lived in that man's chest. She remembered well when she had to get on without her parents, without relatives, and after the collapse of the cave… Without Darkay. His master, tutor and friend. She was frail and saw the same fragility in Phillip Darrell. The elf lady felt the closeness of their stories, she had to overcome it in the name of survival. He had done it his way and she, hers.

"Hey. I owe you an apology" Jupita said openly moving towards Phillip Darrell.

"Wh… What?" due to the their last meeting, Darrell cowered keeping the wheel between him and the elf lady.

"For forgetting that there is always a reason. Sometimes we are blinded by our truth. It arrogant of me, I'm sorry for attacking you."

"Actually, I thank you." the helmsman said, now without shrinking "it was better that way. I hid it for too long, sealed in a shell and my shell was tight, but you know… There are certain things that are hard to get rid of."

Darrell, Phillip Darrell took a while to tell his story. To Jupita it was as if he wanted to admit to himself the need to reveal everything, however he had to go further to justify his acts, so he plunged into a dark past that by his look, it was where he never wanted to go back.

"I wanted to escape the fate that my family imposed on me. I would be much more than a conjurer, another one of the family to follow such path. I never liked books, so I dropped my studies halfway. I thought that that was more than enough to defend myself. I preferred the joy of the halls of the taverns and brothels. I learned to love and to fight when I was cheated in gambling, learned parlor tricks and discovered that I was good. My hands were skillful, agile. I started traveling with nobles and wealthy merchants on their ships. I screwed up with the drinking and with whom I decided to steal at cards, then I was captured by pirates. Stupidity killed the others, and as for me… I survived.”

The steersman took a long swig from a thick neck jug. Morgrinald had stopped close by, to stay away from the side and minimize the nausea and strangeness of the flight, identified the container and by the strong smell was sure of its contents, but resisted the urge. There was no honor in separating a good bottle of its owner, unless he offered.

“Back then” Darrell continued in a somber tone “I knew very little about the sea and even less about reading a compasses or stars. We went through some islands, stopping only long enough to get fresh water, there was no time for hunting or harvesting fruit, they were fleeing. Surely they knew the my family’s reputation.”

“They wanted time to get organized and ask for the ransom.”

“Of course they considered this possibility with any other family, mine however, was most likely to show up with the full force of the magic school and hired thugs in sufficient number for a small war, regardless of the amount of dead floating in the waters.”

“Instead of negotiation, retaliation.” the dwarf added meddling into the conversation “An idiotic way to rescue someone.”

“It was how the family kept its superiority.” Tarson interceded concerned with the possibility of stocky and strong dwarf starting a fight on the boat. “After all, dwarf, the family also owned a small, but noteworthy, commercial fleet.”

“Allowing the family to pay the ransom would be like going back to the magical path chosen by his uncles, right?” Jupita asked shrewdly.

Darrell squeezed his eyes as if disgusted with something.

"I chose to take my chances with the pirates, heck, I want to live for myself. I made a deal with them. They laughed and agreed with me."

"They knew the family; that's why they went so far. Or am I wrong?

"I didn't see any alternative at the time… I knew about a shipment of spices destined to overseas lands, and when and where they would depart. When those poor men recognized me, they allowed me and those bastards to come on board. They didn't stand a chance. I still have nightmares about that day. As I was there, they didn't expect trouble. I asked them to surrender but they drew their weapons. This caused some to be spared thanks to the intervention of the astute Yuri Caleb."

"The fat man with tattooed arms." Tarson translated for Jupita.

"Him again?" the dwarf joked "I have heard about him since we were on the island."

"I adhered to piracy, under the condition that the crew was spared, but two-thirds of men were redistributed in other vessels. They had the option to join us and make a fortune in a single attack or be abandoned in the smaller craft with ripped sails, without oars and support ships to die in a storm or crashing into rocks. The result was obvious. They all wished to survive. I learned about sailing, high and low tide, measurement mechanisms, and finally earned the title of captain of the seas."

"You could have run."

"Without my servants? Never. I confess, however, that I thought about it for a while, at least I would save the few who were with me. I would give the boat to the others and free the servants. However, they were sea wolves by choice, they had salt water instead of blood, they would soon be back at sea and if they were ever found by my family, their her fate would be even worse. It was the third time that my beard had grown to my chest, and I was sick of it. It took years, and there was only one way to stop. So the three of us, I mean, Maqui, Caleb and I agreed we didn't want this fate, so we came up with a new one."

The pause before resuming clearly revealed to Jupita and Tarson the consternation in his breathing. He suffered with the mere memory.

"One day we returned to the pirates' hidden bay and took their ships. A long period without water made the survivors on land surrender. As there were no men capable of leading, we become their sovereigns. So we bought our freedom. We elected men we trusted as captains, we minimized the amount of crew against us choosing the less daring, the cowards and the meek. So it would be easier to control them. Then we left behind those who could stir problems. Over time we found a small village and we left, at least I left my old life behind.

"The village of Miller."

"Earlier!" Darrell corrected. "Before it became a village. There, Yuri Caleb, Maqui Bone Breaker and I became partners as far as cheaters can be."

The girl born in the village of Almokaryr had grown with high standards of behavior, so distance was a good answer, then she turned to the cabin and left.

Morgrinald shrugged, he just offered another bottle he found to the helmsman:

"Explain." proposed the dwarf.

Instead, the helmsman consulted a rugged map scratched in sheep's skin.

“Do you know what this is? Do you know the magic wheel?”

Morgrinald shrugged again:

“Something about the sea, consult the stars, Sun and wind? I was never interested in these…”

“These matters?” Darrell supposed touching the mechanism similar to the wheel. “The divisions present in this are considered degrees north, south, east and west. The standing bone on the wood projects a shadow, and through the degrees you have the direction. Even the shadow shows the way. Would you be willing to follow your own shadow to find your destiny?”

An awkward silence took over.

Inside the cabin, in the crew’s general quarters, a feverish body shook in a hammock. Moved, Jupita caught a thick mountain goat skin blanket and covered him. Dominescu was sweating a lot and she did what she could removing the sweat from his face with a cloth dampened in an iron bowl. His calloused and firm hand stopped the gesture.

“Shhh. It’s me.” the friend said gently.

With that she gently withdrew her hand from his, their fingers intertwined. And with a smile she again passed the moistened cloth on the young bearded man forehead. A lot had happened. Entering the temple, the shipwreck, all that time on the island… It was a shame to see a man who had shown his value in such a short time lying there, bedridden, feverish and dependent. So Jupita bent over and with a hand on his forehead kissed him, a pure and sincere kiss with more pity than love.

Tarson, who had just arrived, saw the scene and left forlornly.

HOURS LATER...

Inside the floating vessel, the sky was different. Seeing the world from that height gave an impression of smallness. The thin air, despite the incessant damp wind brought memories of the past and surviving so many misfortunes, assured a future.

Jupita wanted to be alone with her beloved, yes that was it. She didn't want to hide what she felt anymore. She loved her long-time friend different from the fatherly love dedicated to her master, Darkay. Thus, in the captain's quarters, wearing lighter and gentler garments, her beautiful silhouette thought about everything that happened, the dusk redness seen from the oval window regaled the eyes. And to Tarson-Romanei, the elf, this moment was full of promises of peace, one that lacked for months and months without the beautiful Jupita.

On the deck, with his short legs hanging out, old Morgrinald refreshed himself in the strong wind, the thin air smelled of home. He leaned back in a corner and removed the piece of braided leather from his neck, revealing on one end, a small box with an elaborate clasp and inside, a bit of dark earth. Like every good dwarf, he would always have the smell of land with him, but having a handful of earth from his beloved and nostalgic city was reassuring. He took another sip of the dirty and sweet water the eared ones called liquor and, with no one to curse, relaxed his body, put away his greatest treasure and allowed the beautiful view of the high horizon to rock him into a well-deserved sleep.

Dominescu, in turn, was delirious in the hammock since he had arrived on the ship. Fever and an irritating itch took him completely. Besides, the part hit during the fight with the mermaid pulsed. It was just a kick… One kick in that mouth riddled with sharp teeth. That's was all he could do, but surprise did the rest, she moved away leaving behind a trail of teeth, which included two small ones broken on his shin and calf.

Suddenly, the warning bell sounded. Although weakened, former sailor Dominescu acknowledged the warning, announced by the ringing of the insistent bell. Imminent danger no doubt. Dangers of the route, such as coral reefs and sandbars, storm or attack, but what could it be in the sky? Running, Dominescu hit the deck, despite the fever weakening his muscles. The surprisingly experienced helmsman plunged the ship into thick clouds, trying to buy some time against the voracious and skilled opponent. The sudden change of course made Dominescu fall and slide down the deck wet of water from the clouds. Dominescu rose between two barrels wisely tied by ropes.

Jupita, while gathering a bow and arrows, instantly recalled than the big rat had said months ago at the tavern:

"'This is true! (…) And even after our guidance and help in the plantations space, there were criminal fires without explanation last year'".

Jupita fired unsuccessfully against the dragon that was so red, it became difficult to distinguish from the twilight when it moved away for a new onslaught. Upon returning in a fast curve, it roared loudly, the disciple of Darkay dropped her weapons and acted hastily. Traces of clouds attacked the dragon's eyes and it reacted as if the clouds were slimy webs stopping its onslaught to tear them like thin and old cloth with its agile claws.

Darrell, the helmsman, entered the clouds again. A fierce roar echoed and then nothing else; a suspense between life and death was installed. The silent crew of watchful eyes scanned the fog around.

Tarson and Jupita with attuned ears, common to their race, recognize the rustling of the gigantic wings. Tarson jumped to the helm and turned to the side. The turn made Morgrinald fall and slip on the wet deck in the opposite direction of the turn. However, with his warrior's agility, he rolled and soon stood up just in time to see the tail spines entering the clouds again.

"The fucking winged one is smart men. We need archers!" deep down, Morgrinald admired his opponent and smiled between teeth. "The little red one takes advantage of its weight and speed. That's a well used advantage!"

Jupita, just held on to the sail ropes of the central mast.

A few more minutes of tension and nothing from the sky predator.

"He's gone." said a crew member.

Suddenly there's an impact as if they ran over something and then the boat begins to lose altitude.

Tarson frowned and yelled:

"He's on the hull."

They hear a roar near a sadistic laugh. Next the sound of wood being torn echoed in the air.

"Archers of starboard and port side."

The order was followed to the letter. The crew run to the sides and hit three of its four legs that were latched to the thick hull. The reptile with an evil look fell and disappeared into the clouds, shaking the magic vessel.

Before they could recover, the ship left the clouds and, to their dismay, the sky ahead was clear. The sound of wings now followed them. At the stern of the vessel the cruel opponent grew, the monster kept one of its claws ahead making its intention clear.

Dominescu, though still feverish, still remained between the barrels, he looked at himself and drew a broadsword from his back. A reminder invaded him, the wise words of a dead man. "You will serve it as much as it will serve you." The sword whistled intensely and began to vibrate in his hand… "Believe me, everything has its usefulness". Dominescu, the woodsman and former sailor, raised the sword without hand guard to his eye level. He saw the sails ahead of the mast and prayed for the it to work.

"Fast wind!" he screamed with his powerful lungs.

At that, a sudden storm wind came out of the sword and filled the sails of both masts, lending, with a jolt, some extra speed increasing the distance between pursued and pursuer. The monster roared heavily, but left frustrated. The helmsman and the crew were sure that the celestial reptile, sky predator, wouldn't give up that easily.

"Beast rising on the horizon!" Darrell shouted and the crew echoed while they ran to their posts.

Flying above the ship, the beast could dive straight and in a flyby, rip the vessel with its claws or spew its volcanic breath on them. That was the dragon's intention, Tarson knew it, and the experience of the crew would certainly say the same.

"Waiting for your orders sir!" the helmsman said to Tarson with a firm voice.

Tarson looked at his subordinates. They had been through a lot with that flying ship. Sargauss, a being of the air elemental race, housed in a room in the belly of the ship was what kept them in the air. And having him there was a huge responsibility. Too many lives at risk and there was also the beautiful Jupita.

"Captain?"

The elf pondered. He had lives and measures on a scale. The dragon had to be killed. It was a fact. Dragons were exempt of honor and moral values. Shiny stones and metals to lie down and sleep on after ravaging villages in search of food. That all that seemed to matter to them.

"Tarson!" the helmsman cried. "use the artifact."

"It will cost a month's delay." he replied to Darrell reservedly.

"Otherwise you risk the life of the woman."

Tarson closed his eyes

"Use it" he asked again. "No one will blame you."

The dragon roared loudly to frighten the airmen, however, this was not the first time they faced a dragon in the ample space of the venerated sky. Tarson noticed Jupita's fear, her inexperience would be fatal in this highly dangerous activity. His beloved, and this was clear to him, was not as powerful as she thought she was. He sighed while looking at the lead disc object stuck firmly to the central mast, he ran quickly to it and cut its heavy ties in a single and precise blow.

"Brace for impact on the port side!" the helmsman shouted.

A hail repeated by each one of the twelve brave crewmen.

The captain listened carefully, while he ran with the disc to the ship's stern. The repetition of his command aloud performed by each crew member was so that everyone was aware of the tasks and problems ahead and also, counting the repetitions assured how many men were still alive and/or willing to fight. He positioned himself at the stern. He uttered the mystic words perfectly except the last one. He waited…

The dragon come with its mouth opened, making its choice clear. Teeth big as spears distributed through the huge arcade willing to swallow a house in a single bite. He flung it open showing the infernal furnace in its throat.

"Goddamn winged chicken!" Morgrinald yelled. "I'm one of the legendary Battle Hammers! He who has the blood of Keldorn never fears any flames!"

Some crew members looked at each other after hearing the dwarf's words in a glance of recognition or fascination.

Clouds appeared out of nowhere and grew darker when they were engulfed by a powerful vortex, lightning writhe, thunder moaned loudly, the blackness of the night arose in that circular space, stars showed their beauty and the intensity of their colors, a piece of earth and fire raced from one point to another leaving a trail of dust. It was a portal to a place far from there.

The dragon, surprised by the sudden change of scenery, tried to dodge, but it was too late; its long tail with bone spikes lined at the top, whipped the ship and with the impact the ship swung at an angle of forty-something degrees.

Dominescu held on as he could dropping his sword which slid quickly on the deck, hitting the bulwark and falling out. Morgrinald, rapidly sunk his axe into the wood floor. Jupita held on the ropes with her eyes closed, a repressed memory assaulted her, a passage from her childhood. And, suddenly, silence and a calm wind.

Panting, Tarson raised his eyes, not seeing the opponent but rain clouds clearing and a rainbow emerging gently. Taking deep breaths, he thought about the sacrifice of so many days in the schedule he wished to follow to the letter. He looked at the disc shaped object made of poor metal and craftsmanship that now revealed its unique quality: that was the object that provided Yuri Caleb's quick escape when he tried to imprison them when Jupita, Osiris, the woodsman, and him left that underground place. He escaped in another direction, he went straight to the village. Straight to the place where Darrell worked. Soft hands touched him and brought him back from memory. It was the soft hand of his beloved Jupita. He sighed with relief realizing she was unharmed. Inhaling gravely, Tarson stood up. His posture by itself had a grandeur of its own. The kind common only to kings and legends.

Morgrinald extracted his axe from the ground, and checking the surroundings, noticed the trembling figure sitting in a corner. It was Dominescu.

"What the fuck is this? My rescuer is a coward?"

Dominescu leaned on the dwarf's shoulder and tried to say something, he collapsed in his arms.

"But damn it…" said Keldorn's grandson swallowing his words.

Quickly, he removed one of the gauntlets biting the thick tip of his forefinger then putting his callous hand on the forehead of his fallen ally. Then shouted:

"This man is burning up! Old man, help me! Shouldn't you be by his side? Ah, whatever, don't even bother to explain. It seems your healer skills are required here!"

"Mister Martin, start the count."

A strong commanding hail forced everyone to respond.

"Honey, there were sixteen of us." Jupita said looking around. "counting us, when we boarded."

"I will recount, sir!"

"No need to… Darrell is no longer with us."

In the empty space where Darrell was, the wheel swung adrift.

A long silence honored the death of Phillip Darrell.

Until one of the sailors, one with an eloquent voice uttered by lifting his flute:

"To the sailor, the friend of countless qualities, sea treasure hunter."

"And of sky beasts." said another one, raising his long bamboo staff.

"To the gentle and helpful ally and above all, his patience with vessel newcomers." said Talassas the elder.

"Captain? The ballast stones."

"What about them mister Martin?"

"The ship is unstable."

With so much to lose, Tarson ran to the tall deck, towards the helm.

"Do you feel that on the helm?"

"No. I just saw a few stones fall when that winged beast… Finally. Wouldn't it be better to do a stability test?"

"I don't think making the men run from one side to another is the best idea. Just try to keep the ship on course. But let me know of any other changes."

"Yes, sir. And… Sir?"

Tarson-Romanei, known as "Silver Fists" was noble and his magnanimous posture was enough to impose respect to be called Sir, but he also accumulated the rank of captain. The elf stopped and turned his head to the new helmsman and this, understanding that he had permission for other issues, said:

"Well, the boys and I believe in you, sir. Including mister Darrell."

Squeezing his lips, Tarson laid a hand on his shoulder and said:

"Thank you!"

A long whistle followed by two short ones coming from the crow's nest reached everyone's ears. Excited about this, the crew began to scream:

"The continent! The continent!"

And that was it. From the sails, at any height the massive block of earth, trees and life could be seen. Not that the sea had no life, grace and beauty… Sailing in the open sky was an art and few could survive it. In an enchanted caravel that sailed through the skies, then, it was quite a feat. The crew lived it day by day and had just faced another dragon and yet, there was still great brightness in their eyes. Tarson knew now that he could face anything with them.

Inside the vessel, Morgrinald raised his feet to reach the window, he sighed quietly relieved by the news. It would be good for his sick friend. He had already noticed the crew's stares and silent conversations. They were afraid of contagion and Morgrinald feared epidemic hysteria that usually arose in confined spaces like that. Hysteria was a strong weapon that gained muscles instead of common sense, shortly ignorance and uncertainty would decree that a no was a yes. And it might be another kind of yes. The sick would be killed no matter who or how many defended him.

Sartre went quickly to get more water and wine. He planned to get the patient drunk so sleep could steal some of the disease, at least allowing him to sleep.

"Did you hear that?" the dwarf said kindly. "Dominescu, Slayer of the giant reptiles is coming home. There's a good story to be told with a good wine, sitting by the fire, waiting for the stew to be ready…

"Morgrinald, I'm not going to make it, and we both know it."

"Shut up."

"The wound gangrened, didn't it? Sartre is a good healer, but a terrible liar."

"Hero, it's not always how we wish it would be."

"And I don't wish it was. If it was only the gangrene, he could amputate my leg. He knows I was infected."

"Shit. You're delusional again, huh? I think I'm going to smash your face and pound the fever out of you."

"I'm going to die."

"Bah! I've been there several times and I'm still here and breathing. Once I slept for almost five years. I was the victim of a bloody cane distillate, that's why I say: never drink that shit. Besides, when I woke up, I had a thunderous headache."

In a quick glance, Morgrinald realized that the bearded hero listened with his eyes closed to his exaggerations, possibly to stop the pain. It was clear by the writhing faces he made. So he decided to continue because if death went through there, it might want to take the story instead of Dominescu.

"Once in the dark corridors of a labyrinth, we were subdued by three ogres, one half ogre and a naga. Have you ever heard of this creature? An ogre you should know, because your live in a mountainous city. A naga is a quite ugly creature with a snake body and a head similar to a human. Imagine a large tadpole with the size of a big snake. The ogres had barred Argus, the mercenary. Now, Astrias and I were surrounded, I was stupid and tired of cuts and hits that day. That thing, the naga, had cold and clammy skin. It slipped between old Astrias legs. Scared, he began beating it with his staff, like a woman afraid of a cockroach. The naga got pissed and showed that same ugly grimace of someone shitting. Everyone there moved away, even the ogres were afraid of the mighty naga. Astrias was skillful, in fact smarter than skilled, and he tried to reverse the situation with his spells, trying to capture all of them, but that big headed thing dispersed the spells. Astrias, the idiot, let down his guard. And, as he was in front of me and the place was tight, I couldn't do much. That quick thing dragged and tumbled Argus as fast as it suspended and trapped him between its teeth. However, Argus's ugliness was only smaller than his absurd strength and that's why he grabbed it tightly and strangled her until she dropped him. When she dropped him, he pelted it on the wall. Her blood made a strange painting on the wall. Then Astrias, of the flaming blade, covered our eyes with mists with his magic, and…

"Argh!"

How can he handle so much pain? Morgrinald thought. The human was really surprising. He had never met anyone like that. An example of bravery, too bad he wasn't a dwarf and worse that he was not one of his clan. Morgrinald swapped the wet cloth on the forehead of the bedridden hero, he remembered his fierce look defeating the slave traders without military training. Suddenly a strong grip held his fist:

"I'm dying, so could you at least have the decency to hear the cries of a dying man?!"

Morgrinald sighed:

"All right. Talk."

So Dominescu, with an undeniable certainty of death, confessed to many things Morgrinald, way too many things. Some didn't even seemed to make sense but Morgrinald heard them. It was certainly the fever's voice. Besides, it was the least he could do at the moment.

"I know what you're thinking right now." Morgrinald said changing the tone.

Dominescu's lucid gaze caught his attention when he looked at him:

"There are reasons for saying such things. This isn't the first time I've had this vision. I know where your strength comes from and vow you made in the bowels of the earth.

Morgrinald stiffened for a moment:

"Drink some more water, while I find you some good wine.

"I know who fell in the lava, Morgrinald. And know why you survived, you talk a lot about your grandfather, but you forget the deeds of your mother and father.

The dwarf was hit in the chest with a brutal dose of past.

"Elves? The elves and I?"

"Consider it a dying man's wish."

Pain consumed Dominescu's body.

"Shit! Are you serious about this death thing?"

Dominescu held back the sharp pains, but, instead of talking, he nodded.

"Friend, where I come from there is another way to bypass the pain.

Quickly, he delivered a well placed blow, knocking out his sick friend.

BETWEEN THE SHADOWS...

In the belly of the ship, in a corner, a creature tall as a wolf and curved like evil itself, sensed a new smell that called to it. A slight odor made it sniff like a mouse, zigzagging so the smell won't escape. Going to the door, the creature was surprised with the smoke. Closing its eyes wickedly, it opened the door that gave access to the basement and lower floors, following the smell like a dog chasing a fox. Finally it arrived to the source, the kitchen, at the lowest point of the splendid vessel. A thick brick fireplace on the ground prevented contact of the flame with the wooden floor. The cold iron cauldron seemed to cook something awesome mixed in cereal and thick dry pea. Close, on a long table, dishes of barley porridge and roasted salt pork. There were meats hanging to dry and smoke, that was the only storage place. The eager eyes, and the tongue seemed to enjoy its own lips. His own stomach surprises him uttering a strange and restless sound. It was empty for well over two hours, a real pity.

The cook, at the sight of him, remained with his hand in the huge spoon.

He tried to smile at the cook, as waiting for an invitation.

"You're on your own." he heard in response.

When he agreed, the hungry creature, with a little smirk strummed the air, choosing its breakfast. When he pulled the bread, he heard the shriek of a rat angry for losing its meal.

The cook laughed.

The war here is much tougher than outside, little Demon of the woods…

"Humph!" Hans, the big rat, faced the rat, his rival, and, tilting slightly his head forward, squeaked in equal tone.

The little animal didn't move, and neither did he. The impasse was formed.

"Why fight the rat? Let him get some."

Hans looked annoyed, because he didn't know what animal he was referring to. They continued to squeal and the cook began to feel scared and recoiled his fingers expecting the worst of both.

His hairs stood up slow but visibly, long barbs, hairy knives, but the rodent rival was not afraid. ,Mouses ran yes, but not rats. Rats have twice the size and ferocity, capable of shredding their opponent, especially if they acted in defense of their offspring or their offspring's food, which, of course, was the case. Zao Jung, the cook, retracted the machete used for chopping hard vegetables, because in this case, the best defense was to not be there. He moved away carefully so he wouldn't be considered a third party in that dispute. From his protective corner, Zao watched equality and inequality. The rat squealed, claiming its fair share… Everything for the litter. The black nails of its agile climbing paws scratched the wood nervously, the thick and ugly tail stretched out behind it to help in any attack or escape giving it balance. The nose and whiskers identified dozens of scents and fragrances while the long ears picked up sounds and noises. On the other side, a Demon of the woods. That "carries the madness in their teeth and death on their claws".

Big rat and the rat, the shameless rival, despite the impasse, they were annoyed by the cook's smell of fear. Would he be agile enough to defend himself? Agility in small and closed spaces have very little relationship with immunity: being there was a risk. Escape was another. Hans concentrated, there were only three there, he, his rival and the food. The chunk of food defended as his last, his only, his…

"Precious…"

Suddenly, in a flash, the redoubtable rodent had only half of its body.

"I must have blinked." he said, almost spelling to the incredulous cook.

The remaining body squirmed in its last throes, the inert tail, nails ending in needles, its agility, ferocity was useless against the Demon of the woods. The gray rat was devoured and in an instant. Only at times like these it was understood why the name Demon of the woods. The iris of the wild winner rolled in savoring the victory. When they came back to normal, a bright yellowish glow crossed the iris, only then Zao realized that the glare came from the machete in his hand.

"What's that for? She started it!"

Saying that, the Demon grabbed the disputed prize and the tall hairs of his nostrils contracted. The nose smelled something and so he followed the scent behind a cauldron, pulling out a forgotten pan with six baby rats inside. Zao felt his stomach squirm.

"Oh no!" he whispered in fear and disgust. "Isn't he going to stop?"

But far from what he expected, the hairy Demon tore the bread, the disputed award, chewed it and spat the slime on his hand to place it with love and care close to the hungry ones.

"Don't look me like that! You saw… She started."

"Yeah… Okay! Okay."

"Why didn't she ask?"

Thus, Hans, the creature turned in his direction and smiled amiably:

"What's in the pot?"

Later, on the upper floor, Dominescu awoke, however, it took a while to remember where he was and that he had been knocked out. Deep down, he thanked the dwarf for relieving his pain. Laying on a large hammock made of interwoven strips of rope and wood, he felt his skin burn, something inside him pulsed as if he breathed with hatred in the closed place of the crew's general quarters. Keeping his eyes closed, he tried to control the convulsions generated in his stomach and the more severe pains on his nerve endings. The fever and pains seemed to want to overwhelm him.

"No, nothing and nobody. No, nothing and no one" and, like a stubborn child, he repeated it several times, with wide eyes.

The fever burned under the cold sweat, he felt dizzy and had double vision. Trying to regain control over his sick body, he focused with his eyes closed. He fell silent.

Sartre returned with water and cloth to refresh the body of the poor sick man and clean his already dried wounds. Without the forest plants he could do very little, so he started some prayers in a nice and soft song.

"How am I, healer?"

"You're awake?" he startled.

"So?"

Carefully, Sartre turned him on his to better examine the extent of the damage caused on the island. Then he removed his tall boots.

There were pustules on the open wound.

"Gods. Can you feel this?"

“No.”

Sartre pressed strongly the opened and purplish wound with the tip of his knife.

“You will lose the strength of your leg soon, I’m not sure there will be time to save it.”

“Is there a cure?”

Sartre shook his head negatively.

“The poisonous blood has already reached the heart arteries. You only stand the fever thanks to your great strength.”

“The legends of my people say that blood given willingly by one of the elementals can cure diseases.”

“Or destroy you from inside.”

“If I'm dying it's my choice!” he shouted outraged.

Dominescu opened his eyes in surprise to see Morgrinald leaning against the door frame, eyes opened and attentive. Sartre soon noticed him.

“Yes. Leave us old man.”

Leave the dwarf there, that is crazy! And why did he wished to stay with the woodsman?

“I must follow the fever evolution and minister medicine...” Sartre tried to evade and stay there “the situation has subtle changes that I must accompany and...”

“Sartre? You know and so do I.” Morgrinald had a strange neutral face. With no expression that denounced his actions.

“I have to stay here. If you must talk, you will have to bare my presence.” Sartre feared that perhaps the dwarf was there to end the misery with a swift death, after all, that was how a warrior would treat the wounded.

The calloused hand, although weak now, rested upon his, Dominescu's eyes pleaded in silence and the rude voice complemented:

"Listen old man… Go see some clouds outside."

The right of choice was respected, Sartre patted his weak hand, got up slowly and left. After all, the patient had reached a point of no return. If there was really any medication, ointment or prayer to save him, it was beyond him. Soon it would be over. He would have to tell his parents, because it was his moral duty. So… All that was left was understanding and dignity.

From above the clouds were formidable, although he didn't risk looking over the stern. The strong winds fulled the sails, but on line of the floor where he stood, that part whose name he never got right, the wind was more subtle. He also felt it on his serious face. The swirl of some light and thin strips of leaves on the floor the reminded him of his friend Sargauss, with his voice muffled by the dying moment he said:

"O friend, where are you? I feel your strength near. Why don't you show yourself to me?"

Then his mind ran away with natures and legends. Suddenly, right there, he heard a well known scratching. A blade.

"Oh gods!" Sartre exclaimed in amazement and ran back in despair, but he stops in the door frame.

He wasn't even prepared for that moment, he knew it could be like this, but, in fact, who actually prepares for this? When he looked inside, he saw the dwarf dipping the cloth in the metal basin and wringing out the excess. That was the sound. It was was probably his bracelet scratching the basin. He was impressed. He takes care of him! The fever punished the villager and the dwarf was there to hear his whispers and moans with dignified patience. Sartre put his hand on his heart, which exploded with the fear and hastiness. Suddenly he hears the sound again and now he knew it was the scratch of a blade. Sartre's eyes widened, but he stood still. With his chest heaving, he retreated in slow steps until he collided with the gunwales. Powerless, his legs trembled with what he saw. Something that proved what he knew about the stories of the world… A tragic and dangerous story about everything that exists. A world overlapping another, world above world, with cracks in the middle, giving passage from one to another. About such worlds being created just to prevent the god brothers from killing each other. If they go through the world crumbles, and before him there are always minor agents that from time to time, try to open the crack so that their beloved lord and master can pass. And like the offenders, there will always defend the passage, those who are part of both worlds, the guardians. Nevertheless, the healer's mind dragged him back to the terrifying present where he witnessed Morgrinald's feat. And understands when he sees him do it. A new secret is born there and with it, the certainty of a new sin, or not.

Finished, crushed by thoughts, in pain because of the crude cut on his wrist, as well as by blood loss, Morgrinald sighed, and as he didn't expect any results, he left. When he passed by the old healer, he wondered why he was standing there in the middle of the passage. The dwarf lowered his gaze, he was uncomfortable. No discussions, he wanted to respect the patient. But, when he passed, he felt the old man's hand on his shoulder and heard:

"You did what you could… Thank you."

TRUTHS THAT SEPARATE

On the other side of the caravel, in the ample captain's room, because of the confidentiality promise made to Sargauss he felt fragile, and bitter. Neither he nor his crew should speak of their obligations. The elf lady he knew since he was a boy, hunched her body over a short and narrow table close to the glassed window, and spied the skies.

"Remember when…"

"Sh." the pretty lady whispered. "I think I saw one of our ancestors moving around. They say that from above, where they are in zealous vigil, they only move when they think no one is wtaching…"

Tarson approached the young lady and wanted to touch her, but a pathetic shame, an unpronounced love, directed his hand to the wall and not her soft shoulders. Right behind her he began to investigate the stars.

"Those were beautiful legends."

"Our most noble and beautiful ancestors." She spun around getting too close.

And with that comment and proximity, Tarson held his breath, like a young bird again before its first flight.

"Yes… they say that they use rainbow cloaks, and nowhere is there such beautiful colors."

Tarson didn't even try to look at the stars. And why should he? The colors of Jupita's skin, hair and eyes were all the colors he wanted.

"T…"

"Yes?"

“Do you think Darkay is somewhere over there?”

Tarson had always been afraid to answer that question, even to himself. Darkay was human and not one of his race, neither one of the ancestors. Instead, he picked up the measuring instrument on the low table in front of them. It was a mere piece of rectangular wood and in its center was a thin rope with knots throughout its extention.

“The humans call it "Magical Wheel". With it they can predict the rise and fall of the Sun in the firmament.”

“What's the point of knowing when is dusk and dawn?”

“Do you see the horizon? I put the rope in my mouth and hold it with my teeth.” the rope tied to his mouth gave him a muffled and silly voice.

“Ha, ha.”

“The Shun should tush the upper phart and the…”

“That’s disgusting… I hope you are the only one who uses it.”

“Actually, it tastes like beans.”

Jupita slapped him softly on the chest. Gradually, with a shyness shared by Tarson, they raised their gaze and there, at the back of the eyes where promises, misunderstandings, hurt feelings and secrets. In the privacy of the bedroom inevitable issues took their place.

Despite the joy of the reunion and the escape from a great and smart dragon, in the crew general quarters, Dominescu suffered in silence because it was unfair to worry everyone else with something he caused. The brightness of the full moon invaded the place and showed in the stare of the sailors, their concern of that fantastic craft. Soon, the crew at any time would require action from their captain. A sick man on board with a disease that might be contagious, killed all celebrations when they entered that room. And so the day imposed itself on a busy and depressing night.

Looking at the earth from above was like looking at a live map, and at one point, they recognized the topography of the landscape and the magic vessel descended slowly on a treeless hill.

A small and fast figure jumped out of hiding and from there, in free fall, to the tree tops, surprising everyone. The figure was of Little Hans, whom everyone thought had remained on the island. And no one saw him coming aboard. When the magic vessel stopped, Morgrinald was the first to disembark, jumping to the ground from a height higher than that would risk making a metallic thud and raising a lot of dust.

"Hey dwarf!" one of the crewmen shouted. "You're crazy. You could have died."

"Come down here and finish the job you piece of shit."

"Yes, he is all right."

When he got up, Keldorn's grandson was smiling for having earth under his feet again, but one of the latches of this armor bent and lost its setting.

"Lower Dominescu." Morgrinald motioned to the men on board "Help him lads, carefully."

"I will stay with them." Dominescu said by himself grabbing the gunwales and denying support.

"Damn fever! You said that the fever had dropped." he mumbled to Sartre.

"And it had" he said next to the sick man.

"Someone up there punch him in the head and throw him down, I will catch him."

"Morgrinald, seriously… I'm lucid. They need an experienced man. That is, if the captain will have me."

Tarson was caught by surprise, he had had no time to meet this wonderful man, but his lover told him about his exploits.

"We're going east, beyond the mountains region, woodsman." Tarson told him still trying to understand the reasons for his decision.

"I know a sailor's routine. I'm not dead weight."

What he said first could be true, but his real health state was clear. A wobbly and shaky walk. Quite different from the firm and imposing stance from yore. The brooding elf stared at him with interest.

"I'm a born navigator, elf." Dominescu insisted.

Tarson knew nothing about Dominescu, however, he recognized the lethargy of death before it stroke. If he kept him, he would certainly have some explaining to do to his mates, who feared epidemics… He hated lies, but used them frequently, instead of worrying dear friends.

"There may be risks like the one we just faced." Tarson said loudly.

"In any case, you are heading east and to the east is also the capital of the Great Empire. Consider it a lift. Besides, the wood hull was severely damaged, I was a woodsman for five years and I know the art of carpentry."

"Can you fix it?"

"And teach the others, because I'm going to do it alone, and if I don't match your expectations, drop me off on the way."

The work on board was already hard, there weren't enough people to take care of all the jobs, many there had accumulated more than one task. The healer, for sure, would be an obvious choice, however a carpenter also was welcome, since the damages to the hull could be an immediate liability.

"Seems sensible. And… Necessary."

"Yes."

Sartre passed by slowly and looked deeply at him, and when he begun to climb down the ladder and almost fell, he was aided by Dominescu's hands, Sartre then took the opportunity to ask him:

"Is there a way to persuade you?"

Dominescu smiled and helped with him with the rope and the descent. Sartre had his answer.

Jupita's body was became involved by a bluish white energy. The tips of its feet hung as her beautiful body shape began to levitate. Her hands moved as she swam in midair, the fabric seemed to want to compete with her beauty, but to no avail. The breeze around her took straight into Tarson's arms. To the one that met knew her since her youth and who she never expected to love so much, she hugged him and this time without concern of letting the world know about her love. A slow and prolonged kiss given as a veiled and sacred vow, with her feet above the deck. They looked at each other, Tarson-Romanei-Timbal; the elf; known in some places as "Fists of Silver, placed his hands gently on the face of his beloved to hide and dry her tears, letting the same breeze that lifted her, take her away from the vessel, from him, but above all, away from a danger that could be fatal.

Jupita of distant Almokaryr, disciple of Darkay, elf and woman, was the last to leave the vessel. Tarson and her had been together for a long time and knew each other very well. They felt and feel a huge affection for each other, and the feeling has always bordered between brotherly love and perfect lovers. But, now, they reached a new stage and they knew it and Tarson reflected on how much she grew. However, thoughts and conjectures were crazy dreams without order or invitation spinning in his head.

On deck, Tarson suddenly regained his haughty attitude that his post and mission demanded and gave orders to the crew, and slowly, the vessel turned into a light and majestic farewell. While it was turning, those on the ground could see the damage done by the sky beast to the side of the hull.

When the boat was at a certain distance, the adventurers turned to a trail well-known by Hans who stepped forward screeching with happiness.

"This way, lads. No more bird trip." Morgrinald said, frowning his face and moving on ahead of the others in a clear haste.

"Why the sudden rush?"

"Too much beer, wine and liquor in the bladder."

Everyone laughed and left the dwarf and a troubled bush behind.

Hans rehearsed an heroic and victorious walk, however, due to his short legs, was easily overtaken by Sartre.

Jupita followed but was staring at what now was nothing more than a dot merging with the clouds and felt a little hand holding hers. She looked down and with a sweet smile noticed Hans, who returned the smile and whispered:

"Come, captain's beloved, we have to finish what we started, until he…"

Speechless, the elf lady held rebel tears and her sobs and followed with her friend Hans Ranni Ramiro and Roder.

The walk took two hours until another well-known place to the adventurers.

"Hey! It's the commercial road."

Suddenly the elf stopped in her tracks and two minutes later, a beast roar was heard. Hans fled into the high grass, Sartre picked up a branch from the ground to use as a weapon. And Morgrinald who was evacuating in a broad-leaved shrub, lifted his pants and cursed the evil gods for the tragic and comic play created by them, and there he stood static to gather his bearings while he plucked a leaf.

A thick coat tiger suddenly appeared. Big rat resurfaced from the bushes and bent down to pick up a stone, as he was very close, the large feline also noticed him and soon the tiger reacted, crouching in fear. Hans threw the stone on the ground at the same time that he ran and jumped on top of the beast that dodged him. Their movements were fast, Jupita despaired with Hans' madness, they all turned to their weapons.

"Wait!" Sartre warned. "We know that beast."

The Little One's arm was trapped between the teeth of the fearsome feline. Jupita held her breath. At that moment, Hans stroked its head and laughed when the huge feline beast began to purr.

Sartre crossed his arms, and putting one of his hands under his chin asked:

"If Zork is here, where is the old man?"

"Close, dear friend." said, by surprise, the elderly barefooted man wearing old and tattered robes. "Very close…"

The fraternal embrace reassured the others. Hans started telling their misadventures, but Sartre interrupted him when he noticed something serious in his friend's posture.

"What is it, Zorak? What happened while we were gone?"

"A beautiful woman attacks the unsuspecting at night. Not even locked houses are safe."

"Where did she come from?" Hans asked, stepping forward, fearing for his loved ones.

"Remember your friend, the fatally wounded one, that collapsed in front of everyone?"

"Osiris survived?" Jupita shouted, surprised and happy.

"Actually, she's the beast."

Dumbstruck by the news, they silenced and began to listen.

"A thin and small dagger blade, without handle, was embedded in her chest. An ancient weapon endowed with strange and malignant intentions. Certainly responsible for the condition between alive and dead she is in. She, once your friend, attacked Little Ones and humans at night, not even the horses or cattle are spared. We had to take desperate measures, the dead are now beheaded or cremated because they wake up with the same fury and blood thirst. And there's only one place where she could nest during the day and use as a lair."

"A place we all know well!" Jupita cried "I mean, at least Tarson and I."

"This is where I say goodbye." Hans Ranni said seriously. "I have to see my people, see my wives and children."

"Children? Which ones?" the dwarf asked.

"My third wife. They live closest to the village. I don't even know what I will find, I just know that I must go."

Jupita knelt in front of her little big rat and kissed his thick lips. Due to the weight of the situation, he wasn't even shook.

"Goodbye."

The brave Hans Ranni Ramiro Roder ran quickly through the forest and soon disappeared among the greenery.

Suddenly, while they walked, Morgrinald said:

"He must have climbed the flying ship's anchor, while the crew raised it."

"What? What are you talking about, dwarf?"

"A dwarf!" whispered the old man to his friend.

"That's why the inhabitants of the island laughed. Not because of astonishment or euphoria with the vessel." Morgrinald said rethinking the moment.

"Morgrinald do you think…" the elf lady locked her eyebrows and like someone who interrupts their own thoughts, continued. "Of Course! That's the myth's reason."

"Bah! They never leave mother earth…" joked the dwarf. "Nothing. It's just not easy to see them embark or disembark, that's all. Bastard piece of shit!"

Busty and Morg laughed when they remembered all they went through with the hairy nut. The elf remembered when she met him, his fetish, his arrival on the island, paddling in circles from inside his cage, reaching the sand without getting wet. His desperation of seeing her drowning and his joy, when she managed to glide over the water. The dwarf recalled the stealthy shorty, the "piece of shit" who freed the prisoners of the ship and the night they shared memories, sorrows and liquor. No one had ever accompanied him so decently in drinking. And both, elf and dwarf, revived the unlimited capacity of Hans Ranni Ramiro Roder to get in and out of trouble. Always intact, without a scratch. And above all… his innate talent to create deep and true friendship and always escape the water.

Frantic squeals coming from far surprised the elf lady. How could that be? In broad daylight? Soon the others could hear. From some point northwest, a heavy cloud of black and brownish fragments passes squealing. Wolf bats. Morgrinald only put an open hand in front of his face and a few bats passed centimeters from his face. Jupita scratched the air with her opened hands ahead of her pensive face. When she arched her arms, the flying creatures split as if obeying the movement of her arms. And they were gone.

"A flock of bats in the middle of the afternoon?" the old healer made a veiled gesture upon himself. "A foreboding sign."

"Are there mansions or mausoleums around here?" the dwarf asked in the absence of that, there could only be caves there.

"No. Only a village at the end of the trail." Sartre replied. "Something bothered them."

"Or someone." Zorak added.

"Nothing." Keldorn's grandson said "It could be the collapse of a hall or gallery. Are there many caves around here?"

Silence.

"It's a shame we don't have horses…" replied Sartre completely ignoring the dwarf. "We would arrive faster."

Keldorn's grandson bit his fist but ended up saying:

"Arrive? What do you mean, arrive?"

Sartre was totally absorbed by doubts and fear of what he might see at the village. He was about to ask his hermit friend but seeing that blank stare, like blurry pearls, he concluded that it must have been something serious and sudden. What happened to him during those two or three seasons? Diseases don't consume so quickly. He had been gone for months, he recognized, two or maybe three seasons. Thus, almost by accident, the words just leaped into the air in a fragile sigh, almost inaudible:

"Your eyes…"

The old man of the woods stopped, in a brief movement, he put his hand his friend's back and drew him closer in order to answer very close and in the same tone:

"Good to see you."

And kissed his forehead. Making it clear that he did not wish to worry him, nor the others, for being believed, on account of old age, was difficult enough and if everyone noticed his weakness, it might be quite different.

"Let's go faster, I want to see Osiris."

"Quick to where, child? Where do you want to go?" the old man of the woods asked lightly, to that woman, without raising his eyes.

Sartre, on account of his craft, started thinking about the cause agent of the disease. Mentally he assigns the possible causes although he didn't know how it could have blinded Zorak. He thought about bitter herb and the anil acorns.

"I have a theory. But it's useless, we have to reach the temple before dusk."

"Then your faith may help, because the trail passes through rocks and small hills and is sinuous like a slow river. Now, on the trail of the inhabitants of the forest…"

"You think so?"

"Like I believe in the gods!"

"Show the way, old man! Time threatens to changes the fate of many." Jupita said, hoping for the solution of facts that had been thrown on her lap. Responsibility was a serious weapon and she repeatedly denied it, but life changed constantly and for the first time, she acted without thinking about it.

"A village, right?" Morgrinald asked thoughtfully pushing a thorny shrub aside for the old men could pass.

"Yes, the village where I live."

"Village, small place…"

"With some fifteen families."

"Only children and old people, huh?"

"No…"

"It has two or three pregnant ladies maybe."

"Just a village!" Sartre continued to answer without understanding the value or purpose of the questions.

"I understand… A village with fifteen families. If you count only one LOSER every THREE families, you have FIFTEEN! And they're afraid of an evil woman who walks at night?"

"Morgrinald?" Jupita warned him for she smelled trouble.

"I didn't understand." Sartre said.

"Goddamn cowards! Why didn't they enter the ruins and exterminated the damn thing?" the dwarf asked bluntly.

An awkward silence settled and no one answered.

Jupita was just wondering about the the impossibility of it. If Osiris had lost her legs and arms she would still butt them all to death. She preferred to remain silent because she was still trying to digest that her friend had survived, since Hans' elusive answers on the island about the real meaning of the whistles, she had assumed the worse. She believed her friend to be dead. Now, even before she could deal with her survival, they were already talking about lynching her? It was too unreal, but on the other hand, she had never considered training the people to defend themselves, not even for a moment. Jupita and Tarson's race, regarded as godly, saw the world differently, seeming distant, snobbish, secretly allied to various causes at the same time, however, the insight and simplicity with which the experienced warrior assessed the general situation was suprising.

Suddenly the healer interrupted everyone speaking firmly:

"I vote in a consensus."

Zorak noticed the tone, he had heard such tone before. He knew that things would be well now. Things would be fine again.

"It's evident…" Morgrinald observed with revulsion and weariness in his voice.

"Easy now…" Jupita extended her arms in a clear gesture to separate even the words. "If we decide to go into town…"

Morgrinald covered his forehead with his calloused hand and dragged it over his face to the beard and pulled down hard:

"If we decide? That's enough. It is not my commitment, what's it to me?"

"Dwarf…" Zorak tried to argue.

"Dwarf my ass! It's Morgrinald the blood of…"

"Blood, yes." Zorak tried to add "The blood of children from…"

"Who declared them innocent? You? I? No more heroism! I'm tired and, if in case don't remember, Dominescu can be dead by now!"

"How?!" the sentence hit the elf lady's heart.

"He was hurt. The leg gangrened, hence the fever."

"What?"

"Are you fucking deaf? The woodcutter is dying… He decided to do so away from us."

The elf's eyes dropped to the ground:

"Dominescu was important to me, too."

"Important?" Morgrinald did not quite understand that comment.

"Could you both listen to reason?" Sartre screamed trying draw attention to himself and only when he was sure that he had it, he began to speak again. "Have you considered for one moment that he wanted it to be like this?"

"What?" Morgrinald couldn't believe it "Sure. And what about you old man?"

"I'm not the issue here."

"I'm not the issue!" the northern dwarf echoed in a pathetic parody. And then continued. "Of course it is, and has always been."

"In a few kilometers in that direction, many people." Sartre faced the dwarf. "Good people, poor, but good people and they are in trouble! Dying!"

"It's always like that. Some son of a bit…"

"Hey."

"Some son of a bitch screws up and we have to clean up the mess. Dwarfs, gnomes, elves, and any other idiot. What? Too many things hidden under the carpet?"

"That's enough, Morgrinald." Sartre continued "All I know is that those poor people…"

"See. All they do is whine, begging others to take part in their struggles. Man is nothing more than what he does to himself, mate."

"Look, I know you're upset with Dominescu."

"Don't you dare talk about him, you bastard." with a flick on his chest, Sartre took two steps backwards and fell. Morgrinald looked deeply into his eyes. "Many in that damn village disappeared and because of that, Dominescu got involved in this."

"It was his destiny."

"Ha! I have yet to meet an idiot who doesn't blame fate."

"What do you mean?"

"What do I mean? I mean that it's so beautiful, so cute blame the fantastic… If there's an eclipse, the Sun went out; if there is a fire, it's a dragon's fault and not the idiot who dropped sparks on the dry bush; a baby is born deformed, and we sacrifice the son of the devil; an earthquake is some evil or good earth's god fault. There, they rather blame the gods instead of our incompetence. Not ours: yours!" he said and moved away so Sartre could get up.

"Do you really think so?" Sartre said putting on one of the sandals that came off.

"In their complete lack of sense?"

“That fate does not…”

“Holy shit old man!” interrupted the angry dwarf. “You believe too much and do too little!”

“I…” Sartre thought it was unfair because he gave up a lot and much. Not even on the island he abandoned his mission. He lived for more than twelve years in that village. A humble place where he helped deliver every child. Each youngster and every elderly there had a story with him. And now panicked families fled their homes. “Morgrinald is right. And I never saw someone more naughty and without commitment to image who makes such an effort to create one. Dominescu at least walked with his own feet. I think that's much more than a few know how to do.”

“Feet…” Morgrinald was bitter, puzzled. They would never know how much he was affected by what the old man said. He had his reasons. The answer to that dried in his mouth. Of everyone there, he had saved the ungrateful healer more than once. He never thanked him and never asked why he was there or the importance of his journey. “That's it! The conversation and the group end here. My feet! My feet will take me there.”

“It’s too late for him” Sartre said with a hint of pride in his voice “Even he knows that.”

“Sartre? Friend…” the old hermit was trying to extinguish the flame of agitation, the quick fire of vanity appeased his insane hunger and all that was left were the bitter scars of the ashes.

Jupita however was unaware of the woodsman condition. She was shocked.

“Morgrinald, I…” The elf lady really wanted to say how she felt. She wanted to have spoken with Dom. She even hoped to visit him in the near future. But instead, she babbled, exhaling without forming any real words.

"Humph! You shouldn't have left him" said the barefoot armored dwarf without raising his head. He straightened the twisted clasps that held the wide chest plate and walked by the healer, and said:

"You expect too much from others, 'old man'."

"I only expect what is fair."

"Fair for who?"

Sartre, now began to come back to reason, but there was no way to swallow the words already spoken and deny their existance.

"Morgrinald?" he tried to say.

"Forget it. I have things to take care of in town. Things I started."

"Look… I…"

"Shut up, old man. You were right and I was wrong. You're the best and I'm an asshole."

"I didn't say that…" he muttered regretfully.

"No, you didn't. I just translated it. Take care, busty."

Morgrinald, blood of Keldorn, heavy footsteps seems to scar the ground. And in every step, the certainty of a mistake made in exaltation was greater. Sartre seldom lost his calm or faith. Secretly, he prayed to the gods that someday he may meet the brave grouchy of the people made of earth and fire. A moist and quick scratch on his face outlined a path to the ground. Tears He was surprised he could still produce them. The dwarf, Morgrinald, Blood of Keldorn of the Battle… Well… A fellow with terrible manners, still… He was right. It was time to fight for everything and whomever came. He would no longer beg for mercy and favors.

Jupita felt the weight of the obligations inherited; the weight of the loss of a friend because of a quarrel and another one to death. And, with so much commotion, didn't even notice the difficulties of the old man of woods on the trail. Only the healer noticed when his friend Zorak stumbled and almost fell to the floor and when he stopped his fall, he whispered:

"Come On. Straight ahead. I will help you."

With a grateful smile, he turned to his friend:

"You already have."

"Gods! Are you…"

"Blind? Thanks to my strong immunity, it only blinded me."

The old bush man, in a pure gesture, smoothed his friend's hair:

"You are crucial here."

"Oh no! It's a dwarf disease, isn't it? Tell me, you must. I demand you do!"

"Not in the way you think."

"Not in the way I think? Hold on here. This part of the forest has a stream. I will get…"

"You will get nothing."

"Of course I…"

"Listen"

"Psst! Decidedly. You need care and I will stay here, looking after you and soothing your…"

"The village needs you more than I do."

"And leave you like this!?"

"It would have happened with age… It only arrived earlier. Better so… So I get used to it."

"Bull shit."

"Stop!"

His hands fell to the lap and the pity countenance moved to his feet. Even without seeing, he should know that he was ashamed and hid his moist eyes in his palms:

"I can only save one at a time."

"Oh Sartre, Sartre, Sartre. My friend, my good friend, why are you so hard on yourself? What evils afflict you in this world?"

What could he say? How? He had seen too many things and that made him aware of the world… The true one, drained of dreams, full of interests of nobles and undoubtedly… A world of greed and cheating.

"My actions are useless, Zorak." he confessed to his friend, crushed.

"I can't even imagine what you went through as a slave in overseas lands." said the blind man.

"How did you know?"

"Gódi."

"What?"

"'Who?' Would be the appropriate question. She's just a girl from the Little Ones, but has the potential and the courage of few from any race."

"Shame. I'm ashamed of that. A child had more strength and responsibilities than I."

"Again, harsh with yourself."

Keldorn's grandson's words still echoed strongly in his mind. Part of him wanted to scream, saying he had been kidnapped before he could react. And that he knew Darrel's real family was strong in commerce and all it took was to change the caravan route for the village disappear.

Zorak, with his blank and shaky stare, closed his friend's grieving face with his hands and said closely, in a lower tone:

"The Little Ones made the villagers believed that the old track was cursed. The trail that leads to the ruins of the old temple."

"What temple?"

"That was how they kept the treasure hunters away all these years."

"What temple? What are you talking about?"

"It took some work, but you did it. You and Sargauss. However… He was not found."

"He's fine. He spoke to me. In secret."

The blind man's chest heaved under the weight of the feeling.

"If he didm then you know he will be leaving. You are aware of the the problems his race has with age, right? Thin skin, absence of weight, gradually they become part of the air and vanish."

"Unless…"

"The elf is still young, and doesn't have that strength!" Jupita's voice surprised them cutting into the conversation and in so low and confessional that sounded more like a sigh.

Sartre looked at her stunned. She was walking in front of them, and the gap between them was well over twenty meters, her hearing and voice control were amazing.

"Is Sargauss really responsible for keeping the ship in the air?" The elf's voice sounded clear and crystalline as if she was close to them.

Zorak smiled down to the ground, he wet his fingers and didn't feel any wind. Actually he wasn't even impressed, he was just waiting for the elf lady to say something, she should know of the secrets now, so she didn't hold hers back.

"Right Sargauss supports it with his noble essence."

"So that's what the dragon wanted?"

"Certainly."

Zorak was looking at Sartre while he spoke. And he in turn saw in the unfocused eyes a thick yellowish and disgusting goo which asserted to his dismay, that it represented his friend's unrecoverable blindness.

"And what did he take?"

"I'm not sure!" Jupita's answer was harsh.

"Let it be friend, leave it. Do you know why the air elementals like her hate the dragons? They need them, they need to consume them. Consume them to fertilize."

A low wind whirled and whipped his face as a warning. Zorak tore a piece of the robe that covered his old body to make a blindfold and continued to say:

"The dragoness took some of those Sargauss hid. Creatures, things and refugees from inside him."

"No, she didn't." Jupita lowered her gaze to her own body. "No, she didn't."

Certainty had a strong mark, offensive as a truth too strong to be ignored. Jupita ignored the protocol between the races, and so a strong wind began to swirl, raising dust and clumps of grass, leaves and small dead twigs. Sartre protected his face and Zorak, already blindfolded, kept his stance. The wind quickened, whistled and immediately ceased. When it ceased, the healer saw that

Jupita, disciple of Darkay, from distant Almokaryr was no longer among them and may never return.

BACK TO THE TEMPLE

A group of soldiers was once again on their quiet patrol. Stanislaw Hanverovich, or simply Stan, wished to serve the king his whole life. Such desire, incidentally, so ardent that made him the youngest soldier and a few years later, the youngest officer. Now captain Stan dreamed of the day when he'd be taking the royal standard in into war. Irving, in turn, burned with fever every time, just thinking about the possibility. It was easy to see in Lucrecia's face the evil androgyny and no word emerged from her mouth about the past, mute, without yielding a syllable. But, from what the ugly Endoli Desiderian told him, she was the bastard daughter of the Mansur house, of the Mansur patriarch and, given her cleft lip and birth outside of marriage, her fate was obvious. And about the ugly Endoli, it can be said that his background was equally or more unattractive than Stan's. As for the women, Ellan, July and Nery they didn't even deserve a second look. Neither the three newly assigned boys that didn't dare raise their eyes above their horses. Clear, evident as the whiteness of milk. The latter were just too poor and their coming to the army was only in search of a better salary, with no other ambition, just common dreams of ordinary people. Stanislaw defined them all easily. At least that's how Stan saw it.

Actually Ellan descended from wealthy families, but didn't find marriage. She abhorred the idea of being committed to a convent, apart from having a well equidistant ideas from the clergy and abbesses of the temple of war. That's why she joined the royal guard. She deserved a leadership position only by the force of her family coat of arms and thus had; and for a whole year now, completed in early spring. Nery ran away from an arranged marriage. The elders, including her parents, understood that the chances of finding love were only through shady sheets and the wellbeing of the family came first. Conclusion: the hateful adultery at times would be the solution on both sides. July, the youngest of all, had the most perverse fate: being poor. And worse: cursed by her people, after all, widowhood was considered evil. The acid prejudice created the most bizarre and hideous legends and fear pollinated such insanities in the community, and she, the proscribed in her midst, only hoped that in the distance from her homeland reaped a better fate. As for the boys Tobias, Edgar and Lico, he was right. Poor ones in search of a better future, however their low faces expressed the immense discomfort of returning to their village from where they ran away from their families.

The lack of integration of this newly formed patrol provided a critical weight, silent, with all the gravity of thoughts and expectations. For Stanilsaw Hanverovich, it was a dry hard sip, stuck in his throat. And why wouldn't it? The crude and young woman was given leadership of the patrol in his place by his commanding officer. Was it a test? An insult? There was space for both as a test and as an affront. He thought very deply about this that he didn't even notice that he forced the five-hour on the corporal, Irving, and the three young soldiers. When they arrived at the station, only Irving complained so he ordered him out into the rain.

"Go soak your tongue."

One of the boys laughed.

"You! Drown your laughter there too and, when you get back, you will be "tight" with immediate superior. The same goes for the man outside. Humidity and responsibility, you will learn the meaning of both. Go!"

That was thirty-two hours ago. However, the freshness brought from the close sea, softened everything and ride became easy, enjoyable under the mid-afternoon Sun. Suddenly, screams and roars broke the softness of that afternoon. A quick eye exchange and they spurred their horses and these galloped like they were on the prairies. Despite being in good number, the noise they made on approach on scared all the beasts making them flee. July went straight and started chasing some of the wolves, Nery called her back, while Irving threw up on his horse. Ellan jumped off the horse in motion. Without a doubt, she was the best rider of the entire coast and the most helpful and active in the company.

In the ravine, bloody bodies and their belongings scattered from a small and poor caravan. They were all on foot before the attack, carrying merchandise on their backs.

July returned.

"Are you crazy. Where did you go?" Nery asked.

"To scare things. Hopefully I also scared their leader. Which is good."

"Stop yapping, and help me." Ellan ordered.

Stan went with her to examine the bodies, finally he saw some action and hated it. Every chewed body, every thread of blood. In an outburst, a fallen old man screamed when the dumbfounded officer stumbled on him, but he immediately helped him and heard his last words that resembled a prayer.

"It will be done, old man. I'm going to rip that thing's head off." Stan said with vehemence, with nobility. It was without doubt an opportunity and to the others, an obligation to fulfill.

Therefore, the obligation was obvious to all of them. Carefully they tied the bodies to their saddles and walked to the village from where they came. The bodies of the unfortunate weren't too dirty. Therefore, they must have left from the village nearby and someone may recognize them, and if they spent the night there, someone could may know something about them.

They will pick up a carriage in the village to take the bodies to the chapel as soon as possible because the world was afraid of its dead.

The chapel was one of those places where no one went or visited. Except when there were dead people there. And escorting the dead to their final resting place was a guard's duty. Escorting the dead to their resting place, the so-called "Towers of silence", so the dead would not return. And of course, reporting what happened to his superiors was another obligation, because such a aggressive bunch of animals was a big problem for trading and sooner or later that problem would be the local platoon's problem. They would have take care of both tasks. However, transporting the dead was never easy. It would take them two days. Because the transport animals got scared at the smell of death; predators were attracted by the blood and scavengers by the remains. In order to avoid such problems, they had to find lime to kill the stench during the trip, ropes to contain any restless spirit from the dead and a tarp to cover the murder victims with dignity. They knew that they would find at least horses at the village of Miller, thanks to a royal decree. At least two fresh horses were available to royalty or his army in peace time or otherwise. This was the law.

They could hardly believe once they reached the village. The once buzzing trading post was now engulfed in fear. On arrival they saw a territory recently fortified by a wall of palisades with thorns tied between the spans closing off any passage. A place prepared for war. It used to be the kind of place with a few tens of primitive houses raised by necessity with no concern about the future halfway to the sea that grew both by the installation of an inn and tavern, and as the path to town from there was shorter, the inn was the reason why it became a trading post. Where the locals took advantage of the arrival of caravans and travelers to sell their greens and vegetables.

From the horses in a cross angle one could see the identical houses that seemed minimal straight caves of faded colors when there was any, and bricked in by a thick stroke of branches underneath the parched mud walls that time ruined here and there. Their windows were only ugly holes for ventilation and covered by long pieces of wood and, at the entrances, heavy internal doors without hinges like miniature drawbridges placed upside down, with the only concern to prevent the entry of nocturnal visitors with feet or paws.

To corporal Irving, the village was something curious, because in the rich village around the king's castle the walls were made of superimposed trunks. What he saw was surprising while it saddened the others as a reminder of their own origin.

The uniforms allowed them to pass easily through the recently erected stockade where the green wood evidenced its recent construction. The access gates were formerly the walls of an old and partially collapsed house that narrowed the entrance allowing the passage of only one horse at a time. Except for the local guards, there were few people on the streets, and that had created an ambiguous and partially expected reaction. After all, they were carrying corpses, although the bravest one there snooped around the face of the dead out of obscene curiosity. The desperate people crowded around the soldiers, like flies on meat. The thought itself was not pleasant, the soldiers represented hope and order over the bad shadow of these days.

"These unfortunate people died on the road to the king's city" Ellan shouted, and panic settled in.

Stan looked at her with disapproval.

"We're doomed!" the villagers said and shouted, between sobs and despair. "Surrounded like pigs and slaughtered one by one, save us."

Before anything could be said, fearful eyes and trembling lips multiplied, and suddenly an old woman came screaming with her bell, announcing another happening.

"The moon! The moon. Look to the skies. It will be an early evening."

She warned about an eclipse.

Stan, with a deranged smile on his lips, whispered:

"She will come with the night."

"Hey! You!" Ellan called with all the authority invested in her. "Show us the stable, we require some horses as ordered by the king."

"Sorry, but I don't think you will find any horses available, their owners have taken them." said one of the villagers.

"What's going on here?" Ellan shouted again trying to maintain her authority.

"Some time ago, we requested the help from the king, are you… The help?" said an old man with his hand on corporal Irving's leg.

"Certainly not." captain Ellan replied "but tell us anyway, so we can see if we can help."

"Some months ago, madam, our children and neighbors began to disappear, and it wasn't because o f wolves or lurking animals, at least of the kind we know. Some spoke of monsters, we got help from a missionary of the temple of war and two elves and my son, who also volunteered."

"What happened?"

"We don't know." Madam, they vanished like the others and now our dead and the lost ones came back… But there is no life in their eyes. They became cruel and with them, other dead also appeared. We were able to kill some, but a worse evil came soon after, the woman, the missionary, was seen in the streets and her mouth was stained with blood. Blood of a fallen man."

"Are you delirious, man?" the madness disturbed Stan.

"I wish, sir, I'd rather be a madman and have our kids at home."

"Your kids too, I suppose?" Ellan inquired keeping her eyes on Stan as a silent rebuke.

"You guessed right, sir. Dobrovonski, my oldest, was the only one who came back, but he was dead like the others."

"I'm sorry."

"Thank you…"

"And what happened?"

"July!"

To captain Stan, Ellan's open warning was evidence enough that everything was on the verge of disarray.

"I'm sorry, but we have to find out. Right?" She argued back.

Another fault, Stan thought.

"She is right madam." the elderly said. "I can say that now we know where the others went and where they returned to. A passing by missionary went there, to try to get rid of this evil."

"Alone?" Ellan had a bad impression of this.

The old man only agreed.

"Who?"

"He said his name was Tristan."

"Tristan?" July's eyes almost jumped out their sockets. "Tristan Ivanov?"

"I guess that was the name. So you recognize that valiant soul?"

"Valiant?"

From her tone of irony, July also knew Tristan's real story. Even as a boy, he always had a restless soul. He was a bit of everything and as soon as he managed to grow a beard, he abandoned the city. He never had a profession, so he never settled anywhere. However, when he saved a girl from drowning, he named himself the "Missionary of Hope".

"Yes." July said sarcastically. "Since the lord of the land promised to build a chapel, he has been in places and situations from which few walked away. He calls his immense luck divine protection."

"Regardless madam, he promised to eradicate what he called a vampire. And that was two days ago."

To a shrouded face in the crowd, that was enough and that figure jumped on an empty saddle and the equine galloped more out of fear than the kick in its belly, dragging along corporal Irving that was holding its leash.

"Hey!" the corporal exclaimed.

Noticing the extra luggage, the hooded figure drew a dagger. Irving widened his eyes in terror, but the blade was used only to cut the rein making him fall and roll on the ground.

The one who stole the mount had a single thought. No time for protocols, it had to find the others and warn them about the terrible news.

And it didn't even have to look back. Except for the fallen soldier, the others would be on its trail as soon as they got rid of the corpses tied to their saddles. The initial distance was a provisional and welcome advantage.

WITH HIS OWN FEET

"Walking with your own feet ", that sentence was more firewood to the dwarf's fury.

"How can he be so frail? So weak?"

In the village there were fifteen families and in the Iron Citadel, his homeland, about seven hundred and fifty individuals and some forty children, and the people depended on themselves despite the strict local conditions at the top of the mountain. The seasons were imposing there. And even at the foot of the mountain, the inhabitants life was far from being good or quiet. These neighboring tribes of semi-nomadic nature were subject to snow, stone and broken trees and shrubs avalanches, especially Morgrinald's people… Subject by distance and climate to an immense commercial ostracism.

But they survived… both peoples. The strong and mountain adapted people and the humans that inhabited the base of the mountain.

~"These idiots are weak!" the outrage ran in the dwarf's thick veins and marked the surface of his neck and temples. He lumbered with eyes locked on his beloved soil, his beloved ground, dodging wood or rocks and stomping all the rest.

The dwarf from the Iron Citadel left a heavy and demolished track. Anyone could follow him. He had already been at his destination a few times, but the discussion with the healer was still intense in his mind. He repeated the scene, the whole discussion in his head, and once in awhile, a shrub or a tree were the target of his wrath, and obviously, it lost.

"Dependent. Creep."

Typical attitude of people of questionable character. A fool and other names he could list on his way. However, his memory was an avalanche that took him back to the old days. Back to the cold days, when a white layer covered his body when they were out in the open and went down to the foot of the mountain. Down slope until they found the semi-nomads to trade. Morgrinald liked those humans, they were a discreet, quiet people, that negotiated the meat and the skin of hunted animals at the foot of the mountain. A people strongly adapted to the climate.

Without being able to stop walking and ponder, a serpent, on the road, hissed and bit him. However Keldorn's grandson skin, like those of his race, was hard and hoarse, so the bite didn't even scratch him and he neither noticed the danger nor the attack. Thus, the reptile lost one of its fangs in a useless bite while the dwarf continued thinking of the harmony of that relationship. The dwarfs were exempt of the energy expenditure in hunting and they could concentrate their efforts on mining and smelting. And the hunters took advantage of the opportunity to get valuable stones for other trades that would cover their needs. A mutual benefit.

And Morgrinald never heard his people or the tribes ask for help for simple things. The merchants of those tribes traveled for days, whole months and living off what the land offered: bison skins for the cold, their meat and fat for the stomach, and the bones for soups, knives and utensils. Insufficient for a comfortable life? Yes. But they prospered. Far from it, for the mountain dwellers, humans or dwarfs, life was fragile, both for the lack of food during winter and the summer diseases.

The preciousness of life in such a severe environment was such that children who completed five years of age were seen as winners and a big celebration, sponsored by everyone, gifted the fortunate parents with the best they had to offer. And that was a culture and tradition shared among the mountain dwarfs and the neighboring tribes at the mountain foot.

Suddenly, an odor irritated his nostrils. The characteristic smell of death. He blew his nose and shook his hands to get rid of the rest, but the smell persisted. Then, Keldorn's grandson snapped his knuckles just by squeezing his hand and went to see what it was.

OBEDIENCE AND OBSESSION

"Along with their crew, are those who are supposed to be the guardians of the world and other survivors who managed to escape through the other plains." Zorak of the Hill's speech, nicknamed Old Bushman exuded wisdom. He rested his face on his friend's and, near his ear, reported:

"Keep the bridge between worlds closed."

"I can't, I'm an ordinary person." Sartre felt sweat dripping from his armpits, each one of the old man's words seemed like a piece of meat forced down his throat.

"Anything but ordinary. You're responsible." he replied.

"No."

"Yes, old fool. When the place grew, the Little Ones and I remained vigilant. You know all too well that things happen when you lose interest, the…"

"Someone always comes by at the exact moment you are no longer vigilant."

"Yes. The fissure between the worlds is necessary, it allows them to breath, a point of…"

"It's called weakness, I know it well."

"Weakness? That's an attribute you don't have, you only think you do."

"Praises from an old man."

"Truths to a friend, more blind than I."

His head dropped to the ground, but a loose laughter escaped:

"How long have you known?"

The expression on elderly marked face failed; it became unusual and motionless, a man immersed in mist. The healer feared that it could be an extreme reaction to the poison. Suddenly, the old man looked as if he could still see from behind the whitish yellow of his pupils and said regretfully.

"Twenty three years."

A HUGE CORPSE

Imagining was the field of thinking, a fertile area and so promising as deep the mines in the west. Or a barren and desolate area as a hell of sand and emptiness. Evidently… It depended solely on the thinker. And so, to the eyes of the cynical dwarf, an ability for stating the obvious. To deform, absorb and sweeten everything you wanted to hear.

In the exact field of evidence, an observation employed with due seriousness resulted in concrete, indisputable truths. Henceforth the whole thing had a scary hint of repetition.

A corpse as big as a house, with an elongated neck and crude plates of scales that ran the back of the amazing specimen. On the neck joints, on the abdomen and in the lower part of the long tail, tall and painful thorns, the rest a dense thick meat and for that reason, ugly. Extended up, a not-so-thin but strong leather strap, covered the long and thin bones of a wing that, when healthy, flapped possibly with a hard thud of a sail fabric and certainly would fasten hearts and make men and creatures pray.

On what was left of its jaw, blown up on impact on the ground, teeth like swords and massive molars capable of crushing some stones. When alive, it had dizzying agility for its tonnage, and above all, smart as the one that attacked the vessel. However, there in that situation, irretrievably dead… It represented a different kind of horror.

Part of the muscular body was buried, the ground clearly denounced a straight fall. The hole caused by its weight opened an obtuse and slightly oval crater. From the soft and broken jaws a purple and black tongue, where scavenger birds fought for a piece of it. Besides the birds, which it never tolerated, there were other scavengers and ground profiteers. The blood and meat produced a well courted feast, which in itself made it a very dangerous place. The blood did that very well removing their common sense, be it by famine or thirst it awakened, or by the madness of death, death wish, the kind of desire that takes hold of the minds of the weak, sadists and other types of miscreants.

For Morgrinald, insanity always surrounded everything and awaited cracks in the flesh of the living to install itself, grow and persevere.

Flies and other small animals didn't really bother him. Actually, how could they? Could such small animals make him sensible to any irritations? But he hated the smell, the rotten perfume of death reminded him of the war, the last one, the war of the races. A memory deeper in his soul than in memory. In a critical month, he walked heavily through the valley, hill after hill, with the smell all around him. A place where the dying still defended their banners and Morgrinald split their skulls for mercy, fun or both. War was never a right or wrong place. Being right or wrong neither… A war was a red and gray place where you have little and nothing is known. Through that territory of the fallen, the difference between fortune, glory and victory was never measured with who remained standing. And remaining in that place was to die also. Be it in mind, body, or what's left to be called soul.

Outside his memory, growls vied the real place, however, Keldorn's grandson ignored the scavengers. At first they didn't even look at him, mesmerized by the pleasure of eating and satisfying themselves. Many there fell aside still chewing, others, with their muzzles immersed in hot blood, very hot, were delirious with the strength of that poison and positioned themselves to defend their food. The dwarf tore the axe from his back and punched the side of the double-edged blade, and the metal vibrated horribly and some whined angrily, some remained alert and the rest fled, visibly frightened.

Morgrinald, Keldorn's grandson put his chin between blades and when he muttered a secret prayer, the thick and heavy sound of his voice increasingly reverberated on the blade edges until his voice reached a guttural sound incredibly low and long, confusing the senses. The once determined beasts where now confused between fight or flight. The brave dwarf of the valiant clan scratched the blade on the ground and everything around shook and then they were gone, except the hideous and hated birds who thought they were exempt from his wrath, then Morgrinald stomped the cracked ground hard and the soil caved in here and there beneath that immense carrion forcing the wretched daring birds back into the trees.

"You feathery bitches think I can't throw stones? I do, and very well." he said to himself. "I can also hit. But that will be for later…"

Now he wanted to understand how the beast died. Dragons didn't die of old age, especially females. Dragons were born in a way hard to describe, but the winged reptiles kept the flame within themselves, they were part of that world, this one died, like a grasshopper.

"It crashed to the ground, evidently…"

Obvious so far.

When he touched it, it was cold, despite having fresh blood in its opened flesh.

"Its flame was drained? But how?"

On closer examination, he noticed a blackened spoken stain in the center of the immense chest, that was that the only mark.

"Lightning? In a single spot?"

A quick and sharp pain made him back up a step and find out there, on the floor, the remaining part of the monstrous jaw exploded on impact. To his right, the yellow whitish eye stared at him from somewhere in the afterlife and Keldorn's grandson finally asked the question that irritated his stomach:

"Why?" the question joined his heavy eyebrows.

Suddenly, the sunlight returned strong and a huge circular shadow appeared. Instinctively, he rolled sideways without releasing the weapon in his left hand. As soon as he was positioned, he rose intrigued and recusant. Above, the size of the thorax of a mule, and without being tied to nothing visible, was a thick and crudely polished metallic shield hovering in the air.

PANIC AND TERROR

Agnes Rey, with her plaid sweater, passed beside her little Irving. His body was laid down. The world seemed like a distant draft in the background, a pinkish fish with long purple fins blinked one of its big and bright eyes and leave, being dragged forward and then to the left where it disappeared. His mother reappeared and asked him to put on his sweater. She was saying something crazy like he couldn't be dragged without a sweater, because it would dirty his uniform.

Realizing the madness of the dream, corporal Irving woke up. He squeezed his eyes. He felt his arms, legs and everything else. Alive. After the fall, he should be only a bit dirty, he opened his eyes. A boy at his side was wearing the wreath of branches on his head; an aspiring guard; and only after a moment he realized that he was just looking at his reflection in a polished copper mirror.

By the cloud dust ahead, the platoon was chasing the thief.

The ridiculousness of the situation put him on his feet. He expect quips, but no one was laughing and if they laughed about an attack against an officer and stealing his mount… The would be flogged before being taken to prison.

Actually, no one there could laugh, the place had an almost palpable tension. The sticky air of death and insanity made it clear what the poor villagers insisted on warning: the place was constantly under attack. Attacks from "no-humans", corpses, the so-called "Death in life" by the people of this area. Everyone was abandoning the village, including the scared soul that stole his mount. At that speed, they would have all left by the next full moon.

They would certainly use the clear moonlight, they could travel by night and gain even more distance from beasts. At least, Irving would do that.

One inn, Only one inn opened in the whole damn place. Everything else on the block, as far as one could see, were sealed houses smelling of fear and poverty. Doors and windows were boarded with crosses or a line hanging old charms to ward off evil.

The remaining inhabitants, it seemed, where gathered behind the inn's walls. Pounding on the door, Irving noticed a whisper followed by a strict silence. After some time without response, he decided to insist and pounded again with his closed fist, and one of the charms fell to the ground. Suddenly something heavy is dragged and the wicket opens but no one appears.

"Who's there?" Someone asked from inside.

"You really think that 'it' would say something?" said someone else.

"Shhhh!"

"Shush yourself!"

"Open in the name of the king." corporal Irving ordered.

"What?" he heard some say inside. Soon they were more than two.

Irving lost his temper, he placed his fingers on the wicket and his gauntlet made a quick sound of metal on wood. When he risked putting his head through the crack, a kitchen knife almost scratched his face.

"Step aside, evil creature."

"You fool! Careful!" warned another voice from inside.

"Injuring an officer is an offense and pointing a weapon at him another much worse than…"

Widened eyes emerged at the wicket and collected the knife with the same haste that wielded it.

"Oh, gods, oh gods, oh gods…" you could hear joy in that voice.

Heavy objects behind the door are dragged in a hurry while a second voice warned about the insanity of opening it.

Suddenly, a tuft of some strong and sweet smelling herb was pushed through the wicket by an arm with scrawny fingers and hands.

"Hold it then, if you don't wish me any evil, if you are who you say you are."

"What is this charm old man?"

"See. I knew it."

"Open it, now." the officer demanded pulling the meaningless tuft of grass.

Another moment of silence.

"How many are there?" said the hidden voice.

"What?"

Someone behind him clears their throat. Only then he noticed his new shadow, thanks to the last trouble with captain Stan. The voice inside insisted:

"Pass along the holy herb, if you are pure you won't suf…"

"Take it, for the love of the gods." said another voice.

Soldier Tobias, at his side, obeyed with a silly and brief smile, common to all lacking wits or reason. New recruits tended to nonsense and promptly followed orders and charges. However, he concluded that fulfilling their rites against their fears would be the way enter, so he grabbed the herbs and passed it over his face and raised it. Those somewhere in the darkened inside seemed to have gone back to reason. The wicket was closed and the heavy door was dragged backwards. The movement made the threadbare and beaten hinge cry softly in protest.

"Come in quick." the one arm crippled old man said.

In the low light of the opening they could see that he was bald and unshaved, and his skin was pale as lime and wrinkled, as if life had abandoned him. Irving got scared at that image, because that looked like a damn zombie.

"What is happening? The king finally learned about the creature? Or have you come only to collect taxes?"

"Wong!" a voice scolded somewhere inside that space.

"If you came for money" old Wong said shrugging and dropping heavily the door lock bar, sealing the passage from the outside madness to another inside. "You can have what's left in the pockets of the dead."

"Sir, control yourself." the corporal asked.

"Control myself? Yes, I really should. Now, you guys in the corner with your pants dirty of fear, help this old freak."

The closed door received furniture to anchor it down from three young men who now lifted the heavier furniture and threw against the door.

"And what does it matter?" Wong repeated. "In the morning we will be safe then we can leave. You may take any room you wish, after all, this place doesn't belong to anyone else now."

"What do you mean? I demand…"

"You demand nothing! Your uniform has no authority here little soldier. Unless the king himself has selected someone for this land, and no one wants this damn place. The weather is unforeseen, unpredictable and the crops, they are, are…"

A hard thud of something against the reinforced port killed the discussion.

"It's back. It's back."

Flustered with everything, corporal Irving just put his hand on his weapon and watched the chair tilt and fall from the top and bounce once before standing still. On the other side of the door, another dull thud was heard and everyone became attentive. A sudden breeze revealed, too late, a crack in the wall and, through it, a quick arm pulled one of the refugees, and with the crash, the wooden wall caved in and horror took over everyone. Tobias, the soldier, was prevented from acting by a desperate embrace of one of the refugees asking you him to act. Not to move. The victim was taken and one of the refugees picked up the chair and blocked the crack on the wall, but without locking eyes on the body being dragged along the street screaming.

The old man pelted a packet of fragrant herbs and stuck another bunch in the wall opening.

"Let's go!"

"No."

"What was that?"

"The delusions of an old man and the entire village, little soldier."

The corporal was unsure. What had that been?

"Let's go. Do you think that chair will stop the…"

"Stop, my ass. That's why I put the herbs."

"And that keeps it away?"

"Keeps it away? Don't be stupid little soldier."

"Huh?"

"From the way it breathes, the creature has large nostrils and the herbs smell confuses it. We will leave tomorrow."

The others prayed and sobbed with contagious fear.

"Wait!"

"What? You require a reasonable explanation? You're looking in the wrong place."

"I demand!"

"Psst!" whispered the crippled man covering the officer's mouth. You want her to come back?"

"Her?"

"Her."

"How do you know its a… she?"

"I know a lot of things."

"You're tiring me."

"Great, that way you'll stop asking questions."

The soldier had enough of his defensive answers and pulled him by his remaining arm and thinning hair, and stared at him deeply.

"Are you going to hit me?"

"Maybe. Answer my questions. This place may not have a lord, but it certainly has me as its responsible officer and by the authority invested in me, I can beat you, yes."

Silence reigned. The old man felt the pulsing of the soldier's hand. The officer looked at the thin trickle of sweat dripping and realized something else.

"Wong! That is your name, isn't it?"

The elderly made an angry face to disguise his fear, but couldn't sustain it.

"I'm not sure!" he said, defeated. "We only know that herbs confuse it a bit, and if it wasn't for Abigail's garden we would have died earlier. The monster used to attack during the day. At least in the beginning. Now I think there are more of them. Screams came from several directions past few nights."

"As an officer, I promise…"

"Promise? You want to promise something? Remain alive. Get out of here without trying to be heroes. Be heroic by warning the king. Whatever that thing is, it's growing."

The officer released the elderly mister Wong, who staggered in a half circle, and leaned on the wall with his only hand. As he moved away, the others settled and began to follow him down the narrow corridor. Suddenly, he stopped and held back the line.

"If I were you, I would avoid staying too close to the walls. There is some food in the pantry. All the windows are lock, I don't have to tell you why."

THE CASTLE AND THE KING'S CRY

The life of a rich nobleman would always be, in all aspects, something different from the lives of commoners. Even rich merchants would consider themselves miserable compared to the opulence of certain places.

The title was mostly due to a kinship to the king, ensuring, this way, that the possessions remained in the family. However, there were also the lands conquered or defended by generals and officers who received them as gifts from the king. Thus, a rich nobleman, depending obviously on his relationship and title, held on his property several castles, with dozens of servants and dozens of guards and knights. Beyond the strongholds there was always one or more villages on their lands, under their custody.

On those lands, horses, chariots and carriages circulated on unpaved roads, taking nobles and/or their families, escorted by armed horsemen, while wet nurses, squires and other staff followed behind on foot or on mules.

At that moment, they saw on the road only the peasants going to the castle to pay off their debts. The castle was isolated by a rounded brick wall and an old ravine that covered the entire passage up to the second of three gates. Given the space between the walls, it was easy to understand why it was the Daintghorn family castle. The safest place in the known world. The second passage had a labyrinth of tall walls full of sinuous paths like the bowels of an animal in its interior. That was where the cavalry and its twelve stables were kept. Ahead, the last one walled the castle, where the guards changed shifts once again. Suddenly, a cloud on a clear day made the bored guards speechless. A man hung on a rope was climbing down from a floating ship. Dominescu thought it was a shame to have not gone home, however, the situation was serious and his king should know what the celestial scribe of fate had determined in his book.

Outside the vessel he could the hole in the hull caused by the winged beast which would have been fatal to a common ship perched in water of any depth. It would take three weeks to repair. When he looked around, he realized he was surrounded by spears pointing to his chest.

"I have a message for our king, so run me through or let me pass."

Fearing that this could be a magnificent being from another world or a coming from somewhere in the sky, those in front of him moved aside, raising their sometimes hesitant spears forming a corridor. Nonetheless, after passing by so many guards, they did not spread out but gathered behind him and followed until Dominescu, the "Heavenly Titan" who came down from his heavenly vessel, reached the stair door and closed it behind him.

Each step of the stairs reminded him of his injured leg. It took longer than usual to reach the courtyard, where someone finally stopped him.

"Peasant, please follow me to the bastille."

"I have a message for the king."

"You sure do. Move."

"News about a missing nobleman."

"How dare you take me for a fool?" the man said, motioning to unsheathe his sword.

"Would you kill an unarmed commoner?"

"Are you trying to trick me? Arriving like that, I wouldn't doubt your abilities with words and the number of coins to bribe the bad examples of this army. Come on, state your business, because you will hang if you don't name your accomplices in this insane adventure."

"I'm not lying."

"Then speak, mysterious messenger. What is your name?"

"If you care so much for names, why do you withhold yours?"

"Shit! Now you offend me. Do you want my sword moving around your stomach?"

"That's not what I said…"

"Very well, I will show you my tolerance. Tell me already, what is your message?"

"It is not for you."

"You are pressing your luck, when it doesn't even exist."

Tired and with his leg throbbing, he shouted:

"To anyone who cares to listen! I have an important message for the king and this fellow here would not allow me to deliver it, ignoring its urgency."

"What are you doing you fool, do you want to embarrass me?" He asked wringing Dominescu's clothes.

"No. I wish to be heard."

He let him go.

"Come, I will take you to my superiors."

"No! To the king!"

"Preposterous miserable, if this message is not as urgent and special as you make me believe, I swear to the gods…"

"Swear as much as you want. I wish you no harm, just take me there at once."

Dominescu's eyes exuded seriousness and somewhat, a noble resolute air.

"Ok. Show your hands." he tied then with thin silk that held the pommel of the sword to the scabbard. And walked in front of him.

Maybe the man behind him was maybe a nobleman. However, erasing everything he said would be impossible, because the sun never will rise in the west and eggs would never mend once broken. Given his posture and stance, Dominescu was talking to an officer, because in a single gesture the last of the gates was opened without delay. Then, one by one, the doors and gates were opened for the man ahead of him. In the lobby, a fantastic table was being laid with dishes and cutlery, but he didn't see the king nor the queen.

Surely, at least her would be in one of the rooms, inspecting the details to host the nobles during winter as was custom.

However, before they left, they saw the king in a corner of the hexagonal lobby.

Except for the fine cotton shirt and a thick gold ring with a blue stone in its center, Dominescu would have never believed that this was the imposing king he saw every year during the spring festival. Sitting in a corner like a beggar, with his legs opened and surrounded by empty and fallen bottles. His face was covered by the tapestry displayed on the wall. One hand raised the bottle towards the tapestry and it leaked; as his mouth was obviously hidden; a good wine on an expensive carpet and his blue shirt, staining them in such a way that there would be no way of cleaning them. He was drunk.

"Majesty."

"Get lost."

"There is someone here to see you." the officer insisted.

"I'm glad he got his wish, now get out. I hate him like I hate everyone."

"Your highness?" the officer seemed embarrassed behind his pomposity.

"Never mind." Dominescu decided. "It's no use in his current state, I will talk to the queen."

"With the queen, you insolent?" the officer now made clearer his offense and put his hand on the pommel of the sword. "I'm in charge of this cesspool and I command you and your…"

"To turn around and speak with your queen!" a powerful female voice said suddenly.

"Queen Cecil!" the officer said falling to his knees.

"Madam, with all due respect." Dominescu remained standing only lowering his eyes in respect. Invisible teeth bit his leg. I need you both to tell you what I know."

She was accompanied by her ladies in waiting and the administrator, a kind of bureaucrat, who helped with the details of the castle, from the health and maintenance of the large garden to each royal etched napkin fold. The mighty and haughty woman with fluffy and expensive clothes had a dubious-look in her eyes, when she asked:

"Captain? What about those ties?"

"Caution, beloved mother of all in the kingdom." said the captain of the guard with a sickening and queasy voice. "Peasants only come to the castle during big fairs."

"And also to pay off their debts." she completed.

"Certainly, but I suspect this one's intentions."

Dominescu's eyes are suddenly betrayed. Meeting the king in this miserable situation was execrable, as a boy he had the image king as magnanimous, splendid, and today saw only a momentary or maybe a permanent slave of the bottle. The expensive and colorful tapestry that covered the face and best part of the royal body showed a landscape in the background and revealed a little of the history of the royal family, the Daintghorn clan, being true in each point. Apart from the usual exaggeration of travelers, the men of the family had indeed splendid ports.

When the queen noticed the curious gaze of the peasant, she decided to give him more details:

"In our land the mighty dragon is the resident. Unlike many other dragons, this was the benefactor of the town that took its name. Over a decade ago he held alone the onslaught of the giants of the mountain that came down to the plateau and sometimes the plains, to steal food and fight. These giant men inhabited a large area of the mountain and have a shrine at the top, named after their strange deities. Today, unknown to the citizens of the city, few are left in these parts, in fact, two families, most of women and children. Because of this reduction, they stopped being a danger a long time ago. Now, they occupy themselves only with hunting and defending their territory. To the north, the exiled barbarians and the remaining giants raised a new capital. The capital grew and..."

"Cecil, I don't like that story..." said his drunken majesty.

"A curious inversion of values, don't you think?"

Dominescu realized that she herself had her doubts, and carefully replied:

"I heard that story also, my queen."

"Tell me, man, what are you doing here? What such important words do you bring?"

"I have urgent news about your son." the woodsman said at once, as to not be interrupted.

The term 'son' aroused the sottish king as if he was hit by ammonia coming from the cave of nightly evil from the neighboring kingdom, where tens of bats slept.

"Son? I have a son." he stood up with some difficulty due to massive doses of wine consumed. Today's date was special to the king, exactly five years ago, they hunted together in the royal woods for the first time, Erick Daintghorn and Iurik Daintghorn, father and son.

Cecil, the queen of all the Great Empire, a kingdom so called because nothing in the known world could match its size and splendor, arched her eyes with overlapping hands close to her stomach, and tilted her royal head slightly.

"First Lady of the kingdom, I appeal to your reason, don't let the words of this fool stain your sensitive ears with…"

"Be quiet! Is what I ask of you, my good captain…"

At a brief glance, the ladies-in-waiting withdrew from the hallway. And before another word, the administrator of the castle gave her his hand and supported her while her majesty sat gently on top of an adorned chest. And only then she continued, looking directly at the messenger:

"What can you say, if in you resides and is governed by the truth?"

With a slow look, the peasant realized under the lightness of the gesture of the queen, the concerned and frightened mother, with the stumbling king beside her.

"I know nothing of the truth, madam, but I know about the man that had your eyes."

He respectably lowered his eyes to the stone floor, bowing his head forward.

"On an distant island…" he thought seriously about what to say. He remembered his parents and how it must have been difficult when their children disappeared. He cleared his throat, as if it was possible to dispel the memory and concentrated before proceeding. "I'm going to talk about someone without expensive clothes and shiny adornments and whom never missed such things. Someone who called himself the "Loved child of the Koth's house!"

RUNNING...

The horse was sweaty and bordered on exhaustion, but she had no choice, Jupita, for now the thief rider, was in a hurry. Osiris had serious injuries the last time she saw her, she certainly wouldn't be fully recovered to defend herself. And the Little Ones would surely run from any contact as they were shy and cowardly. Hans was an exception, between coward and hero, he was unique. If Osiris was still bedridden, she would be alone and in trouble. So in the elf's mind, thoughts took the following order: find and save Osiris of the missionary, secondly, find the real responsible for this situation.

For the simple, ordinary people's mind, reality and fantasy were difficult to discern. Leaving only a miscellany of lies, untruths, fears and confusions. Demystifying myths always motivated Jupita and her master Darkay. And she used to state that obligation. The obligation of seeking enlightenment and/or power.

The platoon was still firmly on her trail. Suddenly, up ahead, a tree fell and blocked the chase. From one side of the trail came a dwarf, tying the dual blade axe to his back, and she could see the ornate hammer already on the clip. It was Morgrinald.

"Come."

With the noise of horses getting louder, the dwarf decided ask questions later.

The dust and the foliage raised during the fall of the big tree inhibited a definition of faces for the soldiers, they could only see the silhouettes. Stan, thinking it could be the murderer and her accomplice, he prepared the crossbow but his shot was deflected by the leader with a slap on his elbow.

"We need answers, not more dead."

"Don't forget what the old man said, captain." Stan replied. "The dead are rising, captain."

"Even you believe in the superstitions of an ignorant?"

While they were talking, July turned away and violently stuck the horse's stirrup. In the sudden burst, she had enough space to jump over the fallen tree, and the others went around and continued chasing the fugitives.

"Why the rush skinny?" Morgrinald was on a horse behind by the lady elf, the situation really overwhelmed and bothered him more than the forced intimacy of his hands around her waist.

"And Sartre?"

"The old man is back to his land. Why bother?"

Morgrinald remembered the promise he made to his friend, the woodcutter, and was embarrassed for almost forgetting.

"And Sartre?"

Morgrinald hated it when people played deaf and dumb, so he decided not to answer.

"Who is chasing us?" the dwarf grumbled.

"They will lose us."

She made a sudden turn and went through a side trail amid the trees and thickets.

"No, they won't." Morgrinald could still see them riding with excellence, they were cavalry, not peasants. "Dedicated fans… What the hell did you do?"

Darkay's disciple let go of the reins, opened her arms and lowered her body to the horse's mane. Morgrinald, expecting an accident, gritted his teeth and held on firmly to her.

The soldiers went around the turn following the cloud of dust raised by horse running loose, and exactly because of this cover, they could not see that the rider was missing. From up in the trees, actually floating above them, Jupita, with the heavy dwarf hanging from her waist, could see the immensity of all that green. People died easily and for all sorts of reasons in the forests, because of animals or the weather. The lack of water or food also produced their dead. Hence why the journeys were made in daylight. It seems that the "Knight of Hope", faced with so much green and danger, was his own pioneer. Suddenly, the faint smell of smoke revealed his relative position. There was a wisp of smoke coming from very far away from the village, on a trail that Jupita acknowledged even at that angle. The she focused on that point. The bluish glow, already present on her body, intensified and the lady elf began to float against the wind. Not floating, she was actually flying. In the effort, her body became paler, skin more transparent, slightly showing her veins. Jupita had grown older and she knew it. It was what happened to her people, her race. They slowly lost weight and density.

On the trail, the soldiers reached the horse and Nery easily recaptured the docile and tired animal.

"He's exhausted."

"Spread out. Remember your training."

"Was it a lady elf?"

"Seems so…"

"But, come on… Elves don't steal. They don't care about money or possessions."

"We'll see."

Above, already close to the source of the smoke, there was a clearing opened by dead trees, on the edge of a pond. When the mute dwarf felt the earth under his feet, he let go slowly from the elf's waistline only then he opened his eyes and mouth.

"Humph! Was that necessary?"

The shadow on the elf's face said yes with weight and seriousness. No longer needing it, Jupita got rid of the peasant's hood and threw it upward where a gale of wind carried it away.

Morgrinald listened attentively to what the lady elf had to say as they walked. Just in case, the experienced warrior let elf walk ahead while he covered their tracks.

However, far from what was thought of someone so bold, Tristan, the young missionary, was camped. He was found relaxing, hands behind his head, with a square hat covering his eyes and a leg cocked up with a thin sting tied to his big toe, stretching into the pond being constantly tugged. Suddenly a violent tug ripped him screaming out his resting position. The makeshift hat dropped aside and he was violently pulled into the water. He turned around quickly but his weapon was already out of reach, so he began to dig into the ground trying to stop, but the fish was much bigger than his hunger, he even imagined its size.

Right then, Morgrinald stepped firmly on the fabric rope and Jupita cut it with a dry move of her sword.

"I guess I was lucky." Tristan thought out loud. "the fabric broke off."

To get up, he limped sorely and patted himself to remove excess dirt from the already dirty smock and looked angrily at the pond. Only then he saw the lady elf and the dwarf walking together in his direction. He keeled and thank them smiling, saying:

"My trials were rewarded."

With a dryness that was not hers, Jupita inquired:

"Who are you? And what are you doing camping here, with a village so close? From your clothes, I see you are not poor."

"I was told of two elves in this region. Do you know about them?" he asked the dwarf in his own language.

Morgrinald was impressed and also offended by the coarse accent. He certainly learned from the dwarfs of the north, he thought. His clan never got along with them.

"Speak your language. Your language." the dwarf warned, pointing a finger at him.

"Oh! How nice, a mountain dwarf. I was told that you were ill tempered."

"Hey! I'm not ill tempered."

"My northern friends taught me your language."

"Lan-gua-ge? Humph! They speak a dialect you idiot, a dialect!"

"They also said you would say that."

"Okay. Do you have a name, idiot?"

"I'm the Minister of hope. Knight of mercy…"

"Priest." Jupita and Morgrinald said in unison, looking at each other.

"Yes. On a mission. I came here to rid the people of the village of a vampire and her damn followers. So…"

"Quiet. We have company." Jupita said and drew her sword.

Only elves could hear that well and clearly. The dwarf had his doubts, however. How could they remain sane listening to so many sounds at the same time?

Morgrinald pulled his ax and hit it on his feet, freeing some of the extra weight of the mud from the journey. But the elves weren't the only race with abilities. With his bare feet on the ground, he could sense clearly the vibration of the trotting, its cadence, rhythm, weight, and above all, how many.

"Horses?" Tristan asked about a minute later.

"Humph! I hate horses. Horses, birds and you, busty. Every time I follow you, I end up in trouble."

From her half smile, he noticed she appreciated the joke.

"Wait, they sound like heavy horses." Jupita repositioned herself. They were coming from the opposite side of the echo.

"Or they are loaded, long ears." Morgrinald realized that they reduced the pace and opened in two files in arrow before they became into sight.

Tristan was even happier when he recognized the royal insignia on the soldiers' garments. He then put a hand on the elf's shoulder and stepped ahead of the dwarf.

"Halt!" the captain said to the company and the trio stopped immediately. "What is happening here? Answer in the name of the king."

"I am Tristan, emissary of hope, knight of mercy and lord of justice. I'm here on a mission."

"We know who you are mister Ivanov." July mocked.

"And what about them?" Ellan glanced around quickly and consider them to the be only ones there.

"Captain, I'm Morgrinald of the blood of Keldorn, the clan bearing the stigma of the Battle Hammers." The experienced dwarf said staring into her eyes, being careful not to be prepotent.

"You recognize my rank? Admirable."

"And you?" she asked the lady elf.

"Disciple of Darkay of Almokaryr, just an elf… By any chance the envoys of the king are here to help solve the disappearances issue?"

"Something like that." Stan replied promptly.

"Stan." Ellan said, without looking back.

But he ignored her and continued to speak.

"An elf stole the captain's horse and ran into the woods. Do you know anything about that?"

"Actually…" she shouted just to interrupt him and went back talking in a milder tone "We lost the trail, without a confirmation of his identity, but there were some ethnic similarities." captain Hanverovich tried to politely correct fearing that an accusation without clear evidence against a people so ancient and noble could cause.

"Obviously he jumped off with his partner." Stan said staring at the dwarf.

Morgrinald took a step toward the human with an inquisitive gaze.

"You have something to say big man?"

"Stan." this time she was firmer. "Help July with the horses. Refresh them."

His behavior was inadequate. She was in command and he had to respect her. At the right moment, when it was all over, she would report him to her superiors and have him locked up for a few days.

"Please forgive the heated officer Hanverovich, it has been less than a day since we found the victims of a massacre."

The captain continued staring at the suspects impassive and the dwarf added in lower, though still audible tone when they passed towards the water:

"Two captains in one platoon. Military structure is quite different nowadays."

Stan shrugged. He preferred that than killing him in front of everyone. That was the law of direct offense. He had the moral right to do it.

"A massacre indeed. They were ambushed on the road and it seems it happened last night."

"Night travelers?" Morgrinald asked himself, but it came out aloud.

"Maybe shortly before sunrise. The village of Miller is immersed in terror."

"The village has been helpless since we left?" Jupita could not believe the nobles disregard. Sartre was right.

"I can't answer for something I don't know elf. So you are the hired adventurers. What happened to the other elf and the woman?"

"Why would you need another long ear when you have me, officer?" the dwarf answered rapidly expecting a scene from the lady elf.

"Very well. It's okay." by the betrayed expression on the elf's face, he was surely dead. "Morgrinald, we know the bravery of your clan because one of yours lived a long time with the king's great-grandfather. Their deeds together are legendary. Please excuse the lack of manners. To my right are Lucrecia, Nery, Endoli. Refreshing the horses we have July, the recruits Edgar and Lico. And mounted, the talkative captain

Hanverovich. And I'm captain Ellan, I was recently nominated to lead a patrol in this area."

"Soldiers? Adventurers? Now that we are over with the presentation protocol, follow me." Tristan said, already on his horse and before any word or interruption, shot in front of the group.

Tristan Ivanov rode with difficulty, because of the boil on his ass. What saved him was a doubly cushioned saddle, and his combat clothes. Actually a leather chest piece with burlap sowed inside and full of fleas.

The night before, he washed it and left it to dry on a tree fork above the fire until the rotten wood gave way dropping it into the flames. He woke up in a panic with the smoke, grabbed the supplies bag as it was the only thing he had, and beat the flames until they were extinguished. The bag was destroyed and the saddle was padded, that was all it was good for anyway. Further padding the saddle. In the morning, he was awaken by small and noisy animals stealing his fruits and jerked meat that had been in the bag. Without an alternative, he used what was left of the bag to produce a fishing line, and because of his sore backside, he had to lain to avoid falling asleep again, he tied the line to this big toe.

"Then along comes the damn big fish and almost takes it off. What else could happen?" Tristan was the kind of person that talked to himself all the time. "I prefer to think that the gods impose such adversities, such conspiracy, only upon the chosen ones."

He glanced quickly behind him and seeing that he was still in front, he continued talking to himself.

"The chain of events were linked to produce this moment. Because of the boil, I can only ride a little and for a short time. Result: I had to stop. The fleas made me remove the clothes that I had worn for less than a month and a half. But now, even burned, it serves as protection to the terrible pain in my buttocks. And, as I donated my change of clothes at the village, I learned about the damn vampire. And today, with my mass costume, the gods saw that my cause was solid and so they presented me with the help of two divine illustrious champion races and a platoon of soldiers of the king." Without realizing, he reduced his speed. "I only didn't understand the sign of the fish dragging me, so I must quiet down and contemplate the truth of that sign and suddenly be illuminated with that knowledge."

At sunset they had already set up camp almost at the other end of the pond. The soldiers soon divided the chores among themselves.

"Recruits? To me. You too lady elf. Let's find food."

Jupita saw the opportunity to continue tracking her friend and followed without protest.

Morgrinald had slept too much on the 'flying boredom.' Definitely, boats of any size or purpose were unpleasant, and quite tedious. That's why he pretended to sleep. If the soldiers were smart they would catch the curious doe prowling around there for breakfast. Well, the lady elf went with them, so there was no chance. The dwarf then pulled discreetly the cord around his neck and opened the small box and smelled the scent of his beloved land, his most precious treasure. However, his memory wandering was short lived, because Tristan, got up in a jolt and left. Maybe he went for food, or, most likely, was going to relief himself at the pond side, but Morgrinald always… Eternally suspicious, he followed him. In a few minutes he realized that the fool only wanted to get rid of his previous meal, walking with his legs tight together and farting.

And as Morgrinald would never, in his life, guard a man shitting, he decided to follow ahead and entertained himself watching the shape and color of the stones and checking their hardness by stomping heavily on them. He also felt the smell of the soil, a trait, an addiction of his race. Always in search of riches. He sniffled complaining to himself about this habit and the sum of his observations lead north where a cluster of rocks, at the margins of the water, seemed to watch its forward or backward movement. Morgrinald loved rocks. He was one of the few dwarfs able to read their age and precise their formation. Those dark and round ones had interesting samples so he decided to climb and surrounded himself of hard stones because it would give him a good and nostalgic feeling of a soft and innocent time. In peace, he could revise his goals and establish immediate priorities. From there, the sight of the pond was really stupendous. The golden shine of the sun on the water and everything else. He saw the camp and everyone clearly, a privileged observation post, strategic even. Soldiers in charge of finding firewood had already returned to camp. Then he felt something else with his bare feet…

Something incredible, really huge raised from the bottom of the lake and did it in a slow and agonizing way, like the death of dwarfs by old age. Green long branches revealed heads that moved in the air like reeds in the water. By the pressure on the bottom of the pond, it was something tall, higher than houses and smaller than fort walls. One the heads that occasionally skinned its thorny teeth with long necks connected to a single mud covered block, moved silently towards the camp.

Suddenly a dense swarm of bats passed over him and smeared the sky, a thick and noisy mass that gave life to Dominescu's delusional speech: "Black wings infest the morning, teeth glide over the water…"

"Shit!" Morgrinald jumps from the top of the stones and runs through the trail. "Run father! Move your ass."

In the water… Slowly, the rotten and heavy tuft, pulsating and mobile islet, shed more blood in its own veins as soon as the long tail, ended in an oar propelled forward the two thirds of ton figure. The desire for something to eat was vibrant, intense. A group by the water. It will do… Thus, it prepared the ruse, hiding its many heads and mouths in murky water. Expertly, it moved forward slowly. Its powerful muscles, accustomed with the weight of the water made inertia an easy tool for thrusting or braking. The current ran from one side to another without noticing its impotence compared to the water titan. Two curious heads extended their eyes over the water. The hunger was the same, they shared the same stomach, but there is no way of predicting instinct. The fin caused a slight twitch in the water when braking. One of its future victims was looking at the water. She closed her eyes quickly inhibiting like that the possibility of noticing the danger and the opportunity to escape. Even at striking distance, the mistake could be ignored, but never forgotten. The meters ahead were devoured with intense calm, the prey that watched the water gave up, a common mistake of this species. The beast moved on, the hunger was dizzying. None of the mouths thought of postponing the banquet. It had been months since its last meal and the amount of these biped specimens at the water's edge was unusual.

Other specimens of the group hollered in their vibrant language. She had heard them before and that was why she had to move fast. The cold blood received a new burst of adrenaline, the veins reopened and the muscles warmed up in no time and with this, other more meters were devoured. Throats cracked, apprehensive tongues for sucking lives, even from the bones, whipped meekly the air to savor the scent of prey as they hissed.

In the camp, laziness slowly left Nery's body. Endoli started an extensive and outrageous stretch, making Lucrecia shudder and wake up scared.

July was the only one who just opened her eyes with Lucrecia's turmoil and hostile mumblings. July turned, put her hands under her head and watched the clouds, which seemed to be committed of the same laziness. One of those white ladies stretched, ripped and produced other forms until being ran over by another cloud. With that, its fragments are assimilated by other, more willing clouds. Everywhere you could hear the insectivorous agitation, chorus of crickets, a populous senate of claimants and absolutely hidden in their own corners and areas.

Endoli suddenly ran naked and foolishly spewing water everywhere. Lucrecia, who had already washed herself, shrunk to escape the sudden and icy water. Soon, Endoli, the naked and featherless duck, plunged in.

"You didn't have to strive to be ridiculous you pathetic and childish man." Lucrecia said grouchily. "What are you thinking? That you are in a epic fantasy adventure, you are in the army my dear, the army."

Instead of answering, Endoli simply came up showing his feet, navel and mouth spitting water while he floated. Lucrecia let out a smile and couldn't resist:

"Stupid creature."

She then kicked the water, opening a spray over Endoli's face. Then she jumped on the fool.

On the margin, July lost herself in the sounds, the crickets transported her to the year before. A time of bare feet, thin belly, bony and with bleeding hands from cutting sugar cane. She lain on the fallen mount, admiring the sky and the birds in the crying tree, announcing the end of the day. Suddenly she sprang up. Something was wrong.

"Oh my… What a nap. Better saying, 'stupor'. I heard nothing to wake me up. What time is it?" Nery asked with a crumpled sleepy face.

"Morning! That was the matter. It was morning!"

July stood up like a meerkat looking in every direction.

"Nature calls, right young one? Here." Nery gave her a torn piece of fabric. "Always avoid the broad and slightly frilly leaves, my ass was sore for days…"

"Quiet!"

"I'm sorry. Didn't mean to embarrass you."

Suddenly, on the other side from where Lucrecia and Endoli played, a school of small fish jumped and swam away. The crickets became silent. Suddenly she noticed a tuft of roots and sprouts moving slowly.

Unfortunately, far from there, Morgrinald and Tristan ran by the margin, they jumped over rocks and sandbanks and continued running. Seeing the futility of it, Morgrinald reduced his pace because besides his short legs the soil there was soft. He moved away from the margin and started running again through the bushes.

"Through here, you shit." He yelled to Tristan who joined him promptly. "There is mud and quicksand there. Go, you will arrive first. Warn them!"

Tristan, being much lighter than the armored barefooted dwarf, disappeared between the reeds and tall grasses, of course he could get lost, but it didn't matter, he had to focus on what he had to do. The dwarf had to remember what to do in this kind of situation because he couldn't remember ever facing a being like that in the past. Creatures of the water people were not enemies of his kind, but neither were they friends. The neutrality generated a natural distance between them, so… it generated a dangerous oversight. He wasn't even sure if it was a water creature or a monster swimming in it.

"Lucrecia, Endoli! Get out of the water!" July screamed in face of the looming danger.

"What…" Endoli inquired with his hair over his face.

The tuft bulged from the center and, as it spread, mud and mistletoe ran over a greenish gray, semi-transparent hump that opened to reveal a pupil.

"Shit!" Keldorn's grandson said frustrated through his teeth. While he thought about that, he continued to advance. Even if it was an sentient being, there were no guarantees. He was lost in that sense.

The beast surrounded the soldiers in the water with its heads. And now they shrieked petrified at the cruel surprise. Obviously, they screamed for the dwarf. The big mouth of such a terrible beast close to your stomach was enough to make them cry.

"Think you idiot, think." Morgrinald punched himself trying to concentrate.

"If it was a sentient being of the water, would it negotiate a safe passage for the ones in the water?" Keldorn's grandson had to be cold, analyze and act fast. Even from that distance, he noticed three other heads coming out of the muck spewing water and vapor.

Hearing the screams in the water, Nery ran to her sword, but something slimy hit her when she turned around, making her roll. And now she moaned unconscious.

The dwarf tried to evaluate what would be best. If the creature thought it was worthy of the flesh of the idiots in the water, there was nothing he could do. The meal was laid and served. There was, however, some hope… The dwarf hoped that the creature deemed itself superior and with an inflated ego, expected other treats.

However, there was turmoil and despair in and outside the circle of heads. An additional and unnecessary excitation. He knew that that gave it a huge penalty, after all, stumbling and screaming delineate the area and the others participated in one of those purest states: they would either run or mobilize themselves. The indecision however, was a useful advantage to the multi headed predator. Endoli, surrounded by the immense body, was knocked down and, before he could recover, one of the heads came out of the water and swallowed him by his legs. While he screamed in horror and pain, there was a new bite, this time, up to his stomach. The lustful eyes of the beast were semi closed in ocular contortions of pure pleasure. The damn thing would prolong that in order to appreciate the taste of the meat and the acrid taste of the blood.

At this point the terror dissipated. July took the curved tipped knife stuck by the dying campfire. She was the only one who could do something and the fear was much smaller than the responsibility to do so. She had to rescue the dying body from the big mouth. July felt her blood boil while she ran into the water. However one of the vigilant heads contorted its neck quickly down to the water surface and a reptilian whip motion on the water hit July and launched her over the water producing a spray of water until she hit the margin.

July got up with her hands over her stomach and retreated. She realized there was no way to rescue them…

For the creature, the strange surrounded flesh exuded a whiff of terrified fear and such odor fanned even more the pleasure of the heads. Two of them, in fact, the closest and more interested ones, watched each other. Impulsively, they struck almost at the same time. In the struggle, the flesh and bones break easily, like hard mud thrown on the ground with nerves snapping like watercress stalks. A third jaw smiled at the fleshy leftovers and chewed with slow and depraved manners. The lookout migrated to the middle of the feast and with a brave gesture, butted another neck and hissed to it gutturally. They fought quickly and the other one accepted the post of lookout. With the victim's forearm exposed, with a silly expression of satiety, it rolled with its tongue the piece stuck in its teeth and chewed again.

At the margin, July vomited feverishly. The blow had hurt her gravely and now she fought to remain conscious. She tried to drag herself, however, the reflux and the pain outweigh any other action.

Suddenly, a shadow slowly gained the shore and the water and, when it approached the beast, one of its ugly heads looked up and snarled at it.

In the sky, Jupita came in at low speed, although constant, the impressive figure targeted the beast with airs of a challenge. Majestic and solemn and, above all, sure of her powers and duties to humanity.

From the ground to the hands of this august representative of the people of the air, it was possible to see clear air whirling fillets in a light trail behind her. And, above everyone, immense and dense clouds were piling up and turning dark. Crashing into each other as if answering obediently to the elf's body, which in the meantime revealed, even during the day, an extensive and bluish glow.

Heavy footfalls are heard on the ground and a scream followed and, as the speed increased, it became a long curse, a blunt outrage. Captain Stanislaw Hanverovich ran to the campfire and kicked violently the top of the lit stack. Shards, soot and fire flew forward in a short arc and this hail of fragments, of carbonized wood and incandescent wood surprised and terrorized the multi-headed monster.

"Fire?" Stan smiled, picked up three flaming stick without delay and in a spin, pitched them against the beast.

The projectiles hit the semi devoured body and the head chewing on it. The head retreated terrorized in a jolt. However, the fire on the sticks was extinguished by the water.

Stanislaw Hanverovich, the daring and deranged man, didn't give up. Fitted with two burning firewood logs, began to rotate them beautifully around himself in sometimes tight, sometimes loose circles, walking toward the enemy. The offensive-defensive rotations turned the embers into flames. His ambidexterity guaranteed a magnificent and cadenced long stripes of fire.

In the beast's mind, things flashed by and fear approached. It was inevitable to draw away. Fire was never water's friend, and they killed each other frequently. Was this its time to die? No. Definitely. Not like this, neither by such a weak fire. But withdrawing from such possibility was the right thing to do, and, above all, a ruse to the confident attacker, now entering the water. Retreat and bring him to his death. Step by step he… Although the scam is fatal, the swirl of the human caused a noticeable pleasure in the flames, and the fire began to leap slightly. That meant something and she mother of water, the beast, reptile, understood, but how much did that matter? Soon the soldier would stuff her stomach. The fool with strong arms walked firmly, completely unaware of its ingenious farce. Unaware like all the others, except for the flying biped. She had to be quick, drown the ones she could, then flee with them and savor them later.

In the sky, a single cloud somewhere well above the elf, grew furiously. The shock against other clouds in its path made a brutal sound. There was some time left to flee, however, hunger insisted the beast risk further more. Just a little more while the bold human came towards her… He will die.

Suddenly the muti-headed beast felt the water vibrate. The vibration came from the soil below the water. Was there another from the ancient race? She thought. But for her to feel him there, he must possess a huge power. A guardian? But where? With this new one, danger was real and she had mere seconds to flee and even less time for another strike. Her hurried retreat magnified the human's prowess with the fire and, with this pomp, therefore, was more careless. It was easy for one of her conscious, one of her conscious heads, but now she was afraid. The human was no longer sinking… the ground rose and his steps became firmer. By the action of a guardian or one of the ancients connected to the immutable, hateful earth.

The weight of the mother of the water while retreating would create ditches where she may stumble, and become helpless, vulnerable. And none of that happened. Instead of ditches, holes, a plain and regular terrain. Without the ignoble human knowing, he had the aid of a guardian. Suddenly, the human holding the fire raced aggressively, in a stunning muscle explosion. With his heavy footsteps over her body, he hit one of her thinking heads. Another head was knocked out when it was hit and pinned down by a heavy tree that fell from one of the margins, partially inhibiting her movements. Then a second flame hit her, making her scream and lose another head. The human had beaten one of her consciousness but there was no time for retaliation. She had to retreat and free the pinned head before…

A lightning bolt ran through the fallen trunk and shot brutally her muscles and then she heard the thunder… The damn air one evoked a storm and now the fallen wood burned from inside out. She had to liquefy the immobilized before her entire body was condemned. The water vibrated, her fried, her element denounced the arrival of the ancient and hidden being. The guardian was on the margin, but not there with the humans, he was a bit farther. The haste helped liquefy the dead consciousness, however, the human was still trying to strike it and, even though there was little fire, such moves hurt but in a reflex, one of the consciousnesses hit his body and threw him onto the fallen trunk. Great! That way the cursed air one couldn't stop her. If another lightning struck the trunk, it will toast the human. By the weight of the trunk in the water, the beast realized that the person who insisted in its anonymity was about to reveal himself. But she would prevail…

Suddenly, she was hit by an incessant volley of small rocks that bothered more than hurt. There was no way of measuring the level of expertise or age of the bold hidden one. It was an alert. One that could be ignored, the fallen human was hers. Then a second and third volleys intended almost to the same places and, where they grazed the thick leather, it suddenly began to shred and tear. Even all her eyes could not find him. He toppled the tree and nothing else. If it's a guardian, he does act strangely for one. Usually they tended to show part of their power, using only the power over one of their two elements. Then they would make their entrance, a common intimidation strategy. If the second element was water, would she already been hit? The guardian may not even know of her new condition. Worse, maybe he didn't care. Too many thoughts, she had to concentrate. Having many consciousnesses sometimes caused this kind of conflict.

On the ground, the silt was overturned. The earth foolishly pinned one of her paws and if she freed it, another was held down. That made the mother of water think. The one acting from afar probably came from the immutable womb of the earth and it was just a nuisance, an obstacle. She should therefore, concentrate on the flying biped because if another lightning were to strike, it may be more than a warning. Suddenly a new burst of stones hit her and as she had no arms, she shielded herself with one of the heads already scratched and injured close to the abdomen. Meanwhile, one of her powerful fin was stopped. However, before she could free it, an immense trench opened behind her. When she moved back, she lost her balance momentarily and the paw was suddenly released, furthering even more the stumble. Incredible and amazingly strange the continuity of the inappropriate but efficient actions of the concealed foe. But could she be blind? The human was fallen there, in front of everyone… Clear… Well above, standing out! Could this earth creature be a victim of the demon of madness who spared no one? A mere member of humanity rendered helpless, in the middle of combat, and not for a moment there was a retreat or doubt. Terrible… Doubly terrible, too grotesque, thought the great worm. Whoever is hidden on the margin has forgotten his role as protector. The body of the passed out human, hung high, almost falling into the shallow water. Certainly bones would break, but he seemed uninterested. He wanted blood. All of a sudden she felt the weight of wood in the water again and its awesome power was shown. The fallen trunk of almost 20 meters was pushed against the hydra's body where dense branches stuck in various places. All the eyes closed in sudden pain without really making out the attacker.

The strength used in that effort, didn't even steal a sound. If the tree had its roots in the earth, it didn't matter. Finally the plot was revealed. It wasn't just one of the ancient beings, a master of his element. It was no doubt his element and being or not a Guardian, he was definitely experienced.

On the trunk, the human was very close to the ground... His fainted body slid limply on the surface of the stem but was incredibly sustained by the flames that erupted from the trunk. The human of powerful arms, foolish confidence, now unconscious, was supported and caressed by the flames, without being burned, actually they seem to like him and with his sudden rise the flames grew. The beast, only her, seemed to see the danger of that, and walked away with her superior traction and speed in the water, and when she dived, her escape was complete.

She knew she had almost died... She was almost obliterated, however, she was successful in taking the bodies she had killed. The beast distanced herself, now free and, above all, aware that the greatest danger of all was not the guardian or the master of the immutable earth or the strong flying creature, but what was with them. Seeing and knowing the danger represented by this 'flammable' made her heads smile and laugh with malice and wickedness.

BEGINNING OF THE END

"Report! What happened here?" Ellan could see the huge burning tree fallen over the water. Obviously a lightning from the thunder she heard in the woods before seeing the elf run back to camp. "Why Lucrecia and Endoli took the horses?"

The captain was sitting watching the fire on the trunk and seemed spent. For a moment Ellan's heart accelerated imagining that Endoli and Lucrecia were underneath the trunk, but there was no sign of that.

"Are you okay?" Captain Ellan asked landing her hand on the officer's shoulder.

Stan relived the battle in his mind, and looking at the fire seemed to stir even more this memory, hearing the captain made him even more dismayed. And the flames on the trunk seemed to accompany his outrage. Because it was a stupid question to ask. After all, half of the group was killed by a legendary monster. A mythical beast, thus, inexistent to the community, but with very real teeth and armor. What could he tell her, who saw none of that insanity? The rain washed all the evidence of the battle and the bodies of his fellow soldiers were gone forever. To Stan that was a point of no return. Who would believe? Not even those who survived believed the gruesome truth. The "fact" full of teeth and heads that devoured flesh came sneaking through the water. What he felt near death in front of the multi-headed titan, against the hydra, bordered on the impossible and was running over the boundaries of hatred. With that anger in his throat, his eyes were burning and he saw nothing. Logically, the pain he felt was from the blow and from the fall later. Throat and eyes affected by the smoke and the rest was…

"Officer? How do you feel?" Ellan insisted.

"I'm fine." Was all he said.

"Hey busty! What happened here?" the dwarf asked, arriving gasping, as if his lungs were about to jump out his chest.

From the corner of his eye, he targeted the trembling man with sacerdotal clothes and without holding back, attacked:

"Things could be better if the little priest hadn't got lost. The most this idiot did after raising his robe and show his bent scrawny legs, was run like a lizard with its legs opened.

"You should know sir, that since I was a young man…"

"… like a girl" the dwarf corrected sarcastically.

"… I was always a good runner."

"You ran from anyone, right, you…"

"I demand respect."

"Respect? Do you know what it means or only the pronunciation?"

"At least I ran better that you with those…"

"Those, what?" It was clear that Tristan spoke of the dwarf's short legs, but allowing his mouth to say such insult would be suicide, and silencing in these cases would be leaving him to imagine the end of the sentence, something equally harmful to one's health. So he continued. "Armor parts. Yes, that's it. Do you ever consider taking them off?"

"The little priest running like that was hilarious! Like he had shit himself."

Tristan folded his arms and pouted like a disdainful child.

"My dear friend, I don't believe that was why I dropped behind." he raised his knee and shook his leg while looking at the dwarf's thick but short legs.

"Listen to me, you piece of shit, you lost yourself on the way back. An idiot incapable of coming back over his own foot prints!"

"The why did you follow me?"

"Followed?" Morgrinald inquired quickly and dismissively.

"If a fool leads the way, what is the one that follows?"

"Okay." offended, the dwarf cracked his knuckles. "It's time for a cranial massage." But in a glance, he realized the lady elf stumbling. "Jupita?"

The elf fell slowly, and Keldorn's grandson supported her with a hand behind the neck of the brave lady, but she didn't even touch the ground, just floated.

"Is it over?" she babbled with a, although fixed, look. Maybe she was talking with the guide of the dying.

Even if she was talking to someone else, Morgrinald, with a bitter glare in his onyx eyes, replied.

"Yes."

Fainted in the air, except for her robes a bluish luminescence covered her skin. Where the contrast of brightness with her skin caused curious colors, but to the dwarf, the situation stirred other questions. Questions interrupted by the visible fluctuation. A light breeze passed through everyone followed by chaotic gusts of wind.

"Jupita! No!" Morgrinald was desperate as he hadn't felt in a long time. Without control over her powers and her light weight, the elf would be thrown upwards by her own powers then the fall would do the rest. So he jumped on her, hoping the density of his body would hold her down. The soldiers, not knowing what to expect from that situation followed suit, however, her ability to carry weight without reducing her height, was amazing.

A few meters away from them, Keldorn's grandson saw the captain staring, but his stare was something more than just disdain, however, suddenly he threw a rope over them.

"Tie her." his imperative voice was enough for the soldiers to obey without blinking. While they carried out his order, the captain tied the other end of the rope to a tree.

Meanwhile, unaware of what was happening, July brought the horse blanket and put it over Nery who was burning with fever, after using a damp cloth to clean her face of slime. That was all she could do, she knew no antidotes against poisons neither did she have enough faith for a simple prayer that may have a miraculous effect. With her hand still on her friend's forehead, she ran her eyes over the camp. The foreigner was in a similar situation as Nery, but the attention given to her was absurd. But she decided no to argue about it. Taking care of the wounded after the battle, regardless of status or side, was the right thing for a good soldier to do. She opened passage between them with her shoulders, then saw the strange fluctuation and the rope around the lady elf's waist and without delay, put another dry blanket over her. And curiously, whether by comfort or weight, the lady elf came back down.

"What's wrong with her?"

"Age. Just age." actually it was a way the dwarfs used to say that someone was dying.

Captain Ellan moved away from the group and watched the pond and the birds soaring. Whatever happened, it took place without her presence. Taking the lady elf with her on a hunt was a way of separating her from the group and interrogating her discreetly. How Hanverovich didn't notice the simple stratagem? She acted according to protocol. Divide to control. Every aspiring officer knew this. It was even easier for him, he started out as an ensign. For her, because she was a woman, she started at a lower level. To harden the soul, they said. Whatever the case, her recruit days were hard and she was lucky to raise through the ranks so quickly. She did what it took to conquer and keep the leadership. In her understanding, leading was not only telling people what to do, but a complex enneagram made of several egos. And facing so many different egos was maybe the greatest of all challenges and ignoring that would be like losing this opportunity. But how to deal with someone so intense and sensitive as captain Hanverovich without offending his honor, without diminishing her legitimate authority? After all, they held identical hierarchical levels separated only by a direct order from high command. Ellan would lead.

And now, given the lack of answers to her questions, she concluded that July and the captain were colluding with about Nery's wounds and the desertion of soldiers Endoli and Lucrecia. The defectors took the horses so they could not be followed, thus the journey back would be long. They had a civilian and two members of foreign races, therefore questioning, imposing and punishing would be a breach of decorum, a rude military act.

"Raise camp, we're leaving immediately." Ellan said loudly and they all nodded silently. She went to the captain. "Captain Stanislaw Hanverovich, where are the others?"

What could Stan say? All he knew was that it wasn't him who put out the campfire neither the drizzle, but the elf's flyby. He still remembers the anguish of the unbreathable air, the sand and thin clay of the margin swirling. The woman of the air race had the power of the legends told by the old ones. And out of nowhere, he found out he hated her deeply, for her attitude and even existence. Something as big as the hate for the mother of water. Too many events spun in his fearful and uncertain mind. Thus, he only said:

"They are gone."

"Where to, and by who's order?" Provoking was not her way, but Ellan believed it might work in this situation.

"I wasn't in charge." a growing hatred began to take him over. Thinking about it, he was one step away from losing control, he felt the blood boiling, but suddenly, he took control of it.

"Says who? Better yet: what do you mean by that?"

"I already said." Stan guessed the next questions and scanned the area with his eyes in search of possible battle scars, but the rain brought by the lady elf washed all the evidence.

"That's enough sir." Ellan's voice went up a tone. "You're an officer and as such you should show discipline carrying out your duties. If we were assigned to the same patrol I doubt it was for us to argue all the time!"

Julie pressed her lips unable to blink. She seemed mad. She could tell Captain Ellan the sad fate of Endoli and Lucrecia in the mouths of that monster, but she was trying to keep her sanity. Her short and high pitched breathing on behalf of the horror, and with a shaky and low voice tried to speak to them:

"Nery needs help… She has been poisoned."

"By whom, in the name of the king? Do you have anything to do with this?"

The vivid image of the multi-headed beast in Stan's memory made his skin boil with hatred.

"Somehow? Yes." If Stan hadn't followed secretly Ellan and the lady elf, who he thought to be the thief and had something to do with the old man's assassination, he would have awakened in the middle of the night to check the vigil and they would have been up before sunrise.

"July? Please tell me what happened! I'm fed up of excuses. Was it desertion?"

Desertion was a capital offense. Deserters, when found, were hang without trial. But she saw nothing, she was only certain of their deaths. She heard the sound of bones and death. July decided to remain quiet. The officers were responsible for that terrible encounter. Besides, all they did was stare and challenge each other, the act of commanding was left in second place.

"The implications are the responsibility of those in charge." Stand said in her place. "Whatever it was… July is exempt."

The captain's defense surprised July. However, when she looked at poor Nery, a victim of such insane encounter, she kept her opinion. Someone will pay for Nery and the others. And surely the desertion carried more weight and truth than the attack of an 'inexistent' monster. She would be treated like a madwoman, or worse, an accomplice in desertion or assassination.

"You will be considered guilty, captain!"

"Ma'am?"

"You didn't follow regulation." Ellan crossed her arms behind her back and continued. "When you made camp, you did not establish a perimeter…"

"… You left!"

He was right and Ellan was nervous beneath her neutral face forming questions inadequately. She had fought hard for her current rank and everything else up to there.

The desertion of half of her soldiers under her command would generate problems and consequences that she didn't even want to consider. Now she would put politics aside and keep the authority invested in her.

"What does it matter? You think you are exempt of your responsibilities? While I set up the perimeter, you should have overseen the fire and…"

"And it was done."

Stan owed her respect and if she could avoid this stupid discussion it would be like giving up. Thus she decided to assume a more emphatic and rigid posture.

"The fact is that you should have not followed us."

"I followed by suspicion." He did not forget the lady thief and he still believed it was Jupita and needed evidence.

"A foreigner." she corrected.

"That also."

"You broke the nations hospitality protocol."

"I respectfully disagree."

Ellan paused. The words and the discussion seem to be controlled. Reason now emerged, so she let him conclude.

"Officer or civilian has the civic and especially, morale duty, to keep an eye out for misdemeanors and felonies."

"What are you getting to? Say it."

Stan didn't even lower his gaze, he was intimately stunned with the disarray of his faculties. Unfortunately the patrol captain and leader believed that his actions were just prideful and decided to shut up.

"No? Good. Then we will talk in the presence of our superiors. All I want to know…" she came very close to him and whispered. "Does the dwarf and lady elf have implications in what happened?"

It was clear. The captain kept the protocol of politeness and respect to foreigners and individuals of other lands, even when she bordered confusion. Maybe his sister in arms still remembered the horse theft, thus, a subtle way of admitting that she had her doubts.

Stanislaw Hanverovich's eyes smiled and deep inside, it reassured him somewhat, and he only shook his head negatively.

"Lord Morgrinald? What do you know?"

"I'm sorry captain, I know as much as you. Besides, forgive me for what I'm about to say, but…"

He took a breath to make sure everyone was listening and hollered:

"Quiet." with his fingertips on his temples, he spoke with no reservations. "Mother fuckers! Look around, do you need an audit of who's responsible? Ok. Register the information carefully while we take care of the living, of those present." The mucus released by the Mother of the Water paralyzed and maddened. If he was right, the soldier standing was paralyzed and the fallen one was in the second stage of poisoning. He remembered Sartre and his craft. "We have urgent things to take care of."

"I Agree."

"An easy way to escape…"

"Listen, gang!" Morgrinald tried to establish some sense, in a battlefield these inexperienced soldiers would die in the first week. "Later you may dispute who has the biggest middle finger. For now, mine is bigger." And he showed it in a serious provocation. "There is a competent healer in the village nearby. Tell them Morgrinald sent you."

The dwarf doubted it would have any positive effect on Sartre. The important thing was to get the innocent away from there. Suddenly, he caught himself with his back to everyone staring at the lady elf. The busty lady may take a few days to recover. Morgrinald of Keldorn's blood, as well as all of the blood, never broke a promise, no matter how lengthy or long it was. The thought escaped him in a low tone.

"The elves and I. The woodsman was right."

Captain Ellan, however, had a tough decision to make. Carry the injured and leave the suspects? Never. However, if she took them now and they were bandits they would be victims of the suspects because it would be only her, captain Hanverovich and July to contain the dwarf because nothing or very little could be expected from the recruits. Ellan twisted the pommel of the sheathed sword trying to keep a placid face. Being in a commanding position entailed making difficult decisions subject to complete failure, a mistake prone to laughter and shame, and also, under a different light, it could result in satisfaction and glory of having fulfilled her role. Heroes or villains? These twin weights seemed to play on a seesaw and doubt plagued her brain.

"Captain! I have something to say. There is an entrance to a buried building nearby." Morgrinald pointed the direction with his head and silently, his inner voice was saying; Right there, where I found the rotting carcass of the dragon and right there where I decided to bury it. "There is a good chance there is a lair, maybe there…"

"Gentlemen, your attention is more important than whatever you are doing." Tristan said upon arriving.

Coming from who knows where, the comical character now walked pompously with his nose in the air surrounded by unshakable certainty. Somewhere between being proud of himself and pride. His arrival and appearance were so intriguing that, with this momentary impact, everyone forgot what they were arguing about and what bittered their hearts.

"While walking through the woods of this green hell, I prayed to the protective saint of paths, the patron of good fortune, and because of my dedicated prayer, she offered to guide this poor sinner to the entrance to the beast's lair." Without knowing, Tristan pointed in the same direction as Morgrinald did a few minutes earlier.

Actually, there were no saints or miracles. Tristan was desperate to find a place where he could get rid of yesterday's meal… His stomach had never been very strong and neither were his bowels. All it took was something slightly acid to make him suffer for days with aches that prevented sitting and, therefore, riding. Aware that there could be pain and unpleasant sounds, he decided to evacuate elsewhere. He took advantage of the discussion and ran. When he found a wide crack, he took a quick glance and noticed that the indentation on the ground had a few meters. Given its darkness, it would be the ideal place to defecate without having to bury his feces after. He squatted, lifted his robe and when he started, forced himself to finish faster. "Get out of this body that doesn't belong to you," he said with emphasis and hoped to get rid of his queasiness in a single dump. However, the usually awful sound of gases was increased by an unexpected echo coming from the crack in the ground, a slight scare helped him accelerate what he had already begun. However, the usual grave sounds were overlaid by acute winches. Then, surprised, he dove his head between his legs and the hole and a swarm of bats came out, making him jump from one side to another, mainly to get rid of the ones that entered his robe.

"Father, what are you talking about?" Ellan had to know.

"I found the beast's lair."

Morgrinald had not paid attention to the priest's approximation, but to say that he didn't know his presence was too inaccurate and wrong. Nothing that walked the ground escaped his race's perception, so whenever he could, he walked barefoot. Especially because he was unable to stay away from the ground for a long time both for love to his element as the old superstitions of his people who said that losing such connection could be fatal. Anyway, Tristan had been there for some time, because he recognized his footsteps pattern. The fool put too much weight on one side than the other, maybe he's not even aware of his spine's deviation caused by treading flat and outward. Morgrinald initially classified it as a habit or as a manifestation of his fear, but not... His arrival was connected to a cue. He waited for the right moment to enter with all the brightness of the hero he fought to show he was. The dwarf could refute it, however, unraveling that fraud would mean presenting evidence and revealing more than he wanted about himself. That wasn't the moment to present his real self.

DIVIGATIONS OR PREMONITION?

Tarson was in front of her, the kiss, instead of the the smell of his breath and the smell of his body, only subtle colors. She was floating again, outside the ship saying farewell to Tarson, the crew and the ancient being stored in the bowels of the ship that made it fly, moving away from her. Suddenly she receded without moving, she could see clearly the boat drifting away and diving back into the cave, only a hole at the top identifying the sky and suddenly nothing else. She heard only her heart, she tried to speak, scream but no sound came from her mouth and suddenly, two children ran into her back and passed by laughing. She was no longer in the cave but somewhere with low grass and the children grabbed and fought each other, laughing and whining nonsense.

Another sensation came along, her heart pounded, but there were other sounds also. Jupita was stunned because the vision was an unreality as large as was possible. Then Jupita woke up smiling and perplexed.

"Children?" she inquired in a weak voice.

Everything was twisted and revolved slightly, a mild pain weakened her movements. Jupita realized she had fainted, but only for a moment. From the ground, she heard the last words of the man called Tristan.

"I found the beast's lair."

"Captain! I request permission to take…" July shuddered with hatred for a second. She wanted to say many things, but instead, she just continued. "I'm taking back, in my name and under my responsibility, the poor wounded as soon as I find the horses.

"Soldier July?"

"Dwarf?" and it was he who decided to interrupt her, which further increased the neglect of the captains. You should try to understand what happened, especially the absence of the others while they took care of the wounded.

"They went west. They are still running. You will never catch them."

"I don't have to. Animals, like any other creatures, migrate to places where they feel safe. They are from the nearby village. I will certainly find them there, north wise."

Tristan controlled himself when she left. She had stolen his great scene. July had always been like that, unbearably like that, filthy like now, he remembered her as a kid. Talented and smart. On the other hand, he was grateful that she left, now he could shine alone.

"Ok. Ok. It's time to salvage what we can. The country depends on us."

"Lord Tristan, we still have to find out about the others…"

"Captain, I believe that they obviously went after the luggage animals."

"How can you be sure?"

The knight of hope scratched the top of his head and removed a lice or some insect that was bothering him. He repeated the gesture while he answered.

"I saw them."

Morgrinald joined his thick eyebrows, because the answer had a curious duality. Taking into account what he was doing, he was surely talking to the insects, but to the lady captain, the answer was sufficient to prevent a new interrogation of the unfathomable and bizarre captain.

"Guide us, citizen Tristan. Share your success with us."

"Negative captain. The lady elf is in no condition…" Stan was reluctant because he remembered what he promised the dying old man, he would catch the damn person responsible for the robbery and brutal murders. Although the lady elf had helped the troops against the marine beast, there was still the crime of stealing the horse pending against her. He wanted to stay close.

"I will decide that ." suddenly Jupita was standing, without any one seeing her get up.

"A sudden illness. We may proceed."

In Stan's eyes, her prompt recovery was another reason to keep an eye on the foreigners. These beings, descendants of elementals were different, but were they indeed? Suddenly, the priest tapped his shoulder and moved ahead of the group with his chest puffed with pride and pomp.

Morgrinald snorted, but followed. Again compelled to do things that no one had asked his opinion about. But anyway, he would act as promised to Dominescu. Anyway, that buried building seemed to be the center and beginning of all that tragedy, but while he walked, he was actually intrigued with something else. With the sudden recovery of the lady elf. When they stopped where the talkative Tristan would start some dramatic story of how he found it, Morgrinald looked at the crack, especially at what was around the hole. He was immediately pissed. The footprints around the crack and the other signs of a body rolling on the ground denounced clearly. Lies… And lies. Having found out, he nudged Tristan's elbow and smiled slightly making it clear that he was aware of the priest's little secret. Then he peered the dark slit and kicked a big stone down, widening the crack and allowing the stone to roll heavy and loudly over the natural steps. Quickly, a new flight of bats came out and while the others covered themselves, the valorous and courageous knight of hope dropped to the ground closing rapidly any openings in his robe like someone holding their breath before a dive. Morgrinald allowed himself to laugh uncontrollably. While he laughed, he went down the crack like someone coming back home, followed by Jupita.

The others gathered around the crack in a mix of fear and curiosity. Ellan observed, a few steps behind. To her, the hole was the smallest mystery as she was still thinking about the previous episode and the possibility was blunt… Could the person who boldly stole the horse be actually a woman? After all, corporal Irving's position during the situation, allowed any observation? Breasts or a bundle of clothes? A female face? Another doubt, as it was easy to picture Lucrecia and recall her androgynous shape. With so many "ifs" she had to select something else. And, if the it was a lady elf, could it be Jupita? However, considering it might be a mistake, if the figure had no female traits, she could suspect Tristan, who, incidentally, at no moment, made it clear what religion or deities converged his prayers.

However, all the possibilities bumped into inhospitable territory. Accusing an individual of another nation and especially one of another race would cause at least some discomfort to her superiors, especially if the one who identified herself as Jupita occupied any office or owned status or notoriety. And the dwarf's involvement, because of the dwarfs participation in the past of the Great Empire, would also lower the morale of the kingdom's legion. Without forgetting the third individual they found, Tristan, the missionary that, if charged, would encourage devotees to confront any soldier of the kingdom.

The best she could do was come up with a greater "if…" And what if none of them had nothing to do with the horse theft and they were who they claimed to be? Ellan's instincts fought her reason. In the meanwhile, she decided to investigate the entrance of the alleged lair where the beats involved in the massacres were probably hiding. And thinking about the episode, Ellan focused her eyes on the captain. He was becoming more bizarre by the minute. Could it be because of the sight of the poor bastards killed in the caravan? She had heard about this in the past. The reality of death was too strong and overwhelming for certain minds.

After all, what was understandable in the taking of so many lives? Items of a certain value, a bag of coins opened with its untouched pieces reflecting light in a visible glow and the food had only been touched by the animals. Or he was tormented by what the dying man had told him? Why devote so much importance to the opinion of a dying person? He made a promise then and now he was stuck with the mirage and delirium of a dying man. The old ones called it "the dying men fever". Or was it frustration? Captain Stanislaw Hanverovich was a proud and eager for combat person. A childish idea that still haunted him.

In Ellan's mind, issues and questions with few answers; and of those few based on assumptions from half-answers, from reading the captain's face and speculation. His arrogant silence about what happened in the camp before the lady elf and herself returned and his choice of words. He was an ignorant in both senses. Ignorant in his behavior and for not seeing the Endoli and Lucrecia's intentions to desert. Ellan was sorry for Nery. That illness, whatever it was, stole the liveliness of her thoughts making her act like a fool. And July had a rough time also. The best thing to do, would be to let July take Nery to the village healer. July had lived long enough in the woods to find the way back to the village and find corporal Irving. He would act according to protocol. Then she should investigate a little more... There was a possibility that the sum could be part of something even bigger. Such thoughts sent shivers up her neck.

Lost in thoughts, she didn't even realize that the civilians were the first ones to enter, anyway, better this way... If there were any traps or the whole building was a ruse, they would have time to step back and away from there, regroup and send for reinforcements.

"Captain Hanverovich?" she said in jolt as he was about to enter. "You will cover the back to secure the perimeter."

Captain Ellan adjusted the height of her sword strap, while she passed by him.

"Unnecessary. The..."

"Stay." she emphasized without lowering or rising her voice; looking from the crack to his eyes, she completed in a suggestive tone. "I know that you are capable of following at least this simple order."

That was it. What else could she say? She was outraged with the desertion of two members of the team, an injured carrying a sick and a captain trying to play hero.

DARKNESS

Every time you reached some place like this, the mixture of fear and curiosity grew exponentially. An inevitable torrent of questions arise and that can only be answered by further exploration. As they went down the large steps, they saw the carcass of a large animal. They stopped for awhile and improvised torches of wood and metal wrapped in strips of cloth and soaked them in the dead animal's fat. One of the recruits lit his torch with a flint and the fire was shared among them. As the forsaken place was illuminated, it revealed, amid the stale and dusty air, furniture taken over by fungi, mushrooms and insects that devoured them from inside. That mute world seemed elegant, although decadent as much by the weight of time as by lack of care of its builder's descendants. In other words, no maintenance or improvements. Frightful suspicions widened the mouth and pounded the hears anxious to run away screaming. Only the lady elf, the dwarf and the captain remained placid, Tristan was holding his chin to stop his teeth from clattering, and his fear was easily absorbed by the recruits.

A semicircular metal frame on the ground gave the impression that someday, lost in the past, it had been an imposing chandelier. Judging by the doors, twisted inward, it could be assumed that they were the result of forced entry or the weight of rot on its hinges. The shadow and the slight humidity below that rubble created a unique habitat for insects and crawling creatures.

At the sight of this rich environment, the precaution, the fear that tied the missionary's bony legs, was fiercely beaten by an enthusiastic thirst for treasures. With haste and greed, he canvassed the place and its corridors only to find fallen walls and rubble in steep alleys and dead ends.

Suddenly, in the midst of a promising corridor with tapestries and trinkets hanging on the walls, a low and singular sound grew in an instant, a long floor plate gave way dropping with all who were there to the floor below.

"Are you ok?" the captain's heart screamed in her throat.

"Yes, I'm well." Tristan said.

The recruits pored their surprised and childish faces to the lower floor.

"The priest meant that he's concerned with all of us and has checked our damn health."

Tristan just raised an eyebrow, fully outraged by the dwarf.

"Right. Listen" the captain tried to convey tranquility. "We have no ropes, we will have to walk around. We will meet at the stairs."

"Damn it, it was a trap." Jupita said.

"No, lady elf. Everything here is old, our weight may triggered the collapse."

"I believe the elf! This is a trap made by the evil creature."

"Let's go." Jupita said flatly, thinking about her friend disregarding what the missionary was saying. It can't be Osiris, deep down she knew.

Suddenly five putrid, semi-destroyed bodies groaned loudly and advanced towards the explorers. Tristan's throat locked up. However, when the undead saw the dwarf, they inexplicably seemed to panic and began a slow retreat. Before Morgrinald could cut and dismember the last one, Tristan issued a short and quick scream.

"No."

"Huh, what happened? You wet yourself little priest?" when Morgrinald turned around, he realized that the undead was already far from the light of the torch and he didn't want to run after that thing. He felt the priest's hand poking his shoulder and he granted passage, his eyes were heavy with fear.

Then, the melodramatic missionary raised the front of his torch as if it was the most sacred of swords and declaimed screaming:

"Go evil creature, warn your mistress. This insanity must end."

"There goes the element of surprise." the dwarf said rolling his eyes. "Shut up you robed piece of shit."

"Don't worry my friend…"

"Great, now he thinks he's my friend."

"The enemy of justice will never see herself victorious." Tristan said, ignoring the dwarf.

"Herself? Herself? You can't even speak your own language. You imbecile."

"Hope and justice are the same language. One desire in the heart of…"

"I wish you would shut up!" Morgrinald thought he should have an accident with his teeth.

"How do you expect me to react to these creature's mistress? This maleficent servant of everything that is evil?"

"Priest, contain yourself!" Jupita was trying to listen ahead, but it was impossible with their chatter.

"How do you expect me to contain my holy inspiration?" Tristan asked.

"Inspire on my farthing." Saying that, the dwarf released an unpleasant and loud sound.

"Argh! I shall convert you by the end of this mission. You will see the truth when we stand face to face against the pillar of ten flavors of good people."

"Ten flavors? Trouble? Oh shit! This fellow is worse than the late Hellsing."

"When we arrest this mistress of evil…"

"Stop the mistress." Morgrinald corrected biting his finger. "Elf, can I beat him?"

In response to that, Jupita spun her body and quickly pelted the torch on the undead that was almost escaping at the end of the extensive corridor. The power of the blow caused the body to separate from the head when it fell to the floor. Decapitated, the undead movements ceased immediately. Having done that, she turned to the priest and said between her teeth.

"Keep this in mind. There is no mistress, understand?"

They both remained in rigid silence. Morgrinald smiled evilly pleased, and Tristan gulped agreeing.

"Perfect!"

Between the tiring zigzagging corridors they reached the staircase. On the wall, written in four languages, was a single sentence.

"WHOMEVER YOU ARE, GO BACK OR ACCEPT DEATH IN LIFE".

The staircase was narrow and prevented a rapid descent, the stone steps and a thick mass of masonry resembled a spider's web. At the end of the descent, was a mumbling soft light torch nearing its the end, below, there was a high cavity with nothing inside. Ahead, strange sounds anticipated an unknown danger, then, a sudden gust of wind passed through them and extinguished the dying torch.

In a few seconds, Tristan rekindled it with his flintlock, and retaining the torch in his hands said with wide-eyed craziness:

"Listen to the sounds of evil."

Morgrinald took advantage of the proximity and punched him in the kidney, quieting him. Of course, in addition to the fun of doing that, he wanted to hear and distinguish better the noise.

"The sound increased. Oh shit. It seem to be some sort of metallic gear of a mechanism."

"Traps?"

"Could it be? In this abandoned place?" Jupita inquired doubtfully. "You yourself said that…"

"This way." she interrupted following ahead receding into a lateral corridor where the sound was coming from.

At that moment, Jupita was divided about Osiris. She wanted to re-encounter her friend, but didn't want to see the monster she had become. She fought firmly against this second thought, as the villagers gave them only descriptions full of fear, ignorance, and fear generated by ignorance. Common people tended to always elevate any problem to the status of ancient monsters and demons. That's is why she choose to be an adventurer. Demystify myths and help people. Certainly, the sound was coming from the center of the corridor, most likely from where the flickering light was. She moved ahead easily and before entering, she stopped with her sword in hand and back against the wall. She gestured the others and they attended stopping. Looking ahead, she signaled them again. The dwarf awaited pulling Tristan slightly who answered without reservation or talk.

Then, the disciple of Darkay, in a skilled rotary motion, jumped past the entrance, and rose again with her back against wall on the other side. Her mouth was gaping. It was all in a flash she could hardly see, but what she saw was enough. The location was an old room, in the center, with its back to the door, was an enormous animal, wide as a bull with a brown and armored back hunched over a body. Jupita immediately remembered her friend and tears insisted in blurring her vision. She squeezed the salty juice with her eyelids and with closed eyes her memory came alive.

"Osiris!" lamented the lady elf.

Then, resolute, she launched herself into the long room with many beds. The noise of her entry alerted the tall and wide monster and when it turned its reddish around, it was clear that the noise came from its fantastic and prominent jaws chewing an arm with metallic sheen.

"Osiris!" Jupita screamed desperately and advanced towards the creature with her sword.

"Jupita, no!" the dwarf cried, trying to stop her, as soon as he saw with who and what she was dealing with.

The cornered animal retaliated with a well-aimed blow of its tail, flinging the lady elf on one of the beds around and, with the impact, landed on the floor after a twirl.

The animal fled and Morgrinald only guaranteed its passage, keeping everyone else away.

"What have you done, dwarf?" Jupita screamed. "Do you have stones for brains? You let it escape, you idiot." she said running over the beds.

"The poor thing was only hungry." he said with his arms extended blocking the passage.

"Hungry?" Jupita stared at him pulling one of his beard's plaids.

"Metal. See?" without noticing, the dwarf held the elf's sword by its blade without being cut and pushed away from his chest. "He's docile."

The thing on the floor, chewed and in pieces, was just a metal statue of a soldier, thus, he decided not to follow it.

Morgrinald peered seriously at the lady elf. She had the gaze of someone fighting despair. He knew what it was like. He noticed he confused gaze at the statue. And this temporary confusion made her sit on the bed next to her with the sword still in hand, ready for a fight, but soon her arm fell and the blade touched the worn stone. Then suddenly, Keldorn's grandson, spoke to her:

"Apologies. That's was what you were going to say?"

"Give her a break." Tristan said with a saddened voice. "You came here of your own will."

"Humph! Are you falling in love?" Morgrinald controlled the urge to kick him.

"I thought it was Osiris…" the lady elf entwined her fingers sadly.

"The animal is docile, busty, but it doesn't belong here."

"How do you know?" Jupita had her own ideas.

"I just know."

"What do you mean?"

"I just know. That's all!"

"Affirmations and denials are insufficient now." she screamed and hit the bed where she was at the same instant she jumped out of it.

The echo became the obvious boundary between emotion and reason. Morgrinald, of the most honorable clan that ever existed, realized his mistake. Too many secrets could ward off problems and generate others, far worse. He had seen madness close up and didn't want to be alone again.

"Right. He's not of this world."

"So where is he from? The moon, from the land of demons, the fantasy world of a children's book? Where from, Morgrinald? Tell me!" Jupita inquired.

"I've been in the world where he came from. When age comes and kids don't play with their games anymore, my race forces them to travel to the interior of the earth, deep in the caves and chasms where the fire fights to get out.

"Lava!" Jupita whispered close to his face. "On the island, you knew so much about the volcano there…"

"Dead. The big rock was formed by a much bigger volcano."

"What's this about?"

Morgrinald hears the robed idiot question, but shrugs. He just sat on what was left of the bed beside him and continued his report:

"Tradition requires that they bring back the hottest rock, the hottest fire and upon return they are called adults."

"A tradition." Jupita's voice was no higher than a whisper.

"The problem is that some children saw it as a game. So some take well longer than others to return."

"Tradition?" the lady elf put away her sword. "Children walking alone into chasms?"

"Never! The elders were sent with them, so they could hear the stories of our people and to have someone to prevent them from overdoing it, of childishness."

"Foolishness of dem…" brutally, Jupita kicked the door against the nose of the unwary missionary who went quiet.

beneath the thick beard, Morgrinald sketched a smile from the corner of his mouth, but the weight of his own history stole his humor again.

"When I entered the darkness of the mines of the mountain where I was born, I was anxious to get back. Keldorn, my grandfather, was one of many of my lineage to explore the world. This traveling business, finding other things and places was manic. No. Our mania! It was like a damn leech. It doesn't let go of the skin or flesh. I was lucky that my grandfather took me. He said I was ready, and that Fulbor, my aunt's the only son, wasn't. And alone, in the bowels of the mountain, he told me that he had been to a fantastic land. The ancient homeland."

The dwarf of the combatants clan, paused, picked up his hammer and recalled that it was much more than just a hammer, it was a sacred and ceremonial item, Morgrinald held his nostrils with his fingers and scratched his mustache. The pause was his way to inflate his chest and find the courage to continue, then, in a sigh said:

"I looked for it alone."

"And your grandfather?"

"Keldorn was too old and he died on the way. I was ashamed, elf. Ashamed to tell the family, so I didn't return. I stayed alone. In the dark. Without Keldorn, no family, no comfort, no nothing."

Morgrinald closed the thick eyebrows and looked intensely:

"Without food, water… I became weak, with lung illness…"

Jupita had no way of contradicting him, the truth seemed to pour out of his pores. She shared his fear, the sensation of being alone. After all, she lost Darkay, her master and tutor, to death. However, life gave her Tarson, more than a long time companion, a friend. She understood the foul mouthed dwarf's feelings, but she was never alone for such a long time. What would it be like to live with one's wits alone as company? Noticing that she had lost herself in thought, she returned her attention to the dwarf, who, with a low and heavy head was saying.

"… finally I found the passage. There, I grew stronger and met several types of creatures, including this one. Believe me, the animal is not important!"

Tristan had already reopened the door, and with his face and robe stained with blood from his nose, spoke seriously:

"Okay. I understand. The animal is not important. Let's continue…"

"Not this one!" interrupted the dwarf, much had to be said before proceeding.

"What?" Tristan asked with a swollen nose and emerging confusion.

"Jupita, if this animal found the passage between worlds, other creatures may have crossed the passage too."

"You yourself told me you came through it."

"I passed by the Guardian because it was part of my clan's rite. He allowed my access, even with no one to accompany me."

"Then it means that the passage was breached and the Guardian is either away or dead." Jupita said, uncertain.

"Or it means someone opened it on this side." Morgrinald rose and his look became gloomy looking down the hallway. "Was that sound from the passage?"

Tristan, in the corridor, sees other problems. Clear footsteps and metal noises. He swallowed hard, his voice froze in his throat while he pulled his mace and took a deep breath. With no time for hesitation, he hollered and raced against the damned:

"Fear, evil monsters, before the banner of justice!"

A face emerged from the darkness and before any other move, Tristan was dominated and in a double rotating spin and fell on the floor. A torch was lit and everything became a little more clearer.

"Tristan? And the others?"

"Captain! How nice to see you." he said with her foot on his chest.

Sighing with relief, he laughed out loud and, July swiftly covered the mouth of the unwary. Then he recognized her. You? He would say if she wasn't covering his mouth.

They heard a door creak behind them. And with the torch's light, they identified the dwarf and the lady elf.

"Two of you are missing." Keldorn's experienced grandson noticed immediately.

"Yes, they stayed at the entrance to this place. In case we fail, they have their orders." actually, the recruits could only tremble with fear so when they said that they belonged to a village nearby, she asked them to take Nery to the renowned local healer. So she would have July with her. And in case they didn't return in the next few days, corporal Irving would know how to proceed.

Tristan's mace shone and indicated, through a beam of light, the path to follow.

"Why didn't you mention you had that toy?" July asked, perplexed.

"This? The paths of good and evil without…"

"Shut up!" the dwarf said again, pushing him against the wall, then he heard it too.

It was a voice hard to identify, somewhere between male and female, echoing in the air of that subterranean world. The reaction of each of the humans was different. To Ellan, the beauty bordered on the sublime. To Tristan, such melodic and harmonic power could only come from a chapel or a cathedral atrium. July heard a confusing harmony. Only the old and the descendants of ancient races could have a better understanding of what it was.

Jupita had been hearing low moaning for some time, complaints of pain and agony. Sure it was her imagination, she diverted her hearing to other sounds. She rather keep her ears almost null, almost human, so she could retain some sobriety.

Morgrinald decided to sneak away using his unique skills. Soon the walls and he were one, in the belly of the earth, he migrated to another corner and there began to think better about the death of the dragon. At the time, he clearly understood the cycle that it allowed. How, for example, the small feast with its corpse. Geniuses and fools would arrive sooner or later to the same conclusion… If this "feast" continued, other opportunists would be attracted to the smell and the cycle would continue gaining strength and independence. Well-fed females give more cubs and more cubs meant larger hunting territories. The event would rapidly devastate the village of the esteemed Dominescu. When he cleared a large area of land for the winged and dead creature to be buried, the entrance formed by a wide and long tunnel was revealed. The walls of the tunnel were anchored in polished stone, the type found only to the west of the high mountains. The executors of this immense work, whoever they were, relied on help from the dwarf race, although the woodwork and metal structures, the wildfire in certain points in the hallway, made clear the help of other ancient peoples.

And suddenly from inside of the enormous corpse, two crows flew away scared. With that memory, Morgrinald removed from inside his armor, one of the birds covered with stiff mud. It was dead as well as its twin, the other crow that the dwarf hit too strong with a ball of mud, he ripped off its head and claws and munched the snack thinking quietly on what he would do now. That was too serious. Then, gradually, as he did for years, he remained standing, inert, as much as he could, avoiding only total immobility, as required by his fear and superstition. Isolated from all, he expanded his senses as only those of his race were capable and by being immersed in the earth he felt there was a lot more there than the calmness of the earth, the rigor of the stones and the passages of the commons in the galleries.

The others, without realizing the disappearance of their sullen partner, exploited the major passages, ignoring the recesses connecting to other corridors. Thus, they reached a grand hall illuminated by the glow of thick candles, manufactured with animal fat and tallow. And there, in a buried and abandoned nook, a good distance from the village they can see people kneeling in adoration poses, dividing the space of long benches sown in line. The voice heard before now was clear and sang old rhymes and the vaulted ceiling carved into the rock provided a majestic reverberation. And these faithful, silently prayed. Everyone approached doubtfully. The items, such as a table, reliquary and chandeliers, presented the incredible and venerable age, however, far from real, showing an excellent state of conservation, the metals still shone and not a speck of dust on the furniture. When they approached, they noticed the tuned in eyes and purple lips. All dead and tied by gross frames keeping them in a praying position, praying in a cursed ceremony. Greater horror, however, was on the tabular altar, bodies hung by metal hooks attached to the wall still dripping. The stench of death was unbearable.

"Gods, gods, gods!" Tristan echoed in a shaky voice.

"Shut up, there is something else here. the captain imposed. There was no time for niceties. That was the lair of mad assassins. She immediately remembered the road slaughter, it was all connected.

"Victims of Osiris's hunger?" the priest blessed himself with signs of various religions.

"Here too." July said as she peered into a room next door, where bodies were positioned as if operating things of everyday life.

Tristan approached one of the poor people when he heard something that sounded like a whisper, as he looked closer, the muscles of the dead face contracted creating an infant and sinister smile.

"Aaargh!" the knight of hope was hopeless. "We have awaken the dead! Look!"

"Postmortem spasms." July had seen that before in dead animals, even after they were skinned.

Jupita hears a slight movement behind her, and suddenly in the flickering light of that damned place, Osiris familiar figure emerged. The light of the torches in that foul place made her look ghoulish… And empty.

That robbed the air from her mouth, the memory recalled the air of excitement on her face when the blacksmith spoke of meat hooks and now that was what she saw. Hooks hanging victims of insanity. Disgusted with what she was going to say, but too outraged she said:

"The blacksmith, the hooks. The lack of a chapel. It was a plan, wasn't it? You wanted a temple for yourself and why not this one that is so great? That's why you were interested in the blacksmith. I thought it was only sex. It was what you wanted, you…"

"You were fools coming down here." Osiris interrupted.

"How could you?"

"Did you forget whom I serve?"

The face in front of her barely had any expression, it was completely different from the old Osiris.

Tristan approached, appealing:

"I can cure you. Cure your soul of the evil that…"

"Isn't it the god of war, lover of death and the husband of pain?"

The mute look stole the missionary's thoughts. One by one, they were gone. It was too easy to see that he was hypnotized like a moth around a flame, neither close nor far. His legs wobbled and he fell to his knees.

"Should we tolerate those who invade our domains?" Osiris's wild voice was the harbinger of a new slaughter and her gaze seemed to pierce everyone.

"Oh agent of evil, confess your collaboration and be delivered to salvation." Tristan felt his legs being wet by urine.

"Do you want to blame someone?" There was a mocking look in eyes of the cleric of the god of war. "So I take the blame. As no one else wants it…"

The lady elf, insensitive to that, revealed:

"We have already discovered part of the mystery. It was a gang of slave merchants that took advantage of bums and begg…"

"Jupita! I am the mastermind of the children's disappearance…"

"What?" the word stunned the lady elf.

"Bitch!" Tristan was shrunk and yet he spoke. "So you confess, evil spirit?"

"Shut up." with stunning clarity, Jupita recalled the subtlety employed, Osiris had guided them to the village and not by chance.

"Disappearances? You air dwellers spend so much time in the air that you reverie for days and I took advantage of that."

"Renounce…"

The missionary was interrupted with violence, being pulled and pressed on the wall by the brooding lady elf. Having done that, she turned to her old friend.

"Again. What about the disappearances?"

"One of my envoys arrived weeks before me, but this place already had its structure."

But what was wrong with Osiris? Why so much chatter? She wasn't like that… Never!"

Smart, balanced and cunning. It was almost stupid… Confess? Like one of those villains of novels, children's tales. There was more… But what? A warning? A warning about what? Of what? Let her continue talking, driving this strange theater without known script was the only way to understand and find out what she wanted with this stupid chatter.

"Prefer, may be more sensible to say. I preferred to continue to tear the children from their homes, it was an idea. A quite valid one… There would be a plea for help and that was the entire plot."

"Lair!" Cynic! The truth is that you wanted a temple for yourself. From the beginning."

"Lair?"

"The leader was weak. Charismatic, but weak. His removal or death, being well conducted, would make the place a mess and revolt would emerge from chaos. A whole village of warriors. The place, being a store, the shortest path between the Great Empire and the sea, was already essential in reducing losses of goods. And.."

"With a well paid protection…" the lady elf interrupted, playing along. "Gold and fame would spread through the traders' active mouth. I agree, quite convenient. The place would grow so well that your cancerous divine king would be lord of another land. Nobles would seek the services of specialized warriors and a single slip would be enough to…"

The priestess's eyes sparkled and a crazy bitter voice left her throat:

"War!"

THE SINCERE LECTURE

"From individuality we forget the collective, our own and that is why I cry. Take what you believe is necessary to move. In all these months I was away, I remained in contemplation, trying to find the ones responsible. And I did! And they weren't far. They never were…"

The families, with these well placed words by Sartre, were filled with will and fury. The union of so many made them unstoppable, generals of their souls. Shortly after, the group walked either behind or beside Sartre, the leader of and liberator.

During the march, they passed by their houses, built with sweat, pain and happiness. Among the constructions, some abandoned properties and others marked by grief. They observed everything, thought about everything, especially the power of that union. Amongst them, a hundred stories and tens more should be told by the children and those who disappeared. Unfortunate… such suffering… Lives shortened by mysteries and horrors. A faceless horror, and thus, so strong, so powerful.

But that was the day of the end of its strength, the day to tear its veil. The day evil would be revealed! And the torment of loss was so terrible and bitter that the weight of the journey on the trail of fallen trees, rocks and thorny thickets was not felt. With that poison in their veins, the trail was easily widened and cleared.

Sartre, in a not so late or out of purpose reflection, remembered Marin Bey – the saint. A quiet and reserved woman. Regardless of her past. The saint knew what hope was and would never surrender to any other kind of feeling. Being away from his people for months made him understand her even better. Instead of a humble, kind lady, serene and focused on her chores, he saw, at the time, a woman obsessed by the idea of the return of her beloved. Sartre was never so obtuse of reality, of the essence of that act. Just thinking about the work she did, her quest, the laborious and eternal painting of the doors and the marking of the path, all, without exception, should be called obstinacy and, above all, hope. Indirectly, thanks to this monumental work, people lost in the fog found salvation. An indirect and happy benefit. Maybe that was how the popular saying "Those reborn in faith are guided to salvation" was born.

Now he understood that he never had the privilege of knowing her. Being immerse in the problem, blinded to other possibilities, he didn't comprehend what she told him when they met. "Who gets lost in a soft shimmer of light will never see the sun glow ". He should be like Marin Bey, the saint, a guide. Accept his role as the community leader, be their watchful eye. A community is a single body, and Sartre focused on that thought. Now, if they had to walk to salvation, they would be the walking legs. He remembered the noble Plézoun Raymovick and also the convenience of the equally coward peasant who lived with him. A person who, aware or not, sold much more than his self esteem, his pride and his dignity… As someone far more illustrious said somewhere… "To understand the rulers of a land, just look at its people." Thus, the simpleton peasant was afraid because his ruler was also afraid of everything. And, in the village of Miller, his home, was the same. The villagers fear were solely reflections.

"Of me." Sartre understood that clearly now and it would change on this day. Sartre had no more doubts. The walking legs only needed eyes to guide them. A simple but overshadowed vision as other eyes were also immerse in the problem.

Sartre looked at those following him then turned and gazed ahead with determination. You are not always aware of the strength of the unit, the great strength of will. Such consciousness could only be awakened if he removed himself enough to understand the unit.

"Walk!" he told himself.

Strides to the east, west, north or any other direction, it didn't matter. The solution to such heinous events had begun. And in the hands of every solution, an end…

The trail rose and the steps slipped on humidity or stones. Hands and knees were scraped, but pain and disposition were synonymous. And so they followed, holding on to each other, and, soon, supporting each other.

How surprising life was, walking legs behind a leader. He remembered Lefty, the gnome. Was he the leader of that odd community? Well… Pillar or not, he convinced everyone with few and clear words… Help. And the people moved. Morgrinald, the brave guardian, said it well when they returned to the mainland: "All they do is whine begging others to take part in their struggles".

Sartre, the healer, gone for so long, was back and he returned with hope and strength. And everyone following his steps had their own plans of how to punish the guilty. Plans that gave new breath to the journey's sacrifice. And not an hour had passed and Sartre; the leader of his people; the keeper of hope; the banner of commitment; put his hands on his waist and leaned forward trying to rescue his breath that escaped galloping. And for being the tallest and up ahead, was the first one to see.

"Come!" he said imperatively. "Although from here, it's equidistant, look at what you should see."

The enthusiasm and desire for justice or revenge of those who followed him all the way to the top of that rock smiled indescribably. As soon as they were where they wanted to be, Sartre pointed with his head to the placid and livid lake.

"People of Miller, I declare the journey over! I present to you, not one or two, but all those guilty for our problems. All of the Guardians of Sin!"

The only thing they saw in the cleanness of the lake were their reflected images and, even looking ahead, they would not escape this reality because the sun projected long and ugly shadows on the opposite wall with a series of forks, machetes, clubs and spears.

"Man is nothing more than what he does to himself."

Saying that, they all the weapons dropped to the ground.

THE COMBAT

Somehow clear, during Osiris monologue, the sanctity of the ground was recited and Jupita understood the subtext. They could not or should not do anything there without compromising something, without establishing something. The world in that space belonged to beings and comprehensions far greater than hers. Suddenly Jupita remembered Osiris' threadbare and frayed clothes, and finally the end of the clash that began her convalescence.

"So Osiris now serves another master?"

She would continue to discuss based on her minimal knowledge of religiosity and its devotees. She had no idea of what to do.

"Try what, lady elf? Distract me? Shock me? No, no… Gain time. Gain time because you are out of ideas, support, offensive position."

Jupita thought about where Morgrinald could be. A sudden shiver too over her soul. Maybe she met him before, that was why she talked that way. Support would not come, no surprise attacks…

"You can come out, Tarson."

"He won't come." Jupita said promptly, with a bitterness easily defined as loss.

That surprised her. A tear formed in the eye of the warrior of the god of war. Finally a glimpse of her old friend in that heavy face full of mystery. She looked around, looked at the human bodies hung by metallic hooks, the same ones used in the butchery. Piercing muscle and flesh. From the agonizing sound, it became clear that they were still alive.

"Life taken by cowardice is an impure nourishment and serves only gods that should be forgotten or relegated." She said with hard eyes.

"So you condemn the offering, minister?" Jupita said acidly.

Her outrage was clear, and without understanding, Darkay's disciple held herself back.

"Deliver a few meats in a banquette? What an idea!"

"But…" War does the sam…"

"In war, it's a random factor. The brave, the weak and the innocent die. And those who started it prosper and find a place in life."

"But they die!"

"But they know they can die. That they will. Now, is there any justice in that?" Osiris once again pointed at the shackles, the dying and the dead ones tied and arranged in nasty poses.

Then a flash of memory hit her. Jupita recognized, in the back, or better, in the front of that sinister mass, the broken nose on Maqui's short forehead face. Caleb's right arm, who had lassoed Tarson and feel through the hole.

Among the dead she could still hear the moan and a light and low singing blending to all that monstrosity. The scene, together with the swarm of strong emotions prevented Jupita from understanding from where and from how many the sounds originated. In the meanwhile, Ellan and July were removing the injured from their shackles, giving them water, ignoring those that wouldn't survive. When the lady elf turned back to the cleric of war, she saw her dumping the contents of a bag she carried on her back. It was a load of weapons of all types and quality.

"I found these tools around here."

Some of the dying and hooded figures from the lined pews that were praying nervously came out of their inert poses. July screamed and receded until she reached the wall and shrank into a fetal position. That was just too much for her sanity. Ellan didn't have a different reaction. Astonished, she sought refuge in a corner like an involuntary spectator. They were both common people and saw the world in a common way. The dying became agitated looking at each other.

"What?" Osiris said in a dubious tone. "I decided to stack them… Can't I? Ok." then she kicked the pile of weapons and scattered them.

The sound and sight of so many weapons made the tortured, with some effort, and the hooded torturers arm themselves. That made the cleric of the god of war feel the energy of the place change. With both sides arming themselves, she began a new ritual, and the previous one was no longer a valid sacrifice to Entropia, god of death. Soon he would have no more right to that handful of souls.

A terrible and ugly fight was about to begin. People who never touched a weapon and others who never should have, raising and dropping blades and clubs. The fallen bled, the dying died and the weak, although skillful, survived until hit by a harder blow.

"Now your chatter became obvious, my friend." she whispered, knowing the lady elf could hear her even with all that racket.

"You wanted to annoy them, break the torturers' concentration so the others would act."

Osiris smiled with the malice of a cat. There, although profane, was an altar and they were making an offering. By interrupting the offering with her chatter and provoking the clash of weapons, their attention turned elsewhere. Although it was an ingenious plan, sooner or later, when the gods considered it convenient, such interruption would have a price. In her mind, Osiris thought: rather it be earlier. Then, in a thunderous voice, she said vehemently:

"These bastards are responsible for some, but not all the disappearances."

Osiris moved through the battle untouched. With a dry blow, she hit one of the hooded ones planting her mace like a nail in a rigid wall. Suspended in such unusual and brutal way, the blacksmith of the village had his face uncovered and, astonished, was between not knowing what to do or to finally expect death. But Osiris dropped the mass on the floor and ran her finger sensually over his chin.

"If you recognize this face, my sister in arms." The devotee said, staring into the the lady elf's eyes, good Jupita. "Now you know about the intentions. And if you allow me, here are mine for this one." she immediately screamed her war cry and punched him a few times, then the next and the next opponent.

With a swift and violent spin, she threw one of them against the wall at a highest point and made three figures run away from the huge falling reliquary. Jupita didn't move, maybe too shocked.

Anxious to make herself useful, captain Ellan entered the combat, but she could hardly move among the weapons and confusion. Thus, as quick as she entered, the captain was injured and plunged into the arms of her friend July. Ellan's strong and sweet gaze now reflected the acute pain of death and the uncertainty of what would become of her soul in that place.

Tristan, still squatted on the floor had his shoulder stomped by Osiris and from that extra height, she threw her weapon, hitting the hooded one about to cowardly attack him. So, defended at the last moment by the icon of evil, by the beast, he was stunned. The knight of hope was divided between his own concepts of good and evil. Confused, he sat down and waited for the end of the battle.

Osiris got up from the floor. Few were still standing, those good enough to leave, but they didn't flee. She smiled… Now the mob belonged to her and the god of war. Everyone stopped thinking about dying, they gave up the idea of wanting to die. Not without a fight. A new encouragement took her, it was the grace of her father and lord, the god of war, inhabiting her in this beautiful moment.

And the devotees of death noticed that. Everything would be lost soon. So they continued to pray even in battle. Then she sensed a new presence. A thick layer of dirt and filth started to cover the area like a severe web. Huge forces focused their might on the place. Osiris whirled about herself and hit the nearest priest with a powerful punch producing a harsh and hollow roar when her hand sank the rival's chest. She laughed and ripped a dark goo from his chest resembling more a tumor than a heart, or maybe both. Now the corpse dropped to the ground and fell apart. That wasn't even alive, it was an imitation of life. With that in mind, the champion of the god of war invested on the second rival, however, since the onslaught of the divine warrior, he rubbed his hands constantly which magically produced several boils on his palm as the bubbles of boiling oil. From his wrists, pustules between white and green tore the thin skin and hurled like fast knives towards Osiris. And she, champion of the Great Valley, dodged them skillfully.

Darkay's disciple pulled the air around rapidly.

"Jupita, no!" the cleric didn't want help.

Her manifestation in loud and good sound was a sincere plea. Acting on holy ground would compromise her elf friend like it did with the captain. Since the beginning, her intent was the battle, however, for a reason that only she could understand, they had to begin it, so anyone could join and challenge the champion.

The third hooded individual with and crazy and empty gaze stood still in the background, a standing dead, and suddenly he attacked, fell, convulsed in spasms and raised again to fight.

"Nothing here belongs to us. Let's get out! Save those you can. Let's go then, let's go!" As if that was an irresistible order, the others heard and followed Tristan as they could and regardless of what side they fought for, they abandoned the insane and sinister battle leaving it without an audience.

Then, the same way he had began, the third one became motionless again. And suddenly, the third one began to scream, including the fallen bodies, rolling on the floor in his direction as if magnetically draw to the heinous figure. When they collided with the sinister minister of death, they flesh was fused with his, as if made of mud. And the figure began to grow.

Looking at the bizarre situation, Osiris was knocked over by a body and dragged towards the uno. When her legs touched the meat mass, they sank into it. That made her roar with pain and convulse.

Seeing that, Jupita forgot the plea. From what she knew of the place, of old laws, she dissolved her body in a light gas moving against a single opponent. When the thing was involved by the fog that was Jupita, the thing convulsed as if molested by thousands of insects and started coughing spitting parts of itself. The now gray fog began to take over its respiratory ways, infecting noses, ears and mouths. Soon, severe convulsions took it over while Osiris rolled away. She knew what she had to do… She spat blood quickly and got up imposingly and with her weapon at hand, prayed. The powerful names she pronounced made the place groan and tremble. Standing, she turned to the mass of meat, that, without Jupita, in fog form knowing, was devouring her. At hearing the prayers, Jupita's body regained its shape, regrouping beside the monster.

Osiris' lips twisted downward. That was almost an avatar. The devotee looked at her old friend, her weapon, the Pacifier, the thorny mace that followed her for as long as she could remember and mentally renewed her vows. And before the monster had a chance, she pelted the mace at it. The prayer wasn't over yet, and with firm paces, she moved towards the beast. She offered her hand and it accepted. Then she clamped her mouth trying to suffocated the scream of pain when it touched her.

Far from there, but not far enough to not hear and feel the tremors, the survivors wandered aimlessly.

"This way, lads!" The low light revealed the missing figure; Morgrinald pulled them by the arm, one by one to the upper level where he stood.

"The lady elf…"

"Go straight ahead, you will find a fountain, a kind of statue with big eyes…"

"Dwarf?"

"I know."

Meanwhile, in that place of war and death, Jupita hesitated between existence and reality. Weak, almost dead, she shook her head with her eyes closed and blinked several times, trying to focus her mind. Standing beside her, Osiris was being devoured. Half of her forearm was already inside the aberration and she would be next. Suddenly she felt her friend's foot making her roll.

"Go away."

"No…" Tears rolled freely down her sad face.

"ARGH! Go!"

Jupita wept weakly, although her instinct claimed for life. Suddenly, she noticed in the faint light, a carpet of worms crawled and in the air, flies and beetles surrounded their master. However, Osiris' metal weapon was pulsing, pushing the insects away. In her friend she saw something she had never noticed, an immense burning took Osiris' body and leaked into the place, it was a characteristic ardor, hated by her race. The shock of that revelation terrified her and made her cling to the wall.

"Listen! My name is Osiris and I plea for my blood, my duty, my profession and my love to my god." Saying that, her body stopped moving into the now almost divine creature. "by my real nature, by all my ascendance and by the fates professed by my relatives." Slowly Osiris brought her forearm and her fist back in a raging pull. Her left hand ripped the mandible of the heinous undead and a tall and sudden flame flared and died, like the mass of bodies of the avatar of death. However, in a last spasm of the now disfigured beast, the devotee of the god of war was gravely injured once more. But now in a fatal way. Her eyes turned white instantly.

"NNNOOOOOOO!!!" Jupita cursed and cried held back by Morgrinald who had just arrived. The lady elf softened her essence once more and began to float, and even from there, thunder could be heard.

The dwarf pulled to the ground with difficulty. The elf had her eyes illuminated by the just fury, one that ignored Morgrinald's weight, his plea. And as she floated, she began to drag him. But with unmatched strength, Keldorn's grandson held her and a in a quick motion, grabbed her jaw and stood in front her. Resolute like that, he shook his head in a long negative, then Jupita's eyes went from the immortal glow to the wet brightness of tears and she surrendered at his knees. Keldorn's grandson then carried her out there.

The exit became a difficult path that weighed on Jupita's soul. She didn't have the strength to deal with that.

And the lady elf wasn't the only one shook by the underground events. They screamed hysterically, cried and some, too shocked to utter any sound, for the rest of their days would battle against a contingent of values and beliefs against dementia. After all, how to convey this moment to anyone? Should they? Did they want to? The survivors left with more questions than answers. Their entrance was encouraged by petty desires, ambitions and on their way out, they carried doubts about these values and above all, about their characters. Sobs and cries were valid likewise silence and screaming. That moment belonged to the introspection abyss. Some mined dark corners of their memories trying to extract a more refined truth, a plausible one, like the reason for such villainy. Or they would merely carry the memory and walk around in ignorance in a doubtful hope to retain their sanity and/or their dignity.

Suddenly, a cold breeze from inside hit them. A shiver ran through the humans, they unsheathed their weapons with the quickness of despair and when they turned around, found nothing. Fear's alert waned when they saw that nothing or no sound came from there, so they lowered their rusted and poor weapons.

"The temple demanded its new guardian!" A sexless and powerful voice hollered from somewhere.

At that moment, a spectral form of Osiris appeared.

Frightened by what seemed a continuation of the ill fated episode, the survivors tried to brandish their weapons however, they were too heavy. Still crying, Jupita stood up and gliding slowly, moved towards her friend and tied hands with her.

"She only came to say goodbye." Tristan said loud enough so everyone could hear.

"Humph! She offered herself not to die." Morgrinald said with his arms across his chest.

Far from the others, Osiris, Champion of the Big Valley, devoted to the god of war, and now elected Guardian, revealed to her friend.

"I will summarize because my time is short. While I was recovering… Oh, yes, I convinced the Little Ones to continue making the villagers disappear. I wanted to isolate the problem, therefore, if there was one or more beasts running free, they would have to come out because of the lack of victims. But according to the Little Ones, that was unlikely. So we focus our attention on the village. Weeks before we arrived, the Little Ones were already watching the villagers activities when their own began to disappear. The village had no source of income big enough to create a dispute, except one…

"The tavern!"

"Yes. But, after you went east, the disappearances continued. In a smaller scale, but they continued. The Little Ones assured me there were no animals or beasts involved, so we decided to increase the amount of losses, increase competitiveness and see what would happen.

"And the landlords?"

"It would have been good if they moved their fat asses, secretly, I even wished so, you know… An armaments race, a war drill."

"And the row of devotees…"

"Yes, it also grew. But are you kidding? This land is jammed between the domain of at least two of them and you how politicians are."

"The Little Ones made the kids disappear?"

"I believe that they were only able to carry those."

"Radical."

"Efficient."

"You were always like that."

"You can't judge! You saw only the peak of the plan. Children are precious, period. And about this, I had already sensed its presence, even in the blacksmith. I only had to find it…"

"The location of the precious temple of death."

"It's only worth something now." Osiris smiled with juvenile sarcasm.

Then the friends hugged and soon the new guardian was gone in a veiled and sincere farewell.

The survivors cheered and smiled. The missing children came running and shouting out of the woods, brought by the Little Ones, by Hans Ranni Ramiro and Roder and the legendary hermit known everywhere as the "Old Bushman".

Parents recovered their most precious assets. Cries and joy that claimed all the attention that the cloudless sky should command.

SOMEWHERE BEFORE HERE

… Between the bay and the high sea, sailed the king of the Great Empire. The wind caressed his strong face carved by age. He just peered attentively the horizon, remaining for hours on the helm deck. Watchful over each wave that seem to bow in respect to his majestic figure. All it took was sometime together to understand that the comments about him were truth. Comments that echoed throughout the kingdom almost in verse; a certainty beyond romantic poetry and fantasy stories. Whispers behind his ears said that the silence of his mouth was like an aggressive prayer that sped up the hearts of the living and brought despair to the dead. His voice was sweet, soft and kind like a beloved poet.

As for his subjects, he preferred to keep an open dialog without casts or creed divisions. King Dainthgorn of the cities and places in the west that formed the Great Empire, always said that the greater the distance, the smaller would be the understanding. Everyone loved them and those who didn't have such love for the king in their heart, sealed their feelings in their chest and never spoke of it afraid of the commoners justice.

Having said all of that, could the "meat myth" have any enemies? None! None openly declared, of course. And if there were, they could say that the Dainthgorns have influential friends.

And the captain of the great and beautiful ship was one of those friends. With approximately thirteen hundred square meters of sails on a single vessel, dozens of deadly cannons and liters of the viscous, lethal and flammable oil, the black fire.

The magnanimous lord and father of all in the kingdom, the king, stood imposing as nature made him. The wind whipped his cape and turned the impressive royal figure in its own flag banner. His thoughts, with peculiar weight and swiftness without comparison, agitated him much more than his cape that morning:

"Sartre. Healer and farmer." he said to himself.

He could still hear the echo of the woodsman's words.

"… The old and molded wheat was ground and distributed throughout the region. The greatest problem was the insanity brought on by the fungi. The spoiled product was consumed by many in the region, including his only son. In the mist of a fury attack, the son stabbed Sartre, his father. They rushed him to the closest village healer, where he spent days without a single improvement… Between life and death, all he cared about was his beloved relative. His friends went to pick him up, but it was already too late… the young man, believing he had killed his father had hang himself in remorse. When Sartre, the father, found out, he knelt and prayed for youngster's soul he had love so much. Alone in the world, he imposed on himself the objective of refining his understanding of plants and seeds and moved to a wheat crop region. He resumed his life and, gradually, learned not only the art of farming, but also healing by using herbs, plasters and roots. He learned and taught others.

"Insolent peasant." the king had said when he met Dominescu. "You wish to teach your king how to live?"

"No! But what to live for! My lord."

That was why he was at sea. The woodsman's story about pirates, about his son's shipwreck was convincing, so convincing that if any other one else had brought his son's royal coat of arms, it would not be as valuable. A splendid man, who earned the sympathy of the king, therefore whatever debts Dominescu's family had, were forgiven.

For such, the august king of the Great Empire, lord of esteemed and honored house of Koth, swore in front of his army that he would nail each ship, each frigate or pirate caravel to the bottom of the sea. He would ruin the water rats once and for all. Swearing to help those who really mattered. The people.

Meanwhile, on the fatherland soil, heavy hooves echoed on the trail of stones of the trade route. Jordan; the Just; Commander of the royal order of his majesty, with thirty-five champions of the royal guard at his command, rode in triple row with a mission to investigate the situation in the village of Miller as told by the eloquent peasant. Besides, there was a greater mission to carry out. These knights, the elite troops of the royal guard, for the first time in years, weren't escorting their king, but someone more distinguished… More… Royal.

In a carriage, covered in satin and floral arrangements, Dominescu; poor man with no surname; born a woodsman and dead hero, was finally home.

.End.

BAD VALUES - THE POWER AND THE MEANS

"Your twins raised by the church?" The dwarf asked the elf in the cell, but she remained quiet and sad.

Morgrinald had doubts, but it was Jupita who decided on the tutor. The problem wasn't the faith, but the values. Good and bad values. Some kinds of faith will come and go, but not values. The war against the pirates was a good example. The war of the king of the Great Empire against the pirates began from what the woodcutter Dominescu told the king about the crown prince; how they met and how he died …

That memory ripped a low and bitter roar from the dwarf while he scratched his armpits. Dominescu died in the Castle, what Morgrinald did for him should have saved him but it didn't. Keldorn's grandson had to watch his mind, about the reasons for this, why he died. However, he had push away thoughts about the positives and negatives of vengeance.

Whatever the good Dominescu told the king, it caused a huge value impact. If king Erick was anything like his son, Dominescu's words reinforced his virtues, so that was an excellent example of good values, since otherwise it would just be a case of revenge of royalty for the dead son. In other words, bad values.

Morgrinald, the last member of the clan of the Battle Hammers; bearer of the sacred weapons; sniffled as if it were possible to expel undesirable thoughts from his wide nostrils. And soon another thought rolled through his mind. Was the king aware of what a prolonged war against the water dwellers could cause? The dwarf's hands ran from one side to another on his beard. Certainly no one noticed the water levels dropping in the coastal communities; Morgrinald's thick eyebrows met restless, disturbed with facts and memories. After all, with so many shipwrecked and floating bodies these offensives incited more than offered any solution. Right now , an entire population of mermaids and mermen, of several areas, would be migrating to feed, breed, and deposit their already fertile eggs in the dead and castaways. If these moribund reached the beach, they will be regarded as mentally ill or worthless while the litter in their bodies ate them alive from the inside. Before these poor guys finally die, they will seek water and the litter will hide until they are fully developed. Then that will be the beginning of water counter attack. Because that was how the damn water acted and continue to act. A subtle counter attack, invisible to those with short live spans, like the humans, Little Ones and most of the animals.

Although it acted slowly compared to most standards, the results were always apocalyptic. The water, like most elements, had its allies and beloved ones among the humans. Like pirates, fishermen and, why not, even many of the sailors of the royal fleet.

Like the two prisoners sharing a cell with them, isolated in a corner. They were two old merchants who traded with pirates, that is, land pirates, middlemen of products bought honestly from dishonest people.

These two crazies fed off each other, the fought and caressed each other. For that reason, no one paid them any attention. Morgrinald noticed them as soon as they were locked in the cell along with the other ten. He noticed easily because the isolation marked them as leaders or as problems. And it didn't take long to figure out which one they were or what they were. They fiercely disputed the water, they ran blindly and fighting for the buckets brought by the prison guards and in the following days making it clear that they were "Infected by the water".

And that was it. Keldorn's grandson, the daughter of the wind and the scum of the city locked up in the same cell.

"How nice …" Morgrinald seeped the acid irony imagining, conceiving when the serpent litter of their swollen guts would hatch and kill their hosts to then slither to their next meals. "Actually, busty, your rascals are better off with him, in his church somewhere far from here.

One of the infected squirmed in agony, so it has to be today, in the middle of the night, under the veil of darkness Morgrinald would have to kill him quietly to defend others. However, It was already late. Suddenly, the stomach of the squirming one opened and the litter slithered on the ground.

"Wet nightmares!" Jupita said angrily.

Too late, the dwarf thought. The lady elf also saw them and these water worms were certainly the same kind that evolved in a very short time from annelid amphibians to bipedal reptiles and together, in a blitz attack, razed the village of Almokaryr.

The eyes of the irate elf became white and the aura of her art became so deeply blue that it seemed to color her body. The worms on the floor stopped instantly when they were perforated along with centimeters of rock beneath them. They were air claws. It had been decades since the experienced dwarf saw such display of power. Outside, an array of lightning flared with the slightest wrought of the lady's beautiful face. She roared and the remaining moribund stood straight up with a swollen chest and feverish breathing, turning purple. Morgrinald thought she was compressing him with the air until he noticed the straw on the floor being swept and the other prisoners beginning to suffocate and drop. Actually, it was the contrary. The daughter of the wind was denying air to infected one's lungs, and the others, by pushing the air out of the cell. Morgrinald also began to feel dizzy. He had to stop her, but walking towards her became laborious. The wind hissed so he shouted, asking her to stop before she killed someone else besides the aim of her horror. But Morgrinald noticed it was too late. The humans were already unconscious on the floor. Soon they would be dead.

"This is going to hurt …" Keldorn's grandson shouted before striking her chin so hard it made her fly and hit the ceiling, then her unconscious body floated back to the floor. He caught her and struggled to push her back to the floor.

With her safely on the ground, Keldorn's grandson punched the ground and while he was shaking, he shoved his hand and effortlessly ripped out a block of stone then put the two dead and the drilled worms into the hole and sealed it by returning the large block to its place.

One of the inmates, that didn't faint, quite scared, dropped to his knees after witnessing such display of power and examined the slightly irregular ground.

"So much power. Why don't you escape?" He asked startled.

(…)

ABOUT THE AUTHOR:

I have been writing since my parents forgot a pen between me and a wall. Although my first critique was the quite painful, I never stopped writing after that.

I live in São Paulo with my wife and my alter ego, Jeff.

I complain about the weather, the water shortage, and the traffic just like any São Paulo native, but I will never move away.

Jeff chops sushi with his bare hands and writes occasionally. Obviously, I'm the one who has to edit his writing and make sure he doesn't forget to take his medication, otherwise, he leaves the house naked or wearing a superman costume (again).

In 2014 (and 2018) I was awarded as one of the finalists in Piracicaba's humor short story competition in São Paulo.

OTHERS E-BOOKS AND BOOKS OF THE AUTHOR:

Guardiões do pecado (2015) – portuguese version;

O adereço da estranha árvore (2016) – portuguese version;

Maus valores (2017) - portuguese version.